Praise for the novels of *New York Times*
bestselling author

KAT
MARTIN

"[Martin] produces irresistible novels that blend
the eerie and unexplainable with her own uniquely
sensual and exciting style."
—*Romantic Times BOOKreviews*

"In this intricately crafted novel, a terrific paranormal
story unfolds that is sure to send shivers down many
a reader's spine…. Ms. Martin is a master storyteller."
—*Coffee Time Reviews* on *Scent of Roses*

"A real page-turner…*The Summit* is a superb story…"
—*Romance Reviews Today*

"An edgy and intense example of romantic suspense
with plenty of twists and turns; fans are sure to be
turning pages well into the night to finish."
—*Paranormal Romance Writers* on *The Summit*

"A terrific contemporary romance with an
interesting setting, perfect pacing,
compelling plot, fascinating detail."
—*Booklist* on *Midnight Sun*

"A stunning achievement for such a talented author!"
—*Literary Times* on *Bold Angel*

"For once, here's a paranormal book where the
paranormal element is truly creepy."
—*All About Romance* on *The Silent Rose*

KAT MARTIN

SEASON OF STRANGERS

MIRA®

MIRA®

ISBN-13: 978-0-7783-2554-3
ISBN-10:   0-7783-2554-7

SEASON OF STRANGERS

Copyright © 2008 by Kat Martin.

www.MIRABooks.com

Printed in U.S.A.

To my friends on Rock Creek. What a great group you are! Thanks for all the good times. It's been fun just getting to know you.

One

It was an odd sound, like the wind whipping a heavy wire stretched too tight. She heard it and a tense shiver crawled up her spine. The sun scorched down, hotter than she'd expected. The sky, a washed-out white instead of its usual blue seemed to trap in the heat. There wasn't the hint of a cloud to offer relief.

It was Wednesday, the middle of the week. No one swam in the ocean. No one looked down from the private, guarded cliffs rising up from this deserted stretch of beach. Only a stray black dog, little more than a pindot in the distance, wandered aimlessly in her direction, veering occasionally into the surf to cool its burning feet.

Ignoring the dog and the heat soaking through her red bikini, Julie Ferris turned to her sister, propped up on the sand just a few feet away. "Listen, Laura—do you hear that sound?"

The tall, sleek young woman beside her sat up on her faded yellow beach towel. A sticky breeze coming in off the ocean lifted strands of her pale blond hair. "What sound? I don't hear anything." She reached over and lowered the volume on the radio, extinguishing the low beat of rock music that filtered out toward the sea.

"It's sort of a thick funny buzzing. I think it's coming from someplace over there." Julie pointed toward the west, out toward the breakers crashing in with the rising tide. They were lying in a private cove on Malibu Beach, part of a huge estate owned by Julie's neighbor, Owen Mallory, a friend and her most important real estate client.

Cocking her head toward the odd hum that had begun to resonate along her spine, Julie rubbed her arms, trying to rid herself of the goose bumps prickling her skin. "Now it sounds like it's coming from the east. I can't exactly tell."

Laura shifted in that direction, angling her slender frame and tilting her head. "Kind of weird, isn't it? I can hear it and at the same time, I can't. It seems to be sort of all around us."

Julie dusted clumps of gritty sand from her hands, which were smaller, more petite than the long-boned supple fingers of her younger sister. At twenty-four, Laura Ferris had taken after their handsome fair-haired father, while Julie's dark-red hair, lightly freckled nose, and small pointed chin came from her mother's side of the family. She looked more pixieish than beautiful, though she was attractive. She was proud of her figure and shapely legs, and she thought she had a very nice behind.

"Whatever it is," Julie said, "it's irritating to say the least." For a moment, the sound seemed to heighten and a sharp stab of pain shot into her head. "It's getting on my nerves and giving me a headache." She craned her neck, scanning the empty stretch of beach, careful to keep her eyes shaded beneath the brim of her big straw hat.

Glancing up at the washed-out blue sky, she tried not to stare into the harsh ball of early June sun. "Maybe it's coming from above us...some kind of microwave something-or-other, or a military jet that's flying really high."

At twenty-eight, Julie was more outgoing than Laura, more vivacious, more driven to make the most of her life. Their father had left when they were just kids and the years of bare subsistence gave Julie her relentless drive. Laura had reacted in an opposite way, growing up shy and withdrawn, dependent on Julie to take the place of a mother who was rarely there. As a child, Laura was sickly much of the time—or at least believed she was.

"I don't see anything," Laura said.

Julie scanned the sky. "Neither do I, but that noise is giving me the shivers. Maybe we ought to go in."

"I'm not ready to go in yet," Laura said, sliding down onto her backrest. "Besides, it doesn't seem quite so loud anymore. I think it's starting to fade." She yawned hugely. "It's bound to stop in a minute or two."

Julie rubbed at the irritating goose bumps, trying to ignore the piercing hum that didn't seem to bother her sister. She lay back on the red-and-orange beach towel that read Watch Out For Sharks, which she had gotten at a real estate conference in Las Vegas.

"Turn the radio back up." Julie clenched her jaw, wishing the grating noise would end. "Maybe that rock station you were listening to will drown out the sound." Shoving her sunglasses up on her nose, she settled her straw hat over her face to shade her eyes. Beside her, Laura reached for the volume knob on the radio, but it was no longer working.

"Damned thing."

"Probably the battery," Julie mumbled from beneath her hat.

"Can't be. I just replaced it." Laura gave the radio a whack, but it didn't go on. "They always crap out when you need them." Grumbling, she picked up the book she'd been reading, a Danielle Steel novel about two sisters and the hardships they had suffered as children, a story much like their own early years.

"What time is it?" Julie asked, grateful the noise had finally stopped though the weird vibrations continued. Her body tingled from head to foot, her fingers felt numb, and her heart was throbbing strangely.

At the same time she felt unaccountably sleepy.

Laura glanced down at her diamond-faced wristwatch, a present from Julie last Christmas. "That's weird…my watch has stopped working, too." She grimaced and plopped the paperback book down over her face. "Nothing works when you want it to." The words whispered out from beneath the pages.

"You're not going to sleep, are you? One of us had better stay awake or we'll wind up with a doozie of a sunburn."

But already Laura's eyes were closing.

And as the odd numbing sensations became more intense, Julie's limbs began to feel heavy. Her eyes drifted closed and her thoughts slowly faded. A few moments later, she was soundly asleep.

When the stray black dog sauntered over from the

edge of the surf, dripping water from the hair under his belly, he cocked an ear at the once again softly playing radio. A low growl rumbled from his throat and the thick black ruff of fur at the back of his neck shot up as he sniffed the terry-cloth folds of the two vacant beach towels, the empty backrests, and the cast-off book he found carelessly abandoned in the sand.

He growled again and glanced up, then whimpered and began to back away. Tucking his tail between his legs, the dog turned and bolted off down the beach.

Val lingered a moment in front of the monitor on the narrow metal table, studying the glowing blue screen. He'd been examining his research notes ever since the tests had been completed and all of the data assembled. Nothing he saw on the screen or in any of his other case studies gave him the answers he searched for, answers he so desperately needed.

He shut down the power and the monitor went blank. Panidyne would be waiting for a report and he still hadn't reached a decision. He wasn't usually so indecisive. Back home he tended to be somewhat outspoken, not a particularly desirable trait, considering the position he held. But this time the action he was considering was far too risky, too important to undertake without a great deal of thought.

The fact was, he needed more data before he put his radical notion before the council.

He moved away from the table, a sudden calmness settling over him. His superiors had wanted more testing, but he had disagreed. It was harmful to the subject, life threatening, they now knew.

Two

Julie Ferris shoved open the front door of her office on the corner of Canon and Dayton in Beverly Hills. Donovan Real Estate, a company that specialized in palatial-sized homes and properties, had been a fixture in the area for more than twenty years. Julie had been with the company for eight of those years, starting as a receptionist during her term at UCLA. She never thought she would wind up in a sales position—top sales—she corrected, thinking of the money she earned each year and the plaques that covered her office walls.

She stopped at the receptionist's desk, dark mahogany, polished to a mirror-gloss sheen, the Queen Anne tables in front of the off-white sofa and chairs equally expensive and well-cared for.

"Any messages, Shirl?" Julie asked the voluptuous bleach-blond girl behind the desk, the only thing out of place in the elegant, conservative interior. "I meant to get in earlier, but my car wouldn't start. I had to call Triple A and have them jump-start the battery." She rubbed the bridge of her nose, trying to ignore the painful headache building behind her eyes.

"It's been kinda slow so far," Shirl said as she popped open a tube of bright red lipstick and began to smooth it over her pouty lips. Shirl was Patrick Donovan's contribution to the office staff. His father had founded Donovan Real Estate and run the business for all but the last three years. A stroke had left Alexander Donovan partially paralyzed and his playboy son in charge. Shirley Bingham was a leftover from one of Patrick's numerous affairs.

"There's a call here from Owen Mallory and one from a Dr. Marsh," Shirl said, putting the lipstick back in her purse. "The rest are on your desk."

"Thanks, Shirl." At least the woman was conscientious. She still carried a torch for Patrick, but then so did half the women in Beverly Hills. "Has Babs come in? I've got a client who's interested in one of her listings." Barbara Danvers was another sales associate, and Julie's best friend.

"Sorry, Ms. Danvers hasn't come in yet, but she phoned in a couple of times for her messages."

"If she calls again, find out if she's got plans for dinner. Tell her I'm tired of eating alone."

"Will do, Ms. Ferris."

Julie picked up her burgundy leather briefcase and started toward the door that led to her private office, one of the perks of being in a top sales position. Unconsciously, she rubbed her temple. The headache was building, growing with every minute. They'd been getting worse each day for the past two weeks, the first one hitting after she and Laura had spent the day together on the beach.

That was the reason for the message from Dr. Marsh. Three days ago, she'd awakened with a migraine so severe she couldn't get out of bed. She'd been dizzy and nauseous, the pounding in her temples so excruciating four Advils hadn't been able to numb it. She had gone to see Dr. Marsh that afternoon in an effort to discover what might be causing the headaches, and he had begun a series of tests. The doctor had promised to call with the results.

Lifting the receiver, Julie dialed his number, then waded through a barrage of secretaries and nurses until he finally picked up the phone.

"Julie, how are you feeling?"

"Not so good. My head's beginning to pound. I hope I'm not getting another bad one. What did the test results show?"

"The MRI and CAT scans were clear. No sign of a tumor, nothing like that. The X-rays revealed no spinal problems. As a matter of fact, so far we've found nothing at all that would indicate headaches of the magnitude you've been suffering." He paused and silence descended on the phone. Julie didn't know whether to feel relieved or more worried than ever. "You've been working terribly hard, Julie. Stress can cause any number of problems. Severe migraine headaches are certainly among them."

Julie said nothing. She had worried the headaches might be stress related. Though it would be simpler, in a way she hoped they weren't. She had to work for a living. If stress was the trouble, there wasn't much she could do about it.

"I'm not saying that's what this is," the doctor continued. "There are several more tests we need to run before we'll know for sure. I've set them up for Thursday afternoon at two o'clock. If that doesn't work, just call my assistant and have her reschedule."

"Thursday's fine, Dr. Marsh." Julie said goodbye and hung up the receiver. She needed to return the stack of phone messages on her desk, especially the one from Owen Mallory, but the pain in her head had begun to worsen. So far the headaches had lasted no more than several hours. She could turn off her cell phone and have Shirl hold her calls, then close the door to her office and lie down on the sofa for a while. In a couple of hours she was sure to feel better. By then Patrick might have come in.

Giving instructions to Shirl not to be disturbed, Julie got up from the stack of paperwork on her desk, closed the door and the blinds over the window into the office, then lay down on the overstuffed camel-backed sofa. She had a bone to pick with Patrick over his bungling of the Rabinoff deal while she had been out of town. Typical Patrick, drinking and carousing instead of tending to business. She had promised the Rabinoffs the escrow on their house would close by the end of the month. Now she had to find a way to straighten out the problems and keep her word.

Julie closed her eyes and tried not to think of tall, dark and handsome Patrick Donovan. She tried not to see his disarming white smile, gleaming black hair, and perfect V-shaped body, all attractively packaged in expensive custom-tailored clothes.

Instead she forced herself to think of the wild, drunken parties he favored, the women, the drugs, the careless, reckless spending that was dragging Patrick *and* Donovan Real Estate right down the tubes. It was Patrick's fault the company was near financial ruin. Patrick with his selfish overindulgence, his endless schemes, and self-destructive ways.

As she always did when her mind strayed to Alex's charming, incorrigible son, she worried about the way he was destroying himself and thought what a terrible waste it was.

Patrick Donovan slammed the door of his sleek black Porsche Carrera a little harder than he meant to, then winced at the jolt of pain that shot from his head to his toes. Jesus, what a hangover. Sex and drugs and rock 'n' roll. Sometimes he wondered if it was worth it.

"Take care of her, will you, Monty?" He dangled the keys in front of the little valet who parked cars at Spago, the posh celebrity restaurant half a block down from his office.

"You got it, Mr. Donovan!" The kid grinned like a fool, grabbed the keys and a ten-dollar bill, and slid behind the steering wheel while Patrick continued on up the sidewalk to work. It was late afternoon. He should have been in the office hours ago, but the juicy little blonde he'd picked up at Jack Winston's party last night had kept him up until nearly dawn.

She was into booze, big-time, a cokehead who occasionally got high with a needle, but she was also really built. She knew how to party and better yet, she knew how to screw. The trade-off was worth the price he'd paid for an eight ball of really good coke. And of course he hadn't minded getting a little grilled himself.

"What's up, Shirl?" Resting an elbow on the message center beside her desk, he leaned forward, giving himself a better view of her outrageous cleavage.

She beamed up at him. "I got tickets for Saturday night—The Jersey Boys. Front row seats. I didn't really think you'd be interested, but if you're not already busy—"

"I meant what's going on around here. What calls I've had and whether or not anyone is desperately looking for me."

"Oh." She looked crestfallen. Shirley Bingham had never been long on brains but she was dynamite in the sack. Too bad getting her in bed meant he'd had to employ her. Shirl loved the job and now he didn't have the heart to fire her. He was, however, smart enough to ignore the lure of temptation again.

She straightened in her chair, jiggling her magnificent breasts, and the front of his pants went snug. He might have one helluva hangover, but obviously he wasn't dead yet.

"You've had a lot of calls, sir. I put them in on your desk. Oh, and Ms. Ferris has been waiting for you to come in. She's in her office now."

Julie Ferris. Patrick sighed as he straightened away from Shirl, turned, and made his way past the twin rows of desks, nodding to a salesman here and there as he walked by. If he had one regret in life it was Julie. He'd been attracted to Julie Ferris since the day she'd walked through the office front door eight years ago. She'd been only twenty then, not even old enough to drink. But she'd had a beautiful body and skin like cream, big green eyes, and the clearest, sweetest laugh he'd ever heard.

At the time, she was a junior at UCLA, looking for part-time work. He had convinced his father to hire her on the spot and begun to put the moves on her right away. Eventually he'd convinced her to go out with him, but he was seven years older than Julie, and she was wary of a worldly man like him. When he'd driven her to his apartment after dinner to try his hand at seduction, Julie had come unglued.

"You're drunk," she had said, unwinding herself from his sticky embrace and leaving him sprawled on the couch. "I feel like I've been out with an octopus, and the whole time we were having dinner, your eyes were on every other woman who walked through the door. That might work with the bimbos you've been dating, but it won't work with me."

"Wait a minute, Julie—" He struggled to get to his feet and finally dragged himself upright. "So what if I am a little drunk? We're out to party, aren't we? I only wanted to have a little fun."

"Fun for you, maybe." She snatched her coat off the chair. "Certainly not fun for me." She started for the door. "You don't have to drive me home. If you tried, you'd probably get us both thrown in jail. I'll take a cab."

Julie had gotten home on her own and she hadn't gone out with him since.

He thought of that night as he knocked on the door to her office, then turned the knob and walked in. Things had changed a lot between them since then. He was her boss now. Over the years, she had won his respect and they had come to a sort of understanding. He glanced to where she sat on the sofa, gently massaging her temple. She was usually behind her desk with the phone shoved into an ear.

"You don't look good," he said, noticing the lines of fatigue beneath her eyes.

"Neither do you." She glanced up at his drug-ravaged face. It was hard to fool Julie. She always saw through to the truth. "Another rough night, I gather."

He grinned boyishly, wishing he could charm her as easily as he could the rest of the women he knew. "Kind of. What about you? Not feeling well?"

Julie sighed and came to her feet. As always, she looked at him with a combination of regret mixed with disapproval. It always pissed him off.

"I had a headache," she said. "It's pretty much gone now."

He knew she was attracted to him, but Julie Ferris wasn't the kind of girl who went for one-night stands. She disapproved of the drugs he used and badgered him about his drinking.

"You don't look like you're feeling much better," she said, frowning at the smudges beneath his eyes, the slightly sallow color of his usually suntanned skin. "That stuff is going to kill you, Patrick. How long will it take before you figure that out?"

Patrick stiffened, drawing himself up to his full six foot three inches. "What I do is none of your damned business."

Julie stopped a few feet in front of him, tilting her head to look up at him and fixing those big green eyes on his face. "It is when my clients are involved." Her brows drew together, moving the tiny freckles across the bridge of her nose. "We need to talk about the Rabinoff deal. You really blew that one, Patrick."

"I know, I know." He raked a hand through his wavy black hair, shoving it back from his forehead. "Things just sort of got away from me."

"They got away from you because you weren't paying attention. You're too smart for that, Patrick. If you kept your mind on business instead of Shirl's cleavage or Babs's derrière—"

"Okay, okay, I'll fix it." He didn't tell her it was *her* derrière that usually snagged his attention. "I know the secretary over at the mortgage company. I'll get her to put a rush on the documents. Anything else you want me to do?"

She rattled off a list of items, each word punctuated by a green-eyed glare that scorched right through him. Damn, she was pretty. Not beautiful like some of the women he knew, but cute and smart and sexy as hell. He forced himself not to think of what she'd be like in bed.

After eight years of giving it the old college try, he knew it wasn't going to happen.

Julie lay in the middle of her big pine bed, listening to the pounding of the surf rolling in on the beach, the intermittent throb of a foghorn in the distance. Her bedroom was white, like the rest of the house, with light pine hardwood floors and woven throw rugs in bright southwest colors—a bit of New Mexico on the California shore. The house wasn't huge, just three bedrooms and an office, living room, dining room, kitchen, sunny breakfast room and two-car garage.

It was the wall of windows overlooking the beach, the deck that ran the length of the house, and the privacy of the property that had seduced her into buying it. That and her friend, Babs, nagging her that with the money she was earning, she needed the tax deduction.

Julie thought of the evening she had spent with her friend. A pleasant dinner at The Grill after they'd worked late at the office, though later she had suffered another migraine headache. It was a bad one, leaving her weak and drained, but once she got home it had disappeared. She had slept for a while, then awakened abruptly from an unpleasant dream. Now she was finding it impossible to go back to sleep.

She rolled onto her side, pulling up the covers, plumping her pillow, trying not to think of the work piling up on her desk and hoping the sound of the ocean would lull her as it usually did. Her love of the ocean was one of the reasons she had bought the expensive beachfront property. She had stumbled on to the place while working with Owen Mallory, showing him a series of luxurious homes, hoping he would add one of them to his worldwide collection.

This little house sat next door to the vast estate he had finally chosen, which meant, at his insistence, she had access to a long stretch of private white sand beach.

Julie fidgeted and turned just as the phone began to ring on the nightstand beside the bed. Sitting up quickly, she reached for it with a suddenly unsteady hand. She had always hated late-night calls. They were usually nothing but bad news.

"Julie, are you there?" Her sister's trembling voice crackled over the receiver. "Julie?"

"Laura, what is it? What's happened?"

"I-I'm frightened, Julie. I think somebody is outside my window."

Julie tensed. "Did you call the police?"

"No. The last time I called them, no one was out there. I'm afraid they won't come if I call them again."

"Of course they'll come. It's their job to protect you. Hang up and call them right now. I'll be there as quickly as I can."

"Julie, don't hang up. I'm afraid they'll come if you do."

Julie's fingers tightened on the phone. "You're afraid who will come? The people outside your window?"

"No…I…I don't know who they are."

A knot balled hard in Julie's stomach. Laura had been acting strangely ever since the day they had spent on the beach. Still, her sister lived in a small apartment in an older section of Venice, not the safest place for an attractive single woman. Julie had seen some of the oddballs and riffraff who frequented the zany beach town. She had tried to persuade Laura to move somewhere else, but her sister had refused.

"Listen to me, Laura, do exactly what I tell you. As soon as you hang up, call 911. Make sure the doors and windows are locked, then stay inside until the police get there. I'll be carrying my cell phone. You can call me if you need to. I'll be there as fast as I can." Steeling herself against her sister's protests, Julie hung up and jumped out of bed. In minutes she was dressed in jeans and Reeboks and a navy blue sweatshirt, racing down the front steps and into the garage.

The powerful engine of her silver Mercedes SL convertible, her pride and joy, fired up when she turned the key. It sat next to a nearly new, four-door Lincoln Town Car she used when she wanted to show property.

Julie grabbed her scarf from the passenger side of the

sports car and tied it around her bouncy, just-above-
the-shoulders dark red hair. Then she jammed the car
into reverse, slammed her foot down on the gas pedal,
and peeled out of the driveway. In minutes she was flying down the Pacific Coast Highway, headed toward
her sister's apartment, her heart pounding like a drum
inside her chest.

She dialed 911 on her hands-free cell phone, confirmed that her sister's call for help had been received,
and hung up, praying nothing would happen to Laura
before she could get there.

Laura Ferris finally opened her front door. The officer on the other side had been pounding, cajoling, trying to convince her he was really with the police
department but Laura was too afraid to believe him.

She sagged with relief when she saw his billed cap,
dark blue uniform, and the shiny chrome badge that
glittered beneath the porch light. "I'm sorry, Officer, I
was just so frightened."

"It's all right, Ms. Ferris. Why don't we go into the
living room?" He urged her in that direction and Laura
let him guide her, feeling weightless with relief.

"Did you see anyone? Did you catch them?" She
brushed past the big leafy philodendron that had out-
grown its pot, and sat down on the sofa. The orange flo-
ral fringed throw was a little crooked so she nervously
began to straighten it.

A few feet away, the tall thin policeman stood in
front of her, a man in his forties, a man with experience,
she thought. A man who could protect her.

"I'm sorry, Ms. Ferris. We saw no sign of an intruder,

nothing at all that would indicate a presence outside the apartment."

Laura frowned. Surely she couldn't have been mistaken. She glanced up at the sound of the door swinging open and saw her sister rush in, a small bundle of energy beneath a cap of glossy red hair.

"Julie—thank God you came." Laura shoved a tousled blond curl behind her ear. "This is Officer—" she read the nameplate over his badge "—Ferguson. He says they've checked things out but they didn't find anyone. You'd think the guy would have left footprints or something, but I guess he didn't. Anyway, I guess he's gone."

"You're related to Ms. Ferris?" the policeman asked.

"I'm her sister. I'm Julie Ferris."

"Could I speak to you a moment? In private?"

Julie glanced at her slightly disheveled sister, noticing the pallor of her skin and the tic that had surfaced beneath one dark brown eye. "Yes, Officer, of course." They made their way into the cozy little kitchen, dodging potted plants and ducking behind the red beaded curtain that clattered in their wake.

"You weren't able to catch the man?" Julie asked worriedly.

"There was no man, Ms. Ferris. Are you aware this is the fifth 911 call we've received from your sister in the past two weeks?"

"No…I…I had no idea. She mentioned that she'd called once before, but I didn't know there had been others."

"The dispatch says each call's the same. Your sister's frightened voice coming over the phone claiming someone is trying to break into the house."

"Maybe someone *is* trying to get in and you're just not here quickly enough to catch him."

"Prowlers leave traces, Ms. Ferris. Footprints, loosened window screens, tire tracks—something. There's nothing of that sort here. I hate to have to ask this, but has your sister had any kind of psychiatric problems?"

A tightness pinched in Julie's chest. "She's been to counseling. Her childhood was extremely difficult. She had occasional bouts of depression, but she's never seen a psychiatrist. Are you implying my sister may be suffering from some sort of mental disorder?"

"I'm not implying anything. I'm simply telling you that no one is trying to break into this apartment. It seems to me your sister may need psychiatric help a lot more than police assistance."

Julie mulled that over. Laura *had* been acting strangely. "I'll speak to her, Officer. It was my fault she called you again tonight. I didn't realize she had done it four times before."

"No problem. Besides, it's always better to play it safe. At any rate, good luck with your sister."

"Thank you." They returned to the living room. The policeman said his goodbyes to Laura, and Julie sat down beside her on the sofa.

"Feeling better?"

"Yes…much better. I'm glad you came."

Julie reached over and clasped Laura's hand, gave it a comforting squeeze. "The officer says this is the fifth time you've called the police."

Laura straightened a little on the sofa, began to fidget with the cord of her blue velour robe. "I-I didn't realize I had called them so much."

"Want to tell me about the other times?"

Laura sagged back against the sofa, resting her head against the top, catching her long blond hair beneath her shoulders. "I thought I heard something, that's all. I thought someone was trying to break in."

"You heard noises, something that frightened you?"

"Not noises exactly, more like just a feeling. It was terrifying, Julie. I'm sure someone was out there. I didn't know what else to do."

For a moment Julie said nothing. "You always said you liked living alone. You never used to be afraid."

"I know. It's just that lately…I don't know what it is…I just feel scared all the time."

Julie rubbed her temple, praying the slight nag of pain wasn't the start of another headache. "You haven't been frightened like that since we were children. When did all of this start?"

"I don't know exactly. Not that long ago. Sometime after the day we spent together out at your place."

"The policeman assured me no one was trying to break in, but if you're frightened, maybe you should come home with me, spend a few days in Malibu lying on the beach."

"I'd rather stay here. Besides, I can't take time off from work."

"It's only a part-time job." Laura worked in a little boutique called The Cottage down on Main Street, one of a dozen different jobs she had had since she dropped out of college. "You could always drive in to work from my house."

Laura chewed her bottom lip. "Yeah, I guess I could." She glanced at the door and then at the window. "Maybe if I just stayed there until the weekend. By then Jimmy will be back in town—"

"Jimmy Osborn? I thought you weren't seeing that creep anymore."

Laura straightened, pulling her hand away. "He isn't a creep."

"He hit you, Laura. If you want to be frightened of something, you ought to be frightened of him."

"He just lost his temper, that's all. He promised it won't happen again."

"He's bad news, Laura. Forget about Jimmy Osborn, pack a bag and let's go."

She hesitated only a moment, then she got up from the couch and went into the other room. A few minutes later she returned with a small vinyl suitcase, enough clothes to last through the end of the week. She wouldn't stay longer than that, Julie knew. Laura liked being on her own too much, and even if she didn't go back to dating Jimmy Osborn, there were a dozen more men standing in line to take his place.

As they walked out to the car, Julie caught a glimpse of Laura's strained, wary expression. Her sister glanced over her shoulder, looking right and left, then finally climbed into the passenger seat.

What was the matter with Laura now?

She'd always had a tendency to illness, both real and imagined, but this was something else. Julie wondered if the policeman might have been right, and silently vowed to find the name of a good psychiatrist.

Three

Julie walked out of her office, heading toward the front door at the opposite end of the room.

"Always in a hurry." Seated at his desk, Fred Thompkins chuckled. "I told you what my doctor said about that."

She paused beside his chair and smiled down at him. "He said you have high cholesterol and a heart condition. That you had better learn to slow down. You said that also applies to me, that I should stop and smell the roses. I believe you've mentioned that, Fred."

"Maybe I have…a couple of dozen times." He was an overweight retired math professor who wore funny little paisley bow ties. He grinned above the starched white collar that cut into the folds on his neck. "Unfortunately, you never listen."

"That's because I don't have high cholesterol and I've got bills to pay." More next month, she thought grimly, when Dr. Heraldson's psychiatric bill came in. She just hoped the sessions would be of some help to her sister.

"You still looking for Patrick?"

"I'm always looking for Patrick, for one thing or another. He hasn't come in yet, has he?"

"He's never here before noon. You know that as well as I do."

"He said he'd work on the Rabinoff deal. We've got to get that escrow closed."

"Shirl said he was driving out to Flintridge to see his dad. He's supposed to be in later."

Julie's heart tugged painfully. "I hope Alex is feeling better. He looked pretty bad when I saw him last Saturday." Patrick's father was confined to a wheelchair, the left side of his body paralyzed by a stroke, his speech impaired, one side of his once-handsome face now drooping.

It was tough on a strong, imposing man like Alexander Donovan, and yet he would not give up. Instead, he'd had a therapy room installed in his lavish Mediterranean style mansion. Daily he worked with nurses and equipment to rebuild his aging, ravaged body into something that resembled the powerful figure he had once been.

"He's a good man," Fred said. "This place was really something back when Alex was running it. There wasn't a real estate man in town who could shine his shoes." He shook his head, the lamp on his desk gleaming on the bald spot in the center, fringed by his thinning gray hair. "This place hasn't been the same since he's been gone."

It could be, Julie thought morosely, if Patrick would put as much effort into his work as he did getting laid. He was smart enough, and certainly he was savvy enough about business if he would only apply himself. Instead he was driving the company further and further into debt. Several people on the sales staff had already quit. Babs and Fred would like to leave, but they stayed on for Alex's sake, just as Julie did. She loved that old man. She wasn't about to abandon him, no matter what kind of a jerk his son turned out to be.

"I've got to run, Fred." Julie started walking.

"Why am I not surprised?"

Julie waved at him over one shoulder. "I'll talk to you later." And then she was out the door, heading off to Spago to meet Jane Whitelaw for lunch.

Evan Whitelaw, Jane's husband, was a big-time movie producer. Six months earlier, he had listed his home on Burton Way and it had finally sold last week. Now his wife was ready to start searching for a larger place to live. An estate in Bel-Air, she'd said, but Julie knew better than to listen to what a client said they wanted. You had to listen past what they said, learn to look inside and discover their secret yearnings. That was how she'd made so many sales—listening for wishes, instead of just meeting needs.

She had just reached the outside wall of the restaurant when Patrick's black Porsche pulled up to the curb. There was office parking in the rear of the building, but Patrick liked the valet to take care of it for him personally.

The pudgy youth opened the passenger door as Patrick unwound his tall frame from the driver's side of the car, and a long-legged, willowy blonde stepped out on the sidewalk.

Julie's chest went a little tight, but she forced herself to ignore it. It always bothered her to see him with a woman. Silly. Stupid, beyond belief. Yet she couldn't seem to stop the twinge she always felt watching Patrick squire one of his many one-night stands.

Ignoring the woman, she stopped him before he reached the curb, which gave her the advantage of looking straight into his eyes, the brightest shade of blue she'd ever seen. "I'm sorry to bother you...I can see you're busy...but I have to find out if the Rabinoff escrow is going to be closing on time. Were you able to get those documents drawn?"

Patrick smiled and looked over her head. "Julie Ferris meet Anna Braxston. Anna is a model with the Ford Agency. Julie is one of my top sales associates."

Julie forced herself to smile. "It's nice to meet you, Anna." She returned her attention to Patrick, who looked rested for a change, his tan slacks and navy blue sport coat immaculate as always. "I have to know, Patrick. Will the escrow be able to close by the end of the month, the way it's supposed to?"

He grinned, a slash of white in a suntanned face that would give Tom Cruise a run for the money. "Relax. I told you I'd take care of it. The docs will be ready on Friday. Get the Rabinoffs in to sign them, and the escrow can close exactly the way you planned."

She sagged with relief. "Thank God."

"You worry too much, you know that?"

"And you don't worry enough."

He frowned at her words and for a moment she wondered if he was more aware of his financial problems than he let on.

She smiled faintly at the woman. "Nice to meet you, Anna. Patrick, I've got to run."

"I'll see you back at the office," he said. Julie waved and hurried off toward the posh, high-walled interior of her favorite lunching spot.

Sometimes she imagined he watched her, though why he would when he was with a woman as beautiful as the blonde she couldn't guess. Sometimes she pretended he was different, that he was more like his father, more like the man twenty-year-old Julie Ferris had once believed he was.

He wasn't. He never would be and both of them knew it. As always the thought made her sad.

Laura lay awake in the guest room of her sister's Malibu beach house. The antique iron bed had been painted a dull brick red and an old-fashioned quilt served as a spread. Throw rugs covered the hardwood floors, and a wall of windows led out to a deck overlooking the sea. Before tonight, Laura had envied her sister this house on the beach, envied the privacy afforded by the hundreds of acres of the exclusive Mallory estate next door.

Now she leaned back against her pillow, thinking tonight she wished the house was sitting on a lot in the center of the city. That it was surrounded by dozens of people, that it was the middle of the day instead of so late in the evening.

A series of waves, loud as gunshots, crashed against the shore outside the window, but they couldn't quite block the dense dull hum Laura could barely hear above the roar of the ocean, a noise that had settled like a weight around the two-story batten-board structure. She tried to tell herself it was only her imagination, tried to concentrate on the pounding of the surf and the old Kirk Douglas movie on the television screen, though the volume was turned so low she couldn't really hear it.

It was three o'clock in the morning, dark outside, a cloudy night with no moon. She had always liked staying in Julie's guest room, but tonight the ceiling seemed lower than it usually did, the walls a little closer, the sound of the waves more irritating than soothing. Her palms were sweating, her pulse beating faster than it should have.

"Julie's right next door," she told herself, speaking the words aloud. "All you have to do is call out and she'll come running." Perhaps her sister would come even without the call. If anything was wrong, Julie seemed to sense it. Her sister had a way of doing that. Julie would protect her. Just like she always did.

Then the television set went off and the night light on the wall near the bathroom dimmed and finally sputtered out. Laura swallowed against the fear that was building in her chest.

A whispering noise sifted down from somewhere above her. She tried to cry out, but the sound lodged tight in her throat. She tried to get up, tried to swing her legs to the side of the bed, but her body was rigid, completely unwilling to move.

It was dark in the room, but now the darkness lifted and a blinding light filled the bedroom. Laura's eyes slammed closed against the stab of brightness shooting into her skull. Her muscles strained to move so hard she quivered all over and arched up off the bed.

Help me! Julie, help me! But the words remained locked in her throat and the silent scream never emerged. Then the light began to fade. She heard a noise on the stairs leading up to the deck. Small, scampering footfalls that paused outside the door.

A strangling sensation engulfed her, a terror so great it throbbed through her body in great tormenting waves. She tried to move, but only her eyes responded, rolling in their sockets, darting wildly around the room, then fixing on the door. They were coming for her. She could feel it in every nerve ending, every fiber and cell in her body. They would take her as they had done before, strip her naked, use their cold metal projectiles to invade her body. Until now she hadn't remembered.

Help me! she silently screamed, thrashing like an animal caught in a trap, yet her body never moved on the bed. *Julie, where are you?* But maybe her sister was also ensnared, caught as readily as she. Fresh terror speared through her. She remembered the pain of before, the humiliation she had felt, and prayed it wouldn't happen again. Prayed that if it did, she would be able to endure it.

The shuffling continued outside. They were coming, just as she had feared. When the door slowly opened and she saw them, her mouth formed a stark O of terror and the bile rose in her throat.

Seconds passed. She blinked and they appeared all around her, lining the sides of the bed. Her terror inched deeper, long thin tentacles reaching down into her belly. Circles of blackness whirled, clouding the edges of her mind, carrying her toward the safety of unconsciousness. Finally the darkness overtook her, freeing her from the fear, sealing her mind from what was to come. Laura welcomed the descent into oblivion.

A deep blue glow resonated up from the floor of the examining room, lighting the rounded girders along the curving walls behind his back. A bank of diodes, dials and gauges spread across the console down at one end, and air hissed through vents in a pulsing rhythm that matched the bleeps of the heart being monitored on the glowing blue screen.

Val Zarkazian stared down at the subjects lying on the table. Their scanty night clothes had been removed, and the younger woman had already been examined.

It was the second woman, the one with the dark red hair, who had brought him out from behind the monitors of his research laboratory down the hall.

He surveyed the nude figure tossing restlessly on the stark blue surface of the table, her small hands clenched so tightly the muscles in her forearms quivered. A tongue block had been inserted, but not before she had bitten into her bottom lip, leaving a slight trace of blood.

He studied her with the same objectivity he had used on a dozen subjects before, noting the woman was smaller than average but well-developed, and in healthy physical condition. She was a normal female, except that she was far more resistant to any sort of mental intrusion than most of the larger male specimens who had been brought in for study.

The woman shifted restlessly on the table, fighting the tests with the same fierce determination she had shown on her visit several weeks ago.

He glanced down at a short thin figure in dark blue protective covering, one of the lab technicians, who stood beside the table studying the subject with puzzlement and concern. Behind him, just outside the door, several soldiers milled about, members of the team who had brought the women aboard.

They were troubled by her reaction and rightly so. The first time the study had been done, she had resisted so strongly they thought they were going to lose her.

This time they had done only cursory testing, nothing intrusive into the body, and only the mental scanning that could be done without a probe. He looked at the monitor at the end of the table. The subject, a healthy female in her twenty-eighth year, had suffered normal childhood diseases—what was known here as measles, mumps and chicken pox; a broken wrist at the age of eight; minor scars and healed abrasions.

Her vital signs were strong, but just as before, they had begun to shut down the moment they started their assessment of the brain.

A row of symbols came across the glowing blue screen. *Is it happening again?* The message came from the viewing area where senior officers and staff watched the proceedings.

He confirmed it was so and watched the corresponding symbols pop up on the screen. The last similar case had occurred six months ago, an artist taken from the hills outside Santa Fe. Over the years, there had been quite a number, from a variety of different backgrounds. Neither race nor gender seemed to be a factor in the degree of resistance, which could result in the subject's mental incapacitation or death.

More questions appeared on the screen, one in regard to the proceedings.

Yes, he replied, *the tests have been stopped. We don't want to lose another subject.*

He turned to the short lab technician and ordered him to finalize the tests on the younger sibling, to complete the external examination of the older, and return them both to the point of origin.

The screen on the console began to flash another communication, countering his orders. *You must proceed, Commander. We must discover the cause of the older sibling's reaction. We cannot afford to let her go.*

He had known his superiors would want to continue, no matter how dangerous it was. Probing the outer boundaries of scientific knowledge was the first directive of their mission, one of the reasons others had come here before. It was an accepted fact that furthering that knowledge inevitably demanded a percentage of casualties.

But Val wasn't prepared to lose the woman, or any more subjects in the future.

He turned back to the screen. *There is another, better way. We have the technology. Why should we not proceed?*

The symbols flashed in rapid succession. *Such an undertaking would be dangerous. Who would take the risk?*

He logged in the reply he had thought long and hard about. *I have been working on this project for years. I am the logical choice.*

The Ansor *cannot afford to lose its most valuable research officer.*

All men are expendable in the name of science. It was a basic tenet of their work.

The screen went blank. He waited with less patience than he usually displayed and even a hint of anxiety.

The recommendation will be made to the council at our next session.

Relief filtered through him. He didn't want to see the woman die, and ever since his arrival three years ago, he had hoped for a chance like this. *I am grateful for your assistance.*

A long line of symbols appeared. *I hope you will still be grateful once you are confined in such an uncivilized environment.*

Four

Pain. Excruciating pain. Julie felt the throbbing, pulsing ache well up from the deepest part of her brain.

The slatted wooden blinds over the bedroom windows were closed, yet tiny cracks of light seeped in, stabbing like white hot rays behind her eyes. The hot, damp skin across her forehead felt stretched and swollen as if it might burst. Her lips were dry. She moistened them with her tongue. Nausea threatened, a reaction to the incredible pain in her head.

Julie rolled to her side, her small hands fisting the pillow, her teeth biting into her lower lip. It wouldn't last much longer. It never did. No more than a couple of hours. The brief duration made them bearable, and the fact she had never had them until these past few weeks.

Perhaps it was some sort of virus, an illness that was fleeting. She could stand the pain, if only she knew the cause.

Knew for certain the headaches wouldn't get worse.

A second hour passed. Her body lay on the sheet

bathed in perspiration, but the pain had begun to recede. She felt limp and drained. It was nine o'clock in the morning. She was late for work, had already missed the weekly office meeting. She wished she could just stay in bed, but headache or no, she had to go in. There was too much to do, too many clients who depended on her.

Another fifteen minutes and the last of the vicious migraine—the worst she'd suffered so far—had ebbed away. Julie gripped the pine headboard, used it as a lever to swing her legs to the floor and ease herself up off the bed. As she passed the mirror over her dresser, she paused, took in the dishevelment of her hair, and the pallor of her face that made the freckles stand out across the bridge of her nose. She headed into the bathroom, turned on the shower and stepped in before the water got good and hot.

Perhaps the test Dr. Marsh was giving her this afternoon would provide the answer. A dozen horrible scenarios flashed through her mind, everything from cancer to the brain tumor the doctor had mentioned.

She had to find out. Then again, maybe she didn't want to know.

Julie washed her hair, grateful for the soothing feel of the water running over her scalp. She shaved her legs, lathered her breasts and belly, then moved lower. She felt a twinge as her hand brushed sensitive flesh. It had been so long. Three years since she had been with a man.

Not like Laura. Laura had to have a man, needed one like people need to breathe. And her sleek model's figure and glorious long blond hair made attracting them easy. But Julie wanted more from a relationship than just a sexual fling, and if she couldn't have it she was happy to do without.

She stepped out of the shower and reached for a towel. Her head still throbbed and her hands were a bit unsteady, but her strength had begun to return. Maybe the headaches would disappear as quickly as they had started. She hoped so. With her worry for Laura, the problems she was facing at work, and her burgeoning expenses, she had enough problems already.

She sighed as she walked to the closet and slid open the mirrored doors. Her beige suit would do. She wasn't in the mood for anything but plain-and-simple. She took her time dressing. Her muscles ached and she still felt a little bit shaky. As soon as she stepped into her matching leather pumps, she made her way to the guest room in search of Laura, but her sister wasn't there.

The guest room looked a shambles. The bed was un-made, the sheets thrashed off haphazardly, the bright-colored quilt shoved carelessly onto the floor. Julie crossed to the closed bathroom door.

"Laura, are you in there? Are you all right?"

"I-I'm fine," she answered through the door. "I'll be out in just a minute."

When Laura finally appeared, Julie was stunned at the sight of her sister's pale, haggard face, at the faint purple smudges beneath her brown eyes and the sunken hollows in her cheeks. "My God, are you sick? You should have said something." She set her palm on Laura's forehead, checking for any sign of temperature, but the skin felt cold and slightly damp instead of warm, as she had expected. "Get back in bed. I'll go down and get you something to eat."

"I-I'm all right, Julie. I'm just a little tired is all."

"You look like you're a lot more than tired. Maybe you've got the flu or something."

"Maybe. That's kind of the way it feels." A hint of embarrassed color rose into her ashen cheeks. "I-I was bleeding this morning…from inside. It wasn't much, just a trace or two. You don't think it's anything serious, do you?"

"I-I don't know. Has it happened before?"

"Only once. The morning after we suntanned in the cove on the beach."

"I think we'd better have Dr. Marsh take a look at you. I have to go in for a few more tests this afternoon. You can come with me."

"You're still having those headaches?"

"Bad one last night. I finally took some sleeping pills and eventually fell asleep. I must have slept pretty hard once I did."

Laura frowned. "I had a terrible dream last night. I can't remember it now, but I remember at the time it was really scary."

"It probably is the flu. You'd better stay here through the weekend, at least until—"

"No! I-I don't want to stay here. As a matter of fact, I'm going home this afternoon. I'll feel better sleeping in my own bed. That's probably all that's wrong with me. Too much dampness in the air."

"I don't know, Laura. Dr. Heraldson thought staying here was a good idea. And now that you're sick—"

"I'm going home, Julie. I promise I won't call the police or do anything crazy, okay?"

Julie looked at her hard. "Are you sure about this?"

"I'm sure."

"And you'll go with me to the doctor's this afternoon?"

"I said I would, didn't I?"

Julie sighed. "I don't mean to be pushy. I'm just worried about you is all."

"I know that." Laura walked over and hugged her. "Thanks for caring so much. You've always been there for me, ever since Dad took off. Mom wasn't much of a mother, but you were always there. I appreciate it. I don't know what I'd do without you." She smiled. "But I promise I'll be okay, so you don't have to worry."

Julie fidgeted, smoothed the skirt of her tailored suit. "I guess neither one of us got a good night's sleep last night."

Laura just shrugged, but she looked uncomfortable with the subject. For some strange reason, Julie was uncomfortable with it, too.

"I'll be back to pick you up around noon. In the meantime, why don't you go back to bed for a while? You'll be all right until I get here, won't you?"

"Sure," Laura said lightly, "I'll be fine." But as soon as her sister left, she got up and bolted the doors. She checked and locked all the windows in her bedroom, then locked the ones in the rest of the house. She didn't open them, not even when the sun came out and the day turned warm. Not even when the temperature began to climb into the nineties and she began to perspire in the closed-up, airless bedroom.

"I'm worried about her, Babs." Julie shifted restlessly in the black leather chair behind her desk. "I can't figure out what's wrong with her."

Seated on the opposite side, Barbara Danvers made

a rude sound in her throat. "You're always worried about your sister and there's always something wrong with her. Until she takes control of her life, there always will be." Black-haired and dark-eyed, Babs had just turned thirty. She'd been married three times, to a banker, an actor and a successful television producer. She was divorced again, worked too hard but didn't really have to, not after the settlement she'd received from Archibald Danvers two years ago.

"You're too tough on her, Babs." Julie sat forward in her chair, propping her elbows on the desk. They were working in her office, going over the Richards file, an estate in Palos Verdes that Babs had listed and Julie had sold. "You know the kind of life Laura's had. A father who was gone by the time she was five years old, a mother who was never home. No supervision, no direction, never enough money to make ends meet. It's a wonder she hasn't had more problems than she has."

"I hate to remind you, but Laura had the same childhood you had and look at the difference in the way the two of you turned out. You put yourself through college. You're a successful real estate agent with a lovely home on Malibu Beach. Laura's a twenty-first-century hippie."

"Hardly that."

A sleek black brow arched up. "No?"

"Just because she's had a number of different jobs—"

"She hasn't worked more than three months in a row since I've known her. How much did you spend on Laura's medical bills last year?"

"That isn't fair."

"I'll tell you what isn't fair. Having to work the kind of hours you do to support your sister's hypochondria."

Julie glanced away. "This is different."

"I'll just bet it is. What does the psychiatrist have to say…Dr. What's-his-name?"

"Heraldson." Staring through the glass into the main part of the office, Julie jumped up from her chair as Patrick strode in, grateful for the chance to avoid Babs' last question. She almost wished she hadn't brought the subject up, but maybe she needed a dose of Babs's honesty. "I have to speak to Patrick. I have an offer on one of the units in his condo project."

"Brave girl. You're actually going to sell something Patrick Donovan's involved in?"

Julie jerked open the door without responding. Another shot of Babs' honesty right now was more than she could manage. She hurried out into the office, running to catch up with Patrick's long-legged stride.

"Sorry to bother you, Patrick. Have you got a minute?"

"Sure, come on in. Shirl said you wanted to see me." He led her into the plush interior of his spacious office, remodeled since the days when the place had been his father's. Instead of the understated mahogany and beige used throughout the rest of the building, Patrick's office was bold and energetic, done in electric blue and black. Julie took a chair in front of his black lacquered desk, settling herself in one of the deep leather chairs, and Patrick sat down across from her.

"What can I do for you, love?"

Julie glanced up from the manila file folder she'd been rifling through. "I asked you not to call me that. Save it for Anna, or Charlotte, or another one of your bimbos."

He leaned back in his chair, crossing one long leg over the other. "My, we're testy today, aren't we?"

She looked up at him, saw the usual dark shadows beneath his eyes, as well as a puffiness she hadn't noticed before. Some of her anger at him faded. "You look like hell, Patrick. You've got to start taking better care of yourself. If you won't do it for yourself, do it for your father."

He said nothing to that, but his shoulders sagged a little, and some of his cockiness faded. "He's not doing so well, Jules. The doctors are afraid he might have another stroke."

"Oh, God, Patrick."

"I'm sure he'll be all right. The old goat's too tough to die." He smiled but it came out a little shaky. "You said you needed to see me. What about?"

Escaping the painful subject of Alex's failing health, Julie pulled the thick sheaf of documents out of the file she'd retrieved from her briefcase. "I've got an offer on one of the units in your condo project. Mr. and Mrs. Harvey are interested in buying number thirty-three."

His long fingers tightened around the burgundy Mont Blanc pen he was holding. "I thought you said you didn't like the project, that it was too shaky, that you wouldn't put one of your clients into the development until it was almost full."

"I think the construction could be better. You skimped too much as far as I'm concerned. But the Harveys insisted I show it to them. They like the location—so do I for that matter. Santa Monica is growing and this is very near the beach. Besides, you said the units had finally begun to sell. The last time I checked the board it looked like over fifty percent of the project was now sold out."

Instead of looking happy, Patrick looked grim. "Condos aren't your normal dose of poison, Julie. Are these people friends of yours? How did you wind up working with them?"

"I got them on a floor call while I was covering for Fred. Mr. Harvey is a retired aerospace engineer. They made a little money buying and selling houses when the market was good. That's why they're purchasing a condo. They plan to pay cash for it, and whatever is left will be a nest egg for their old age."

Patrick said nothing for the longest time.

"I thought you'd be happy," Julie said. "I know how much that project means to you. You risked everything when you decided to build it."

His shrugged his wide shoulders, rustling his custom-fitted Oxford-cloth shirt. "In the beginning, I may have felt that way. Not anymore."

"Why not?"

"Because now other people are involved. When I couldn't get the construction money I needed, I had to take in partners. Lately they've been calling most of the shots."

He shoved back his chair and came to his feet, then leaned toward her over the desk. With those piercing blue eyes and hard jaw, he could look darned intimidating when he wanted to. "I'll give you a word of advice, Julie—I shouldn't but I will. Put your clients in some other deal. Something that isn't so risky. That's all I'm going to say on the subject and if anyone asks, I never said anything at all. If your people won't listen, that's their problem. If they still want the property on Monday and the price is right, they've bought themselves a new home."

"You took an offer from Fred's clients, why don't you want this one?"

Instead of giving her an answer, he turned away. "I've got to go." Reaching behind him, he jerked his black Italian-cut sports jacket off the wooden valet in the corner. "I just remembered something I have to do."

"Wait a minute, Patrick, I don't understand why all of a sudden—"

"See you later, Julie." And then he was gone.

Julie stared after him, wondering how he always managed to leave her speechless.

Val tried to concentrate on the screen, review the notes on his latest experiment, but he felt restless. In nearly half a lifetime, he hadn't learned the virtue of patience. He wondered if he ever would.

For the sixth time since his arrival in the lab, he turned to his message file, hoping to find some news, then sighed inwardly when he found nothing there. It had been nearly a full month since the council had agreed to his plan. Initial preparations had been made. Now he was forced to wait.

The mission could not be accomplished until a suitable donor was found. In order for that to happen, a death had to occur. Sophisticated computer calculations had come up with a list of possible candidates, people who lived or worked in close proximity to the Ferris subject.

The data had shown a ninety-percent probability that one of the primary donor candidates would face a life-threatening occurrence within ninety days; a seventy-percent chance it would happen in less than sixty; and a fifty-percent chance it would happen within thirty days from the date the calculations were made.

Unfortunately, it hadn't.

Unfortunately for him, he reminded himself, but not for the donor. Still, there was nothing personal involved. Now that the project was underway, he just wanted to get on with it.

He punched up a row of symbols. Though he knew the information well, he found himself returning to the donor file. The Alexander Donovan candidate was predicted to be the most likely. He was the eldest and in the worst physical condition. He was also the least desirable. He had no use of his legs and less access to the Ferris woman than the others.

The Fred Thompkins candidate was closer to the subject since he worked in her office. His heart was unstable and he could suffer a heart attack at any time. Unfortunately, as with the previous candidate, he was still much older, and he had only limited subject contact.

Perhaps, he thought, he should be grateful that so far nothing had happened. It was the Patrick Donovan candidate he really wanted as the donor. Physically the younger Donovan was within his prime years, just as Val was. Donovan's body was physically abused, but with a little effort on his part, it could be returned to the superior specimen it once was. The man was intelligent, appeared to have plenty of the trading currency used on Earth, and worked in close proximity to the subject.

As her superior, he even had a certain amount of control over her. It was only logical Val should prefer Patrick Donovan over the others.

And from what their sensors had discovered, not

only did Donovan have a weak wall in his heart that was on the verge of collapse, his behavior patterns were conducive to hurrying the event along.

Val couldn't help a small throb of excitement, a rare emotion in his experience, rare, for that matter, for anyone from his planet. Science was everything there. Discoveries were made daily, hourly, becoming almost mundane.

But this was different. Experiencing a new world— not from the outside looking in, as they had been doing for hundreds of years. But from the inside—from an actual functioning position within the world they studied. Though he would technically be there to discover the reason for the Ferris woman's exceptional resistance, it was the knowledge of Earth in general that Val found so intriguing.

He punched in the symbols and opened another computer file, deciding to reread the reports he had requested, observations, limited though they were, made by his predecessors during their brief stay on Earth. There wasn't much, he knew. The process called Unification had only been done a few times, and never for any duration.

Still it was something. When the time came for him to go, he wanted to be prepared.

Patrick Donovan reached for the rolled-up hundred-dollar bill lying on the acrylic coffee table in front of the sofa in his penthouse apartment. "How 'bout another little toot, baby?"

Anna Braxston smiled. She was a classy piece of ass, no doubt about it. In her long, slinky, black-sequined dress, her blond hair piled up in soft waves on top of her head, she looked like she'd just walked off a page out of *Vogue*. She was almost as tall as he was in her high-heeled shoes, though the shoes had come off long ago, along with the dress and all but the skimpy little peach satin teddy she was wearing.

"Thanks, honey." She set her cigarette in the over-flowing ashtray, a fine thread of smoke drifting up. He'd been trying to quit, but what the hell? He reached over and took a long lung-filling draw, let the smoke drift out through his nostrils.

Anna took the rolled-up bill, leaned over and snorted a long line of powdery cocaine up her nose. A second line followed. She wiped the residue away, leaned over and rubbed a coke-laden finger across his lips, but he was too far gone to feel the numbing sensation.

He poured a shot of tequila into his glass and tossed it back, grimaced at the fiery taste, and took the bill from her hand. Another line of coke disappeared, then another. She was after him to do a speedball—half heroin, half cocaine. He wasn't sure he was ready for that…then again, maybe later….

He leaned back on the gray wool sofa, felt her long supple fingers running through his curly black chest hair. He was already hard. She unzipped his navy blue slacks, the only clothes he still had on, reached inside his fly and freed his erection, then began to gently stroke him.

"You like that, don't you," she purred. It wasn't a question. She'd have to be a fool to think he didn't. Sex was the only thing he liked more than booze and drugs, the only thing that still gave him the kind of kicks he'd always needed. Everything else seemed bland in comparison, and he had tried them all.

Sports cars when he was in high school. Motorcycle racing after that. He had run the European circuit two years in a row, staying on to ski the winter in St. Moritz. He'd gotten his pilot's license, bought an old P-38, had it completely refitted, flown it in the Reno Air Races and come in third, then gotten bored and sold it for less than he'd paid for it. He'd tried skydiving. Not bad. Especially after he had done it high on cocaine.

With no responsibilities, no one to answer to but a father who was buried to his bushy gray eyebrows in work, and more money than any kid his age had a right to have, he figured why not enjoy himself? And so he always had.

Anna's lips moved over his hardened length, stroking him like a pro. His muscles flexed. He thrust upward and groaned. When she stopped for a moment to help him slide on a condom, he propped his back against the sofa, pulled her teddy off over her head, cupped her buttocks, and dragged her up on top of him, spreading her long legs until she straddled him.

"Oh, yes," Anna whispered. "Give it to me, honey."

He'd give it to her, all right. All she could take and more. He thrust his tongue into her mouth, felt her soft little breasts pressing into his chest. Her nipples were hard and distended. She was slick and hot, gloving his erection neatly.

"Hand me a popper," he said as he flexed his hips, moving in and out with a slow rhythm that had her panting and squirming. She picked the drug up off the end table, neatly broke the capsule in half, and shoved it under his nose.

God, what a rush.

He ground himself deeper, thrust into her harder, fought to hold his climax in check. He liked it this way, being in control, setting the pace.

Doing something to please somebody besides himself.

But then he liked it just about any way he could get it. Not very personal, he supposed. Not very meaningful. Just more kicks to keep him going, something to help him tolerate the empty, vacuous days.

Something to distract him from the money he was losing, the father he'd disappointed, the mess he had made of his life.

Coming in from the parking lot, Julie walked in the back door of the office just in time to see Patrick walking out the front.

"Patrick! Patrick, wait a minute! I've got to talk to you!" She was late getting to work. She'd gone by to see Dr. Heraldson, Laura's psychiatrist, who had asked for a meeting to discuss Laura's childhood, hoping he might uncover something that would help him understand what Laura was going through. Dr. Marsh, their family physician, had found nothing physically wrong with her, but Laura's paranoia had continued to increase, and her nightmares were getting worse. Julie wished she knew what to do.

She glanced ahead to Patrick's tall retreating figure. "Damn it, Patrick!" She raced down the sidewalk in pursuit, but didn't catch up with him until he'd reached the corner. "Where the hell are you going in such an all-fired hurry?" Panting with exertion, she leaned against the lamp post, watched Patrick's long dark fingers punch the button on the light so he could cross the street.

"I've got a lunch date with Anna." He turned to face her, winked, and flashed her a cocky, wicked grin. "Want to come along?"

It was the first time today that she had actually seen his face, and something clenched hard in her stomach. "My God, Patrick, what in the world have you done to yourself?"

His fine black brows drew together in a frown. "Give me a break, will you? So I'm a little washed out. I haven't had a chance to catch any rays lately."

He started across the street, but Julie caught his arm. "This is serious, Patrick. Your face is so pale it's practically blue. Something's wrong. Are you sure you're feeling all right?"

"I'm fine. What did you want to talk to me about?"

"More problems with the Rabinoff closing. I thought maybe you could help." She stopped him the minute they reached the curb on the opposite side of the street. "Patrick, your health is more important than any closing. Something is seriously wrong with you. For once in your life, please, will you listen?"

He stopped in the alley outside The Grill, a nearby restaurant that was a local haunt for movie higher-ups: producers, directors, agents, a few hopeful starlets and a lot of hangers-on. "I've got a little heartburn, okay? I'll be fine just as soon as I eat."

Julie's face turned nearly as pale as Patrick's. "You're having chest pains?"

"Heartburn. That's all it is. I took some Maalox tablets. In a few more minutes, they'll kick in and I'll feel great."

"Patrick, listen to me—" She took a deep breath, terrified he wouldn't, since he never had before.

Before she could finish, Patrick swayed and leaned against the wall, one hand flat against it, the other sliding up the lapel of his coat, stopping somewhere near his empty breast pocket. His breath seemed to catch on a heavy gasp of air, and his eyes looked suddenly frightened.

"Julie…" The words passed through lips that were dry and the same pale color as his face.

"Oh, my God!"

His legs turned to rubber. He swayed and slid down the wall, coming to rest slumped over at the bottom. Beads of perspiration popped out across his forehead and dampened the black hair at his temple.

"Somebody help us!" Julie looked frantically toward the people passing by on the sidewalk just a few feet away. "Please…somebody call 911!" A few heads swiveled in their direction, but no one ran into the alley or even started walking their way.

Julie fumbled with her purse, finally found her cell phone and made the call herself. She was shaking by the time she finished.

She forced a note of calm into her voice. "Take it easy, Patrick. Help is on the way." She didn't know if he could hear her, but it gave her a feeling of being back in control. Up ahead, the valet in front of The Grill had just hopped into a big white Mercedes-Benz and driven away.

No help there.

She didn't know CPR. For years she had been going to take a class, but there never seemed to be enough time. Leaving Patrick on the sidewalk, she raced to the shiny brass doors of the restaurant, pulled one of them open and rushed inside.

"Please, you have to help me," she said to the dark-haired maître d'. "Patrick Donovan's on the sidewalk outside. I think he's having a heart attack. Is there some-one here who can do CPR?"

"I know Patrick," the man said. "He's too young to be having a heart attack. It's probably just gas or something."

"It isn't just gas! You've got to help us! Patrick may be dying!"

He went into action then, telling her not to worry, hur-rying toward the paging system and asking if there was a doctor in the house. Julie raced back outside. By now a small crowd had gathered. She shouldered her way to-ward a man in a navy blue suit leaning over Patrick's now unconscious form.

"A-are you a doctor?"

"No." The slender man stood up and backed away. "I'm a stockbroker. But I checked for a pulse and I couldn't find one. I don't think he's breathing."

Julie swallowed past a growing lump of fear. "Do you know CPR?"

"I'm afraid not."

"Is there anyone here who does?" When no one in the small, worried crowd answered, she steeled herself. She had seen it done, but she had never tried it. Still, someone had to do something and fast. "Well then," she said, forcing a note of authority into her voice. "Get out of my way so I can get to work."

They wouldn't let her ride with him in the ambu-lance. She wasn't his next of kin, after all, and he still wasn't breathing on his own. His heart had not re-sponded to her clumsy efforts at CPR and the ambulance seemed to have taken forever to get there.

Julie drove like a woman possessed all the way to
Cedar Sinai Hospital. She hadn't called Patrick's father
yet, afraid the news might cause Alex to have another
stroke. Better to wait, see what the doctors had to say.

Better to pray that Patrick was still alive when she
got there.

On trembling legs, she shoved through the glass
doors into the reception area and hurried toward the information desk, stopped at the counter, afraid to ask,
afraid she already knew the answer.

She had called Babs on her cell, had found her at the
office, which wasn't too far away. Now the sight of her
friend's purposeful, no-nonsense strides as she pushed
through the front doors into the lobby gave Julie a shot
of courage. She took a slow, bracing breath and worked
to calm her thundering heart.

With a small silent prayer, she turned toward the
desk and spoke to the gray-haired receptionist, who
looked at her over the top of her gold-rimmed reading glasses.

"May I help you?"

"Yes. I'm here to inquire about a friend…Patrick Donovan. They just brought him in." The woman began to
search the names on her computer screen while Julie
stood tensely, running her tongue over her trembling lips.

"How is he?" Babs asked when she reached Julie's
side.

"I-I don't know yet." They both turned to stare at the
woman.

"His condition is listed as stable," she said, the age
lines around her mouth puckering unbecomingly. Too
many years in a job where it was all too easy for people

to become merely numbers. "He's been taken to intensive care, but he can't have visitors, only immediate family."

"We *are* immediate family," they both said in unison, then looked over at each other and grinned, light-headed with relief. At least he was still alive.

"I thought you said he was a friend," the woman reminded her tartly, her rheumy eyes suspicious above the rim of her glasses.

"Well, he is," Julie agreed. "But he's also our brother."

The receptionist eyed her with suspicion, but one hard look from Babs and she pointed a bony finger down the hall.

"Take the elevator up to the third floor. Follow the signs. They'll tell you where to go from there."

"Thanks," Julie said as they walked away, thinking it was time she called Alex, but first she wanted to speak to the doctors.

Babs pushed the elevator button. "At least he isn't dead," she said with her usual bluntness.

"He nearly was." Julie nervously plucked a speck of lint from the front of her pink linen suit. "His heart had stopped and he wasn't breathing. I was afraid he wasn't going to make it."

"It's the damned drugs and booze. We've both been telling him for years that one day it would kill him."

"Maybe now that this has happened, he'll listen. Sometimes a close call with death can make a person change."

Babs flashed her a look of disbelief. "Don't get your hopes up, honey. Nothing is going to change Patrick Donovan. Between his motorcycle races and his skiing, he's had half a dozen close calls. He hasn't changed a lick and this time won't be one bit different."

Five

Commander Valenden Zarkazian lay quietly beneath the clean white sheet on the hospital bed, listening to the beeping sound of the heart monitor attached by wires to his chest. The curtains were drawn so that only a sliver of light fed into the darkened room, dimly illuminating the stark white walls and dull gray linoleum floors. He was lying on his back, his mouth and nose covered by a plastic oxygen mask, his arms resting limply at his sides. A needle dripped clear liquid into a vein in his wrist.

He was glad for the quiet, the undisturbed moments to gather his thoughts and come to grips with where he was and what he was feeling.

To discover exactly who he had become.

It was the oddest sensation, lying there in the darkness, one that, with his limited information, he hadn't completely expected. His body lay still but his thoughts were in turmoil. His mind was a jumble of information, his senses bursting with memories, images, and sensations—both tactile and internal—the forces so powerful they nearly overwhelmed him.

It was easier to deal with the physical aspects of his incredible journey, the weight of a body influenced by Earth's heavy gravity, the pulsing of a heart inside the cage of his chest, the in-and-out motion of air rushing to and from his lungs. Those things he had expected. He had been studying the human form for years; he was well prepared for the physical transition he would make.

It was the invasion of the mind, the onslaught of memories and emotions he was ill-prepared to deal with, the meshing, the mixing, the overwhelming oneness he felt with Patrick Alexander Donovan.

The astonishing fact was, in a way he hadn't expected, he actually *was* Patrick Donovan. He knew everything Patrick knew, every thought he'd ever had, every fear, every need, every wish. He knew the man's strengths as well as his failings. He knew the depth of his depravity as well as the heights of his goodness.

Fortunately, considering Patrick's somewhat weak, self-destructive personality, it was Val Zarkazian who was now in control.

It was Val's strength of will, Val's sense of purpose, Val's set of values that would rule Patrick Donovan's heretofore misused mind and body.

He settled his head against the pillow, feeling the slick white smoothness of the case, smelling the stringent hospital odors, and trying not to think of the prickle of pain in his wrist where the intravenous needle pumped fluid into his body. Instead he let himself absorb the memories, the experiences that had been the sum total of Patrick Donovan's life.

Val knew most humans had not been born into the privileged existence Patrick had, yet from the images he received of the boy's lonely childhood, he wondered if other, less advantaged children were not far better off.

He wondered about Patrick's father, the man Patrick had loved so much, a man too busy after the death of his beloved wife to pay attention to his only son. A man Patrick had always admired, yet also resented. A man who in the past few years had tried to reach out to him. Unfortunately for Patrick, by then it was too late.

He wondered about the mother who had died when the boy was ten years old, at the stepmother, a society woman, a beautiful "social butterfly"—to quote one of Patrick's own thoughts—who dressed him up in blue blazers and showed him off to her friends, who bought him dozens of expensive toys, but abandoned him to a nanny until he was big enough to be left on his own.

Big enough to get into trouble. Big enough to turn to sex and drugs.

Val wondered about the former. On Toril, the planet he came from, generations were perpetuated by test tube births. Male and female were paired genetically, then linked together after their maturity to form a loosely regulated, monogamous family unit. There was no such thing as sex, not in the sense of the physical linking that Patrick had apparently enjoyed so much.

Drugs Val understood. He was a scientist, after all. He knew their debilitating effects, the totally destructive power the misuse of drugs could unleash. In that regard, there was no need for experimentation. Only a need to repair the damage to Patrick's ravaged body that the drugs, alcohol, and off-and-on smoking had caused.

Val stirred restlessly on the hospital bed. Now that he was here, there was so much he wanted to do, so much to see, so much to experience. There was nothing he could do to hurry things along; he couldn't afford to alert them to the fact that this Patrick was somehow different than the Patrick he was before. The change would have to be gradual. Believable. Allowing Val to emerge, to become an acceptable part of Patrick without destroying the essence of who Patrick was.

It would happen all in due course, he told himself. Patience had been a virtue he had tried hard to cultivate, yet already he found himself *straining at the bit*, as Patrick would have said, itching to be free to get on with his work. Patrick's body had been physically repaired, the massive damage to his heart had been undone at the moment of Unification. By a physical weakness, an instant of good fortune for Val, and Patrick's own reckless nature, the perfect vessel had been provided for him to continue his work.

It was the chance he'd been waiting for.

The chance of a lifetime.

Val clenched his hands into fists, testing the dexterity, feeling the smooth glide of muscle between skin and bone. Careful not to disturb the needle in his wrist, he held them up in front of his face to survey the long, dark, tapering fingers, the short, blunt, neatly manicured nails. It was one thing to know Patrick's thoughts, another to experience exactly what a human male was feeling.

There was so much ahead of him. So much to learn, so much to explore. Of chief concern was the Ferris female. In the next few hours, he would search Patrick

Donovan's memory banks for every thought, every recollection of the woman the man had ever had. Soon he would begin, but not yet.

Instead Val closed his eyes and willed his turbulent thoughts to rest. He would start with something else, something that would help his host's battered body regain the strength it needed. Something he could do right here in this quiet, barren room. He would begin by experiencing the phenomena humans called sleeping. He closed his eyes and allowed the sensation to begin.

Alexander Donovan gripped the sides of his wheelchair as it rolled down the busy corridors of Cedar Sinai Hospital pushed by Nathan Jefferson Jones, the big ex-football tackle who served as his male nurse. The pair made an odd combination, Alex thin and frail with a leonine mane of snowy hair; Nathan, brawny, bulging with muscle, his head completely shaved and as shiny and black as a bowling ball.

While Alex was left-brained and fixated on work even after the stroke his stressful life had caused, Nathan lived for the moment, always smiling, cheery in the face of nearly any adversity. Keeping Alex going when he sometimes so badly wanted to just give up and let the good Lord take him away.

"There's Julie, Mr. D." Nathan pointed down the corridor. "I figured she'd be waiting right there, in front of Patrick's door."

Alex shifted in his wheelchair, relaxed a little when he saw the small, red-haired figure beside the door to his son's hospital room. Things were always better when Julie was around.

"Alex! I'm so glad you're here." She hurried toward him, walked over and hugged him hard. He could only hug her back with one arm, but it felt good to absorb her warmth and reassuring strength.

"How is he? Have you seen him yet?" The words came out a little slurred, since one side of his mouth didn't move, but Julie had grown used to his affliction and easily understood.

"I peeked in on him as soon as they would let me, but Patrick was sleeping. Babs was here with me until just a few minutes ago. She had to leave for an appointment but she stayed until the doctor came. He says the news is all very good."

"Thank God," Alex said, his bent frame sagging with relief. Standing next to his chair, Julie absently rubbed her temple. Alex frowned, worried she might be getting another of her recent migraine headaches.

She smiled, but it looked a little forced. "How about you? Are you okay?"

"By the time you called, Patrick was already out of danger. I suppose I should be angry that you didn't call me sooner, but I know why you did it, and my doctor would probably argue you did the right thing."

"I didn't want to upset you any more than I had to. I did what Patrick would have wanted me to do."

Just then Dr. Manley, the cardiologist who had been caring for Patrick, walked up, a slight, dark-haired man wearing spectacles and a long white lab coat. "You're Alex Donovan, Patrick's father?"

"That's correct. And this is Ms. Ferris, a close family friend."

"Ms. Ferris and I have already met," the doctor said.

"What can you tell us, Dr. Manley? What has happened to my son?"

"First let me say that your son can look forward to a full recovery. I want you to know that right from the beginning so that as we speak, you won't be unduly upset."

"I understand your concern for my health, Doctor, but Julie has already spared me the worst of it. Now if you will, I'd like you to tell me exactly what you know."

The doctor glanced down at the papers on the clipboard he held in a pair of elegant, long-figured hands. "At exactly 11:45 a.m. this morning your son suffered a massive myocardial infarction. We believe it was drug-induced, a toxic reaction that usually occurs from an overdose, but in this case was caused by an accumulation of drugs taken over a number of years in smaller, but still harmful doses."

He glanced down at the chart. "The drugs produced hemorrhage and cardiac arrhythmias. Cardiac dysfunction occurred, causing damage to the ventricle and the adjacent portion of the inter ventricular septum, which at first we believed might be too extensive to repair, or that by the time we were ready to operate, it would be too late."

The doctor studied a note on the paper, then looked up. "Fortunately, once your son reached the hospital and we began our series of tests, we discovered the damage to the wall of the heart was minimal. The electrocardiogram showed surgery wasn't necessary after all."

Alex said nothing for the longest time, but his insides felt knotted up inside him. He had known about Patrick's drug use for years, but his son had never been an addict. Alex had tried to convince himself Patrick would eventually mature, assume more responsibility, and outgrow his fascination with alcohol and drugs. Obviously, that hadn't happened.

Alex felt defeated in a way even his stroke had not accomplished.

"How long will he have to stay in the hospital?" he asked.

"A couple of days. He'll need to take it easy after that for several weeks—and he'll have to stay off drugs."

"Of course," Alex replied automatically. But in his heart, he knew his wayward son never would.

"Perhaps he'll slow down a little now," Julie said gently. "People can change, you know, even people like Patrick." But the look in her pretty green eyes said she didn't really believe it any more than he did.

"I'm afraid I'll have to excuse myself," the doctor said. "There's another patient I have to see before I leave. If you have any questions, I'll be in my office tomorrow."

Alex watched him walk away, took a steadying breath and turned toward Julie. "Shall we go in and see him?" he asked with tender affection.

He had known Julie Ferris for the past eight years, had been her mentor in the real estate business and come to love her like the daughter he never had. He knew she cared a great deal for his son. But not enough to overlook his many failings. Even Alex couldn't hope for that.

Julie took hold of his thin, veined hand, lacing her fingers through his. As Nathan shoved his wheelchair through the door, he noticed how tired she looked, the tight, strained lines around her mouth. It appeared as if she had slept in the wrinkled pink linen suit she wore. Perhaps for a time she had.

Julie held the door so Nathan could push him into

the room. Surprisingly Patrick's eyes were open when they walked in.

Julie left Alex's side and moved toward him, clasped one of his dark hands in her own. "We've been so worried. How are you feeling?"

"Better." He smiled at her, but it looked strained and unsteady. "I'm glad you're here. I should have known you…would be." The words sounded rough, husky, as if he had trouble forcing them out.

"Your father's here, too." Julie stepped back as Nathan wheeled Alex closer to the bed.

"I got here as soon as I heard," he said. "Julie was playing protector. She didn't call me until she knew for sure you'd be all right."

Patrick smiled again, a little less stiffly this time. "She spends more time watching out for other people than she does watching out for herself."

"Are you kidding?" Julie squeezed his hand. "If I didn't have someone to look after, I wouldn't know what to do with myself."

"You can look after me any time you like," Patrick said, and for an instant, he seemed surprised he'd said the words, then he relaxed and looked up at her. "The doctor says I'll be out of here in a couple of days. You can look after me back at the office."

"He also says you're supposed to take it easy. If it takes Babs and me, Nathan, Alex and Dr. Manley all put together, we're going to see that you do."

Patrick said nothing to that. He was watching her strangely, staring into her eyes as if he wanted to reach down inside her. Color crept into her cheeks. Her hand fluttered nervously when she withdrew it from his.

A noise in the hall disturbed them, drew Alex's attention to the opening door. "I'm sorry," the stout nurse said, "but all of you will have to leave. It's time for Mr. Donovan's medication. He needs peace and quiet, and as much rest as he can get."

Patrick made an disgruntled sound in his throat.

"I'll be back to see you in the morning," Julie said. "In the meantime, get some sleep—and Patrick?" A fine black eyebrow arched up. "For once in your life, do what the doctor says."

But Julie's admonitions had never had much success in controlling Patrick's excesses. Alex wished his son could learn to control himself.

Sitting at her desk, going over the Whitelaw escrow file, Julie answered the phone and was surprised to hear the sound of Patrick's voice coming through the receiver.

"Julie?"

"Patrick? You're feeling well enough to use the phone?"

"Yes…in fact they're releasing me today." Since his heart attack, his voice sounded a little huskier than it usually did, a bit gruffer, yet at the same time more refined. Perhaps it was the oxygen he'd been forced to breathe…or maybe it was just her imagination.

"That's wonderful, Patrick." She had gone to see him during visiting hours every day, but after the first time, she had stayed only briefly. As soon as word got out of Patrick's illness, the corridor outside his room had been clogged with his legions of women, which was why the next words that came from him over the phone were so surprising.

"I was wondering…if you weren't too busy…if you might be able to pick me up."

Something unfurled in her stomach, a mixture of wariness and pleasure. Julie ruthlessly forced it down. When she spoke to him next, a note of tartness rose into her voice. "I thought Anna, or Charlotte, or—"

"If you don't have time, I understand. I know how much work you have to do."

She felt churlish and silly. She and Patrick were friends, after all. Of course she'd be happy to pick him up. "I'm not that busy. What time are you being released?"

"Sometime after two. They didn't exactly say."

"All right, I'll be there at two."

"It might be later. I can call you after the paperwork's done and I'm ready to leave. It won't take long for you to get here."

"I'll be there at two. I can imagine how eager you are to get out of there. Maybe I can hurry things along." If it hadn't seemed so foolish, she would have sworn she could feel him smile as she hung up the phone.

As Patrick had predicted, the paperwork wasn't finished when she arrived at the hospital at two-fifteen. Patrick was still in bed, fidgeting nervously, ringing the bell for the nurse for at least the tenth time since noon.

"Sorry," he said, "I should have insisted you wait for my call."

"Don't worry about it. I'll speak to the nurse and see if I can't get them to hurry."

A few minutes later, she returned with the news that Dr. Manley had just come in and signed the release forms. The nurse would be there in a few more minutes to help him get dressed. As soon as he was ready, he could leave.

"I don't need the woman's help," Patrick grumbled, swinging his long, suntanned legs to the side of the bed. The sheet slid away. Julie noticed the white cotton hospital gown had bunched midthigh and that his bare legs were muscled and covered with a dusting of fine black hair. "She's more overbearing than a…than a…"

"Drill sergeant?" Julie supplied.

He seemed to ponder that. Then he smiled. "Exactly. I'd rather do it on my own." But when he tried to stand up, his legs turned suddenly unsteady and a shaft of weakness rippled through him.

"Here, let me help you."

Patrick swayed precariously as she drew near and only the arm she slid beneath his shoulders kept him from sprawling on the floor.

"Thanks," he said softly.

He was staring at her oddly, studying her with those striking blue eyes. Something fluttered in her stomach, sent a thread of heat spiraling through her. It made her notice how handsome he was, even with his hair slightly mussed and the ugly white hospital gown sliding off a wide, tanned shoulder. It was ridiculous and yet she couldn't deny that physically, she had always been attracted to Patrick.

His glance shifted, came to rest on the place where their two bodies touched. She could feel the heat shimmering between them and apparently so could he. His whole body stiffened and impulsively he jerked away, nearly knocking them both to the ground.

"For heaven's sake, Patrick, take it easy. If you keep

that up, you're going to land us both in a heap. Why don't you just stand still and I'll get your clothes. You can sit in the chair and put them on."

He simply nodded. His face looked flushed and even his ears were red. She couldn't imagine Patrick Donovan being embarrassed in front of a woman, but it certainly looked as though he was. She took her time removing his shirt, shoes, and pants from the tiny closet, giving him a chance to collect himself. The items were freshly laundered, she saw, not the clothes he had been wearing when he'd been brought in. Anna or Charlotte or one of his whoevers must have brought clean clothes from his apartment. She wondered why he hadn't asked the woman to pick him up.

Setting his garments on a table beside the chair, she pulled open the door. "I'll be right outside if you need me. All you have to do is call out."

"I'll be fine," he said stiffly, and began to rifle through the clothes.

Outside the room, Julie sat down on a narrow gray vinyl bench. Watching patients and nurses, doctors and visitors making their way down the hall, she toyed with the strap of her purse and hoped Patrick was truly all right.

A few minutes later, the door opened up and he walked out into the corridor, smiling as if he was pleased with himself for simply getting dressed, though she couldn't imagine why he would be.

"I'm ready if you are," he said.

Julie came to her feet. "I'm afraid you still can't leave. You'll have to go out in a wheelchair. The nurse says that's hospital policy." It occurred to her that for a man recovering from a heart attack, he certainly looked good.

In navy blue slacks and a short-sleeved, knit pullover sweater, he could have just stepped off of a billboard.

Patrick stared at her and frowned. "A wheelchair? Why would I have to do that?"

"Because they don't want to get sued if you should fall."

The nurse walked up just then, a big beefy woman in her fifties. "That's right, Mr. Donovan, that's the way it's got to be, and if you want to blame somebody for it, blame the shyster lawyer who sued us for damages and won."

He had nothing to say to that, just sat down quietly and let the woman wheel him away. Julie was a little amazed. Patrick was anything but meek, especially when he didn't get his way. Then again, maybe the heart attack had left him weaker than he looked.

Val let the woman push him into the elevator and the stainless steel doors slid closed. Beside him in a soft peach suit, Julie Ferris fidgeted with the strap of her over-the-shoulder purse.

He tried not to look at her. When he did, he thought of the way Patrick Donovan's body—his body now—had behaved when she had unwittingly pressed against him to steady his wobbly legs.

He understood what had happened. He understood an erection—theoretically.

The soft feel of her breasts had triggered a memory of her naked, thrashing on the blue-veined curlon examination table, her small, well-formed body fighting the invisible force that had held her in place.

The meshing of that memory with those Patrick Donovan carried, heightened by the close physical contact, had caused his reproductive organ to grow momentarily hard. He knew it meant the male of the species was physically aroused, that he wanted to mate with the female and deposit his sperm.

He just hadn't understood the way the sensation would make him *feel*.

He said nothing as the nurse wheeled him silently down the hall, but soon his thoughts of Julie Ferris were swamped by more pressing sensations. The noise of footfalls in the corridor, the soft thud of rubber-soled shoes mixed with the crisp slap of leather. The dull roar of mingling voices, some of them low and speaking in whispers, others raised in heated debate as they hurried through the halls. The odors he had noticed in his room earlier were magnified a thousand times out here, some of them so strong they made his nostrils burn.

As they approached the front doors, sunlight streamed into the reception area. Val blinked several times, wincing as the bright rays stabbed painfully behind his eyes.

"Take care of him, Ms. Ferris," the nurse said, pushing the wheelchair out through the automatic doors and onto the wide cement steps in front of the building. A strong female arm helped him stand up. "I guarantee he'll be a handful." She winked and Julie smiled.

He watched the woman walk away, saying nothing, too caught up in the sights and sounds pressing in on him.

"Are you sure you're okay?" Julie asked, her expression worried, her eyes fixed on his face. She linked an arm through his, helping to steady him. "All of a sudden, you look kind of pale."

Val ran his tongue across lips that felt rubbery and numb. Even if he could tell her what he was feeling, he couldn't possibly begin to describe it. There was no way to express the riot of colors—the bright green of the lawns and trees, the azure blue of the sky, the stunningly vivid red of a sports car roaring past them on the street.

"I'm fine, Julie. I'll just be glad to get home."

She studied him with concern. "The car's right out front in the passenger loading zone. We don't have far to go."

She said nothing more and neither did he. He could barely function for the jagged sensations ripping through his head. Toril was a planet of peace and serenity. There were no bright colors, no loud noises, no pungent smells. It was a pastel world, a world of grays and browns and a few muted blues, a palette of shaded colors that seemed amazingly washed out in comparison to the splashy, vibrant hues that enlivened the world of Earth.

Aside from the clothes he had seen on the subjects they had been studying, and what they had observed of the planet through their surveillance devices, he had never experienced anything to compare with the rich display spread before him like a banquet for the eyes. On Toril, the sky was a nondescript white, the plant life, even in blossom, brightened to no more than shades of weak pastel. People dressed in solid colors of those same watered shades, the styles varying little between social orders, the three different races, or male and female gender.

Here it seemed as though each individual tried to carve out his own identity by the color and style of his clothes. It gave the place an atmosphere of constant festivity, a parade of vibrant stripes, prints, and plaids all run together in a mishmash of design and color that splashed against the inner wall of the eye.

They had nearly reached the curb when a car horn blared and he stumbled backward. Another horn answered then another and another, driving the cacophony straight into his head. His hands came up to cover his ears, and beside him he felt Julie stiffen.

"Get in the car," she commanded, opening the door and easing him in. Noticing his growing pallor, she moved the seat back a little and helped him settle his long legs inside.

The car was small, a Mercedes, Patrick's memory said. But the top was up and so were the windows. When Julie closed the door, some of the loud noise abated. As she eased herself into the driver's seat, snapped her seat belt then his, Val leaned his head back and closed his eyes.

"You don't look good. Maybe it's too soon for you to leave. Maybe I should take you back inside."

His eyes snapped open. He sat up a little straighter in the seat. "I'm fine. I just want to go home."

"Are you sure, Patrick—and don't lie to me. I'd feel terrible if something else happened to you."

He turned his head in her direction, an odd tingling warmth in the pit of his stomach. "Would you?"

The color rushed into her cheeks. He knew the surge of blood was caused by feelings of embarrassment. He understood the sensation, since it had already happened to him.

"Of course, I'd care. We're friends, aren't we?"

"Yes…friends." But in his head, something said friendship wasn't all that Patrick had felt for Julie Ferris and it was never what he'd wanted.

Val lay back against the seat as the car rumbled to

life, the funny vibrations running up his back and shoulders. In the confines of the car, a faint, sweet fragrance drifted over from Julie's side of the car, a smell so subtle he hadn't noticed it before.

"I like the…perfume…you're wearing," he said, testing the word on his tongue.

"It's Michael Kors. Your father bought it for me last year for my birthday. It's expensive, but it's definitely my favorite."

"Mine, too," he said, inhaling deeply. There were no vile smells on Toril, not like the ones he'd noticed in the hospital, or those drifting up from the gutter he had whiffed as he'd slid into the car. But there was also nothing like the soft sweet fragrance of Michael Kors, either. He liked the way it mingled with Julie's own special scent, giving her a softly feminine fragrance all her own.

The small car hummed along. Val settled back in the seat, stretching his long legs out as best he could. Outside the window, the landscape of Beverly Hills slid past in a blur of sound and color. Automobiles of every design and hue crammed the streets to overflowing. People crowded along the sidewalks, hurrying to destinations he couldn't begin to guess. Buildings rose up from the pavement, their storefronts shaded by bright canvas awnings, the windows glowing with vibrant signs made of…*neon*…yes, that was the word.

"We're almost there," Julie said, turning the car off Wilshire onto Oakhurst Drive. Just past Burton Way, she slowed the engine, turned, and pulled off the road, stopping in front of the heavy metal fence that enclosed the parking garage. "I found this with your clothes."

She held up a small square box Patrick's memory

said opened the door to the underground parking. "One of your lady friends must have come by and picked it up along with the rest of your things."

The woman called Anna, he recalled. A tall, slenderly built blond female who had come to see him several times in the hospital. She had kissed him, he recalled, not an unpleasant sensation, but when she had reached beneath the covers to stroke his sex, he'd nearly had a second heart attack.

Patrick's memory had kicked in, enlightening him on their recent acquaintance—and the fact the woman was a great deal of the reason that, aside from the part of Patrick that Val had absorbed, the living, reasoning essence of Patrick Donovan was gone.

Still, the transformation was not as he'd expected. With each passing hour, he felt a subtle shifting, a reaching out, a melding of consciousness as new information, more of Patrick's being was fully absorbed. He had expected to be solidly in control, less vulnerable to the thoughts Patrick once had, the emotions he had experienced.

Instead it was if he and Patrick had merged, begun to form a third, distinctly different being. It frightened him. Made him worry what residue those changes might leave inside him.

Fear. Val could taste it in his mouth.

It was an emotion unknown to the people of Toril.

Six

"But I don't want to come out for the weekend, Julie. I'd rather stay here."

"Come on, honey," Julie coaxed her sister over the phone, "it's my birthday. Babs is coming for dinner on Saturday night. Owen's in town. He's promised he'll stop by. We'll have ourselves a party."

"I-I don't know…."

Julie rubbed her temple, trying to ignore the headache that had built behind her eyes. "Come on, Laura, please? The weather's going to be clear. We can lie out in the cove and no one will bother us. You can tell me how your sessions with Dr. Heraldson are going."

"He wants to hypnotize me."

"So?"

"I don't want him to, Julie."

"Why not?"

"I-I don't know. I just don't like the idea."

Julie took a steadying breath and slowly released it. "We'll talk about it when you get here."

"It'll be too late by then. Tomorrow's my appointment."

"Well...if Dr. Heraldson thinks it's a good idea, maybe you should do it."

"I suppose so. I guess it couldn't hurt." A pause on the phone. "I'd forgotten it was your birthday."

"Does that mean you'll come?"

"Of course I will."

"Great. Can I count on seeing you Friday night? We could go out for a bite of dinner."

"I can't, I've got a date. I'll drive out Saturday afternoon."

A date, Julie thought, praying it wasn't with that no-good Jimmy Osborn. Her head throbbed even harder. "I guess if that's the best you can do, it'll have to be good enough. I've got a couple of properties to show on Saturday morning. If I'm not home when you get here, you know where to find the extra key."

They both said goodbye and Julie rang off thinking about Laura. She was worried about her, but then as Babs had said, she usually was. Walking into the bathroom, she opened the medicine cabinet and searched the shelves, looking for the plastic bottle of painkillers Dr. Marsh had prescribed for her migraines. This one was shaping up to be a doozie.

Her hand shook as she pried off the lid and dumped a couple of capsules into her palm. A third fell out. For a moment she was tempted, then she thought of Patrick's drug abuse and where it had finally landed him, and slid the third pill back into the bottle.

Thirty minutes later, the medicine had still not kicked in. Pain shot into her skull as the phone beside the bed began to ring. She reached over and lifted the receiver.

"Julie? It's Patrick."

The headache was getting so bad it was starting to upset her stomach. She dampened her dry lips with the tip of her tongue, thinking she might throw up. "Hello, Patrick. How are you feeling?" It had been a week since Patrick's release from the hospital. He had been taking it easy, as the doctors suggested, surprisingly circumspect for Patrick.

"Better than I have a right to. That's why I'm calling. I'm down at the office. I thought you'd be in. I figured you might want to go over the Rabinoff file."

"I'm afraid I'm not feeling well, Patrick. But the escrow's all set to close. I don't think there'll be any more unforeseen problems."

"You're sick?" He sounded suddenly worried. "What's the matter with you?"

"Another one of my headaches. This one's pretty bad and nothing seems to help. I took some of the pills Dr. Marsh prescribed, but—"

"I'm coming over. I'll be there in just a few minutes. Lie down and take it easy till I get there."

"Patrick—you can't drive all the way out here. You probably shouldn't be driving at all. Besides, there's nothing you can do the doctor hasn't already done."

"Maybe there is. I have hidden talents you wouldn't believe. Besides, you helped me, didn't you? I owe you one." He hung up the receiver before Julie could say any more.

Val knew what was wrong with Julie Ferris. Her resistance to their scanners had been painful and immediate. The brutal headaches that followed were not unexpected, since they had occurred in subjects like Julie before. But the vicious assaults had lasted far longer than they had predicted, perhaps because, unlike the others, she had been taken aboard a second time.

Val felt a shot of guilt, a feeling he had never really known. When he'd made the difficult decision to bring the older sibling back aboard, he had known there might be complications. He wished he could explain, reassure her that the headaches would soon disappear. But he wasn't exactly certain that would happen. It was one of the things he'd been sent here to observe. Grabbing his coat off the wooden valet in the corner of his office, he started for the door.

In the meantime, he knew the cause and what to do to treat them. At least he could ease some of her pain.

Shoving open the office door, he walked down the sidewalk toward the pudgy young man in front of Spago's who parked Patrick's car, and handed him a couple of dollar bills. He had driven the shiny black Porsche for the first time that morning—an antique mode of transportation he found fascinating. He was grateful Patrick knew how to handle the car and had enjoyed every second behind the wheel.

Patrick was a very good driver, he had discovered, with what seemed a natural ability to handle the vehicle on the route through Laurel Canyon. Later he had cruised Mulholland Drive.

All along the way, a fierce blue sky curved above him, brightened by clouds so white and incredibly lovely it made him feel funny inside. At the top of the hill he'd parked the car for a while and simply stared out over the landscape. Wildflowers in vivid purple and saffron gold, poppies in scorching red-orange. A large brown bird, a goshawk, his memory recalled, spiraled down off the mountain, coasting on the currents of the wind.

Afterward, he jotted down the experience in the journal he was keeping, filling the pages with words written in Patrick's bold hand. It was the only way he could think of to capture the unfamiliar feelings, the subtle nuances of his thoughts. He had been making reports to his superiors, of course, communicating with the *Ansor* team through normal space channels.

But there was just no Torillian way to describe what was actually going on.

The journal would have to do that. When he returned to the ship, the pages could be scanned, translated by computer into words and images far more detailed than his logical, straightforward mind could manage.

Val tipped the valet for the second time that day, vowing to start parking the car himself in the office parking lot, then slid into the deep red leather seat of the softly purring sports car. He stepped on the gas, relaxed his mind, and let Patrick's well-honed driving skills take over. He knew the way to Julie's house and the fastest way to get there. Avoiding as much of the traffic as he could, he pulled onto Pacific Coast Highway and roared along the beach to Julie's batten-board, ranch-style beach house.

He spotted it clinging to the side of a cliff, a two-car garage on the bottom, forming a two-story structure, the walls of the house draped with shocking-pink azaleas. If he hadn't been so worried, he might have smiled.

Instead he parked the car in the driveway, knocked on the door, and a few minutes later, Julie Ferris let him in.

"This is silly, Patrick. You shouldn't have come."

But she looked so pale he was glad he had. He felt responsible for what was happening to her. *Was* responsible. There was just no way around it. Still, science was all-important. The *Ansor's* mission was all-important.

And yet when he looked at Julie, he wished there could have been some other way.

"Why don't you lie down on the couch?" he said gently. "I give a great massage. Why don't we see if it will help?"

"I don't know, Patrick...."

"Come on, Julie, please. Do it for me?"

A hint of uncertainty appeared in her face. She had always been wary of Patrick and yet they were friends of a sort. "All right. What have I got to lose?"

A few minutes later, she was lying on her stomach on the sofa, her pale blue terry-cloth robe covering her primly from neck to ankle. Val knelt beside her, began to massage her shoulders.

"I must be crazy," she mumbled when his hands moved a little bit lower, kneading the muscles across her back. "If you try anything, Patrick, I swear I'll never forgive you."

He flushed a little at that. Partly because he had begun to like the feel of her small woman's body beneath his hands and partly because the heavy male part of his anatomy was coming to life again.

Val swore something Patrick would have said. "I promise my intentions are completely aboveboard."

"They'd better be."

He continued his deep massage, working upward again, toward the muscles in her neck, reaching the area at the base of her skull that had been his objective from the start. His fingers sifted through her hair. He couldn't believe how soft and silky it felt, while at the same time it was bouncy and vibrant, shimmering with life and substance.

Her skin was soft and smooth to the touch. When he had seen her that night onboard the ship, he had never noticed the satiny texture. But Patrick must have noticed it at least a hundred times, and because he had, now, so did he.

His hand shook, felt a little unsteady. The blood pumping through him seemed to thicken, pool low in his belly. He forced himself to ignore it.

Beneath his hands, a tiny vessel throbbed under an obscure layer of flesh. He searched it out, applied a gentle pressure, and felt the tension begin to ebb from Julie's body.

"Better?" he asked, feeling a little more in control.

She made a purring sound and nodded. "I can't believe how much."

He continued to work on the vessel, knowing exactly how much blood to let flow and when to cut back.

Julie's body relaxed even more. "How on Earth did you learn to do that?"

It wasn't on Earth, he thought. But he just smiled and didn't say it. "I'm just glad it's working."

"Uhmmm, it's working, all right. My headache is almost gone." She yawned hugely and her eyes drifted closed. Her breathing smoothed out, grew deeper. A few minutes later, she was asleep.

Val eased away from her, oddly reluctant to leave. He crossed the room to a serape-draped chair several paces away and sat down to watch her, taking advantage of the chance to study her unobserved. He made mental notes of her posture, the way she curled up in the robe like some small warm-blooded animal. He studied her breathing, watched the way it caused a strand of dark red hair to float beside her ear.

He assessed her small feet and hands, the soft pink polish on her fingernails and toes. He knew what she looked like beneath the robe, but he tried very hard not to think of it. When he did, his stomach muscles tightened and he started to grow hard again. Eventually he drew out the journal, began to use Patrick's words as well as his own impressions to describe what he'd learned—and how watching her sleep made him feel.

He wasn't at all happy with that discovery. He felt warm all over, somewhat sexually aroused, and precariously close to losing some of his precious control. Since control was the thing he needed most, he vowed to be more careful in the future.

In the end, he left Julie a note on the rough-hewn bleached pine coffee table in front of the sofa, then let himself out, pushing the button on the doorknob to lock it behind him. All the way home he wondered if his reactions to Julie belonged wholly to Patrick—or if some part of them could have belonged to him.

Brian Heraldson, Doctor of Psychiatry, sat behind the desk in his walnut-paneled, book-lined office on Galey Avenue in Westwood. He leaned back in his chair, his long fingers steepled in front of him, his thick brown eyebrows drawn together in a frown. Brian was thirty-five years old, divorced three years ago, over it now but wary of relationships that involved any form of commitment. His practice was everything—employer, friend, mistress—and he was good at what he did.

He was open, objective and concerned. To him psychiatry wasn't just a job. It was a guideline of how to live and a deep responsibility. And so he pondered his newest patient, Laura Maxine Ferris. The most beautiful woman he'd ever seen.

He was uncomfortable thinking of that. It was highly unethical to become involved with a patient. And he staunchly believed in those ethics. He wouldn't allow the physical attraction he felt for Laura to stop him from giving her the help she so desperately needed.

Unconsciously, Brian stroked his neatly trimmed beard. He had grown it ten years ago, when he had first gone into practice. It had made him look older, more mature, gave his patients more confidence in his ability to help them. Since that time, he had grown so used to his bearded appearance, he couldn't imagine how he would look without it. He wondered if Laura Ferris was attracted to men who wore beards, then prayed most sincerely that she wasn't.

Leaning forward, he pressed the button on the small, digital tape recorder sitting on his desk and Laura's soft feminine voice floated out through the speakers in the compact machine.

She was telling him about her childhood, describing the day her father had left them, how terribly sad they all had been. "Mama cried the most," she said. "I held onto Daddy's leg when he opened the door and begged him not to leave. I said, 'Don't go Daddy, please,' but he only shook his head. I remember the way his hand stroked through my hair. It was exactly the same light blond as his and his eyes were brown like mine. I started to cry and he looked like he might cry, too."

"What about your sister? What did she do?"

"Julie just stood there and watched him pack his things. She was leaning against the wall in the corner, staring at Mama and me. She saw us crying and for some reason it made her really mad. She started shouting at Mama and me, telling us to let him leave. She said, 'Let him go! He doesn't want us anymore—let him leave!' She ran over to Daddy and told him to go away. She said she didn't care if he ever came back. I don't think Mama ever forgave her for that."

The chair squeaked as Brian sat up straighter. "Your mother thought it was Julie's fault your father left you?"

A sad look crossed her face. "Not really. She just wanted someone besides herself to blame for driving him away."

"What about you? Did you blame your sister?"

Laura smiled faintly. "No. I knew Julie loved Daddy more than any of us. That was the reason she didn't cry. She was afraid if she started, she'd never be able to stop."

Brian punched the stop button on the recording machine, bringing the tape to a whirring halt. He felt Laura's pain a second time as he listened to her story, felt sorry for the lonely little girls who had only each other to love.

He'd been seeing Laura three times a week since she had been coming in for treatment. There was lots of ground to cover but she seemed to be responding very well and they had developed a nice rapport.

He fast-forwarded the tape, coming to the hypnosis session she had finally agreed to that had taken place yesterday afternoon. He had wanted to start with her childhood, hoping to pinpoint the catalyst responsible for her recent paranoia, which had apparently started only a short time ago.

He wanted to know if something frightening had actually occurred, something Laura had suppressed, something perhaps she was afraid to remember. Had she been assaulted, raped, or in some other way abused? Or was the paranoia a result of some earlier problem that had only just now begun to surface?

In either case, a single incident might have occurred which could have brought her fears to a head. He pushed the play button and leaned back in his chair, listening carefully to the final part of the session. Under deep hypnosis, he had taken Laura backward through time to the day several weeks ago when she had first become frightened.

He knew when she had reached it by her sudden rigid posture, the long slim fingers clawing into the arms of her chair.

"Where are you, Laura?" he asked gently.

She only shook her head.

"Where are you? Laura, you don't have to be afraid. Just tell me where you are?"

Her face grew pale. Her eyebrows drew tightly together. Her hands were shaking, her knees trembling beneath the folds of her loose-fitting paisley cotton skirt. "Hospital," she whispered.

"You're in the hospital?"

She nodded stiffly, her arms still gripping the chair.

"When, Laura?"

"June. I went to Julie's house. We took a day off from work to lay on the beach."

It didn't make sense. As far as he knew, no accidents, no emergencies, nothing like that had occurred. "Did Julie take you to the hospital?"

She shook her head. "No."

"How did you get there?"

"I don't…I don't know."

This wasn't going the way he planned. He took another tack. "All right, Laura. You're in the hospital. Tell me about it. Tell me why you're afraid."

She chewed her bottom lip. For the longest time she didn't speak, just stared straight ahead as if she were there again. "They took off my clothes," she finally said. "I was naked. It was cold in there…so cold." She started to shiver.

"Go on," he softly urged.

"They washed my body with something like alcohol, but it was slimy and it didn't have much smell. When they washed between my legs, I started to cry."

Brian stared at his patient in silence, turning over what she had said. "What happened next?" he asked, suddenly not sure he wanted to hear.

"I tried to fight them, but I couldn't move. I couldn't lift my arms. They bent my knees, pushed up my legs. They shoved something cold and hard up inside me. I tried to scream, but nothing came out."

Brian's own hands started to shake. "Go on, Laura."

"I begged them not to hurt me. 'Please don't…please don't hurt me.' But they couldn't hear. They pulled the metal things out from inside me and stuffed something rubbery into my mouth. I could feel it tickling the back of my throat and I started to gag. I was afraid I'd choke if I threw up. I closed my eyes as tight as I could, tried not to think about the thing in my mouth, tried to ignore the crunching sound inside my head when they shoved a little hard thing up my nose."

Brian rubbed the back of a hand across his lips. "What else do you remember, Laura?"

She didn't answer. Just sat there shaking.

"Laura? Tell me what else you recall."

She shook her head. "Nothing else. I don't remember why I went there. I don't know how I got home." She started to cry then, soft little sobs that jabbed at his insides. He knew he should press her, try to discover how this wild delusion had gotten started, but he was fairly certain he knew.

Her medical history said Laura hadn't been inside a hospital in years, not since she was seventeen years old, pregnant, and unmarried. Her boyfriend had convinced her to have an abortion, but his choice of practitioner wasn't the greatest. Complications had set in. Fortunately, her sister found out what had happened and had taken her to a reputable doctor, who had seen she got the proper care.

It was all in her medical files.

All but the trauma the incident must have caused.

Brian turned off the tape and leaned back in his chair. Two more days until her next appointment. Another hypnosis session might prove interesting. Then again, it was certain to be hard on her. Perhaps it was too early in the treatment for any more trauma. He would have to give it some thought.

Then again, more time spent thinking about Laura Ferris might be the last thing he ought to do.

* * *

Julie checked the time on her Rolex watch. It was only 10:00 a.m. She was feeling pretty good this morning—no headaches for the past two days—and there was a two-hour break in her schedule before her luncheon with Evan Whitelaw and his wife, a meeting to discuss the escrow instructions on the Beverly Hills estate they had just purchased.

Julie smiled to think of the sale she had made. True, the house was bordered by Bel-Air, but it wasn't technically *in* Bel-Air, as Jane Whitelaw had insisted. Her smile broadened as she thought of how glad she was she had talked the woman into a quick look at what had turned out to be the Whitelaws' perfect home.

Heading out of her office, she walked past where Shirl Bingham sat filing her nails at the reception desk.

"If anyone's looking for me, I'll be upstairs in the fitness center. I'll be back before lunch to check my messages."

Shirl just nodded and continued filing her long red nails. Julie thought of the fit Alex Donovan would have pitched if he had caught her, but company image was hardly a concern his son would have.

Julie walked out the front doors, into a different entrance of the same building, and stepped into the elevator. She got off on the third floor and went into the health club. For a number of people who worked nearby, the place was well maintained and convenient and not too overly large. Julie had been attending aerobics classes with a fair amount of regularity for the past three years.

She went into the locker room, changed into a pair of black shorts and a tank top, tied the laces on her Reeboks, then went into the weight room to warm up on one of the five stationary bikes. She stopped dead in her tracks when she looked over and saw Patrick on the treadmill, his tall frame drenched in sweat.

"My God, will wonders never cease." She stopped beside the machine, grinning with disbelief.

"Hi," he simply said. His face glistened with perspiration. A curl of damp black hair clung to his forehead. She had the strangest urge to reach out and brush it back out of the way.

"I didn't know you were a member here," she said.

"I wasn't. Not until a couple of days ago. I thought, since it was so handy, it would be a good way to get in shape."

Her grin slid away. "Are you sure you're well enough for this? I thought you were supposed to take it easy."

For a moment he looked uncomfortable, then he smiled his charming white smile. "I am taking it easy. I'm in bed every night by ten, no smoking, no drugs, no liquor. I'd say that's about as easy as it gets."

One of her eyebrows shot up. "In bed by ten? I don't doubt that. The question is with whom? Let's see—could it be the lovely Anna? Or are you back with Charlotte? Or maybe by now there's someone new."

A flush crept under his tan. Julie couldn't believe it.

"Suffice it to say, I'm staying out of trouble. I'm getting myself in shape, just like the doctors said."

She didn't believe it, of course, or if by some miracle it was true, that it could possibly last. She studied him, struck by a sudden thought. "That wasn't your car I saw in the parking lot this morning when I got in?"

"I came to work early. I had some business I needed to catch up on."

Julie fell silent, for the first time allowing herself to really take a look at him. She had never seen Patrick in so few clothes, nothing but a pair of damp, clinging white shorts that hinted at the considerable bulge of his sex, a red tank top, socks, and running shoes. With every stride he made on the treadmill, long corded muscles bunched in his legs. His waist was lean, his shoulders very wide, more thickly muscled than she imagined, and the dark skin across them appeared surprisingly smooth. Curly black chest hair glistened with beads of perspiration above the scooped neck of his tank top.

"I hope you like what you see," Patrick said softly, his blue eyes suddenly intense, and this time it was Julie's turn to blush.

"I'm sorry. I didn't mean to stare, it's just that I-I… that seeing you here was so unexpected."

"I'll be through in a few more minutes. Why don't you finish your workout, and afterward—how about lunch?"

Lunch with Patrick? "I-I'm meeting the Whitelaws, going over their escrow instructions." Had she heard him right? Was he actually asking her out? He hadn't done that in years.

"If you can't go to lunch, what about dinner? We'll go someplace quiet where we can talk."

This was crazy. Patrick hated quiet restaurants. He wanted to be where the action was. The hottest see-and-be-seen he could possibly find.

"Talk about what?" she asked dumbly, sure she was missing something. "Is there a problem I don't know about at work? Is one of my clients upset? The Rabinoff deal had a few shaky moments but I thought they were happy in the end."

Patrick slowed down, finally stopped jogging altogether, and stepped off the machine. "Nothing's wrong, Julie." It was amazing how much taller he seemed when she was wearing flat-heeled shoes. He wiped the sweat from his face with a white cotton towel. "I just wanted some company. I thought you might want some, too."

"I don't believe this, Patrick." Unconsciously, she took a step away. "We decided years ago we'd be far better off as friends. We both know what it is you expect from the women you take out. You also know that's not what you'll get from me. I think the best course is the one we've been on up till now."

He studied her for long, quiet moments. She couldn't ever remember him looking at her quite that way. "I'm asking as a friend, Julie. I don't expect anything more."

She felt foolish then. Of course it was friendship he expected. He had half a dozen beautiful women he could call on a moment's notice. The only reason he had ever wanted her was because she had always said no.

And aside from an unwelcome physical attraction, she certainly didn't want him.

On the other hand, after the scare he'd had, Patrick might need a friend very badly. Besides, it might be pleasant to spend the evening with a man for a change, instead of a client, Babs, or her sister.

"How about it?" he pressed.

Julie smiled. "I can't go tonight, but tomorrow night would be fine. I've got appointments until eight. After that I'm all yours."

He cleared his throat. "Right. Great. So shall I pick you up at your house or will you still be down at the office?"

"The office. I'll be there all afternoon. Now I've got to run. I've missed fifteen minutes of class already. I'll see you back at work."

Patrick just nodded. He used the towel around his neck to wipe away more sweat as he watched her walk away.

Julie had the strangest feeling, one that had nagged her off and on since he got out of the hospital. Patrick seemed different lately, in at least a dozen ways. He even looked a little different, more mature somehow, more commanding. And his attitude toward her had somehow changed, though in exactly what way she couldn't be sure. Perhaps the evening he planned would shed some light on the subject. If it did, maybe she would find some way to help him stay away from booze and drugs. If nothing else, she owed that much to Alex.

Julie decided firmly—she would help Patrick if she could.

Seven

Sitting behind the desk in her office, Julie hung up the phone with a shaky hand and slowly came to her feet. Brian Heraldson, Laura's psychiatrist, had just called. He said he needed to see her. He said Laura had just left the office, having finished her second hypnosis session. He said it was important that he and Julie speak.

On the surface, that didn't seem all that ominous. As Laura's sister, she had offered to help in any way she could, knowing he might want input from the only immediate family Laura had left. Yet there was something in his voice, something urgent, perhaps even fearful, that turned Julie's stomach upside down.

She pressed the intercom button, told Shirl she'd be out for a while, then left through the rear door leading out to the parking lot. Westwood wasn't far. In minutes, she was standing in front of the receptionist's desk, asking the pretty little brunette to tell the doctor she was there.

"He'll be right with you, Ms. Ferris," the young woman said, probably a UCLA student doing part-time work, since the campus was just blocks away. The same sort of work Julie had done.

She glanced around the office, liking the soft gray carpet, the muted tones, and the Impressionist paintings on the walls that made the room feel warm and not sterile.

"Hello, Julie." Dr. Heraldson stood in the open doorway leading into his private suite of rooms. "Please come in."

She smiled uncertainly as she moved past him, her heart beginning to throb inside her chest. "I came as quickly as I could. Laura's all right, isn't she? She was able to drive herself home?"

"Laura's fine...at least on the surface." He firmly closed the door. "I've asked you here in the hope that you might shed some light on a subject that has me somewhat concerned." He indicated she should take a seat on the light-gray overstuffed sofa. "I want to play a tape for you. I don't normally do this and certainly not without the patient's permission. Laura has given her consent, and I'd like your opinion about what she has said on the tape."

"Of course. I want to help Laura in any way I can." She sat down on the couch while the doctor walked to the chair behind his desk. He was a good-looking man, she saw, with his thick brown, slightly too-long hair and neatly trimmed beard. She wondered that she hadn't noticed that when she had first met him, the day Laura's sessions had begun, or the second time she had stopped in.

"I'm not going to play it all. Some of it is extremely personal." He stopped the tape, backed it up a little, ran it forward again, and then pushed the button. "This is the tape I made the first of the week, her first hypnosis session. Here's the part I wanted you to hear."

Julie sat unmoving as Laura described the first time she had been afraid. It was the day they had suntanned on the beach. At first it was the same as Julie remembered, then Laura's story turned different. Laura said that after the beach, she had gone to the hospital, which of course wasn't the least bit true. Julie's skin began to crawl as her sister recounted her terrifying experience, describing in vivid detail the humiliating examination she had been subjected to, the way her body had been stripped, washed, and probed.

Unconsciously, Julie clasped her arms across her chest, waiting for the gruesome tale to finish. She jumped when the doctor pressed the stop button, abruptly ending the strained, terror-stricken voice of her sister on the tape.

"It isn't true, you know," Julie said softly. "She didn't go to the hospital. After she left my house, she simply went home. I called her later, so I know she got there safely."

"I didn't think this had actually occurred. At least not on that day. There was nothing in her medical files and nothing on the admission forms she filled out when she started treatment."

"I thought under hypnosis, people were supposed to tell the truth."

"They tell the truth as they perceive it. I think Laura may have confused another event in her life, perhaps the abortion she went through some years ago. At least that was my feeling until the session we attempted today."

"She told you about that?"

He nodded.

The abortion wasn't something Laura liked to discuss. At seventeen, the pregnancy and botched abortion was just another incident in a lifetime of mistakes.

"You said that was your feeling until today."

"That's right."

Julie's stomach began to churn. "So what…what happened today?"

"I think the best way to tell you is simply to play the tape."

Julie just nodded. Her insides felt tied in knots. There was something strangely unsettling about what Laura had said, though she knew it wasn't the truth. Sitting back on the sofa, she concentrated on the soft whir of the recorder, her chest feeling leaden. Dr. Heraldson skipped the first part of the session where he had done the hypnosis and the conversation leading up to the subject he wanted to discuss. He started the tape at the part where he'd asked Laura about her trip to the hospital the day they had gone to the beach, and if since then, she had ever been frightened like that again.

A long nervous pause ensued. Then, "One night I thought I heard them. I thought they were there, outside my bedroom window. I called the police. They searched outside, but no one was there. A few days later, I thought I heard them again. I was so scared…I didn't know what to do. I called the police again, but they never found any trace of them."

The doctor's deep voice came softly over the tape. "Who did you think was out there, Laura?"

"I don't know. The people from the hospital I guess."

"Have you seen them again?"

She swallowed so hard Julie could hear it on the

tape. "Yes…They came for me at Julie's. I should have known they would—that's where they came for me before…there on the beach. I shouldn't have stayed with Julie."

Julie sat up straighter on the sofa, her stomach clenching tighter.

"Tell me what happened," the doctor said.

"I-I heard them outside on the balcony…footsteps…little scratching noises. I knew it was them. Oh, God, I was so frightened. I wanted to hide. I wanted to run. But I knew they would find me wherever I went. It was dark outside. When the lights went off, I wanted to curl up and die. A few minutes later, a bright light filled the room, so strong it hurt my eyes. Then it was dark again." Laura made a soft choking sound of despair. "That's when they came into the bedroom."

There was the sound of the doctor's chair moving. "Go on, Laura," he whispered gently, "this is only a memory. You're distanced from it. The memory can no longer hurt you."

She seemed to relax at that. "I don't know how they got in. One minute they were out on the deck, the next they were there, standing all around the bed. I couldn't move. I couldn't even scream. They stared at me for the longest time…then they carried me away."

The doctor cleared his throat. "What else do you recall?"

"Nothing until I woke up. I was there…in the hospital. They stripped off my nightgown and washed my body with the same wet slimy stuff they rubbed on me before. They parted my legs and probed inside me. It hurt a little, but mostly I was embarrassed. I don't think they really meant to hurt me, but I hated them just the same. I hated them for what they were doing. I laid there naked and I prayed they weren't real, that what was happening was only a nightmare. I prayed that I would wake up, but in my heart I knew I wasn't dreaming."

The doctor said nothing.

The tape whirred in the silence of a pause. "There's something more," Laura said, "but I-I can't seem to recall what it is." She must have bent her head for the sob that slipped from her throat came out muffled and ragged. Then she started crying.

Julie jerked when the tape recorder went off, looked up from the hands she'd been gripping in her lap, and returned her attention to Brian Heraldson. She wished the blood would flow back into her face.

"Now you can see why I called."

She moistened her lips. Her mouth felt like cotton. "Yes."

"Is there anything you can remember about either of those occasions, anything that might help explain the things Laura has said?"

"No. It makes absolutely no sense. The day we went to the beach, we both fell asleep for a while. Afterward we packed our things and went back to my house. Neither of us felt very good. Probably too much sun. Afterward I had a terrible headache, but other than that, nothing extraordinary occurred."

"How about later, the weekend she spent with you after the incident with the police?"

"As she said on the tape, she was afraid someone was trying to break into her apartment. She was frightened.

That was the reason she agreed to come home with me in the first place."

"How did she behave that night? Did you notice anything unusual?"

"Not really. We ate an early supper—lemon chicken. It's one of her favorites. We had a glass of wine and talked for a while out on the deck, then we both went to bed. I was having another one of my headaches, so I took some sleeping pills. I seem to recall seeing a very bright light that night, but it could have been anything…perhaps a spotlight on one of the beach patrol Jeeps. After that, I guess I must have fallen asleep. I don't remember anything until I woke up in the morning."

"How was Laura then?"

Julie frowned as she recalled Laura's pale face the following day. "Now that you mention it, she did seem kind of upset. I thought she was getting the flu. I took her to see our family physician that afternoon."

"I read Dr. Marsh's report. The bleeding she suffered coincides with her memory of the physical examination she believes she experienced—but the body has been known to assist us in our delusions."

"What do you mean?"

"It is not uncommon in cases of trauma for marks to appear with no physical contact, burns, bruises on the skin, that sort of thing. Psychosomatic manifestations can cause all sorts of problems."

The doctor caught her worried gaze and came up from his chair. "I can see that you are upset and that wasn't my intention in bringing you here." He rounded the desk and walked toward her. "We've only just started Laura's therapy. She hasn't heard the tapes. I wanted to speak to you first, find out as much as I could. I've decided to play them for her during her next session. Perhaps hearing them will help her remember what it was that unleashed her fears in the first place. At the very least, since none of this actually occurred, she'll be able to understand their groundless nature. Then we can begin delving into her feelings about the abortion."

Julie rubbed the bridge of her nose, trying not to notice the headache that had started to build. "You really believe that's what this is about?"

"Don't you?"

"I don't know. It was extremely traumatic for her at the time, but I really thought she'd gotten past it. "I'm not really sure what to believe, but I'm very worried about her."

"I know you are, Julie. And your concern is one of the things that's going to help her get well." He walked her to the door. "I'd prefer you didn't discuss this with Laura, at least not yet."

"All right. And if there's anything else I can do, please just call." He showed her out the door then closed it softly behind her. All the way to her car, Julie's stomach churned to think of the terror going on in her sister's beautiful head.

Commander Val Zarkazian took a last look at himself in the mirror above the black teakwood dresser in the bedroom of his penthouse apartment. Already his face— Patrick's face, he corrected—had lost its pallor. The dark, clean-shaven skin was once again robust, without the trace of puffiness Patrick's drug abuse had caused. The running he did each morning left his chiseled features lean and his jawline firm. There was even a newly acquired, glossy vitality to his wavy black hair.

Remembering the first Earth subjects he had seen, he never thought he would come to like his human appearance. But he did. As Patrick he felt…substantial. A solid mass of muscle and bone. He felt male and masculine in a way far different from anything he had experienced on Toril.

Where he came from, male and female gender were different, yet very much the same. Though he was larger than his female counterparts, any variation in size, shape or thinking was inconsequential. They all worked at the same tasks, were equally well-educated, and shared equally in the raising of the offspring they were assigned, test-tube children resulting from their genetic match.

Until he'd come here, protective feelings toward the female of the species were heretofore unknown, as was deference to her as an expression of politeness. Even more importantly, he had never known this craving, this hunger to mate with a female. It was something he couldn't quite grasp.

And yet he found this division of the sexes, these powerful feelings of maleness, exhilarating beyond anything he could have imagined.

He straightened his patterned silk tie and turned away from the mirror, crossing the artistic, sparsely furnished bedroom, past the king-sized pedestal bed, his black shoes clicking on the polished hardwood floors. Modern art lined the walls: nothing too expensive, just new young artists with an eye for color and form. Patrick's contemporary tastes corresponded with the simple lines in the world Val had come from, making it easier to accept this place as his temporary home.

On his way out the door, he passed the platter of cold-cuts and crackers—a favorite of Patrick's—that he had been determined to eat. He picked up a piece of salami, felt his stomach swim with nausea, and laid it back down on the plate. Consuming Earth food had been one of his most difficult adjustments. Everything was too spicy, too hot or too cold, the texture so different from what he was used to it almost made him gag.

Still, his body needed nourishment. He had to keep trying. He took a thin slice of chopped ham, rolled it up and took a bite, forced himself to chew, grimaced and swallowed it nearly whole, then continued on into the living room. All the while his mind remained fixed on the evening he would spend with Julie Ferris.

It was crucial he increase his involvement with her. He was there to study her in her natural environment, see what he might learn. Physically he had found nothing different about her, from other female subjects, but the testing had been minimal. He needed to study her habits, her likes and dislikes, what foods she ingested into her stomach, what sort of care she took of her body. Through Patrick's memory bank, he already knew a great deal. Tonight would provide another study opportunity.

At 8:00 p.m. he arrived at the office to find her still at work, a phone to her ear as she bent over her desk. She was standing with her back to him, scribbling something on a piece of paper. A small brass lamp on the edge of the table reflected the reddish sparkle in her hair. Dressed in a powder-blue suit with big pearl buttons, she smoothed the knee-length skirt that hugged the curves of her bottom. The tailored jacket didn't quite reach her tiny waist.

Watching her, Val's groin tightened. His blood began to thicken, pulse in a slow throbbing rhythm through his veins. Damn! His body was readying itself, desire sliding through him, making him hard against the front of his pants. He focused his attention on the map of Los Angeles County Julie had pinned to one wall. He studied the streets, memorized the names of the ones he didn't already know. By the time she had hung up the phone, he was damp between the shoulder blades but back in control.

Julie turned to him and smiled, her pretty pink lips tipping up at the corners. "Sorry I'm late. I meant to be through by the time you got here."

"That's all right. I enjoyed watching you work."

She looked at him strangely. "You've been watching me work for the past eight years."

His face went warm. "I've always liked watching you. I just never told you." That was the truth. Patrick wanted Julie—hungered for her—but only on his own terms. Since he couldn't have that, he had ignored his feelings for her. Val intended to use those feelings to his own far different ends.

She glanced away, started rearranging the papers on her desk. "I guess we'd better go." She straightened the papers into an orderly pile and turned to face him with a smile. "I haven't eaten since noon and you're probably starving."

He wasn't hungry, of course. On Toril, people ate far smaller quantities of food, and certainly not as a form of enjoyment. But his body needed sustenance. He would force himself to eat. "I wasn't sure what time you'd be finished, so I haven't made any reservations. I thought we might go over to Trebecca. It's quiet and I know how much you like Italian."

Her smile broadened. "And I know you aren't that crazy about it. Why don't we try that new little Japanese restaurant down the street? It's supposed to be very good."

Japanese. He hadn't tried that yet. Italian definitely didn't set well. He wondered how hard it would be to get down Japanese-style dishes and hoped the portions were small. "Sounds good to me if we can get in."

"Are you kidding, Patrick? There isn't a place in this town you can't get in."

She was right. Patrick knew how to grease a wheel. Enough greenbacks and he could manage just about anything.

Val found himself frowning. Even his thoughts were beginning to sound like Patrick. Then again, perhaps that was good. He wanted to absorb the culture, learn about Earth in a way none of his people ever had.

"Come on," he said, sliding an arm around Julie's waist. "Let's get going. It's getting kind of late, and I'm hungrier than I thought."

The restaurant was just a short drive away. Val tipped the maître d', who promised he would find them a quiet table in the rear. A few minutes later they were seated on the floor on tatami mats in front of a low black lacquer table with a hole cut underneath for their legs. Sort of the American version of sitting Japanese-style on the floor.

The waiter handed him a menu. As soon as he started

to scan the items listed, the thought occurred that Patrick hated Japanese.

He'd never told anyone. Eating sushi was chic. He wasn't about to admit he didn't like raw fish. Instead he had simply avoided places like this.

Val smiled across the table at Julie. "I'm not much of a connoisseur. Why don't you order for both of us?"

She eyed him a little bit strangely. Patrick rarely relinquished control. "All right." When the tiny Asian waitress came up to the table, Julie ordered several kinds of sushi as an appetizer, followed by soup and a stir-fry shrimp and vegetable dish. The first course arrived and Val hesitantly placed two of the artfully designed sushi rolls on his plate. When he didn't begin to eat, just sat there working up his courage, he felt Julie's gaze on his face.

She started grinning, her wide green eyes bubbling with mirth. "Why didn't you just tell me you didn't like sushi? It isn't a crime, you know."

"What makes you think I don't like it?" he said blandly.

"Probably because you aren't eating it. You're just staring at it like it's going to crawl off the plate."

A faint smile tugged at his lips. Determinedly, he picked up the small roll of rice and fish, placed it in his mouth, and slowly began to chew. It tasted surprisingly mild, not at all what he had expected. In fact it tasted a great deal like *bizcal,* a food eaten on Toril.

The second bite was equally light and easy for him to handle. He finished the sushi and started on the clear, thin soup, which was a little too salty for his taste but not unpalatable. The main dish was mostly vegetables, the sauce pleasantly mild, as long as he avoided the soy sauce. He ate one of the shrimps, whose texture wasn't a favorite, but the rest of the meal fit his palate better than anything he had tried so far.

"I think you're beginning to like it."

"Actually, it isn't too bad. Maybe I just needed you to do the ordering."

She smiled prettily, glanced down and saw the fork in his hands. "Oh, no you don't. Chopsticks only. If you don't know how to use them, I'll show you."

Patrick knew how, of course. In fact he was a pro. Though he avoided Asian food whenever he could, he wasn't about to be embarrassed in front of one of his women.

Val, on the other hand, thought the lesson might be fun. He fumbled with the long black pointed sticks. "I'm afraid I'm not very good. What's the trick?"

"It's simple. Just hold them like this." She showed him several times, but he still couldn't seem to master the technique. Getting up from her side of the table, Julie walked around and knelt on the floor behind him. He could feel her breasts pressing into his back as she leaned over his shoulder, the warmth of her small fingers wrapped around his long dark hands. The faintly sweet smell of her perfume drifted around him.

"Not that way." She carefully adjusted the stick. "When you hold them too low, it means you're from one of the peasant classes. Nothing but the upper crust will do for you, my boy."

He held the sticks just right, wriggled them a time or two to show her he had finally gotten the hang of it, then picked up a bite of food.

"Perfect." She grinned with pleasure and started to

rise, but before she could escape, he caught her hand and brought it to his lips.

"Thank you," he said softly.

For a moment she seemed frozen, then she eased away. "Y-you're welcome."

She returned to her place across from him and went back to working on her food, careful to keep her head down. It allowed him a moment to watch her, to study her as he had come here to do. She was a lovely young woman, both inside and out—everything he knew about her said so. But what was different about her, different about the other subjects like her?

What did a male artist from Santa Fe have in common with a real estate lady from Beverly Hills? Mentally he went over the list of those who had fought the testing in the same violent manner: a retired army colonel, a housewife and mother of three from Detroit, an Italian immigrant who owned a pizza parlor in New Jersey. What was the common link they shared?

"Do you ever go to church, Julie?" She didn't as far as he knew. She worked at least three Sundays a month. But maybe there was some other form of religion that gave her that incredible inner strength.

She looked at him strangely. For Patrick, it would have been a very odd question indeed. "No, I don't. Not that I'm opposed to church or anything. It's just that my father and mother weren't religious so I never went to church as a child. But I do believe in God. I think God is all around us. That He's part of everything we do. Perhaps at times He even directs us."

"What about your sister? Is she religious?"

"I know she believes in God. She's not quite as philosophical about it as I am, but she's definitely a believer." She tilted her chopsticks against her plate. "What about you, Patrick? You've never mentioned church before. What do you believe?"

He smiled at her softly. "I believe God is everywhere in the universe. That He's the link we all have to each other. In God's eyes all of us are one. Space and time are one. All matter is part of the same whole. And yes, I believe He guides us, if we're smart enough to listen."

Julie just stared at him. "I've never heard you talk this way. I never knew your thoughts ran deeper than which party you were going to next or which woman you were going to seduce."

A cautious voice warned he should back off, assume Patrick's lighter persona. But he didn't want to. He wanted Julie to glimpse the person he was inside. "Maybe my brush with death gave me time to think, see things in a different perspective."

"I hope so, Patrick. I really do."

They spoke of lighter subjects after that, the weather, sales in progress at the office, nothing consequential yet it helped to round out the picture of her that he carried in his head.

She glanced down at his empty plate. "All right, admit it. You liked the food after all." Julie smiled at him across the table.

"It was great. We'll have to come back here again."

Her warm smile faded. For a moment she just looked at him. "Patrick, are you sure you're feeling all right?"

He leaned forward, gently took hold of her hand. "I haven't felt this good in years. What about you? Any more headaches?"

Julie sighed. "As a matter of fact, I had one late this afternoon."

He frowned, not liking the news. "What does the doctor say?" No that it mattered, since no one could possibly discern the cause. Still he was curious.

"They haven't found anything physical. Dr. Marsh thinks it's stress. After what happened today, I figure it probably is."

"Today? What happened today?"

She took a sip of tea from the small, hand-painted teacup on the edge of her bamboo place mat, then set it back down on the table. "I went to see Dr. Heraldson, my sister's psychiatrist. Laura's been having some problems. Today I listened to a tape of her last two hypnosis sessions. It was—" She broke off and looked up at him. "I don't know why I'm telling you this. You're hardly interested in hearing my personal problems."

Val squeezed her hand. "You're wrong, Julie. I am interested. Tell me what happened with Laura's psychiatrist." He knew the girl had been seeing a doctor. She was wearing an implant, a tiny tracking device. They knew everything about her.

"I'm really worried about her, Patrick. If you could have heard her on that tape…God, she said the craziest things. She talked about hospitals and being examined…she sounded so frightened. I can't imagine what could be wrong with her."

"She'll be all right. She has you to help her. What more could she ask?"

Julie smiled faintly. "That's a very nice thing to say." She studied him a moment, then a guarded look appeared. She was wondering at his motives and the smile slid from her face. She pulled her hand away. "I've really enjoyed the evening, Patrick, but it's getting kind of late. I've still got a long drive home."

He squelched an urge to suggest he drive her. Moving too fast would only make her more wary. "All right, I'll take you back to your car." She relaxed a little when he didn't press her. They talked about trivial subjects on the way, and a few minutes later they were standing in the parking lot behind the office.

He took her key and unlocked the door to her little silver coupe. "I had a good time, Julie." He helped her slide in, then stopped as an odd thought occurred. "Tomorrow's your birthday, isn't it?"

"Yes, how did you know?"

"Before his stroke, my father used to take you out to dinner every year." He smiled. "Since he isn't well enough to do it this year, why don't I fill in for him?"

She shook her head, nervously chewing her lip. "I appreciate the offer, Patrick, I really do, but I'm afraid I can't accept. I'm having a few people over. Babs and Laura, Owen Mallory has promised to stop by."

He frowned. "You're not involved with Mallory, are you…on a personal level, I mean? I know he's always had an eye for you, but I never thought you were—"

"Owen is one of my most valuable clients. Beyond that he's a friend, nothing more."

Relief swept through him. A different sort than he had expected. It bothered him and suddenly he felt uneasy. He forced himself to smile. "Then you won't mind if I stop by too? I promise to bring a bottle of good champagne."

"I-I don't know. I don't think that's a good idea."

He arched a brow. "Why not?"

"Why not?"

"That's what I said."

"Because…because…" Her chin went up. "You know very well why not. Because you're you and I'm me. Because you're my employer. Because we work together, that's why not."

"We're also friends, aren't we?"

"Of course, but—"

He closed the door to her little Mercedes, cocooning her inside. "I'll see you tomorrow night," he said loud enough to be heard through the glass. "Lock your doors," he called over his shoulder as she rolled the window down, but he kept on walking away.

Tomorrow night he would see her again, watch her actions within the familiar setting of her home. So far he hadn't a clue as to why she had reacted so differently to the study probe than her sister. Perhaps if he saw them together…

But as he climbed into his car, it wasn't studying Julie's behavior that occupied his thoughts. It was the way her jacket had pressed against the fullness of her breasts, the compelling pink shade of her lips. Just sitting at the table, he had been hard off and on all evening. Thinking about it now made him hard again.

Val used one of Patrick's favorite swearwords. By now his benefactor would have assuaged his sexual needs with one or more of his numerous women—a fact verified by any number of incredibly graphic memories. Recalling them, Val knew what to do and exactly how to go about getting it done. Every day since he'd left the hospital, women had been calling him, offering their condolences and a whole lot more. But unlike Patrick, Val was interested in only one woman. He wondered what it would be like to take Julie Ferris to bed.

Eight

Julie woke up Saturday morning feeling a little out of sorts. She was twenty-nine today. A year away from thirty. The big three-0. It didn't make a woman feel good.

Which was one of the reasons she had given herself the day off. A birthday came just once a year. She deserved a little present to herself, and time off to do whatever she pleased was what she wanted most.

The last thing she wanted was to work.

Chances were slim, but she might run into Patrick at the office.

Julie felt a tightening in her chest just to think of the supper she had shared with Patrick last night. God, those eyes. A bright cornflower blue. Beautiful eyes that had seduced dozens of women. For years she had taught herself to ignore them. But then not once in the last eight years had he looked at her the way he did last night— as if there was no one else in the room. Maybe not anywhere else on the planet.

He seemed so different since his heart attack, so much…stronger. That was the word.

He had always been physically attractive, but the attraction went only surface deep. Beneath the chiseled face and athletic body was a self-centered, hedonistic, hopelessly destructive individual. The Patrick Donovan of last night was not the spoiled little boy he had always appeared. He was a man, and Julie found herself helplessly drawn to him.

It was dangerous. Almost as frightening as Laura's terrifying delusions. Patrick hadn't really changed. Not deep down inside. Sobered for a while, perhaps, been forced to face the consequences of his self-destructive ways.

But under it all, he was still Patrick. Nothing on Earth was going to make him change.

Determined to forget about Patrick at least for a while, she spent the morning in a lounge chair out on the deck, soaking up sunshine, listening to the pounding surf, and reading a spicy romance. It was set in England, a love story so poignant it brought tears to her eyes. It was pure fantasy, she knew. She would never meet a man like Ethan Sharpe, the tall dark hero in *The Devil's Necklace*, but she was a sucker for happy endings, and even after the bad luck she'd had with the opposite sex, she was still optimistic that for some women, that kind of love really existed.

Which brought her back to thoughts of Patrick. Julie set the book aside.

For the next few hours she worked in the kitchen, getting ready for the intimate dinner she planned. She liked to cook on occasion, and when she did, she was better than passably good. With her father gone from home and her mother busy working, she'd made dinner for their small family every night, though most of the time her mother's meal went into the oven to be reheated later on.

Julie was lifting the lid on a pot of boiling water, ready to add the seasoning to a batch of wild rice when she heard the doorbell ring. Wiping her hands on the apron tied over her strapless black cocktail dress she opened the door to find Laura standing on the porch.

Babs had just pulled her yellow Cadillac STS into the driveway. The table in the dining room glittered with her best Lennox china and Waterford crystal, stuff she had purchased for herself when she'd finally accepted the fact she might have to wait a long while to fill out her hope chest with a wedding.

"Happy birthday!" Laura gave her a hug and Julie hugged her back, perhaps a little harder than she usually did. She hadn't seen Laura since her meeting with Dr. Heraldson. Seeing her now, she could almost hear her sister's anguished words as her frightened voice came over the tape recorder.

Julie forced herself to smile. "I'm another year older but somehow I don't feel any wiser."

"Never fear," said Babs when she reached them, "I'm worldly-wise enough for all three of us." She leaned over and hugged Julie. "Happy birthday, honey." She was dressed in a black St. John knit, the color and simple rhinestone trim complementing the onyx shade of her straight-cut shoulder-length hair.

Julie smiled. "Let's go in. It's great to have both of you here." They walked together into the kitchen, where Julie opened a bottle of Far Niente chardonnay. "I thought we'd drink the good stuff tonight."

"Might as well," Babs said, "you only live once."

"If you don't mind, Julie, I'd rather have white zin. I know where it is." Laura opened the refrigerator, knowing Julie always kept a bottle of the sweet blush wine just for her.

Babs just grinned. "Good idea, honey. Nothing worse than wasting good wine on a Boone's Farm drinker."

Laura laughed. "Come on, Babs, I'm not that bad."

"No you aren't. Besides, if you're smart, you'll never develop a taste for expensive wine. Once you do, it's impossible to go back to the cheap stuff."

Julie said a silent amen to that. She had learned to appreciate fine wine when she had been dating Jeffrey Muller. During their two-year affair, she and Jeff, head of the L.A. division of Panasonic, had made half a dozen trips to the Napa Valley to replenish his extensive wine cellar.

Like most of their trips, they usually ended up with Julie in tears.

She shook off the notion. She never thought of Jeffrey anymore. He had stolen the last of her innocent dreams, thoughts of a husband and family, but three years had passed since then. She was successful in business and even if she didn't feel completely fulfilled, she was satisfied with the independent life she now lived.

She glanced at Laura, wishing her sister was as capable of coping with her problems as Julie had taught herself to be.

"All right," Babs said, "I know you're Miss Efficient, but there must be something we can do to help."

Babs was right, there wasn't much to do. Julie set them to work at a couple of minor last-minute tasks, but for the most part the meal was ready. Chicken dijon, wild rice, broccoli hollandaise, salad with an herb-balsamic dressing, fresh strawberries drizzled with Grand

Marnier for dessert. Nothing fancy, just good healthy, relatively low-cal food.

"What time is Owen coming?" Laura asked, drawing Julie's gaze, which darkened with concern at the sight of her sister's drawn expression. In her simple blue silk dress, her hair pulled into a tight chignon, on the surface, Laura seemed calm enough. But Julie couldn't stop thinking of the tape Dr. Heraldson had played.

"Owen promised he'd be here by seven," Julie said. "He ought to be arriving any minute." She studied Laura more closely and as the minutes slipped past, began to notice a slight restlessness, a subtle tension about her. What was she thinking? Julie wondered. Why was she so afraid?

The doorbell rang a few minutes later. "That's probably Owen now."

It was. Silver-streaked light-brown hair, darkly tanned and athletically built, at forty-five Owen Mallory looked thirty. He was English, wealthier than Donald Trump, but the Earl of Finance, as the press often called him, wasn't nearly so flashy.

"Good evening, Julie. Felicitations on your birthday." He leaned over and kissed her cheek.

"Owen, it's so good to see you."

"Bit of a jam on the freeway. Poor Arthur was in a tither." Arthur was Owen's chauffeur, an aging black man who lived in one of the cottages on his employer's huge estate.

"I'm just glad you could make it."

"Wouldn't have missed it, dear girl. As a matter of fact, I'm planning to spend a bit more time at Oceanside." The name he had given the palatial manor next door. "Perhaps we'll finally have a chance to see a bit more of each other."

Julie smiled. "That would be wonderful." She had always liked Owen Mallory. He'd been a pleasure to work with and even taught her a thing or two about investing. "At any rate, it's always good to see you."

"What about me?" Patrick asked from the doorway, poking his dark head inside. "Aren't you glad to see me, too?"

"Patrick…" A flush rose into her cheeks. "Yes…of course I am."

He handed her a bottle of Dom Perignon and a small bouquet of red roses. "Happy birthday." But instead of a kiss on the cheek, he bent forward and softly kissed her on the mouth.

Julie's stomach fluttered then dipped like a roller coaster. It was a short kiss, hardly immodest. Dear God, she couldn't believe it affected her the way it did.

"Y-you two know each other, of course."

"Of course," Owen said, glaring at Patrick. She wondered why he was frowning, then remembered the men had once had real estate dealings. From Owen's obvious dislike, it was apparent it hadn't worked out.

"Why don't you both come in?"

Owen walked past her into the living room, but Patrick lingered a moment. He was staring at her lips, his skin a little flushed as if he was slightly unsettled himself. Then he smiled. "What can I do to help?"

"Everything is pretty much under control. There's wine in the kitchen. Liquor in the bar if you prefer. I know you're usually a Chivas drinker."

"A glass of club soda would be fine."

She arched a brow. "You aren't drinking?"

"You weren't surprised the other night."

"That was different. We were eating Japanese. I just figured tea went better with sushi than scotch...although I guess you could have ordered sake."

"Club soda. That's what I'm drinking these days. It's not as good as Dom Perignon, but it's not all that bad either."

She smiled brightly. "That's terrific, Patrick. I'm really proud of you."

The five of them talked for a while, sipped wine and ate hors d' oeuvres, then went into the dining room and sat down at the long, glass-topped, bleached pine table. Owen poured the Dom Perignon, filling everyone's glass but Patrick's. Patrick filled his with soda and lifted it in a toast along with everyone else.

"Happy birthday, my dear," Owen said. "May you have many, many more."

Soft notes of Brubeck jazz floated in from the CD player in the living room. As they began to eat, darkness settled in. Tall white candles in cut-crystal holders flickered in the breeze blowing in through the windows, bathing the room in soft yellow tones. Outside the ocean rolled onto the beach.

They finished the meal in warm conversation, then Babs helped Julie clear away the plates and they returned to the table to linger over dessert. All but Patrick sipped a cup of dark French roast coffee, Laura's heavily laced with cream. Outside the window, the rhythmic pounding of waves against sand set up a soothing lull that contributed to the pleasant atmosphere.

Pleasant, it seemed, for all of them but Laura.

So far only Julie had noticed her sister's furtive glances toward the thickening darkness outside, the way she had begun to shift uneasily in her chair. Laura let her coffee grow cold and started drinking more wine, filling her glass to the rim with the last of a bottle of chardonnay that sat open in the middle of the table.

Seated in a chair beside her, Julie reached over and clasped the hand Laura unconsciously fisted in her lap. It felt cold and clammy, damp with perspiration.

"Laura, honey, are you all right?"

Patrick had noticed Laura, too. He was watching with an odd intensity and more than a little concern.

"I'm fine, Julie. I guess I'm a little stressed out is all."

"Hard day at work?"

"Yeah…I guess so." She glanced toward the windows and nervously bit her lip. "I've decided to go home after supper. I've got some things to do in the morning. You understand, don't you? You aren't upset?"

"You brought an overnight bag. I thought you were going to stay."

Laura glanced toward the doors leading out onto the deck. "I've got to go."

Julie forced herself to smile. "It's all right. You don't have to stay if you don't want to, and of course I'm not upset." She squeezed Laura's hand, let go and rejoined the table conversation, not wanting to draw any more undue attention to her sister. But from the corner of her eye, she watched the way Laura crimped her napkin, picked at a loose thread in the hem. Every few seconds her eyes darted to the blackness outside.

Someone laughed, but Laura's face went rigid. "What's that?" she said, breaking into Owen's tale of a chaotic week he had just spent in London. "Wh-what's that funny sound?"

Everyone paused to listen. "I don't hear anything," Babs said. "Wait a minute…now I do."

It was a thick, dull humming, a sound in the distance that seemed to be moving toward them. As it neared, it grew louder, making a buzzing sound above them, compressing the air and reminding Julie of something…something…but she couldn't quite think what it was.

"It's them! They're coming!" Laura jumped up from the table, jerking backward so fast she knocked over her chair. It landed with a clatter against the wooden floors.

Julie stood up, too. "It's all right, Laura. There's nothing to be afraid of. We'll just go out and see what it is."

Laura just stood frozen, her face drained of color as the heavy dull buzzing drew nearer. Then a bright white light filled the room, illuminating everyone at the table, throwing their features into shadowy contrasts of light and dark.

"Nooo!" A high-pitched scream tore from Laura's throat. "I won't let them take me! Oh, God I won't let them hurt me again!" She started to run, but tripped on the chair and went sprawling, came up on her knees and began to slide across the floor till she hit the wall and backed into a corner.

Babs reached her first. "It's all right, honey, no one's going to hurt you. It's only a helicopter." The *whop, whop, whop* of the blades now sounded directly overhead.

"Laura, it's okay," Julie soothed as the searchlight moved on and the chopper roared off down the beach, taking the dull hum with it. "It's one of those sheriff's helicopters." Kneeling at Laura's side, Julie pulled her sister's shaking body into the circle of her arms, trembling nearly as badly as she was. "They fly over every once in a while, remember? That's probably what happened the last time you were here."

Laura gulped back tears. "How—how did you know about that? Do you remember what happened? I remember, Julie. I remember everything. I didn't for a while but now I do."

"What's she talking about?" Babs asked.

"Something she told Dr. Heraldson. Something she believed happened to her the last time she came here."

Laura looked up at her with big dark, tear-filled eyes. "Did I tell Dr. Heraldson what happened? Is that why he wanted you to listen to the tape?"

"Yes. He said you were frightened by something that happened to you at the hospital. You told him you'd been taken there the day we spent out on the beach. Since we both knew that hadn't really happened, he thought maybe I could think of something else that could have frightened you that day."

"I know what frightened me. Just now…when I heard that noise, I remembered everything…everything that happened. Every terrible, agonizing moment."

Patrick stepped into the circle just then. "It's obvious Laura's upset. The evening's over. We've all had a lovely time. Why don't we give Julie a chance to talk to her sister in private?"

"Julie?" Babs questioned with a pointed glance at Patrick. "Are you sure that's what you want? Maybe I should stay." Babs had had a brief affair with Patrick years ago, but had wisely been one of the few who had ever dumped him, which was probably the reason they had been able to stay friends.

Julie looked at Laura, whose face was still so ashen

the blue veins in her temple showed through. Her limbs were quaking, her hands balled into fists.

"I think Patrick's right." Unconsciously Julie rubbed the back of her neck, feeling a dull throb of pain. Damn, a headache was the last thing she needed. "I'd appreciate it if you all went home. I think my sister could use a little time alone."

Owen reached over and gently squeezed her shoulder. "I'm only just next door. Not a bit of trouble for me to come back if you need me."

"Thank you, Owen. I'm sure we'll be okay."

Patrick saw them all to the door, surprisingly considerate for Patrick. He waved a brief goodbye and then they were gone.

Julie breathed a sigh of relief. "Now…" Pasting a smile on her face, she turned and helped Laura to her feet. "Why don't we go into the living room? I'll fix you a cup of hot milk and you can tell me what this is all about."

Laura nodded dully. Julie led her into the living room then returned as promised with a cup of steaming milk. Laura accepted the cup, wrapping her hands around the mug as if to relieve a chill, but didn't take a drink.

"Feel like talking about it?" Julie said gently, sitting down beside her on the sofa.

Laura's dark gaze turned in her direction. "I thought you said you heard the tape."

"I also said it didn't make much sense. You said you were in a hospital, but you weren't, at least not on the two occasions you described."

"Not a hospital, Julie." Laura stared off into the distance. Julie had never seen such desolation. "A spaceship. The day we went to the beach, I was taken aboard a spaceship."

Julie took the news like a blow to the stomach. In Laura's twenty-four years she'd said a lot of crazy things, but this was the wildest yet. The throbbing in her head continued to build, escalating to an ache than ran down her neck and stabbed into her shoulders. "I'm afraid I don't know what to say."

"Just say you believe me, Julie. No one else is going to. If you don't, I don't know what I'm going to do." Laura started crying then, hugging her arms around her stomach, bending over as if she were in pain.

Julie smoothed back silvery strands of her long blond hair. "Maybe it would be better if I didn't believe you. Then we could investigate this whole thing together, find out what really happened."

"I know what happened," Laura sobbed. "It's happened two times—both when I was here. I wasn't dreaming, Julie. It was nothing like a dream. It was a nightmare but it was real."

Just then the doorbell rang, and both of them jumped.

"I'll go see who it is," Julie said, trying to slow the battering of her heart. Before she could get up from the couch, the door swung open and Patrick leaned through the doorway.

"Can I come in?" He still wore his dark suit, but the tie was gone and his shirt had been unbuttoned, showing a triangle of smooth dark skin.

"I thought we agreed it would be best for Laura if everyone went home."

"What I meant was everyone but me." Patrick strode purposely toward them. Oddly enough, she was glad to see him. "Besides, I had a feeling you were getting one of your headaches."

"I am."

"I helped before. Maybe I can again."

Julie just nodded, starting back toward the living room, Patrick following closely in her wake.

"Feeling any better?" he asked Laura, pulling a big orange-and-red striped ottoman over in front of the sofa.

"I may never feel better again."

"Want to tell me about it? Believe it or not, I can be a very good listener."

Her chin went up, a gesture she and Julie had inherited from their mother. "Go ahead, Julie. Tell him what I said. I'm sure he'll get a laugh out of it."

Concerned blue eyes swung in Julie's direction. It was a look she hadn't expected, a look that promised understanding.

Julie sighed. "Laura believes she's been taken aboard a spaceship."

For a moment he said nothing. "Is that all? I thought it was something important."

Laura smiled faintly, and Julie plunged ahead. "She's convinced it's the truth. She believes it totally and completely." She took a deep breath and rushed on, suddenly defensive of her sister. "She isn't the first person to claim such a thing, you know. I've read articles about it in the newspaper. I don't remember exactly what they said, but I know it's called alien abduction. It isn't absolutely impossible. Just because it can't be verified doesn't necessarily mean it's not the truth."

A corner of his mouth curved up. "No, I don't suppose it does." He studied her a moment, then returned his attention to Laura. "On the other hand, wouldn't it be more comforting to believe that perhaps it was some sort of trick, some illusion of the mind? Then you could work through the problem and come to some solution. You wouldn't have to constantly be afraid."

Laura mulled that over, sat up a little straighter on the couch. She smoothed a wrinkle from the lap of her blue silk skirt. "It would be more comforting, Patrick. It would be the best news in the world. Unfortunately it wouldn't be the truth."

He took hold of her hand, clasping her slim fingers tightly. "How can you be so sure?"

Laura bit down on her lip, which had started to tremble. Fresh tears rolled down her cheeks, and Julie's heart turned over. Dear God, she wished she knew how to help her.

"I don't know why I'm so sure," Laura said. "I just am. I suppose once you remember something that awful, something so terrible it paralyzes you with fear, it just won't let you pretend it isn't real."

"What do you think Dr. Heraldson will say?" Julie asked gently.

"I-I don't know. I'm sure he'll think I'm crazy, just like everyone else." She got up from the sofa, stood there staring out the windows.

"You're not still thinking of going home?" Julie asked as Laura eyed the door.

"Stay here, Laura," Patrick softly commanded. "I promise you'll be safe. Tonight there's no reason for you to be afraid." There was something in the way he said it. An authority that gave the words a ring of truth.

Laura looked into his eyes for several long moments, then she nodded. "All right I'll stay here." She turned away from him. "I'm awfully tired, Julie. I think I'll go to bed."

"That's a good idea. After a good night's sleep you'll feel better." Julie rubbed the bridge of her nose, trying to ignore the piercing pain behind her eyes. "We can talk again in the morning."

Laura stopped and turned. Her dress was wrinkled and long blond tendrils of hair had come loose from her chignon. "Good night, Patrick."

"Good night, Laura."

"I'll check on you before I go to bed," Julie called after her, feeling a tug on her heart at her sister's forlorn expression, not far from tears herself.

As soon as Laura left the room, she reached over and turned down the lamp, the bright rays of light suddenly painful. Her head was pounding, throbbing like a hammer against the anvil of her skull. "I'm so worried about her, Patrick." She massaged her temple then felt Patrick beside her, easing her down on the couch.

"Hush," he whispered. "No more talk about Laura. At least not tonight. I want you to relax." He urged her onto her stomach, then began to massage her shoulders and neck.

"It looks like there are two Ferris women who need looking after tonight."

She took a deep breath and slowly released it, feeling a deep relaxation as Patrick kneaded her muscles. "Ummm," she mumbled, grateful for the power in his long-fingered hands. Two months ago, she would have been afraid to let him touch her, sure he was only after the chance to get her in bed. Now whenever he looked at her, she read concern in his eyes. Concern… and something she couldn't quite name.

His fingers slid into the hair at the nape of her neck and a few seconds later, the pain began to ease. "Magic hands," she whispered. "Now I understand why women find you so irresistible."

"I've been telling you that for years."

He worked on her for another fifteen minutes, until her body felt boneless and her headache was completely gone. But instead of falling asleep as she had before, this time she sat up on the sofa and Patrick sat down beside her.

"Thank you for coming back."

He smiled, softening the sharp angles of his face. "I never intended to leave. I just knew the others wouldn't go if I tried to stay." He reached toward her, ran a long dark finger down her cheek. "You look a little better." Eyes as blue as the sea fixed on her lips, and a ripple of heat shimmered through her.

"I am…thanks to you."

"I'm glad." His hand moved beneath her chin, tilting her head back with a firm but gentle pressure.

Her eyes slid closed as he bent his head and covered her mouth with a kiss. Julie's breath caught, seemed to swell inside her chest. His lips slanted softly over hers, molding them perfectly together, and a faint shudder passed through him. The kiss was firm and warm, yet not as demanding as she would have expected, the brush of his tongue seemed hesitant, almost a little uncertain. Before she was ready for the kiss to end, Patrick pulled away.

He glanced down at his lap and her eyes followed. She saw that he was aroused. When he realized she had noticed, a slight flush rose over the bones across his cheeks.

"You have very soft lips," he said.

"I-I shouldn't have let you kiss me."

"Why not?"

Julie sighed. "I'm not what you're looking for, Patrick. We both know that. I never have been."

"How can you be so sure?"

"Because I've known you for more than eight years. In that entire time, all you've ever wanted from me was to take me to bed."

"I still want that. Right now I want it so much it hurts. But this time my reasons are different."

"Different?" She looked into his eyes and fought a sudden urge to run. She shouldn't be listening to him. She knew the kind of man he was, no matter what he said. "How…how are they different?"

A tender smile curved his lips. "I want to make love to you so that I can know you. I want to discover what you're thinking, what you're feeling. If I'm inside you, perhaps I can know you in a way I never have."

Julie's stomach tightened, soft heat sliding through her, seeping lower down. My God, the image he stirred: Patrick on top of her, stroking her breasts, burying his hard length inside her. Her body trembled, shuddered with desire for him. Dear God, no wonder women flocked to his bed.

Julie got up from the sofa, turning her back on him. "I don't…I don't want to talk about this. Please, Patrick… I think you ought to leave."

Patrick stood up, too, but instead of heading for the door, she felt his hands on her shoulder, turning her to face him. He pulled her into his arms and kissed her. There was nothing tentative, this time, nothing the least bit uncertain. This kiss was all fiery heat and pent-up desire, hard-soft lips and a hot, demanding tongue. Taut muscle bunched against the fullness of her breasts, making her nipples tighten and throb where they pressed against his chest.

Patrick deepened the kiss, taking her mouth as if he owned it, stroking deeply, making the heat in her stomach slide hotly through her limbs. It had been so long....

And never, ever like this.

Her fingers curled into his shirt, her heart hammered, and her mouth molded itself to his. For a moment she kissed him back, tasting the roughness of his tongue, feeling the seductive pressure of his lips, breathing in the subtle male scent of him. Hunger swirled through her, and a need so strong it shook her to the very core. Then doubts began to seep in, blocking the numbing haze of passion. Patrick's hand on her breast sent a fission of heat straight through her, but with it came a cold hard dose of reason.

You shouldn't be doing this! Damn, she had to stop this from happening before it was too late!

Pressing her palms against his chest, Julie broke away. Breathing too hard, her legs trembling, she backed up several paces, angry at herself for what she had almost let happen yet insanely, in some strange way, disappointed that it hadn't occurred.

"Don't ever...don't ever do that again, Patrick."

He looked at her but didn't relent. She couldn't recall when he had ever appeared so formidable. "I'll promise you only this. I won't do anything you don't want me to do."

A funny little sound slipped from her throat. Julie tried not to feel the hot burst of hunger. "Please go," she said.

He stared at her for long, silent moments, his shoulders a little stiffer, his posture straighter, drawing his tall frame even more upright. "I want to help you with Laura. We can't let what's happening between us affect what's good for her."

What's happening between us? What was he talking about? Dear God, she couldn't afford to let anything happen between them. "How could you possibly be good for Laura? For thirty-five years, you haven't been good for *yourself.*"

His mouth curved cynically. "Perhaps that's exactly the reason. Maybe I know better than anyone else what it is to feel so alone." The clock on the mantel ticked into the silence. He glanced off toward the windows. "Or perhaps it's just that I want to help *you.*"

"I don't need your help. Laura and I will be fine on our own." She walked over and opened the door. "Good night, Patrick."

He moved toward the opening, paused a moment in front of her, and his hand came up to her cheek. "You're frightened of me, Julie, but you don't have to be. I won't do anything to hurt you."

Julie glanced away from him but said nothing more, just stood in silence while he made his way out onto the porch. She watched him descend the stairs, feeling shaken and oddly alone, wondering how her life had suddenly turned upside down.

Wondering what in God's name she was going to do about it.

Nine

Brian Heraldson sat across the desk from the petite red-head and the tall slender blonde. Laura Ferris had insisted her sister come along when she listened for the first time to the tapes of her previous sessions. She told him about the incident at Julie's birthday dinner and repeatedly said that the experiences she remembered had actually occurred.

She was even more convinced when she heard herself on the tape of the previous sessions.

As the tape came to a close, tears welled in her eyes. "They took me," she whispered, the wetness beginning to roll down her cheeks. "They stripped off my clothes and stuck their instruments inside my body, just like I said on the tape." She sat there on the gray leather sofa, clutching her sister's hand. "I remember the shuffling sound of their feet on the deck and the next thing I knew they were standing there in the guest room. They didn't come in through the door—they were just suddenly there."

"Take it easy, Laura," he said when she began to cry harder. "You're safe in here. No one's going to hurt you."

Her head came up. She wiped her eyes with the tissue Julie gave her. "You think I'm safe? Well, I don't. I don't think I'm safe anywhere. I think they can take me whenever they want."

He sat forward in his chair, hoping to deflect her hostility. It bothered him to feel it directed toward him. "What happened after they came into the guest room? During the hypnosis session you couldn't seem to recall."

"I remember much more since the night of Julie's birthday party. I know they carried me across the deck and down the stairs, across the sand to a place beneath the cliffs. They wrapped me in something…it was pliable, flexible somehow, and it molded itself around me. I remember floating upward, lifting through the air, watching the house recede beneath me. I don't remember anything else until I woke up in that terrible room."

She sniffed several times, then started crying again. Julie tightened her grip on Laura's hand.

"They examined you…is that right, Laura?"

She nodded, her head hanging forward, a curtain of long pale hair falling over her dark brown eyes. Brian ignored a rush of pity, and an unfamiliar tightening in his chest.

"I felt humiliated…violated. I wanted to kill them for what they were doing."

"What did they look like?"

Laura's head came up and so did Julie's. Apparently it was the first time anyone had thought to ask.

"I'm…I'm not sure. I don't think they all looked the same. The ones who came into my room were shorter than the others. And those all looked pretty much alike. They were kind of like soldiers, I think."

"Go on," he urged gently.

"They had big round heads but their chins were sort of pointed—you know, kind of like the pictures of aliens you see in cartoons, except there was nothing funny about them. And they had huge black, bottomless eyes."

"Bottomless?" he repeated. "What do you mean?"

"I mean, when you looked into them, you couldn't see anything but darkness. Like a great black pool so deep you couldn't see the end."

"What were they wearing?" Julie asked, studying her sister with renewed interest.

"Dark blue coveralls. Their skin was leathery and gray." She shivered. "The others were taller. I don't remember much about them, but in time maybe I will. The images are returning, getting a little clearer every day. In a way that's what frightens me most."

"You're afraid of what you'll recall?" Brian asked.

"Yes. The more I remember, the more certain I am that this really happened." She shook her head. "I also know that if I mention it, if I tell anyone about it, they're going to think I'm crazy, that I'm some kind of freak."

Julie turned her gaze in Brian's direction. He noticed that her gray slacks were damp where she'd wiped her sweaty palms. Listening to Laura, Brian found his own palms sweating.

"I know all of this sounds absurd," Julie said, "but is it possible, Dr. Heraldson, that what Laura thinks happened is real? I read something in the Sunday *Times*…I remember there was a picture on the front of the Parade section, a drawing of an alien like Laura described. I remember they interviewed a number of different people who claimed to be victims of alien abduction."

"Is it possible Laura might have read the article, too?"

Laura shook her head. "No. I never read the paper. I don't even watch the news. They never report anything but bombings and murders—why would I want to watch that?"

"Is it possible, Doctor?" Julie pressed.

It was a question Brian had been asking himself since Julie had called him at home Sunday morning. She had told him about Laura's wild reaction to the helicopter the night before and he had suggested she come in first thing on Monday.

"I'll be honest with both of you. I don't believe in alien abduction. I don't think Laura was taken aboard a spacecraft full of little gray men. I believe the problem is rooted in Laura's childhood, that whatever it was may have been magnified by the abortion she experienced during her teenage years. Odds are, something happened fairly recently to set these long suppressed anxieties in motion."

He sat forward in his chair. "On the other hand, there is a growing number of people who claim to have experienced phenomena like Laura has described. I would be remiss in my duties if I discouraged either of you from investigating the possibility that Laura's experiences are real."

The women stared at him in silence. Brian spun in his chair, pulled open a lower desk drawer, and began to ruffle through the files. When he found what he was looking for, he pulled out the folder and laid it on his desk.

"A colleague of mine, a doctor named Aaron Newburg who went to school with me at USC, had a patient claiming to be a victim of alien abduction. After extensive treatment, the patient remained convinced the events were real. Dr. Newburg put him in touch with a man named Budd Hopkins. Hopkins is touted as one of the main forces behind investigating UFO-alien abductions. Since he lived so far away, Hopkins referred the patient to a psychologist protégé of his named Peter Winters. Winters runs a therapy group here in L.A. for people who claim to be victims."

Laura straightened, drawing herself up on the sofa. "I don't believe what I'm hearing. Julie said something Saturday night about other people who believed this had happened to them, but at the time I was too upset to listen. Now you're telling me the same thing. If people say they're being abducted, why won't anyone believe them?"

"I'm telling you there are other people who *claim* this has happened. That doesn't mean it's true. In my estimation, the best thing you could do would be to accept these fantasies as delusions and work with me to arrive at the root of the problem. However, if you think it would make you feel better, perhaps you should speak to Dr. Winters. At least among members of his group, you'll be able to tell your story without fear of ridicule."

Laura bit her lip, her courage suddenly fading. "I don't know…what do you think, Julie?"

The older sister looked pensive, dark-red eyebrows drawn together above the bridge of her upturned, lightly freckled nose. "I think we should definitely speak to Dr. Winters. It couldn't hurt and maybe it will help."

For the first time that day, Laura smiled, and Brian felt the warmth blaze right through him.

"Yes…" Laura agreed, "let's talk to him. That's exactly what I want to do."

Brian ignored an unexpected feeling of abandonment, thinking in a way this might be best. So far, he'd been able to keep his attraction for Laura Ferris under tight grips, but every time he saw her, a little more of his control seemed to slip. Perhaps it would be better if she went to someone else, placed herself under another doctor's care.

He resolved then and there, no matter the outcome of Laura's meeting with Peter Winters, he was through as her physician. If she came back to him for treatment, he would refer her to somebody else. And he would stay away from her himself. The last thing he wanted was involvement with a patient. Especially one who believed in little gray men.

"Well, what do you think?" Laura asked Julie the moment they walked out of the psychiatrist's office. "Did I do the right thing?"

"I imagine it's too soon to tell." Julie unlocked the door on the passenger side of her little silver car, then walked around to the driver's side and let herself in. Maybe she should have listened to Dr. Heraldson, supported him in his efforts to convince her sister her memories were just an illusion. She remembered only too well Laura's emotional turmoil in making the decision to have the abortion.

But Tommy Ross was a drifter, a beach bum headed for bigger surf in Hawaii. He'd had no money, no job, and even if he had, he was already long gone before Laura found out she was pregnant. She was only seventeen. Julie was in college, working part-time to pay for books and tuition. Geraldine Ferris, their mother, earned barely enough to put food on the table and cheap clothes on their backs.

And Laura's health wasn't good. Even if she'd let the pregnancy run its course, the doctor said odds were she would miscarry before she reached full term. It seemed a good decision at the time—the only real answer to Laura's dilemma. She had been upset about it, of course, a little bit frightened of what would happen to her in the hospital, but not, Julie believed, to the extent that it would later cause something like this.

Julie thought again of Brian Heraldson. Maybe she should have backed him up, convinced Laura this was all in her head, but something held her back. It was only a feeling, a niggling, intuitive something that made her want to know more before she formed a solid opinion.

"Dr. Heraldson said he would set it up for me to attend the meeting," Laura said. "Do you think he might come along? I mean…it might be nice to have him there."

For a moment Julie's gaze swung away from the road, caught a glimpse of Laura's pretty face. "You like him, don't you?"

"I trust him. I don't know why, but I do."

Julie smiled. "So do I. But I think, at least at first, we ought to do this alone. Dr. Heraldson's mind is already made up. He doesn't believe this could have happened and that might influence your thinking when you speak to Dr. Winters."

Laura sighed. "I suppose you're right." They drove along in silence for a while. "Patrick was really nice about this. He doesn't believe me, of course, but at least he tried to help. He's certainly changed since his heart attack."

Something warm slid into Julie's stomach. "You know Patrick. I'm sure his reformation is only temporary. For his father's sake I wish he'd change for good, but we all know he probably won't."

"For his father's sake?" Laura pressed. "Or for yours?"

"Don't be silly. I have no interest in Patrick, none whatsoever." But she couldn't stop the tiny flutter in her heart or the stirring of hope at Laura's words.

On Tuesday morning, Val sat at the kitchen table in his penthouse apartment, poring over the pages he had just written in his journal. Much of it recounted the happenings at Julie Ferris's birthday party, the reaction Laura Ferris was having to what she called "the abduction."

Val frowned as he recalled the events of that night. They had known Earth subjects were often severely affected. He had seen their reactions when they were carried aboard the ship: crying and screaming, begging and pleading, shrinking into themselves in terror. He had seen the follow-up studies, showing their tendency toward suspicion, paranoia, insomnia, and manic-depressive moods. He had seen all of this, and yet he had never understood the way they truly felt.

He had never understood because he wasn't able to experience those feelings himself.

Not until now.

Val scrawled more words on the blue-lined pages of his notebook.

Emotion is the key. Humans experience their world in a different way than we do. They are governed by feelings, rather than logic. They are not objective in the same manner we are. Their experiences are absorbed, internalized rather than simply perceived. That is the reason they react so violently to our studies. They cannot understand that our need is simply to learn, to understand, and even if they could, they would perceive it as a hostile invasion. Here, the individual's rights come first.

Val set the pen aside and studied the last line he had written. On Toril, there was no such thing as individuality, no perception of privacy, independent thinking, or personal rights and freedoms. Everyone worked for the common good, existed as a part of one common humanity.

Here, the closest Patrick's memory banks could come to the sort of communal existence was to liken Torillian society to a group of bees within a hive. They all pulled together, reacted as one. There was no dissension, no discord. They discussed things, made a decision based on the common good, then acted to carry out that decision. From emergence until death, five hundred years later, they thought of themselves as one, all part of a common entity.

It was as hard a concept for a human to accept as the concept of individualism was for a Torillian.

Val stretched his long legs out in front of him, raked a hand through his still-damp, black hair. He had run eight miles this morning at 5:00 a.m., long before the streets were clogged with traffic. He was as fit and trim as the twenty-year-old Patrick Donovan who had raced motorcycles and skied the double black diamond slopes.

He felt good about that. He liked the way his body responded, the way it obeyed his commands. He liked the power in his muscles, the exhilaration when the blood surged full-force through his veins. He liked breathing in great, deep lungfuls of air and feeling the tightness of the sinews in his long lean legs.

He liked being a man, feeling a man's wants and needs.

Perhaps more than anything else, he liked the way he felt when he kissed Julie Ferris.

Val shifted against a surge of heat to his lower anatomy. It happened whenever he thought of Julie and it was beginning to drive him crazy. No wonder Patrick took so many women to bed. The man's powerful masculinity exuded great demands and it was only Val's Torillian drive for monogamy that kept him from giving in to them.

Sighing with frustration, he set the journal aside, picked up his leather briefcase, and headed for the door. He'd been going to work early every morning, sifting through ledgers and contracts, reviewing the real estate files Patrick had assembled through the years. He understood the business. After all, he knew everything that Patrick knew. During the time he played the part, it was necessary he do the same things Patrick would do. He just didn't approach those things in quite the same manner.

Still, for as long as he was Patrick, he was expected to run the company.

Which left him sitting in his office behind his black lacquered desk late that afternoon when the door swung open and a tall, well-dressed man in a navy blue suit walked in. Another man followed, shorter, stockier, with coffee-cup ears and pockmarks over the lower half of his face. From their slightly hostile manner, he knew exactly who they were and why they were there.

"Come in, gentlemen. I've been expecting you."

The taller man stopped in front of the desk. With a smug, self-assured smile, he turned and braced a hip on the edge. "You have, have you? Does that mean you've got the rest of the money you owe us?"

"You know I don't. I presume that's why you're here."

"That's right, Donovan, that's exactly why we're here."

Val dug into Patrick's brain, hoping he could put all the pieces together and make some sort of sense out of them. Hoping Patrick's real estate knowledge would be enough to guide him through the mess the man had gotten himself into. "I take it you're with Westwind Corporation."

"Hell, no. Sandini sent us. The guys running Westwind are just working stiffs. They do exactly what we tell them."

"And that is…?"

The second man checked the door, made sure it was tightly closed. "That is, keep writing those phony sales contracts on your worthless condominiums. Keep shuffling the mortgages off to that insurance trust and collecting the money for the sale of useless pieces of paper."

Val's brain sorted out the information, which Patrick already knew. More and more he was able to assimilate Patrick's knowledge. In a way, he actually *was* Patrick Donovan. And because that was so, he was only a little surprised at the extent of the fraud the men were committing.

Val had run across Patrick's involvement in the Westwind scam in a far back corner of his mind, where Patrick had mostly pretended it didn't exist. His pet project, a huge condominium and time-share development near

Santa Monica beach, had gone sour before it ever got off the ground. Patrick had sold his soul to raise enough money to build it—finally giving up a large percentage to men named Tony Sandini and Vincent McPherson, the unofficial owners of a sham company called Westwind Corporation, guys Patrick referred to as "big-time Chicago money men."

Patrick had been certain the project would be a winner. There were millions to be made, he believed. But the condos weren't finished while the market was red-hot and now interest rates were creeping up and there was a big market downturn. The units were completed, but the construction was so shoddy nobody wanted to buy them. They were sitting there empty, most of them still unsold.

And Sandini and McPherson wanted their money.

"So what's the problem?" Val asked, dredging up thoughts Patrick had had right before he died. "Westwind is creating the phony paper, discounting it and selling it. Sooner or later you'll make back the money you've invested and a handsome profit to boot. Everyone involved will get paid and disappear, and you'll be home free."

"That sounds real good, but the fact is the insurance trust isn't buying any more of our notes. Pennsylvania Life just merged with Metropolitan and they aren't buying, they're selling."

"So find someone else."

"We already have," said the man in the navy blue suit.

"You've found someone else to buy the discounted notes?"

The stocky man grinned. "Yeah, that's where you come in."

Val shoved back his chair and stood up. "I told them I couldn't help them when I signed over the deed to the property." A deed Patrick had given to Westwind Corporation, in lieu of foreclosure, a transfer just before his heart attack meant to shield him from the fraud the men were committing and hopefully keep him out of jail. But Sandini and McPherson wanted their money and they expected him to do whatever it took to insure they got paid.

"I can't afford to be connected with Westwind when all of this finally comes down," he said, repeating what Patrick had once said.

"Yeah, well, that's just too damn bad." The stocky man flashed him a look that said he enjoyed making him squirm. If Patrick's involvement was discovered, this kind of fraud would send him straight to prison.

Sooner or later, someone would discover the condo buyers weren't real. They weren't making their payments on the notes because the buyers were just names and credit applications churned up from the recently deceased files of a local Social Security branch. Big Brother knew everything about everyone. And with a little computer wizardry, so did the Westwind Corporation.

The tall man pulled an expensive cigarette case from the inside pocket of his suit coat. He took out a smoke, snapped the lid closed and lit the cigarette with a flick of his shiny gold lighter.

"Mr. Sandini doesn't expect all that much," he said, releasing a lungful of smoke into the smoke-free office. "A word or two from you, a personal tour of the property ought to insure the deal goes through."

"Who's going to be buying the notes?"

"The Ventura County Teachers' Pension Fund."

Val's chest tightened. "That's reaching pretty low, isn't it? Teachers are just average people working to save for their retirement. They can't afford to lose that kind of money."

"Yeah, well those are the breaks," said the stocky man.

"Sorry, Donovan, but as Jake here says, that's the way it goes. The teachers' fund is looking for discounted mortgages to invest in and you're gonna help them."

He said nothing, which both men took for consent. They weren't used to anyone going against them.

The taller man smiled. "That's more like it. Westwind will tell the principals to give you a call. You can set up a meeting whenever it's convenient. Just be sure it gets done posthaste. We need this whole thing wrapped up no later than the next few weeks."

Val followed them to the door of the office. He watched them walk past the row of desks, out through the reception area, pausing only long enough for the guy named Jake to make a lewd remark to Shirl about her breasts.

Julie walked in just as the men walked out, eliciting a thorough, appreciative glance from the man in the navy blue suit. Val's hand clenched on the door frame as an odd, unexpected anger swept through him. His jaw went tight and his pulse began to race a little faster. Not liking the strange sensation, he took a deep breath and replaced his harsh expression with a smile.

Starting up the aisle, he headed toward the little redhead who had just walked in.

Julie watched Patrick walking toward her. She didn't like the tingly, breathless way she felt when she saw him. She didn't like the swirling in her stomach or the increase in her pulse. Thinking of the way he had kissed her the last time she had seen him, she started walking faster, hoping to reach the safety of her office before Patrick could intercept her. Unfortunately, his long legs moved him up the aisle faster than her shorter strides could carry her out of his way.

"I was hoping I'd be here when you came in." He smiled, but concern marked his features. "How did it go with your sister?" He knew about the morning meeting with Laura's therapist, Dr. Heraldson. Patrick had called last night to see how Laura was faring.

"It went all right, I guess." She kept on walking past him and the sleeve of his chocolate-brown sport coat brushed lightly against her breast. Just that small contact made her nipple peak. She turned so that he wouldn't notice, stepped into her office and reached for the door. Patrick stepped in and closed it for her, sealing them both inside.

"What happened? Did she listen to the tapes?"

Julie nodded. "She's more convinced than ever the abductions were real."

"Surely you don't believe her."

Julie sighed. "Not really. But I'm trying to keep an open mind." She leaned over her desk, grabbed a couple of files and crammed them into her burgundy leather briefcase. "Which is why I've got to run."

"Where are you going?" His jacket was unbuttoned, his tie off and his shirt partway undone. An image flashed of his sweat-soaked torso on the running machine at the gym, of lean hard muscle and smooth dark skin.

"I'm off to the library. I want to do some research on UFOs. I owe Laura at least that much." She started to walk past him, determined to ignore the way his eyes absorbed her every movement.

"Why don't I come with you?" He caught her arm. "Maybe I could help."

Julie shook her head. She felt short of breath, even a little bit dizzy. "I-I don't think so, Patrick."

"Why not? Believe it or not, I know my way around a reference department. Which library will you use?"

"UCLA. As an alumni, I'm still allowed to check out books. I've never done research on UFOs, but I'm sure they'll have the latest available information."

"Sounds like a good place to start. I'll drive you over."

She meant to protest, she really did, but he was tugging her toward the back door and she couldn't seem to think of a reason he shouldn't come. In minutes his shiny black Porsche was flying down Wilshire Boulevard, turning in to the small university town of Westwood, then winding its way up Hilgard to a back entrance that allowed them to park not too far from the library doors.

Patrick knew his way around the campus nearly as well as Julie. He had never attended but she figured he must have dated dozens of coeds who did. Her spine went a little bit rigid and she glanced away, hoping he wouldn't notice, but he did.

He pulled her beneath a tall, broad-leafed sycamore just outside the thick glass doors leading into the library building. "What is it, Julie? Something's wrong all of a sudden—I can see it in your eyes. Tell me what it is."

"Nothing's wrong." She started forward, but he caught her around the waist, bringing her body up close to his.

"Tell me."

She looked up and all she could see was blue. Incredible blue, delicious blue, the deepest blue eyes she had ever seen. "I was just…I was thinking of you and your women…all the pretty young coeds, the dozens of women you've slept with over the years. I don't know why you're here, Patrick. I don't understand what you want."

His blue gaze never faltered. "I want you, Julie. I think that's fairly obvious by now."

She swallowed, turned her face away. "Why? Why after so many years?"

He caught her chin, forcing her look at him. "I've always wanted you. I told you that before. But now I want more than just your body. I want to know your mind…your soul." He kissed her then, there beneath the towering tree, a soft, sweet kiss that turned hot and sultry and ended with her clinging to his neck. Patrick deepened the kiss and the heat of his hands seemed to burn through her clothes. She could feel the jutting ridge of his sex, the hot, moist throbbing of her own.

"Why don't we go back to my apartment?" he urged softly in his deep, sexy voice. "You can do your research another time."

The words rolled over her, compelling in their intensity, the unspoken message clear. *I want you, Julie. Now.* It made her already pounding heart trip even more loudly, made an odd weakness slide in to her limbs. She didn't dare give into it. Dear God, this was Patrick Donovan! She must be going crazy!

It took all her will to pull away. Julie wet her burning lips, glanced around with embarrassment to see how many students had been watching their heated display. No one showed the least bit of interest. Passion was an everyday occurrence at UCLA.

"I'm sorry, Patrick. I-I shouldn't have done that. We both know I haven't the slightest intention of going home with you."

"Why not?"

She stepped a little farther away, needing to put some distance between them. "I've told you *why not* a dozen times. Because it could never work out between us. Because I'm not interested in a quickie affair."

"Neither am I."

"Since when?"

"Since I discovered it was you I really wanted."

A splinter of heat ran through her. "I have to go in. You can come if you want. If not, when I'm finished, I can catch a cab back to my car." Without a glance in his direction, she started through the heavy glass doors. She didn't have to look to know Patrick walked behind her. She could feel his imposing presence with every step he took.

How could that be? When had Patrick Donovan become so commanding?

She pushed the thoughts away and brought her mind back into focus. She had come for a purpose. The afternoon was nearly over. She needed to see it done. Heading to the information desk, she asked a gray-haired woman to direct her to the section that included books on UFOs, close encounters, and alien abduction.

"That would be just down that aisle all the way to the back."

"Thank you." She wanted to get an overview of books today, then she would go on the Internet for magazine, and newspaper articles that would provide more recent information on the subject. Patrick helped her search the long row of volumes. She checked out all she could carry and left with an armload of books. Patrick frowned at the heavy stack she carried, lifted them out of her arms, and started walking toward the door.

They reached the car and he settled her inside, then stacked the books on the narrow ledge that served as the Porsche's back seat, pausing briefly to pick up a heavy volume and read the spine. "*UFO Encounters: Sightings, Visitations, and Investigations.*" He lifted another. "*UFOs: Operation Trojan Horse. UFO Crash at Roswell. UFO Experience. Flying Saucer Conspiracy. Visitors from Outer Space, Are They Finally Here?* Christ, you've got more than a dozen. Surely you aren't going to read them all."

"I certainly am. I can't help Laura unless I understand what she's afraid of. Since it happens to be spaceships and aliens, this is the stuff I need to read."

He thumbed through the volume on top of the stack, which was filled with color photos of UFO sightings. "Well, if nothing else, it ought to be entertaining."

Julie just smiled. "No doubt it will."

Patrick closed the door to the passenger side of the car then walked around and slid behind the wheel. It was still light but after seven by the time they turned down the street that led to the parking lot behind the office.

"How about dinner?" he asked. "I found another good Japanese place over in Century City."

Julie shook her head. "I've got a meeting with Owen Mallory first thing in the morning. He's thinking of buying some investment property. You know how sharp he is. I want to be prepared. I want to be bright-eyed and bushy-tailed when I see him."

Patrick grinned. "Bright-eyed and bushy-tailed?"

"That's just an expression."

The smile slowly faded away. "Mallory wants more from you than a real estate deal. You know that, don't you?"

The hackles went up on the back of her neck. "Owen's a very good client, Patrick. That's all he is and he knows it."

In the parking lot, they pulled up next to her car. Patrick dumped the books he'd unloaded into her trunk and slammed the lid. Turning, he slid an arm around her waist and drew her against him. She could feel the long sinews of his thighs, the heat of his hands, the ridges of muscle across his stomach.

"If you won't let me take you out to dinner, let me take you home. It's going to be a beautiful night. I'll stop and pick up something to eat and later we can walk on the beach."

"I told you I have work to do," she said, but the words did not come easy.

"What are you afraid of, Julie?"

"You, Patrick. The person you really are, the one you've locked away. We both know that person is still in there. Sooner or later, he's bound to reappear."

"I don't do drugs anymore. I don't drink or smoke. That man is gone, Julie. I'm a different man now—I won't do those things again."

"What about your women, Patrick? Anna Braxston was in your office this morning. You probably spent the night with her last night."

"I didn't spend the night with her. I'm not interested in Anna Braxston."

"Why not?"

"Because she isn't you."

She shook her head, but her pulse was thrumming in her ears and her hands had started to tremble. "I have to go." But she didn't want to. She wanted to stay with Patrick, to touch him, hold him, let him hold her. Dear God, it was the most frightening sensation she had ever experienced.

"All right, I'll let you go. But I don't really think that's what you want, and next time, I'm not going to let you pretend."

She stared at him, her thoughts in turmoil, then slowly turned away. He watched her climb into her car and start the engine, stood there as she drove away. She could see his tall figure in the mirror, long legs splayed, arms folded over his chest. Was it possible he really had changed? It seemed unlikely, yet the man she'd just left was a different person than the one she had known for the past eight years.

Perhaps this time he really had changed. It was hard to imagine, but more and more she was beginning to believe finding out might just be worth the risk.

Ten

~~~~~~~~~~~~~~~~~~~~~~~~~~~~

Julie stayed up well past midnight. As soon as she got home, she began going over the real estate investment information for her meeting with Owen Mallory. She went over each project she intended to present to him, but it was hard to concentrate when her thoughts kept straying to Patrick and the kisses they had shared, the things he had said to her.

It took a good deal of determination not to dwell on her growing desire for him, but her sister's problems were far more pressing. Thinking of Laura and her terrible fears, she turned next to the books she needed to read. Though the hour grew late, once she got started, they were just too fascinating to put down.

She had never thought much about UFOs, one way or another. It never actually occurred to her that such things might really exist. Now as she perused the volumes scattered all over the pinewood floor in her bedroom, she had to admit the possibility of life on other planets didn't seem quite so far-fetched.

And she wasn't alone in her thinking. All through the ages, men and women had postulated whether other life forms might not exist. Sightings of odd "air ships" and ancient astronauts went back to the beginnings of man.

In more recent times, in the 1970s, an author named Erick von Däniken proposed a theory in his book, *Chariots of the Gods,* that the planet might have been visited by extraterrestrials a number of times over the centuries. Perhaps advanced otherworldly cultures had been instrumental in building the great pyramids of Egypt, or assisted with the massive statues on Easter Island, or been responsible for the incredible landing strips on the South American plains of Nazcar, all mysteries that had never been sufficiently explained.

Another book discussed an occurrence in the Forties. Right after the Second World War, a number of sightings stirred the first modern interest in UFOs, and in July of 1947, one of the most controversial mysteries of recent times began. The Roswell incident. Fascinated, Julie read the article about the highly publicized crash of what was believed to be a UFO, her breath catching when she noticed an interview with a man present during what was purported to be one of the government's biggest cover-ups.

An officer named Lee Beeson, a retired colonel in the Air Force, lived in nearby Thousand Oaks, just a few miles north of L.A.

She continued to read, voraciously scanning each page, until several hours later when she began to yawn. Closing the volume she had nearly finished, she glanced at the clock and groaned to see it was almost 1:30 in the morning. She would be tired tomorrow, but the knowledge she'd gained had been worth it.

She knew a great deal more about UFOs, and she was going to track down this Colonel Beeson who lived in Thousand Oaks. With any luck at all, she would get a chance to speak to him. It would be extremely interesting to see what he had to say.

"I wish I knew what to do, Patrick." Fred Thompkins stood in front of his desk, clutching a file in his thick-fingered hands. "The sellers have agreed to accept my clients' offer but they want more down payment than they've got. My guy can't really afford it. It would take every last cent out of his savings, which would leave him high and dry at tax time and in really bad straits if anything unexpected came up."

Val ran through his memory banks, searching for solutions to similar problems Patrick had come up with over the years. The man's real estate knowledge was amazing. It was a shame he had never used his capabilities in a positive way, never wanted to work hard enough to become successful.

"How does his future income look?" Val asked. "Any upcoming bonuses, anticipated pay increases, that sort of thing?"

"He's in the advertising business. From what I gather, bonuses are commonly awarded. I think that's how he came up with some of the money he's using to buy the house."

"See if the seller will carry a second trust deed as well as a first. Make the second all due and payable in three to five years. Once the money's been repaid, the buyer's equity position will improve and his payments will go down. And the seller has the property as security. He won't have much risk."

Fred Thompkins grinned above his plaid bow tie. "You know, that just might work. Thanks, Patrick. I was hoping you'd be able to come up with something."

"Let me know what happens, Fred."

Fred blinked at the final words. Patrick had always been good at problem solving, but concern was something he rarely bothered with. "I'll do that. Thanks again."

In seconds, the heavyset agent had crossed the room and slipped out the door, moving faster than expected for a man of his size and age. As soon as the door eased closed, Val got up from his chair, crossed to the inner window, and looked out through the blinds that shielded his office from the main working area.

According to Shirl, Julie was due in any minute. He'd been out when she had called the office, but it seemed she was looking for him. Her meeting with Owen Mallory was over, but apparently by the time they had finished, she had one of her migraine headaches. If they weren't so damned painful—and he didn't feel so damned guilty—he might have been grateful.

At least she trusted him to help her in one way.

Unfortunately, the headaches were also dangerous. On the Internet he had learned that twelve million Americans suffered from migraine headaches. A number of studies had shown that people who had them also had a greater chance of having a stroke in their later years. Though Julie's headaches seemed to be coming with less and less frequency, he didn't like the idea that the *Ansor*'s study probe had caused them and that it might mean serious injury long after he was gone.

Looking through the window, he saw her walk in just then, carrying her burgundy briefcase and an armload of books he recognized as some of the ones she had checked out of the library. She was smiling, which he took as a good sign. He left his office and headed up the aisle in her direction, stopping beside her in front of Shirl's desk.

"I got your message," he said. "How are you feeling?"

The smile went broader. "Thank God, my headache's gone. The doctors never found out what was causing them, but the good news is they seem to be going away."

"I'm glad you're all right, but I have to admit I was looking forward to giving you that massage."

A soft flush rose in her cheeks. "It won't be necessary now, but I really appreciate the times you've helped. I'd love to know how you do it."

"Years of study," he teased, but this time she didn't smile.

"Yes, well, it's fortunate for me it wasn't necessary, since I'm running short on time. I just need to get off a letter, then I've got run."

"Where are you headed?"

"I'm on my way to Thousand Oaks. Ever heard of the Roswell incident?"

Val's stomach tightened. He'd heard of it, all right. The accident was a moment of infamy in Torillian history. Fortunately, on Earth, the whole event had been covered up, buried by a government recovering from a terrible war, mired in fear of a future that included the atom bomb, and a situation they worried might be even more threatening. Since the Roswell incident, world governments had adopted an ostrich, head-in-the-sand sort of policy that gave interstellar visitors free rein. It also kept the various governments from having to deal with a matter they were as yet unprepared to handle.

"I've heard of Roswell," Val said. "I saw a movie about it on HBO."

"Yes, well, a lot of people think a spaceship really crashed that night in the New Mexico desert. They believe the government knows it happened and has simply covered it up."

"And you believe that?"

"I don't know. I'll know better how I feel after I've talked to Colonel Beeson."

"I take it this Beeson lives in Thousand Oaks."

She grinned. "You got it." She brushed past him, hurried into her office and sat down behind her desk. Her computer was already on. Taking out a piece of letterhead stationery, she slid it into her printer, typed the letter, then used her mouse to hit the print designation button, and waited for the finished letter to appear.

Val propped a shoulder against the door frame, watching her efficiency with quiet admiration. "I'm through for the day. I'd like to go with you." Her head came up. He steeled himself for a no and silently prepared his rebuttal. The refusal never came.

Instead she studied him a moment while the printer quietly hummed.

"Shirley mentioned that Charlotte Rollins was looking for you this morning," she said out of the blue. "Charlotte says you've been ignoring her. She says you've been acting very strange and she's worried about you."

"Charlotte is no longer my concern."

"Meaning you aren't sleeping with her?"

"No, I'm not. As I said, she's no longer my concern."

"And I am?"

"Yes."

Something flickered in her leaf-green eyes. She fumbled with some paperwork then looked up at him. "All right, Patrick. I'd love some company this afternoon."

"And dinner afterward?" he pressed.

"Yes."

He wasn't exactly sure what had just happened, but he felt certain it was something important. "My car or yours?" he asked, backing off a little, giving up a bit of control and Julie a little space.

"Mine." She wheeled back her chair, jerked the letter out of the printer, stuffed it into the envelope she had already addressed, and tossed it into the out-bin. She smiled. "Come on, let's get going. I don't want to be late."

He found himself smiling back as she dragged him out the door, down the hall to the rear of the building, and out into the parking lot. He wondered what other surprises the day might hold in store.

Colonel Lee Beeson lived in a small, unassuming white stucco house in an older subdivision just off the 101 freeway in Thousand Oaks. He was a man in his early eighties, average in height but exceedingly fit and trim, with a full head of steel-gray hair.

"Come in, come in," he said, holding open the screen door while they stepped up on the porch. "It's been a while since anyone's asked to come by. Living by myself, I get a little lonely. Best thing about what happened in Roswell is it brings me a little company now and again."

"Thank you for seeing us," Julie said.

"Like I said, it's nice to have someone to talk to once in a while."

She introduced Patrick and the two men shook hands, then they walked into the living room. The house wasn't large and the room was a little bit dark. It smelled musty, as if he rarely opened the windows. Colonel Beeson moved a stack of newspapers off the sofa so they could sit down then took a seat in his worn, but comfortable-looking brown recliner.

"I s'pose you want to hear the whole story."

"Yes, if you don't mind, Colonel." Julie pulled out a small steno notebook, rested it neatly on her lap.

"No one calls me colonel anymore. Still, after so many years, it has a nice familiar ring to it." Releasing a long slow breath, the gray-haired man leaned back in his chair. When he started talking, it was obvious he had told the story a number of times before, but that made it no less interesting.

"I was only a shave-tail lieutenant back then," he started, "on perimeter duty the night it happened. July, it was, of 1947. I remember it was hotter than a pistol. I was wiping my forehead with a handkerchief when I first saw the light, sort of a silver streak across the sky, then a flash when it hit the ground. I radioed it in, of course. Thought it might be a small plane going down, or more likely, a meteor or something. A couple hours later I wound up in the recovery party."

He shifted, suddenly looking up. "I forgot to

ask…you all want some coffee or something? There's some Coca-Cola in the icebox."

"We're fine," Julie answered for both of them.

The colonel simply nodded, settled more comfortably in his chair. "All together that night, more than a dozen soldiers were dispatched to the site where the craft went down. I saw the wreckage up real close and I saw what was in it."

"What did it look like?" Julie asked when he paused.

"It was all in pieces, you understand, but some of them were pretty fair-sized. There were some odd sort of beams with funny markings on them. Looked like Egyptian hieroglyphics, but nobody could figure out what they said. Other pieces were shiny, like silver, but when you picked it up, it was light as a feather. One of the guys said it would have to be light in order to withstand the forces of acceleration."

"How big was it?" Patrick asked.

"From what was left, near as we could guess about fifteen feet. We figured it must have been disk-shaped when it was whole. We didn't see any windows."

"You said you saw what was in it." Julie leaned forward on the sofa. "What was it you saw, Colonel Beeson?"

"Not a what, Ms. Ferris, a who. There were four of them, little tiny fellows no more than four feet high. Gray they were, leathery skinned. Big heads, small bodies, hands with long thin fingers. Some of the men loaded them onto stretchers and they were taken away in an ambulance. We never saw them up real close but near as we could tell, all of them were dead."

Julie felt a chill move through her. "A story about it appeared the next day in the newspaper, isn't that right?"

He nodded. "Some reporter from the Roswell *Daily Record* heard about it from the ranchers who reported the crash that night. They were the first ones there. A reporter called someone at the base and at first nobody thought to deny it. By the following day, the brass had all been flown in and things began to get sticky. All the guys in the recovery party were told to keep their mouths shut—in no uncertain terms. Top secret, they said. Classified information of the highest priority. Anyone who was the least bit uncooperative didn't last long in the Air Force after that and left with the threat of a treason prosecution if they talked about a secret operation."

"But you lasted," Patrick said. "So you must have kept your silence for a number of years."

"That's right. I never said a word till I retired and all this talk about Roswell began to resurface. I was older by then, more open to what it might mean. I started thinking maybe the government ought to start telling people the truth about what happened. I had grandkids to think about. I started wondering how many more UFO incidents were being covered up and if that was the smart thing to do."

Julie scratched a few words in her notebook. "In one of the articles I read, it said that more than five hundred people in some way connected to the Roswell incident have now come forward."

"That's right, counting the office staff, officers' wives, children of the people who were involved at the time it occurred."

"If the Roswell incident really happened," Patrick said, "why doesn't the government just admit it? After all, it happened over sixty years ago. What difference could it possibly make now?"

"Every difference, my friend. Once the truth is out and an extraterrestrial presence is confirmed as a fact, every facet of government will have to be directed toward the problems that go with it. They'd have to consider military defense, communication with another life form, protecting the public from possible alien diseases—the list is endless. What head of government wants to deal with all that?"

Julie said nothing and neither did Patrick.

She thought of Laura and nervously shifted on the sofa. "Do you think it's possible they could still be out there? Watching us, I mean…perhaps even studying us?"

He grunted. "Anything's possible, I guess. I know UFOs are real. That's about all I can tell you. The rest you'll have to figure out for yourself."

Julie stood up and so did Patrick. "Thank you, Colonel Beeson."

"Don't thank me—I enjoyed the conversation. Kids all live pretty far away. Don't get down here very often." He walked them to the door. "Helluva story, ain't it? Be a damned good tale, even if I just made it up."

Julie's head snapped around. "You didn't, did you— just make it up?"

Colonel Beeson chuckled. "I was there, remember?" He didn't say more and she didn't press him. It seemed the truth was always a nebulous thing.

They left the house and Patrick opened her car door, went around and climbed into the passenger seat. "You didn't really believe that old man, did you?"

She had pondered that question since the moment she met Lee Beeson. "Frankly, yes I did. At least the part about the ship itself. I've read other accounts that agreed with that part of what he said. And there were quite a number of them. Hundreds of people say the Roswell incident really happened."

Patrick shrugged, moving the long sinews across his shoulders. "It's possible I guess, but even if it is the truth, that doesn't mean your sister was abducted."

"No, but it certainly gives the theory more credence." They were driving through the mountains, taking the back way home to her Malibu beach house. "Did you know that in the piney woods of east Texas in 1980, two women and their little boy claim they drove under a UFO that was taking off? They suffered radiation burns that are fully documented, and radiation sickness that lingers even today. The weirdest part is they sued the U.S. government for damages. Even in the '90s the suit was still going on. I haven't read how it ended."

"Why would they sue the government?"

"Because as the disk took off, twenty-three military helicopters rose out of the woods to surround the craft and follow it away. They obviously knew it was there, so they must have known there was danger. Dozens of other people in the area saw both the object and the helicopters, but the government denies any of it ever occurred."

Patrick released a slow breath of air. "I'm afraid I'm still a skeptic."

"Why? Why are you and so many other people so sure this couldn't be real?"

He smiled. "The answer's very simple—physics."

Julie frowned. "Physics? What does physics have to do with this?"

"Well, if you remember back to your college days, it's a basic principle of physics that an object can't travel faster than the speed of light. Since that is the case, even at a hundred and eighty-six thousand miles per second—almost light speed—it would take space travelers hundreds, even thousands of years to get here. That makes the whole thing damned hard to swallow."

Julie mulled that over. "Okay, that makes a certain amount of sense. We'll put the topic on hold till I can gather some more information." She looked over at him and smiled. "In the meantime I'm starving. You said you'd buy me dinner. I'm heading toward Malibu. I thought we'd pick up something we could take home…maybe later take that walk on the beach. What kind of food shall we eat?"

Patrick grinned. "How about Japanese?"

Julie rolled her eyes. "I think I've created a monster."

They drove along in silence for a while, winding their way through low rolling hills covered with stiff shrubs and wavy brown grasses. The sun felt warm on Val's face, but a cool ocean breeze made the heat of the day bearable. The top was down on Julie's little Mercedes.

Val glanced over at the woman who drove with expert skill through the winding mountain passes. She wore a gauzy white scarf tied around her dark red hair and she was smiling, enjoying the challenge, the speed, and perhaps, he hoped, the company of the man who sat beside her.

All afternoon she had been different. He had felt the subtle shift from the moment she'd agreed to let him come along. She seemed a little more relaxed than she usually was, as if she had made some momentous decision and now had simply to carry it out.

They stopped for Chinese takeout, the closest they could find to Japanese along the way, then sat out on Julie's sundeck to eat it, accompanied by tall glasses of Perrier. A bottle of Pouilly Fuisse Owen Mallory had brought over the night of her birthday party remained untouched on the counter.

Val had stripped off his jacket and tie and unbuttoned the collar of his blue Oxford shirt. Julie had changed into a sleeveless flowing caftan that fell close to the body, outlining her feminine curves. The paisley silk whispered against her skin as she moved, and it was all he could do not to reach out and touch her.

By the time they'd finished eating, darkness had fallen and the moon had come up, a huge white glowing orb that hung over the mountains to the east.

"It's beautiful, isn't it?" Julie stood beside him at the rail, listening to the roar of the waves against the shore several stories below.

"Magnificent…"

"I saw you watching it the night you came to dinner. I hadn't realized you were such a romantic till I saw the way you stared at the moon."

A brow arched up. "And just how was that?"

"As if you had never seen it. As if you had just discovered it and found it completely fascinating."

He smiled, thinking she was nearly correct. There were no moons on Toril, and studying it from space wasn't the same as watching it rise, seeing it turn everything in its path a shimmering silver.

"It's quite a sight," he said. "I don't think I could ever grow tired of seeing the way it lightens the sky, or does something as simple as reflecting the scarlet in your hair." He reached up, wrapped a bouncy dark red curl around his finger, felt it slide across his skin.

Julie turned a little and he cupped her cheek in his palm. "You and the moon. Both of you so beautiful." Bending his head, he kissed her, felt her soft mouth tremble under his. Inside his chest, his pulse began a rapid thudding. At the same time his blood seemed to thicken and grow sluggish. It pooled low in his belly, making him hard, making the hunger he had learned to suppress rise up with primal force.

"Patrick..." Tilting her head, Julie molded her mouth to his, fitting their lips perfectly together, opening to him and urging him to deepen the kiss. He drew her bottom lip into his mouth and sucked it gently, then tasted her deeply with his tongue. The walls of her mouth felt smooth and slick, her tongue rough and sensual, making the heat slide into his groin. His arousal strengthened, pressed insistently against the front of his pants. He couldn't have imagined the incredible sensations, the building power of his desire.

The loose flowing robe she wore dipped low in back. He ran his hands over her skin, tracing the smoothness, allowing the pleasure to slowly seep through him, savoring each new sensation. Tilting her head back, he kissed the column of her throat, trailed moist kisses across her shoulders. He worked the zipper down the front of the caftan and eased the garment down to her waist, baring her lovely milk-white breasts.

A jolt of heat spiraled through him, made the perspiration break out at his temples. Bending his head to a dusky tip, he felt it tighten beneath his tongue, and a groan slipped from his throat. His body pulsed, felt hot and heavy, throbbed in a way he wasn't prepared for, and his hands grew suddenly unsteady. He opened his mouth, took more of the rounded swell, sucking deeply, then filled his palm with the heavy, hard-tipped fullness. He could feel her quivering even as she clutched his shoulders, began to work the buttons on his shirt.

He kissed her again, deeply, erotically, letting the unbearable heat burn through him, wanting her and fighting to stay in control. He felt her hands on his chest, tracing the ridges of muscle across his rib cage, twining through his curly black chest hair. She stripped the shirt away then worked the buttons on his pants and slid down the zipper, her fingers trembling, suddenly a little uncertain.

His hands shook as he cupped her breasts, ringed them with his tongue, and a rush of fire speared through him. His loins felt heavy, full, his shaft rock-hard and pulsing. Taking her mouth in a ravaging kiss, he stroked deeply into the sweetness inside, wanting to possess her, craving her like a drug.

He was shaking all over, on fire with need, his control badly slipping. When she touched him again, wrapped a small hand around his sex and began to stroke him there, waves of pleasure broke over him, and a need so great he had to clamp down on his jaw to keep his body from exploding.

Panic shot through him, making his heart race even faster. His blood was pumping, burning through his veins, his skin felt flushed and damp, and his body tingled all over.

He groped for control, tried to wrest it from the depths of his mind, but all he could think of was burying his hard length inside her. He wanted to tear off her clothes, drag her down on the deck, force her legs apart and thrust himself into the place between her legs. His mind was a swirling haze of passion, his body thrummed with heat and need, pulsed with a hunger so strong he could taste it on his tongue.

His hands tightened on her shoulders. He searched for the strength he needed, the means to regain his control, but found nothing but primitive, mind-numbing hunger.

Fear splintered inside him, devouring his tenuous hold on reason. What if he hurt her, lost control completely and took her by force? He had to stop, had to gain control of himself, couldn't allow himself to rage so wildly out of control. His grip grew fierce, his eyes dark and forbidding. With a last determined effort, he jerked himself away, worked to drag in great breaths of air.

"Patrick?" Julie stood trembling in the moonlight, her green eyes luminous and uncertain. "Is something wrong? Did I do something…?" With shaky hands, she caught the front of the caftan and pulled it up to cover her naked breasts, clutching the fabric protectively around her.

"No." He shook his head, his voice ragged. "No. It isn't you. It's me." Turning away from her, he grabbed his shirt off the floor and shrugged it on, fumbled with the buttons, gave up and tucked the tail into his pants, then zipped them up. He raked back his hair and started for the door, barely aware that Julie followed.

"Where…where are you going?"

"Home. I'll catch a cab from the shopping center down the street."

Her chin came up. "I brought you. I can take you home."

He only shook his head. "I need to walk. I'll get home all right. You don't need to worry." He was out the door before she had time to argue.

If he lived five hundred years, he would never forget the confusion and hurt he saw on her beautiful face.

Eleven

Gripping the thin silk caftan over her breasts, Julie stared at the front door Patrick had just closed behind him. She could hear his heavy footfalls on the stairs leading down to the street. Her chest hurt. Tears spilled over her lashes and trailed down her cheeks.

"Oh God, Patrick, what did I do?" But silence was her only answer. For the last eight years, she had harbored a secret physical desire for Patrick Donovan. She had fought it, defeated it, filed it safely away. But since his heart attack, things had changed.

It had been easy to refuse the selfish, hedonistic man he had been. But this new Patrick, this gentle, caring, concerned Patrick Donovan was a man she could not resist. She had been frightened of the risk she was taking, but it never occurred to her that Patrick might be having reservations, too. Or perhaps he had discovered he no longer wanted her the way he had believed.

Blinking back a fresh round of tears, Julie walked into the living room. She grabbed a tissue, her hands still shaking, dabbed at her cheeks and blew her nose, then sank wearily down on the sofa. Her heart still pounded. Her insides tingled. The ache of unspent desire throbbed through her veins.

What had just happened? What had she done? Julie clamped down on the urge to cry again. It never did any good and usually made her feel worse. Besides, she should have known something bad would happen. He was Patrick, after all. What had she expected?

Still, she hadn't been with a man for the past three years, not since she had ended her affair with Jeffrey Muller. Once she had made the decision to sleep with Patrick, she had wanted everything to be perfect. The time seemed right: a beautiful night, a full moon, the soothing sounds of the sea battering softly against the shore. She had wanted Patrick so very badly, and at first he had seemed to want her. She didn't know what had gone wrong or how she was ever going to face him again.

Her throat ached, and her stomach churned with embarrassment at Patrick's cold rejection. She rubbed her temple, hoping it wasn't the beginning of a headache, thinking that the way things had been going lately, she shouldn't be surprised by anything that occurred.

First the terrible migraines, then Laura's paranoia and outlandish claims. Now there was Patrick and the awful realization that nothing between them would ever be the same.

She thought of his behavior and her own erotic desires, felt her face go warm with humiliation. She stiffened her spine. The headaches were slowly getting better. She was sure in time they would disappear. Her sister needed her help—she would do what she could to take care of her.

As for Patrick…Patrick Donovan could go straight to hell.

* * *

Val paced the bedroom of his apartment, stopped and turned and paced the length of the room again, his shoes making a squeaking sound on the carpet with each of his long, agitated strides. Before he'd left for work that morning, he had completed his required communication with his superiors using a small, powerful device the size of a credit card he carried in his wallet.

As soon as he had returned home tonight, he had begun work on his journal, which lay open on the desk a few feet away, the pages overflowed with words he had written about what had happened at Julie's. Personal impressions he wasn't yet ready to share with his superiors aboard the ship.

I thought I was prepared. I was not. My experience with Julie Ferris was more intense, more powerful than anything I had imagined. More than any Torillian could begin to imagine. Combined with the things I've learned since my arrival, along with the knowledge in Patrick's memory banks, it has made me see these people in a different light, understand them as I never have before.

I try to find the words but they do not come easily. Suffice it to say that although there are ways our cultures seem the same, their world is nothing like ours. They are nothing like us. Perhaps in simplest terms, I could say that passion dominates their nature. It is there in all they do, in everything they feel. They are absorbed by it, swallowed by it. Each of their experiences is more intense because of it. At times it controls them. Their passion stirs anger, fear, murder, and even wars, driving them to lengths we cannot comprehend.

He paused for a moment, thinking of the words he had written, thinking of the things he had experienced tonight. Though he had not actually completed the act of sex as he had intended, the passion he had experienced had given him an insight into feelings a Torillian could not fathom. For the first time he was beginning to understand the intense degree of emotion humans felt.

He paced the floor thinking of all he had learned, all he had yet to learn, thinking of Julie Ferris.

Wanting her still.

His body continued to throb with the ache she had stirred, still pulsed with the heat of his desire for her. He could feel the weight of her breasts in his hands, recall the erotic taste of her skin. He wanted her more than ever, craved to know the full extent of what he might discover from their joining. But now, because his body's needs had frightened him so badly, he had destroyed their growing bond, and the odds weren't good he would be given a second chance.

Val felt another sweep of emotion, this one tightening a hard knot in his chest. He wasn't sure what it was, a mixture of pain and something deeper, more intense.

He didn't know how to ease it, how to make it go away.

And part of him was afraid to find out.

Julie didn't see Patrick all the next day, which was the only stroke of good fortune she'd had. Laura had called early that morning. Dr. Heraldson had arranged for her to sit in with Peter Winter's abduction group at 7:00 p.m. that evening.

"I was kind of hoping you could come with me," Laura had said over the phone.

Julie pondered that. "I would have to rearrange my evening appointment with the Harveys. They're supposed to sign the escrow papers on the condo they just bought, but I can probably meet with them tomorrow." She still felt funny about steering them away from Patrick's condo project, but she had rarely seen him so adamant on a subject as he had been that day, and the condo the couple had finally purchased might turn out to be the better deal.

"I'd really like you to come," Laura urged.

Julie heard the anxiety in her sister's voice. "Then I will. In fact, I'll pick you up. Where will you be? At home or at work?"

A long silent pause. "I'm not working at The Boutique anymore."

An equally long pause on Julie's end. "Why not?"

"I didn't like working so late. I didn't like coming out of the building after it got so dark."

Julie thought of her sister cowering in terror the night of the birthday dinner, and her heart went out to her. "I'm sure you'll find something else. In the meantime, this will give you plenty of time to work with Dr. Winters. I'll pick you up at six."

She rang off, worked for a while on her escrow files, showed a big Palos Verdes estate to a friend of Owen's who was thinking of moving, then bought a couple of submarine sandwiches she and Laura could eat on the road, and set off for Venice Beach.

Dr. Winters's abduction group was meeting at a residence in Long Beach, not that far away. It turned out to be a lovely two-story home that backed up to one of the scenic canals. It wasn't what she would have expected. Neither was the group of people who had gathered to discuss their fears.

"I'm Robert Stringer." The owner of the house waited for them on the porch and invited them in. "You must be Laura, and this must be your sister, Julie."

"I'm Laura," her sister corrected, since the man had reversed their names. "This is Julie."

"Hello, Mr. Stringer," Julie said, wondering if being shorter made her a more likely victim than her taller, more willowy sister.

"It's just Robert. We're all friends here." He was a dignified man in his early forties, the head of Digital Associates, a big computer software company. The last person she could imagine believing in alien abduction.

As they walked into the foyer, a small man in jeans, penny loafers, and a long-sleeved white button-down shirt stepped forward. "Welcome. I'm Dr. Winters."

Peter Winters led them forward and introduced them to the rest of the group seated in the living room. Carrie Newcomb, an attractive young woman in her late twenties, was a hairdresser who had moved to L.A. from Phoenix. Leslie Williams was African-American, tall and willowy with intelligent dark eyes and a warm, broad-lipped smile. She worked for Xerox in the sales and marketing division, driving up for the meetings each week from San Diego. Matthew Goldman, a thin, nervous man with a tic, was unemployed; and fiftyish Willis Small was the successful author of a dozen books on gardening.

An interesting mix, Julie thought, people without

any apparent connection. The only one there with an obvious disorder was Goldman, the man with the tic, who
in less than fifteen minutes proved to be either a fake or
a schizophrenic. Julie wasn't sure which, but she was
betting on the latter.

"Since the group is open to anyone who wants to
come," the doctor said, taking a chair at the head of the
circle, "I'd like to open the discussion by turning the
meeting over to whomever might have something they
wish to say. How about you, Leslie?"

The cocoa-skinned woman smiled. "I'm happy to
say it's been a good week for me, since I slept better than
I usually do. I'm feeling stronger, less frightened since
I've been coming here. I want you all to know how
much I appreciate being a part of this group."

Dr. Winters smiled. "Thank you, Leslie. We're glad
to have you with us. Anyone else?" He turned to Robert
Stringer. "Since we have a newcomer with us tonight,
perhaps you wouldn't mind, Robert, repeating for us the
story of your abduction."

Julie didn't know why Robert Stringer had been sin-
gled out until she saw the way his story began to affect
the others. Where all but Goldman had appeared calm
before, now they had all begun to fidget in their seats.
Perhaps for most of them, repeating the tale was like re-
living it. The occurrence was just too traumatic.

"As most of you know, I was working in Denver at
the time it happened…my first encounter with the Visitors. My oldest son, Tommy, loved to fish, so for the
weekend, the two of us had traveled up to a small mountain lake near Crested Butte. It was such a pleasant sum-
mer day we had taken the top off the Jeep. It was nearly

dusk when it happened. We had already caught our limit and were heading back to camp when we heard an odd sort of buzzing. It wasn't like anything either of us had ever heard before. It was rather unsettling, irritating you might say. It was sort of thick and heavy, and at first we couldn't decide where it was coming from."

An prickle of uneasiness ran along Julie's nerves. She had heard a sound like that the day they were at the beach.

Robert Stringer shifted a little in his chair. "I pulled off the road when we realized it was coming from directly above us. The object we saw was disk-shaped, made of highly polished silver. It looked massive, hovering right over our heads. Both of us just sat there, staring at the object in awe. I remember little Tommy reaching out to grasp my hand."

Leslie Williams started crying.

A chill raced down Julie's spine.

"What happened then, Robert?" Dr. Winters gently prodded.

"That's the last I recall until I woke up on the ship."

"And once you were there?"

"They stripped off my clothes. I remember trying to fight them, but I couldn't move. I remember looking frantically for my son. I never saw him, but somehow I knew he was there." Robert Stringer's throat moved up and down, but no sound came out. With obvious effort, he dragged himself under control

"Can you go on, Robert?"

He nodded, rubbed his palms on the sides of his pants. "They placed me on a cold metal table and bathed me in something…it was slimy and I remember it smelled a little like cheddar cheese. It was wet and colorless and it made me start to shiver. I was lying flat on my back. They lowered some sort of machine over my head and attached it to my forehead with what looked like some type of electrodes. It was reading something, my thoughts I think. It was learning everything about me. When they were finished, they inserted a metal probe down my throat and another into my rectum. They forced me to climax then took a semen sample. I remember I cried. I couldn't stand having them touch me."

Julie swallowed against the dryness in her throat. Her hands were shaking. She glanced worriedly over at Laura, saw tears spilling onto her sister's cheeks. She wanted to go to her, comfort her, but she had to see this through. Julie bit down on her lip and forced herself not to move.

"What did they look like?" the doctor asked softly.

"There were several different types. Most of them were little, less than four feet tall. They had big heads and large dark eyes, and they were dressed exactly alike. At the time I remember thinking they were soldiers." He moved restlessly now, crossing his legs, then straightening them out in front of him. "There were others there, too. Taller, thinner. They were the ones giving the orders, though I wasn't able to hear them."

"I could," one of the others said softly, her voice scratchy and low. Julie turned to see Carrie Newcomb leaning forward in her chair. "Their mouths didn't move, but I could hear them speaking, telling me not to be afraid."

"They were devils," Goldman snorted, "with pointed ears and long spiked tails. They've consigned us to hell and they're going to make sure we get there."

"We all know your opinion, Matt," the doctor said firmly. "Why don't we let Robert finish?"

Goldman sat back in his chair. It was obvious the others wished he wasn't there.

"I don't remember much more about that particular time," Robert continued. "When I woke up I was back in my car and it was almost morning. My son was asleep in the passenger seat. He doesn't remember anything that happened to us, and I hope he never does."

"How...how can you be certain he was taken?" Julie asked.

Robert Stringer leaned forward. He rolled up the sleeve of his shirt. "Do you see this?"

"Yes. It looks like a tiny isosceles triangle."

"When I awakened that morning, this mark was on my forearm. My son has one just like it on his."

Laura made a strangled sound in her throat. Julie turned in her direction in time to see her unbuttoning the cuff on her blouse. When she turned it back, Julie saw the small triangle. *Oh, dear God.* A knot clenched in Julie's stomach. Laura's face was as pale as Dr. Winters's white shirt.

"Laura?" Julie stood up, her mouth dry, her chest so tight she could barely speak. She started in her sister's direction, but before she could reach her, Laura's eyes rolled back in her head and she slumped sideways on the sofa.

"Damn it!" The oath roared out from the end of the room. The sliding door slammed open and Brian Heraldson strode in, his face as dark as thunder. Obviously he had been listening. "I was afraid something like this would happen."

Peter Winters gripped his arm, stopping him before he

reached the couch. "Were you also afraid your patient's fears might actually be real?" He pointed to the tiny mark on Laura's arm, holding Brian's gaze for long disturbing moments, until Laura's soft moan broke the silence.

Brian tore himself away. "Laura?" He sat down beside her on the sofa. "Just take it easy. It's Dr. Heraldson." The bearded doctor rested a hand on her forehead and Laura's eyes fluttered open.

"Brian?" She sat up on the sofa a little too fast and swayed against him. "Oh, Brian, I'm so glad you're here."

He cleared his throat, looking a little uncomfortable at her familiarity. "Yes, well, after I arranged for you to come, I decided that maybe I should be here. I spoke to Dr. Winters about it. I never meant to actually come in, but…"

"I'm glad you did."

Julie watched her sister with a mixture of pity and concern, her insides leaden. Had Laura really experienced the terror of being abducted, the awful invasions of the mind and body Robert Stringer had described? Though her sister had never met the man before, their accounts were amazingly similar. Still, if Laura was a victim of abduction, where had Julie been during the time her sister was taken?

She glanced down at her forearm. No triangular shape marked her skin. Surely if she had been there on the beach or in the house when the abduction occurred, as Laura's memory suggested, surely they would share some common recollections of the incident. But Julie remembered nothing.

"If you were listening," Julie said to Dr. Heraldson, "then I presume you heard Mr. Stringer describe his abduction experience. Obviously it's very similar to what Laura has told us."

The doctor nodded grimly. "Having read other such accounts, I thought perhaps it would be. On the surface the evidence for abduction looks convincing, but you have to understand there are other possible explanations."

"Such as?" Julie asked.

"Shared hallucination, for one. All of the supposed victims might be sharing an imagined event—rather like two people having the same dream. In centuries past, people hallucinated fairies and malevolent angels who took these same sorts of liberties with their bodies. Today we see movies about aliens and UFOs and hallucinate spacemen. Or it might be caused by a medical problem."

"A medical problem? What sort of medical problem?"

"It's called temporal lobe disorder."

"What's that?" Laura asked.

Dr. Winters answered. "There are a number of diseases of the mind that can lead to hallucination. Temporal lobe epilepsy, as it is also called, is only one of them. It is often blamed for psychic and religious experiences, feelings of déjà vu, anxiety and panic attacks. Visions that occur because of this disorder can be extremely vivid, containing even sounds and smells."

He turned a hard smile on Brian Heraldson. "Of our group, only Willis Small has been tested for this disorder. He does not have it. What Dr. Heraldson might not be aware of is that most of the people who have reported the abduction experience and been tested for temporal lobe disorder have also been found to be free of the disease."

Brian eyed him coldly. "Schizophrenia as well as paranoia are also associated with hallucinations," he said defensively.

"True. And no doubt there are those to which that diagnosis would apply." The smaller man's glance strayed to Matthew Goldman, the nervous man with the tic. "But the majority do not."

Julie shifted her attention to Dr. Heraldson. "What about the triangle on Robert Stringer's arm?"

"As I told you, the mind and body often act as one. The former influencing the latter to a degree that is often difficult to believe."

"You're saying her mind made the mark appear."

He simply nodded.

"Or it's possible these people are telling the truth," Peter Winters said.

Heraldson didn't answer. He glanced from Julie to Laura, who still leaned against him. "Whatever the case, I think Laura's had enough for the moment. Perhaps it's time she went home." There was tenderness and concern in his expression, and perhaps something more. Dr. Heraldson was Laura's psychiatrist. Julie frowned at the implications.

He helped Laura up from the sofa, then returned his attention to Julie. "I know what you're thinking. I want you to know I've disqualified myself as Laura's therapist from here on out. I don't believe I can remain as objective as I should be."

Julie relaxed a little at that, grateful for the doctor's professionalism. Heraldson helped Laura to her feet, then together with Julie they walked toward the door.

Carrie Newcomb stopped them in the entry. "It's always worse in the beginning," she said to Laura, reaching out to squeeze her hand. "The fear never really goes away, but after a while you begin to accept it. Things get better after that. And Dr. Winters is terrific. He's always there to help when you need him."

"That's right, Laura," Winters said, coming up to join them. "Talking about it can be very therapeutic. I hope we'll see you here next week."

"We'll have to see about that," Brian said coolly, and Laura's head came up.

She focused on Peter Winters. "I'll be here, Dr. Winters—you can count on it."

"Laura—" Brian started, but the smile she flashed in his direction seemed to cut off his next words. "We can talk about it later," he said gruffly. "In the meantime, I'll drive you home…that is, if it's all right with you."

Laura looked at Julie, then back to the tall bearded man. "I'd like that, Dr. Heraldson."

"Brian," he corrected. "I'm not your doctor anymore. From now on we're just friends."

Laura smiled softly. Her cheeks still held a trace of her earlier tears, but some of the color had returned to her face.

Julie squeezed her sister's hand. "Call me if you need anything." She watched the two of them walk away, worried about Laura yet grateful her sister had a friend like Brian Heraldson to lean on.

Then another man's image came to mind, taller, darker, more sensually handsome. She wondered what Patrick Donovan would have thought about the events of the evening. His opinion might have mattered if things had worked out differently between them.

After his icy rejection, she told herself she didn't really care.

* * *

Walking over to the built-in bar in Patrick's office, Val reached for a crystal decanter of scotch. "Still a Chivas drinker?" he asked the tall, statuesque woman in black who had just walked into the room. Onyx hair framed a beautiful oval face, a cloud of black that set off her pale, nearly flawless complexion.

Felicia Salazar smiled, lifting a small heart-shaped round mole near the corner of her mouth. "You always did have a good memory…at least for the important things in life."

He felt a trace of amusement, appreciating another of Patrick's many talents. "On occasion it's a handy thing to have."

She walked up behind him, rested a long-fingered hand on his shoulder. "What else do you remember, Patrick?" She brushed an imaginary piece of lint from his navy blue sport coat. "The night we made love on the terrace of our room in Puerta Vallarta? We drank champagne that night, do you recall? You poured it onto my breasts then licked it off while we sat on the edge of the pool. God, you were so romantic."

She bent forward till her breath feathered over his ear. "Or perhaps you remember something a little more erotic…like that time in Century City when you pushed the elevator stop button between the eight and ninth floors of Daddy's new office building. The walls of the elevator were mirrored, do you remember? We could watch each other while we did it. I remember how hard you were, how you forced me into the corner and shoved up my skirt. You buried yourself so deep I came almost instantly. You *do* recall *that*…don't you, Patrick?"

He swallowed, his hands a little unsteady. He remembered, all right. The erotic images had him hard again, just thinking about what they had done.

Her smile turned more exotic, her thick-lashed eyes going dark. She reached down and cupped his groin. "Yes…I can see you do." She bent forward and kissed him, stuck her tongue inside his mouth.

Val kissed her back, enjoying the hot sensations washing through him, opening himself up to them. Felicia Salazar had just returned to the States from Brazil, where she had been living with her third husband. They were separated, she said. She was lonely. She was looking to Patrick for company.

He deepened the kiss, sliding an arm around her waist and pulling her against his groin. He cupped her buttocks, massaged the firm globes through her short black skirt. It occurred to him that although his body was aroused, he was far more in control than he had been with Julie.

Felicia slowly ended the kiss. "I'm sure your couch would suffice, darling, but I've an appointment at one, and I'm too greedy to settle for just a few minutes. My limo will pick you up at eight. We'll go somewhere special for dinner then go back to my suite at the Penn. We can fuck like rabbits all night, then have breakfast together in the morning." She kissed him again. "No strings. No expectations. It'll be just like old times."

Val's dark eyebrows drew together. It was Julie he wanted, not Felicia. He was even more determined to have her, but if they did make love, he couldn't afford to make another mistake. Even though he could relive Patrick's experiences through his memory any time he

wanted, it wasn't the same as having actually done it.
He wanted desperately to do things right this time and
there was only one way to insure that.

He smiled. "All right. Sounds like the perfect evening."

Felicia ran a long red nail down his cheek. "It will
be, darling, I promise."

She left him then and watching her walk away, he
pondered his decision. He felt uneasy about it. Something didn't feel right. Still, it seemed the sensible thing
to do, the most logical way to achieve his final objective.

He had a couple of phone calls to make. When he was
finished, he left his office and headed toward the receptionist's desk up at the front.

"What time did Julie say she'd be in?" he asked
Shirl Bingham.

"Actually, she didn't say. She said she had appointments all day. She called in a couple of times for her
messages, but I didn't get the impression she was going
to actually come in." Behind him the front door swung
open, ringing the bell on the top. "Babs just walked in.
You might try asking her."

He turned in her direction. She was dressed impeccably in wide-legged lemon-yellow pants and a black-
and-yellow top.

"Hi, stranger," he said. "How was Mexico?" She'd
gone to Acapulco for three days with her latest flame,
a polo player named Renaldo de la Garza.

"Hot." She rolled her pale blue eyes. "I must have been
out of my mind to go down there this time of year. All
we did was drink Margaritas and vegetate in the pool."

"Sounds like real tough duty."

She grinned. "Yeah, well, somebody's got to do it."

Val smiled. "You wouldn't happen to know where I might find Julie?"

"Not right now, I'm afraid. I talked to her though. She said she'd be working late. Maybe you can catch her tonight at home."

Not tonight, he thought, he planned to get laid—to coin a phrase from Patrick's vernacular. Then again, perhaps it was better this way, to wait to straighten things out between them when his night with Felicia was over. "If you happen to see her, tell her I need to talk to her, will you? Tell her I'll be in my office all day tomorrow."

"Will do." One of Bab's sleek dark eyebrows arched up. "By the way, I saw your ex-girlfriend out in the parking lot. She says she's back on the loose."

"So I gather," Val said.

"I guess we both know what that means."

"Do we?"

"Sure. It means wild nights and partying. It means the old Patrick is on his way back in."

"I told you, I'm through with alcohol and drugs."

She fixed him with a cold-eyed stare. "Try to remember that, will you, Patrick? You've really been a nice guy lately. Even Fred's starting to like you. Don't screw things up."

Val didn't answer. There was only one thing he wanted from Felicia Salazar. He wanted a lesson on how to make love. No strings, she'd said. No expectations. As soon as the lesson was over, that would be the end of it.

He left the office at five, headed home, wrote in his journal for a while, then changed to go out for the evening. He wasn't as nervous as he had expected to be. He had tuned in to Patrick's memories of sex with Felicia, something he didn't have with Julie, and he intended to use them to guide him. When the limo driver called from the lobby, announcing Felicia's arrival, he shrugged into his double-breasted black silk Armani jacket and headed downstairs, looking forward to the evening with a calm he hadn't expected.

The limo driver held open the door of the long white Lincoln stretch limo and Val climbed in. The slender black-haired beauty was waiting for him in the back seat, extending a frosty champagne glass in his direction.

Val accepted the glass. His body was in perfect physical condition. He would never take drugs, but in contrast to Babs's and Julie's fears, he knew a drink or two wouldn't hurt him, and tonight he needed to appease the lady he was with if he was going to accomplish his purpose.

"Thanks." He took the crystal goblet from her hand and settled his tall frame next to her on the cushy gray leather seat.

"You look marvelous, Patrick, the best you've looked in years."

He smiled. "I gave up the dope and the booze. This is the first drink I've had since my heart attack."

"I heard about that." She rested a hand on his leg, ran it halfway up his thigh. "It doesn't look like it's slowed you down any."

He leaned over and kissed her on the lips. "I guess we'll find out a little later on."

They drove to the bar at the Four Seasons hotel, one of the current celebrity hot spots in L.A., ordered an extravagant meal at an intimate table in the dining room, then returned to the limo.

Conversation with Felicia was limited at best, mostly sexual overtones about what she intended to do to him once she got him in bed. By the time the meal was finished, considering how little both of them ate and the uninspired dialogue between them, he wondered why they had bothered going out at all.

They returned to the car and the chauffeur started back to the Peninsula, Felicia's luxury hotel.

"Damn." A sudden thought occurred, and Val pressed the intercom button that connected the back seat to the driver, who was sealed behind a darkened window in front. "I need to swing by my office. There's a file I've got to have." To Felicia he said, "I've got a meeting first thing in the morning."

She arched a brow at a move so out of character for Patrick, then gave him a petulant glance. "Not too early, I hope."

His mouth curved faintly. "No. Not too early." The big black Lincoln stopped at the rear of the office and as Val climbed out, Felicia pulled his head down for a kiss.

"Hurry back," she said in her deep sexy voice, and he smiled.

"I'll only be a minute."

As soon as he returned, they were off, the driver pulling into the long sweeping drive of the Peninsula hotel, a uniformed doorman helping them out of the car. Felicia's suite, in a separate row of town houses in the rear, was richly decorated in muted peach and cream. Marble and gilt, lavish and expensive. The minute the door was closed, he found himself wrapped in her arms.

"I must have been crazy not to bring you straight here," she said, kissing him fiercely, dragging her fingers through his hair then biting the side of his neck. "In fact, I should have let you screw me in your office. That's what I really wanted. I just thought it would be nice for us to get reacquainted a little bit first."

They were never really acquainted, Patrick's memory said. They had used each other. That was the way each of them wanted it.

Val kissed her deeply. His body stirred, continued to harden, but there was none of the hot, lusty fire he had known when he had kissed Julie. He felt Felicia's hands on his crotch, stroking him through his slacks. He worked the zipper at the back of her black cocktail dress and she stepped out of it, stood in front of him in a garter belt and black nylon stockings. She wasn't wearing a bra. And she wasn't wearing panties.

For a minute he stood there frozen. His loins were thick and heavy and yet he sensed there was something wrong. His body wanted him to take her, but the man he truly was, the man he seemed to be losing, said no. He wanted to have sex with her, to finally reach release, but his mind remained strangely unmoved.

Something is wrong, he thought again, more and more uneasy. With Julie his body and mind had worked as one, each heightening the sensations of the other. Now he was dealing with just his physical needs.

And something else bothered him.

It was an odd sensation, a gut-deep awareness that he was somehow failing Julie. He labeled the feeling betrayal, a violation of trust, a word that meant disloyalty and deceit. They were simply not acceptable to the man he truly was.

Felicia had his shirt stripped away and his pants unzipped before the full implications hit him. Sex was different than making love. Sex was physical. The animal act of procreation. Making love to someone required a form of caring. It was Patrick's way to stay removed from emotional involvement, to remain uncommitted, unconcerned and uncaring.

It wasn't Val's way and it never would be.

He grabbed her slim wrist as she reached inside the waistband of his shorts and Felicia's dark head came up. Her lips glistened with moisture, her eyes were glazed with passion, the brown of the irises nearly as dark as the pupils. His body craved release, ached to quench this hunger that had been with him for so long, yet his mind could not be swayed to that end.

For the second time in a matter of days, he was leaving a woman who wanted him in her bed. But for two far different reasons.

"Patrick?"

"I'm sorry, Felicia, this isn't going to work."

"What…what are you talking about?"

He began to ease away. "I said this isn't going to work. Too much has happened since we were together last. Too much has changed."

"Wh-what's happened? What's changed?"

"I have," he said softly, easing himself farther away. He reached down and picked up her dress, then handed it over to her. "I'm sorry things didn't work out. I hope you'll try to understand."

"Understand?" she repeated, her back going rigid. She stepped into her dress, reached behind her to zip it up. "I understand, all right. I understand you're a real son of a bitch, Patrick. Just like you've always been."

He drew on his shirt, buttoned it up and tucked it in. "I'm sorry, Felicia, I really am."

"Get out of here, you bastard."

He didn't say more, just opened the door and stepped out into the hallway. When he reached the lobby, one of the guys at the front desk waved a farewell, and a uniformed doorman hailed a cab for him outside the entrance to the hotel.

All the way back to his apartment, he reviewed what he had done, going back over each precise moment. Of all the decisions he had made, he had never been so certain he had done the right thing.

Twelve

It was silly. Absolutely idiotic to be crying about a man like Patrick Donovan. But Julie couldn't help it. Not since the moment she had left the office at 10:00 p.m., climbed behind the wheel of her car, and seen Patrick pull up in Felicia Salazar's fancy limousine. Julie knew who it was—with a plate that read *Feline l,* it wasn't hard to figure out. Besides, she had seen the woman kissing Patrick when he had opened the heavy car door.

God, just thinking about it made her stomach roll with nausea.

Julie took a nerve-calming sip of the brandy she had poured herself when she got home. No wonder Patrick hadn't wanted her. Why should he when he had a beautiful, exotic creature like Felicia dying to crawl into his bed?

God, she felt like a fool.

She drank some more of the brandy, tilted the glass and drained the contents, then coughed as the burning liquid fired down her throat. Damn him! Damn him to hell! What in the world had ever made her believe he had changed?

Grateful to the alcohol for the numbness that began to seep through her body, Julie went to bed and eventually fell asleep. She tossed and turned, woke up at least four times, then lay awake till the alarm went off at 5:30 a.m.

All morning she felt groggy, drained and out of sorts, but she dressed in a pale peach pantsuit, grabbed her briefcase, climbed in her car, and headed in to work. She was tired of hiding. Patrick had made a fool of her, but she hadn't actually gone to bed with him so she still had the remnants of her pride.

And now that she knew the truth, she would arm herself against him more fiercely than she had ever done before.

She saw him at ten o'clock that morning, when he walked in with Ron Jacobs, one of the newer salesmen in the office. They were talking about selling the Weatherby estate, a listing Patrick had apparently just helped Ron get, and both of them were laughing, heady with their victory over half the other agents in Beverly Hills who had been trying to do the same thing.

Even at a distance, Patrick's rough male voice sent an unwelcome fission of heat sliding through her. She tried not to notice how fresh he looked this morning, not at all as if he had spent the night thrashing around in Felicia's bed. She tried to ignore the hurt that welled inside her, making her want to turn and run.

"Hey, Julie!" Ron approached as she walked past Fred Thompson's desk. "Did you hear? I just got the Weatherby listing—thanks to Patrick. You should have seen him. He was really terrific."

"That's great," Fred said, grinning. "Congratulations, boy. Now all we have to do is get the damned thing sold for you." It was Saturday morning. Fred wasn't dressed for work. He had only just stopped in to pick up some paperwork on one of the properties he had sold. Instead of his usual suit and colorful bow tie, he wore khaki pants and a T-shirt that read Math Students Do It By The Numbers, apparently a leftover from his teaching days.

"I've seen the property," Julie said, keeping her eyes on Ron, refusing to glance at Patrick, who stood just a few feet away. "I was there a couple of years back. I might be able to show it for you. I've got a client coming in from New York on Wednesday afternoon whose husband's with NBC. He's being transferred to the West Coast office. The place might be perfect for them."

"Great," Ron said. "I'll get you a copy of the listing and make arrangements for you to get in. Just let me know what you need." Ron was thirty, a college grad who'd always had trouble working for others. He seemed to have found his niche in the real estate business, where his employer, for the most part, was himself.

"I'll let you know as soon as I find out the details," she said. Two months ago, Ron had been grumbling about changing offices, still new enough to need a certain amount of guidance that he wasn't getting. Lately Patrick had started to help him. Now it looked like he just might stay.

She still didn't look at Patrick, not that it mattered. She could feel those intense blue eyes focused squarely on her face.

"Did you get my message?" he asked, forcing her to acknowledge him. "I'd like to talk to you as soon as you've got time."

Her chin came up. "I'm afraid I'm busy right now."

She smiled sweetly at the others. "If all of you will excuse me…"

Fred eyed her with interest as she started to walk away. Ron waved and headed for his desk to start processing his listing. Patrick simply fell into step behind her. When she reached her office, she started to close the door, but his foot slid into the opening.

"I only need a minute." His long body moved forward, forcing her backward into the room.

Julie pasted on a smile. "I'm afraid I don't have a minute, Patrick. I've got an important appointment. I have to leave." She stared up at him, determined not to falter, having to tilt her head back since he was so damned tall. "We'll have to talk some other time."

Patrick closed the door, the resounding thud as hollow as the feeling in her stomach. "We have to talk now." Intense blue eyes bored into her, bright with determination.

She held her ground a moment, then wavered and backed away. "We don't have anything to say." Turning toward her desk, she fumbled through some papers, then began to stuff them into her briefcase.

"I think we have a lot to say. To begin with, I want to explain what happened the other night."

She turned, a cynical smile on her face. "That's kind of you, Patrick. While you're at it, maybe you'd also like to explain about spending the night with Felicia Salazar. I have a feeling that's a far more interesting story."

Patrick's black eyebrows drew together. She could see he was wondering how she knew.

"I saw you with her. I was working late. I had just gotten into my car when the two of you drove into the parking lot." She snapped the latch on the briefcase, hoping he wouldn't notice the way her hands were shaking. "Now may I leave?" She started for the door, but Patrick blocked her way. In the light slanting in, his face looked ominous, cheekbones darkened by shadow, eyes a darker blue and swirling with some turbulent emotion.

"I was with her, yes. But I didn't sleep with her."

"Give me a break, Patrick. The woman had her tongue halfway down your throat in the parking lot." She reached for the doorknob, but he caught her arm.

"I didn't have sex with her, Julie. I give you my word."

"You give me your word," she repeated sarcastically.

"Yes."

She stared up at him. His expression never faltered. How could he seem so damned sincere? Then again, of all the things he was, Patrick was never much of a liar. "You didn't sleep with her," she repeated.

"No."

"Why not?"

"Because I didn't want to. I discovered it was you I wanted. No other woman would do."

She scoffed at that. "Oh, yeah. You wanted me so badly you walked out and left me standing half-naked in the living room, feeling like an absolute fool."

His hands came up to her shoulders, holding her firmly in place, yet his touch was strangely gentle. "I don't blame you for being angry. I know I made a mess of things. That's why I had to see you."

With an effort, she broke free. "Get out of my way, Patrick. I've heard all I'm going to."

He didn't move.

"I'm warning you, Patrick. Get out of my way or I just might do you bodily harm."

He almost smiled, a corner of his mouth curving faintly. God, he was so damned handsome.

"What time will you be through?"

"None of your business."

"Listen to me, Julie. One way or another, you're going to hear me out. This conversation isn't over until you listen to what I have to say." He stood immobile for several seconds more, then reluctantly moved away.

Julie turned the knob and jerked open the door. "Tell it to someone who cares." Squaring her shoulders, ignoring the knot in her stomach, she brushed by him and walked out into the main part of the building.

Fred and Ron both looked up as she passed but neither of them said a word. Several other salespeople had come in. The smell of a fresh pot of coffee drifted out from the small employee lounge. The phones were ringing, people scurrying about. If they noticed the tension between her and Patrick they didn't show it.

Julie worked hard all day, filling every spare moment, trying to keep her mind busy and her thoughts from straying to Patrick. Still, when she wasn't thinking of Laura, worrying about what might be happening to her sister, she couldn't help thinking about him.

The formidable man she had left in her office was far stronger than the Patrick she had known, far more determined—and far more appealing.

She wondered what he could possibly have to say.

Damn it, there was nothing he *could* say. She had practically thrown herself at him and he had turned away, rejected her flatly for Felicia Salazar.

There was nothing more to it, there couldn't be.

Still, she couldn't stop remembering the way he had

kissed her that night beneath the moon, fiercely hot, yet achingly tender. Even in his passion, he hadn't been demanding as she would have expected. In fact, he had seemed almost shy. She could still see his face when he had finally turned away, taut with some strange dark emotion. If she had to name it, she might even call it fear.

It was impossible, completely out of character. Yet whatever it was, it stirred her in some way, tempted her to hear what he wanted to say. She shook off the temptation. Patrick was too smooth, too polished at handling women for her to risk herself that way. She had done it once and look at the price she had paid.

No, she wasn't letting Patrick come near her.

If she saw Patrick coming, she would run like a deer the opposite way.

Val wiped the sweat from his brow with the towel that hung around his neck and kept on running. It was six o'clock Monday morning. He had already run ten miles, but today it wasn't enough. Not after the dream he'd had, the erotic images he battled every time he had fallen asleep. Images of the times Patrick had made love to Felicia. Only it wasn't the dark-skinned Brazilian beauty he saw in his vision—it was Julie. She was naked and responsive, pressing her lovely full breasts into his mouth, clawing his back and begging him to take her.

He had gladly obliged, dragging her down on the floor and spreading her wide for him, driving himself inside her again and again. Still he'd awakened hard and throbbing.

Shaking off the images, he jogged on, rounding the corner of Alden onto Elm, his feet padding rhythmically, returning him to his apartment. Once he got there, he stripped off his sweat-drenched clothes and headed for the shower, pausing only a moment to add a few more lines to the journal entry he had made earlier in the day.

The water felt good raining down on his head, soaking away the soreness in his muscles, draining the last of the sexual tension from his body. He toweled himself dry, shaved, and dressed to go into the office.

It took a load of concentration, but eventually he forced his mind to focus on work. Several calls came in, the last one with Sarah Bonham, chief administrator of the Ventura County Teachers' Pension Fund.

"Mr. Starky over at the Westwind Corporation suggested I call you," she said. "He thought, as the former owner and developer of the Brookhaven condos, you might have some pertinent information. We were hoping you'd have time to show the members of our executive committee around the site sometime this week."

"I'd be happy to," he lied, then was conveniently unable to find time in his busy schedule for them to meet. He would call them next week, he assured her, knowing full well he had no intention of setting up an appointment.

If he stretched the time out long enough, chances were his sojourn as Patrick Donovan would be over and without his assistance, hopefully the deal would never be made. The teachers wouldn't have squandered the money in their retirement fund and Patrick wouldn't be around to go to jail.

He drummed his fingers on the desk next to the phone. Then he smiled. Sandini and McPherson wouldn't be pleased when they discovered their fraudulent plans had been thwarted. Perhaps he would leave this place with the knowledge he had done at least some small measure of good.

Of course, that wasn't really his purpose. His objective was to study Julie Ferris, and since his arrival he had been hard at work.

By using the modem on the primitive computer in his office, coupled with the ship's sophisticated computer banks, he had collected a number of files on her. He had locked into the Internal Revenue system and pulled up all the records associated with her Social Security number, which was easily obtained through Donovan Real Estate's accounting department. It was amazing what he had found.

Since the number had been issued during her junior year in high school when she had gotten her first job, he could track her employment record. She had worked since she was sixteen, starting as a clerk at the gift-wrap counter of a Macy's department store. She had earned enough to put her through college, where another computer bank had turned up the fact she earned mostly straight A's and graduated at the top of her class. Her financial records were there: bank accounts, school loans, home loans; even medical information could be accessed by the claim forms she had submitted to the insurance companies.

From what he could discover, Julie lived a conservative life. She earned far more than the average American, but she saved a good deal, and paid her bills on time. Because of its location on Malibu Beach, the house she had purchased was expensive, though in style it was fairly modest. The clothes she bought were tasteful, but not at the upper end of the scale.

Medically, she seemed healthy, rarely needing more

than a yearly physical. Her checking account showed a good chunk of her earnings went to pay her sister's bills.

He had pages of information on her, but the fact remained: even with all the data he had collected, the tests they had run on subjects like Julie, and all his earthly observations, he could find no accounting for why Julie Ferris and a small percentage of others should have the mental wherewithal to resist their sophisticated brain examinations.

Val raked a hand through his wavy black hair, stood up and walked over to the window that faced out into the office. Down the hall, the object of his thoughts appeared, walking in through the back door as she usually did, without a wasted step, full of energy and purpose. But Val had a purpose of his own and he was determined to see it accomplished. He set his jaw and started for the door.

Julie saw him coming, his long legs eating up the distance between them. He was dressed in a perfectly tailored dark gray suit, a French-cuffed white shirt with his initials on the pocket, a gray and burgundy striped tie. He was the kind of man women noticed on the street, yet since his heart attack, his looks had taken on a different dimension. There was a solidness about him that wasn't there before, an air of command and purpose. He seemed wise beyond his years, filled with confidence and self-possession.

It made him infinitely more attractive.

It made Julie even more wary. She wanted to run for the door.

Patrick smiled as he approached her, softening the

lines of his face. "I'm glad I caught you. How about lunch? There's a nice little Mandarin restaurant—"

"God, Patrick, don't you ever eat anything but Asian food? I'd think you'd get tired of it after a while."

A black, well-formed eyebrow arched up. "How about The Grill? It's only across the street. We can eat and be back in an hour."

"No thanks. I've got too much to do." She started walking and this time he didn't stop her. She went out a couple of times on her usual appointments and errands, but whenever she came back in, he seemed to magically reappear. He asked her to join him for coffee, though she knew he'd been avoiding caffeine. He asked her to go for a drink after work, which she flatly refused.

At seven o'clock, she left the office, only to find him standing next to her car in the parking lot. His Porsche sat parked in the space beside it, the big engine growling and the door ajar.

Julie walked past them both. "Good night, Patrick," she said as if he would simply disappear.

"Wrong." He caught her arm, spun her around, and took a big step toward her. "I happen to know you don't have anything scheduled for this evening, which means you finally have time for me."

"Now you're the one who's wrong. I don't have time for you—nor will I be able to fit you in at any time in the foreseeable future."

A wolfish smile curved his lips. It was unlike any smile she had ever seen. "You aren't avoiding me this time, lady. You're going to hear what I have to say. You're coming back to my apartment where we can talk and no one will disturb us. You're going to get in my car and

I'm going to drive you. If you don't, I'm going to haul you over my shoulder and put you in the car myself."

Julie's mouth dropped open. Patrick had never spoken to her like this. She couldn't believe he was actually threatening her, but she could see very well he meant every word.

"Well?" he said ominously, taking a threatening step closer. "What's it going to be?"

Julie stiffened her shoulders. "Obviously, Patrick, if it means that much to you..." She started toward his Porsche, pulled open the door and slid into the seat, her nose stuck into the air. Patrick closed the door behind her.

Catching his satisfied expression, she almost got out again. Might have, but one look at the hard-edged, determined lines of his face, and the idea flew right out the window. Furious yet strangely intrigued that he would go to such lengths, she settled herself in the seat, waited for him to get in, and let him drive her away. A few minutes later they reached his apartment on Elm Street, just off Burton Way.

They rode the elevator to his penthouse in silence. Patrick unlocked the door and they walked in.

"How about a drink?" He shrugged out of his dark gray suit coat and tossed it over a chair then casually loosened his tie. "You look like you could use one."

Julie glanced around, refusing to look at him. "I'll take a glass of white wine, if you have one."

She hadn't been back to his apartment since their one disastrous date eight years ago. Julie studied the masculine tones of black and gray, the sculpted acrylic coffee table in front of the gray wool sofa, all accented tastefully by the bright splashes of color in the modern art on the walls. The room was furnished sparsely, yet the place had a surprisingly comfortable feel.

A fact that shouldn't have surprised her. Patrick had always had marvelous taste.

Which made her think of Felicia Salazar. She was frowning when he returned with a glass of white wine. His own stemmed crystal glass was filled with Perrier.

"Whatever you're thinking, it certainly looks unpleasant."

She flashed him a tight, mocking smile. "Actually, I was thinking of your girlfriend, Felicia. I was admiring this room and your exquisite taste…in both decor and women."

His expression looked almost amused. "I'm glad you like my apartment—and Felicia isn't my girlfriend. I don't think she ever was."

"You don't think?"

"All right, I used to enjoy her in bed. As nearly as I can recall, we never shared anything else. I realized that the other night. I'm no longer interested in that sort of bonding."

Bonding. It seemed an odd choice of words. Julie toyed with the rim of her glass, running her finger around the edge as she sat down on the sofa. "Why am I here, Patrick? What exactly do you want?"

He took a seat beside her. Vivid blue eyes fixed on her face. "I think you know what I want. I think you want it, too."

Julie said nothing. She was suddenly remembering the way he had kissed her that night on the deck above the sea. She could almost feel his hands on her breasts, the way his tongue had ringed her nipples. Inside her lacy white bra, they began to pucker and tighten.

"If you wanted me, then why did you leave?"

He studied her over the rim of his glass as if he needed time to choose his words. "Believe it or not, I was frightened."

"You? Why on earth would you be frightened?"

He reached out and a long dark finger moved along her jaw. "I'm not certain exactly. It all seemed so unreal. I've never felt this way about a woman. I've never wanted a woman so badly. I know it's hard to believe, but it's the truth."

Julie just stared at him. It couldn't be true. It could not possibly be.

"I know the kind of woman you are," he continued. "I know the gift you offered came at a high price to you. I was frightened of what it might mean."

Fear. She had seen it that night in his eyes. As impossible as it seemed, Patrick was telling the truth.

"Making love to you meant I cared for you, Patrick. That I saw something in you I never saw in you before. I was beginning to believe in you. I was beginning to think you might actually have changed, that you might really have feelings for me." She glanced away, a tight ache building in her throat. "When I saw you with Felicia I knew I'd made a mistake." Tears threatened. She pressed her nails into the palm of her hand so she wouldn't start crying in front of him.

He turned her face with his hand. "I wasn't a mistake. I do care, Julie."

"You don't have to lie, Patrick. I know the way you are…the way you always will be. I was a fool to believe you could change."

Leaning forward, he pressed a soft kiss on her lips.

"I have changed. What you thought you saw was real. I didn't sleep with Felicia. I didn't want to. I discovered the only woman I want is you."

Her throat constricted. She blinked and a tear slowly rolled down her cheek. She was afraid to believe him. She didn't dare. Yet she couldn't stop the hope from rising. "Do you mean it, Patrick?"

"I've never lied to you, Julie." He lifted away the drop of wetness with a single long finger. "I want you, Julie. I have for a very long time."

Julie shook her head. "Oh, God, Patrick, I'm so frightened." The minute she said the words, his arms went around her, drawing her against him and holding her close.

"Don't be, Julie. Please don't be afraid."

It felt so good to be held like this, wrapped in Patrick's arms, comforted by his solid strength. She felt protected, secure and, little by little, no longer afraid. She looked up at him, saw his eyes had turned a darker shade of blue. "I want you, too, Patrick. I need you so much."

He kissed her then, a powerful, drugging kiss that said how much he desired her. There was tenderness there, in the soft stroke of his tongue, the gentle way he tasted the corners of her mouth. Then he was kissing her deeply, thoroughly, making the blood race through her veins and her stomach flutter and tighten.

Her skin tingled and her nipples puckered. He unbuttoned her blouse, slid his hand inside the cup of her lacy white bra, and began to massage her breasts. It closed in the front and he popped the hook with ease, lifted the heaviness into his palm, used his thumb to gently abrade her nipple.

"Patrick…" It was all she could think to say as he

bent his dark head and took the fullness into his mouth, laving her then suckling gently. The other breast beckoned. He ministered to it and she arched her back, silently pleading for more.

"So beautiful," he whispered, his tongue circling her nipple. He bit down gently and a shot of pleasure roared into her bloodstream. "I want so much to be inside you."

Through the hot, wet haze of desire, she hardly noticed her clothes being stripped away, that she was naked and clinging to his neck. His own clothes followed a few minutes later: shirt, shoes, socks, and slacks, leaving him in snug dark burgundy briefs.

She drew away from him, wanting to see what he looked like. He was all suntanned skin and smooth rippling muscle. A thick furring of curly black hair covered the slabs of sinew on his chest.

Patrick reached for her, drew her against him and kissed her again, filling his hands with her breasts, driving his tongue into her mouth and sending damp heat into the core of her. She was wet and ready, restless and aching with desire for him.

His fingers circled her navel, slid lower, forged a path through the tight red curls at the juncture of her legs. He shifted on the sofa, and she noticed a tension in his body, a straining of the muscles across his chest. There was a difference in his touch now, what felt like a hint of uncertainty. Still, he threaded his fingers through the dark red curls above her sex, separated the plump slick folds with obvious pleasure, and sank a finger inside her.

Hot, fierce need, and spiraling warmth. Julie arched against his hand, her fingers biting into his shoulders. Her head fell back on the arm of the sofa and he kissed her so thoroughly she began to writhe against him. He trailed kisses along her throat and over her shoulders, kissed her breasts and her belly. All the while he stroked her, using his talented hands to make her arch and squirm.

"My God, Patrick," she whispered, barely able to speak for the heat roaring through her.

The tension in his body seemed to ease. Naked now, he tore open a condom she didn't realize he had and took her mouth while he coaxed her legs apart and settled his body between them.

"Easy, love," he whispered when she moaned. She had never let him call her one of his pet names, but it felt so right somehow, as if the name belonged only to her. He claimed her lips in a hungry kiss, laved her breasts, tugged on the ends, then started kissing her again.

She could feel his arousal pressing intimately between her legs and suddenly wished she had touched him there, acquainted herself with his solid male length. She arched her hips, expecting him to drive himself inside her, but he didn't move.

He was collecting himself, she realized, feeling the fine tremor that passed through him. He was becoming uncertain again, and the notion was so endearing she reached between their bodies, gripped him firmly, and guided him inside.

Patrick groaned and slid himself forward, burying himself so deeply she bit down on her bottom lip. He paused and she could hear his labored breathing, feel the thunderous roar of his heart. It was pounding as if it would tear through his chest. He made no further moves and suddenly a terrifying thought occurred.

"Patrick…dear God, are you all right? Your heart's not—"

His low, gruff chuckle cut her off. "I'm fine, love. Believe me. I have never felt better in my life." He moved then, slowly, sensuously, easing his hard length out then thrusting deeply back in. Hot wet kisses followed, waves of heat washed over her, and a sweet piercing ache settled low in her belly.

She was burning inside, on fire with need and wanting. Dear God, she couldn't get enough of him. She clung to his shoulders, arched upward to meet each of his thrusts, and felt his hand slide under her bottom to lift her and drive himself more deeply inside. Then he was pounding into her, riding her with a deep thrust and drag, carrying her toward the pleasure she craved. She could feel him straining, feel the flexing of his buttocks as he drove himself inside, then she was slipping over the edge, tasting the hot sweet spirals of climax.

Crying his name, Julie clung to him, trying to survive the fierce onslaught of passion. Several more pounding thrusts and Patrick's tall frame went rigid. He clenched his teeth, making the muscles stand out on his neck, threw back his head, and shuddered with his own massive release.

Neither of them spoke. Patrick slumped on top of her, his lean, solid body covered by a sheen of perspiration. Julie smoothed back the damp hair clinging to his forehead, pressed a soft kiss against his cheek.

"My God," he whispered with something close to awe.

Julie knew exactly what he meant. This time she was the one who laughed. "I swear, Patrick, if I didn't know better, I'd think you were new at this." His muscles

OFFICIAL OPINION POLL

Dear Reader,

Since you are a book enthusiast, we would like to know what you think.

Inside you will find a short Opinion Poll. Please participate in our poll by sharing your opinion on 3 subjects that are very important to all of us.

To thank you for your participation, we would like to send you your choice of **2 FREE BOOKS** and **2 FREE GIFTS!**

Please enjoy them with our compliments.

Sincerely,

Pam Powers

Editor

P.S. Don't forget to indicate which books you prefer so we can send your FREE gifts today!

What's your pleasure...

Romance?

Enjoy **2 FREE BOOKS** that will fuel your imagination with intensely moving stories about life, love and relationships.

(OR)

Suspense?

Enjoy **2 FREE BOOKS** that will thrill you with a spine-tingling blend of suspense and mystery.

Whichever category you select, your **2 FREE BOOKS** have a combined cover price of $13.98 or more in the U.S. and $17.00 or more in Canada.

Simply place the sticker next to your preferred choice of books, complete the poll on the right page and you'll automatically receive **2 FREE BOOKS** and **2 FREE GIFTS** with no obligation to purchase anything!

We'll send you two wonderful surprise gifts, valued at approximately $10, **ABSOLUTELY FREE**, just for trying our books! Don't miss out — **MAIL THE REPLY CARD TODAY!**

Order online at
www.try2free.com

YOUR OPINION POLL
THANK-YOU FREE GIFTS INCLUDE

▶ **2 ROMANCE OR 2 SUSPENSE BOOKS**

▶ **2 LOVELY SURPRISE GIFTS**

DETACH AND MAIL CARD TODAY!

OFFICIAL OPINION POLL

YOUR OPINION COUNTS!
Please check TRUE or FALSE below to express your opinion about the following statements:

Q1 Do you believe in "true love"?

"TRUE LOVE HAPPENS ONLY ONCE IN A LIFETIME."
○ TRUE
○ FALSE

Q2 Do you think marriage has any value in today's world?

"YOU CAN BE TOTALLY COMMITTED TO SOMEONE WITHOUT BEING MARRIED."
○ TRUE
○ FALSE

Q3 What kind of books do you enjoy?

"A GREAT NOVEL MUST HAVE A HAPPY ENDING."
○ TRUE
○ FALSE

Place the sticker next to one of the selections below to receive your 2 FREE BOOKS and 2 FREE GIFTS. I understand that I am under no obligation to purchase anything as explained on the back of this card.

Romance

193 MDL ENU5

393 MDL ERW4

Suspense

192 MDL ENUT

392 MDL ERWS

0074823 |||■|||■|||| |||■|||| |||■||| FREE GIFT CLAIM # **3622**

FIRST NAME

LAST NAME

ADDRESS

APT.#

CITY

STATE/PROV.

ZIP/POSTAL CODE

(TF-RS-08)

The Reader Service — Here's How It Works:

Accepting your 2 free books and 2 free gifts places you under no obligation to buy anything. You may keep the books and gifts and return the shipping statement marked "cancel." If you do not cancel, about a month later we'll send you 3 additional books and bill you just $5.49 each in the U.S. or $5.99 each in Canada, plus 25¢ shipping & handling per book and applicable taxes if any.* That's the complete price, and — compared to cover prices starting from $6.99 each in the U.S. and $8.50 each in Canada — it's quite a bargain! You may cancel at any time, but if you choose to continue, every month we'll send you 3 more books, which you may either purchase at the discount price...or return to us and cancel your subscription.

*Terms and prices subject to change without notice. Sales tax applicable in N.Y. Canadian residents will be charged applicable provincial taxes and GST. Books received may vary. All orders subject to approval. Credit or debit balances in a customer's account(s) may be offset by any other outstanding balance owed by or to the customer. Please allow 4 to 6 weeks for delivery. Offer available while quantities last.

If offer card is missing write to: The Reader Service, 3010 Walden Ave., P.O. Box 1867, Buffalo NY 14240-1867

BUSINESS REPLY MAIL
FIRST-CLASS MAIL   PERMIT NO. 717   BUFFALO, NY

POSTAGE WILL BE PAID BY ADDRESSEE

THE READER SERVICE
3010 WALDEN AVE
PO BOX 1341
BUFFALO NY 14240-8571

NO POSTAGE
NECESSARY
IF MAILED
IN THE
UNITED STATES

went tense. "Not that it wasn't completely wonderful...*you* were wonderful, Patrick."

He relaxed then, wedging himself beside her on the couch. Sliding an arm around her, he pulled her back against his chest. "It was better than wonderful. It was incredible." He shifted a little so he could see into her face. "And in a way I *am* new at this. Everything in my life is new. I haven't made love to a woman since I got out of the hospital."

She looked up at him. "Really?"

"Cross my heart and hope to die."

Julie pressed a finger against his lips. "Don't say that, not even kidding. I'll never forget the way I felt when I saw you lying on that sidewalk. I never want to feel that way again."

Patrick said nothing, but a dark look crept into his features. Julie wondered what he was thinking and a shadow of fear moved through her. It was as if he felt it, too, for he dragged her beneath him and began to kiss her again, press hot sweet kisses along her throat and shoulders. He stroked her breasts and the plump, slick passage between her legs, then sheathed himself and slid deeply inside her again.

He took her with fiery need, yet his kiss was so achingly sweet tears burned her eyes. She prayed she had done the right thing in giving herself to him. Only time would tell.

Julie wondered what tomorrow would bring.

Thirteen

❧❧❧

At four o'clock in the morning, Val's eyes snapped open. He lay next to Julie in his king-sized bed, wide-awake. Where he came from, there was no such thing as sleep; they had evolved from the need for sleep more than ten thousand years ago. But his body here on Earth demanded it in order to stay healthy.

He had learned to sleep for a couple of hours, a normal sleep cycle, but when the cycle ended, instead of falling into a consecutive period of sleep as most people did, he usually awakened. He would pad around the house for a while, read, or write in his journal, then return to bed and try to get another two hours of rest. Sleeping that way, in short intensive cycles, six hours was enough, but the task took maximum effort. It was a battle he constantly waged. Like eating Earth food, it was a fight he couldn't afford to lose.

Stretching his long legs out beneath the sheet, Val lay back against the pillow. Julie's red hair curled just inches away from his nose. He reached over and brushed a soft strand away from her cheek, then pressed a light kiss on her temple, thinking he had probably slept more soundly tonight than he had since his arrival. Recalling the reason, an erotic tremor slid through him, settling low in his groin.

His mind replayed the incredible experience he had shared with Julie, more intense than he could have imagined. Their bonding had been so powerful, so consuming, there were times he wasn't sure he would survive it. It was Julie's encouragement that had overcome his fears and enabled him to continue. In the end, with Patrick's memories to guide him, they had both attained unimaginable pleasure, a feeling so new, so acute Val had thought he might actually come apart.

He smiled as he remembered, his body beginning a now familiar pulsing, a steady throbbing heat that stirred his arousal and made him go rock-hard.

He wanted her again. His memory said it wasn't surprising. Patrick's virility, combined with the newness of the experience and Val's own heretofore unexplored sexuality, set up a hunger that left him burning with desire for her. He would get up for a while, then wake her when he returned, take her again as soon as he came back to the bedroom.

His strides grew longer on the way to his study. He closed the door, picked up his apartment keys from the top of his black teakwood desk, silenced their soft jangling, bent and unlocked the bottom drawer he always kept carefully closed. Inside were some of Patrick's personal files. Beneath them, Val kept his journal, as well as the small communications device he usually carried with him. Tonight, with Julie in the apartment, he had locked it away in here.

He picked up the device, flipped it open and saw, to his surprise, the small red light was on. Glancing toward the door to be sure he had closed it tightly, he responded to the call and discovered he was being summoned immediately to the *Ansor* for a meeting with his superiors.

He keyed in his response. *Must wait at least another six Earth hours.* Time enough to get Julie up and dressed and returned to her home. For some odd reason, he found the notion of her departure disturbing.

A new row of symbols appeared. *Request your arrival now, Commander.*

He thought of Julie, his mission, and what he had learned of his subject that night. *Not possible*, he put in. *Request six-hour delay.*

The screen remained blank a few seconds longer than before. *Six hours confirmed.* The *Ansor* signed off and the powerful device went dark.

Val turned off the instrument and locked it in the drawer. The transfer to his ship would be made from his apartment at ten o'clock tomorrow morning, though his human form would remain behind in a state of suspended sleep. With luck, he would be back in time for lunch. He smiled to think what Julie might have to say about the speed of his upcoming journey.

Brian Heraldson listened to the empty ringing at the opposite end of his cell phone, finally gave up and ended the call. Damn, he knew she was there. He would give her another hour to cool off, then dial her number again.

If she didn't answer the next time, he would drive over there and make her let him in.

He grumbled something at that. Not exactly a gentle bedside manner. More like an aggressive alpha male determined to resolve a conflict with his woman, a thought that sat no better that the first. Damn, Laura Ferris was getting under his skin and he didn't like it one bit. He didn't like the hot rush of desire he felt whenever he looked at her, and he didn't like the fact that he was worried about her.

He didn't like the argument they'd had any better. A discussion that had started over lunch the day after he had driven her home from Long Beach, an argument about her attendance at Winters's alien abduction group that had turned into a shouting match and wound up with Laura slamming her apartment door in his face.

For God's sake, he was supposed to be a trained psychiatrist. Instead he had reacted like a worried spouse. Well, he wasn't her husband, but the worried part was correct. And on a far too personal level. Thank God, he'd been smart enough to end his professional association with her.

He thought about the fight they'd had, escalating the moment they left the intimate Venice Beach restaurant and continuing all the way to her apartment. "It has to be something else," he'd said. "There are no such things as aliens."

"You're the one who suggested I see Dr. Winters."

"I know, but that was before I heard those supposed *abductees* talking."

"Those people are telling the truth."

"The truth as they see it. But the fact is, there are at least a dozen explanations—we'll find the one that fits and work this thing out."

"All your so-called explanations add up to the fact that I'm crazy."

"I never said that."

"Delusional. Hallucinatory. Paranoid—maybe even schizophrenic—that's your answer to this. God, I couldn't even say that word until this happened."

"You're having emotional problems. That doesn't mean you're crazy."

"I'm *not* having emotional problems. I was abducted, just like Robert Stringer and the rest of the people in that group."

"Matthew Goldman is schizophrenic."

"All right, all right, not him. But the others have all been victims. Whether you believe it or not, it happened. And you know what else?"

"What?"

She stood in front of him in the living room, her hands set with determination on her hips. "I think my sister was there, too. In the back of my mind, I remember seeing her there. How do you like that?"

He didn't like it. He didn't like it one bit. "My friend Aaron Newburg is a competent psychiatrist. More than competent, and he'll keep an open mind. Promise me you'll see him."

"Go home, Brian."

"Promise me," he said, backing toward the front door Laura had opened.

"I'm not promising anything. I'm going back to Dr. Winters's group. I'm going to hear what the others have to say. That is the only promise I'm making." She backed him out on the porch. "Goodbye, Brian."

"Damn it, wait—" But the door slammed solidly in his face and that was the last conversation they'd had.

Now, sitting at the desk in his office, Brian picked up his coffee cup, found it cold and full of thick black dregs, and set it back down on his desk. Laura Ferris had him spinning in circles. He didn't like it, but he couldn't seem to stop.

Now she was dragging her sister into this whole unbelievable mess. He vowed not to mention it to Julie and hoped Laura would have sense enough to forget it.

Hovering twenty-five miles above the surface of the Earth, the *Ansor*'s green-and-red sensor lights flashed in the rim of its silver shell. It was disk-shaped with the exception of a rounded surface that rose at the top, rather like a bowl turned upside down. It was difficult to see in the daytime, and often mistaken for a satellite or passing aircraft at night. Inside the ship, three hundred crewmen attended their myriad duties, keeping the ship operational and on course.

In the science wing, Commander Val Zarkazian stood at the end of a long rectangular table, its clear, hard surface allowing him to see through to the spongy dark blue floor. Around him all ten members of the ship's High Council had come together to hear his progress report and discuss the observations he had made during his time thus far on Earth.

Val glanced down at the journal resting in front of him on the table. Reviewing the thoughts he had transcribed each day, he finished a brief summary of what had transpired to date, excluding the mating ritual, which he wasn't yet prepared to discuss, then sat down to an extensive round of questions. By the time his superiors had finished, he was beginning to tire, and becoming more and more uneasy about the direction the meeting was taking.

One of the ministers spoke up from the far end of the table, his voice vibrating with disapproval. "We appreciate your thoroughness, Commander. You've presented an interesting array of observations, but a study of your surroundings was only your secondary assignment. Your primary task was to study the female subject Julie Elizabeth Ferris. What you have told us so far—what all of this rhetoric comes down to, is that you have gained little more insight into the human in question than you knew before."

"On the contrary," Val argued. "I believe I've made great strides in understanding the subject, as well as others of her species. These people, though extremely primitive by our standards, are far more complex than we at first imagined. As I mentioned in my report, they are creatures of intense emotion—a subject Torillians understand only in the abstract. More and more, I'm coming to believe it is these emotions, in one form or another, they use to resist the probe."

"Emotion…" Calas Panidyne, his immediate superior and head of the council, ran the word distastefully over his lips. "Feelings are not unknown to us, Commander. Torillians experience pleasure and displeasure, happiness and unhappiness. I can't see how human emotions—"

"It is the degree of emotion they experience, sir, that makes them so different. Where our spectrum of feelings might be likened to gently rising hills and shallow valleys, theirs would be more closely equated to towering peaks and nearly bottomless pits. They feel things with such intensity it colors every thought, every reaction, every response they make."

"Even if emotion is the key," said one of the female members of the council, "that still doesn't tell us what sort of emotion accounts for the resistance presented by the Ferris female and others like her."

"I suggest we bring the subject in for more testing," the minister said to the group. "Every hour Commander Zarkazian remains on the surface heightens his element of risk. Unification is still in the experimental stages. We don't know what side effects might occur once the commander is permanently back aboard. Testing the woman—"

"No!" The negative cracked across the table like a meteor hurling through space. Even Val was stunned by the force with which he had spoken. He was angry, he realized, knowing now what had caused the unexpected outburst. Anger had no place on the *Ansor*. It was an emotion that did not exist on Toril, hadn't for ten thousand years. He couldn't be angry, he told himself. Only Patrick Donovan could do that and Patrick wasn't there.

Val forced himself under control and prayed his associates would not suspect what had just occurred.

"What I meant to say is that finding answers is never easy. It is bound to take some time. Every day I encounter vast amounts of useful information. In a few more Earth months—"

"Weeks, Commander." Panidyne studied him with

fathomless dark eyes. "This study was never designed to be a long-term project. We were hoping a brief interlude might help us resolve a problem that has arisen a number of times and assist in ending any further loss of life. However, if your observations cannot give us what we need, we shall be forced to resume our tests."

Val's mouth felt dry. The thought of Julie being returned to the *Ansor*, of her continued resistance and the near certainty of her death, was enough to make him sick.

"Perhaps you're right," he conceded, not meaning a word of it. "However, in the time remaining, I am convinced I'll be able to find the answers we need. Assuming that is the case, there'll be no need to subject the woman to further examination."

Panidyne smiled blandly. "That would certainly be the preferable solution."

Val forced himself to return the emotionless smile. "Then you may count on it, sir. Which means the sooner I'm back at my task, the better the odds for success. If the council has no more questions, perhaps I might be excused to return to my work."

"Does anyone have anything else to add before we end our session?" Panidyne asked.

At the negative mumble from the group, Panidyne turned in his direction and excused Val from the meeting. Fifteen minutes later, he was gone from the *Ansor* and back in his penthouse apartment. He was exhausted, more so than he would have expected, and yet adrenaline pumped through his veins.

Since he was once again linked with Patrick, he told himself it was all right that he was still angry.

And that he was afraid.

* * *

Babs pounded with vigor on Julie's office door, turned the knob without waiting for her petite friend to answer and walked in. As usual Julie was on the phone with a client, the receiver clamped between her ear and shoulder. Her cell phone was ringing in her purse.

Babs was undeterred. She was used to Julie's back-breaking schedule. Taking a seat on the sofa, Babs crossed her legs, pulled a fingernail file from her newly purchased Dolce & Gabbana bag, and began a feverish attack on a rough-edged red polished nail.

Julie finished her second call, then with a glance at Babs, punched the intercom button and instructed Shirl to hold anything new coming in. She turned off her cell phone, as well.

"All right, I know that look, Babs. What's going on?"

The look Julie referred to was one of exasperation tinged with an edge of alarm. "I came here to ask that same question of you, my impossible friend, but I'm afraid I already know the answer, which is the real reason I'm here."

"What are you talking about?"

"In a word—or I should say two words—Patrick Donovan."

A flush crept up Julie's throat. "What about him?"

"You're sleeping with him, aren't you?"

The flush increased, fanned up into her cheeks and down into her breasts. "I'm not sleeping with him. I slept with him. Once. You're always telling me a little casual sex would be good for me. You ought to be happy I took your advice."

"Casual sex with Patrick Donovan? Come on, Julie,

who are you kidding? It might have been casual for Patrick, but it certainly wasn't for you."

Julie straightened in her chair. "What's that supposed to mean?"

"You know very well what it means. You've always been physically attracted to Patrick, maybe even a little in love with the man you believed he could be. Until lately you've been smart enough to realize that Patrick isn't going to change, that loving a guy like that can only lead to heartache. What I can't figure out is why you've suddenly weakened. Just because the man had a heart attack—"

"That isn't the reason." Julie rolled back her chair and stood up. Rounding the desk, she walked over and sat down on the sofa. "Patrick *has* changed, Babs. Surely you've noticed the difference. In a lot of ways, he's the same man he was, but in other, more important ways, he's different. Patrick says I mean something to him, that he wants more from me than just sex. I have to find out if it's true."

Babs hardened her heart against the wistful, hopeful expression on her best friend's face. "He was out with Felicia Salazar the other night—did he happened to mention that? I suppose he wants more than just sex from Felicia, too."

Before Julie could reply, a sharp knock sounded, and Patrick walked in. Ignoring the women on the couch, he headed straight for Julie's desk, laid a stack of files on top, then turned to Babs.

"Felicia was a mistake," he told her bluntly.

"How did you—"

"I didn't sleep with her and I don't intend to, not her or anyone else."

"You were listening," Julie accused but there was no bite to the words.

"I didn't mean to eavesdrop. I heard you through the door." Patrick smiled at Julie. "How about dinner? I'm taking up cooking as a hobby. I'll fix something special if you'll come over after work."

Julie's smile turned radiant. "I won't be done until eight. If you can wait until then I'd love to come."

"Eight is perfect." He looked at Babs, his expression surprisingly earnest. "I know we've have had our differences. I know you're worried about Julie, but you don't have to be. I'm not going to hurt her. As long as we're together, Julie's the only woman I have the slightest interest in."

Babs said nothing, just sat there in shock. Perhaps Patrick *had* changed—a little. It was the "as long as" part that bothered her. Babs wondered if Patrick actually believed that when he stopped seeing Julie, she wasn't going to be hurt.

After a supper of simply cooked vegetarian dishes and a magnificent several hours of lovemaking, Julie awoke in Patrick's bed. Turning toward where Patrick should have been, she discovered the place beside her was empty. The bedroom door was closed but a sliver of light leaked in at the bottom. Padding naked to the closet, Julie grabbed one of Patrick's half-dozen expensive designer robes, this one a thick blue terry, and pulled it on, made a pit stop in the bathroom, then followed the light to its source, Patrick's office down the hall.

"Patrick?" She knocked lightly and tried the knob, was surprised to find it locked. She knocked again, "Patrick are you in there?" She heard the sound of papers being shuffled, then footsteps approaching.

He smiled when he opened the door. "Sorry, love, I couldn't sleep. Thought I might as well get some paperwork done." His hair was slightly mused, several onyx strands curling over his forehead. Dressed in a burgundy silk dressing gown that hung open to his waist, he stepped into the hall, closed the door behind him, and eased her into his arms.

"Perhaps now that you're also awake, we can find a way for both of us to get some rest."

A long kiss followed, rousing her from the last remnants of slumber. She could feel his arousal beneath the robe, feel the heat of his hard, lean body, and desire rose sharply. She hadn't come for this, but she liked the idea, tilting her head back, allowing his mouth to move unerringly to the sensitive spot behind her ear, along her neck and down her shoulders. Long fingers worked the sash on her robe. He lifted a breast into his palm and teased the nipple, then lowered his head and took the fullness into his mouth.

Julie moaned and arched toward him, heat sliding through her, dampness building between her legs. His hand moved over the flat spot below her navel, parted the folds of her sex and he began to stroke her. With expert skill, he worked the sensitive bud until she was moaning, pressing herself against him. She expected him to carry her back to the bed, to make slow languid love to her. Instead he opened his robe, lifted her up, and impaled her on his hardened length.

A hot, deep-tongued kiss, her legs wrapped around his lean waist, he surged into her, filling her completely. Julie clung to his broad shoulders, her nails digging in, her mouth finding his for another ravaging kiss. Heat and need washed over her in great numbing waves. She climaxed twice before Patrick allowed himself to follow. She clung to his neck until the tiny ripples of pleasure finally faded away.

Patrick kissed her softly, then let her slide down his body till her feet touched the floor. Chuckling softly, he carried her down the hall to his bedroom.

"What are you laughing about?" she asked as he settled her beneath the covers in his big bed, then slid in beside her. "It isn't particularly reassuring, you know, to hear a man's laughter just minutes after a round of wildly heated sex."

"That's what I was laughing about."

"What? The fact that we had wildly heated sex?"

"No. The fact that having it at two o'clock in the morning, standing in the hall, seemed like such a good idea."

Julie just smiled. No wonder women were so drawn to him. Patrick was an incredible lover, passionate, inventive, determined to give as well as take; his appetite for lovemaking seemed nearly insatiable. And after eight long years, this new, incredible Patrick was hers.

At least for the moment.

The thought drained the smile from her face.

Val faced Julie across the breakfast table in his apartment. It was a sunny room, done completely in white from the Formica countertops to the shiny white enamel appliances, efficient and state-of-the-art. In a white terry robe as snowy as the kitchen, Julie's dark red hair looked appealingly tousled, her face still flushed from the lovemaking they had enjoyed just before they climbed out of bed.

It was amazing how easily he had slipped into Patrick's routines. Well, his more pleasant routines at least. Val no longer felt threatened by the mating ritual Patrick valued so highly. He had, in fact, come to enjoy it a great deal himself.

And bonding with Julie was enormously enlightening, increasing his awareness of her, his understanding of her innermost feelings, wants and needs.

Val looked over the top of the calendar section of the *L.A. Times* he was reading to study Julie's shiny head bent over the real estate section. Seeing her nearly enveloped in the folds of his robe, he couldn't help smiling at the charming picture she made.

Charming and vivacious and so full of life. Just looking at her made him feel alive in a way he had never felt before. He thought of the mate he would eventually take back home. She would stir him no more than a friend or a sister. Not like here. Here people lived, people died, they mated, they bore children, but they rarely remained unmoved by anything that occurred.

His mind returned to his meeting aboard the *Ansor*, to the facts he had presented, and he knew that he had failed to make them see. Panidyne wanted more testing. Julie was in danger.

I won't let them touch her, he vowed. *I won't let them hurt her.* Yet he knew if his mission failed, there would be nothing he could do.

"My sister called the house this morning," she said,

breaking into his thoughts. "She left a message on my answering machine."

He lowered the paper. "I hope she's all right."

"She sounded all right. Sometimes it's hard to tell with Laura." She folded her section of the paper with a snap and laid it on the table. "She bought a gun, Patrick. She says it makes her feel safer."

"Where the hell did she get it?"

"I'm not sure. Somebody she knows knew somebody who had one for sale."

"Does she even know how to use it?"

"I guess she's taking some sort of class. With Laura's psychiatric problems, I certainly don't approve, but the truth is I own one myself, so what can I say?"

Val didn't answer. Finally he sighed. "In this town, maybe you need a gun."

"I took a class way back when. I go in for recertification once a year."

He nodded. Antique weapons like guns didn't exist on Toril. There was simply no need for them.

"Laura's abduction group is meeting again tonight at the Stringer house," Julie continued. "Laura wants me to go with her."

"Are you going?"

"Yes. Whatever the truth is, whatever might have happened to her, my sister needs all the support she can get."

"Then I'd like to go with you."

She cocked an eyebrow in his direction. "Why?"

"I told you why. Because I want to help her. You said yourself, she needs all the support she can get." Of course that was only partly the truth. He wanted to study Laura, determine the extent of trauma she and the others in the group had experienced as a result of the *Ansor*'s testing. Living as Patrick, he was beginning to understand as he hadn't before the magnitude of what they were doing to the people they brought aboard the ship.

Julie shook her head. "I don't know. This whole thing is pretty far out. I have a hard time believing you'll keep an open mind."

That was the second reason he wanted to go. To discourage the sisters' belief in Laura's tale. Fostering the public's growing concern about UFOs only made the *Ansor*'s mission more difficult.

He gave her one of Patrick's winsome smiles. "I promise you I'll listen as objectively as I can. I really would like to go with you."

Julie smiled. "All right. We'll go together. I could use a bit of support myself."

Fourteen

The meeting was almost ready to begin when Julie and Patrick arrived. Laura, who had mended fences with Brian Heraldson and agreed to his plea to let him join her, was already seated next to him on the sofa in the living room, a white-carpeted, silk-draped area that looked out over the channel.

Julie introduced Patrick as a friend of hers and Laura's then, at Dr. Winters's urging, they went in and sat down with the others.

"It's good you all could make it." Dressed in jeans and a long-sleeved white shirt, the doctor surveyed the room full of familiar faces. "I hope no one had an exceptionally difficult week."

The gardening expert, Willis Small, shifted a bit in his chair. "I'm afraid mine hasn't been all that pleasant. I've had several disturbing dreams this week, Dr. Winters."

"Dreams that involved the Visitors?" he asked.

Willis Small nodded. "I don't remember too much. I dreamed I was taken aboard one of their ships. They did some testing. I dreamed they took a semen sample and I remember seeing several woman they'd brought aboard. I think the women were pregnant. They were begging the Visitors not to take their unborn babies."

Leslie Williams, the tall willowy black woman from San Diego, leaned forward. "Are you certain, Mr. Small, that you were dreaming? Are you sure what you're telling us didn't really happen?" Her voice dropped to a whisper. "That is exactly what happened to me."

Willis fidgeted nervously. "It must have been a dream. At one point, I remember waking up and walking downstairs to get a glass of water. Then the dream picked up again when I went back to sleep."

"The part about going downstairs could have been a screen memory," Robert Stringer put in. "For years after my abduction, I thought my son and I had stopped for several hours at an inn for dinner on the way back from our fishing trip. It used to bother me, since we had gone fishing in the first place because we wanted to cook fresh trout for supper. Why would we go to a restaurant when we had exactly what we wanted to eat in the trunk of the car? Then I started to remember."

Laura inched up her hand.

Dr. Winters nodded in her direction. "Go ahead, Laura. You don't have to be shy. You can say whatever you wish."

Laura fiddled with a strand of her long blond hair. "I-I may have had a screen memory. Under hypnosis, I told Dr. Heraldson that I had been taken to a hospital on the afternoon of my abduction. It wasn't the truth. I haven't been in a hospital in years."

"It could have been any number of things," Brian

Heraldson quickly put in. "Trauma, perhaps, over problems in your youth."

He was alluding to Laura's abortion, Julie knew. It was a plausible explanation. She wondered if the theory might not be correct.

Patrick spoke up just then. "I came here for Laura and Julie. I don't know much about what any of you might have experienced but I've read that childhood trauma can surface in any number of ways. If what happened was painful enough, I imagine it might even come out as a belief in alien abduction."

"That's right, Patrick," Brian said. "It's called False Memory Syndrome. It's like a screen memory, only in this case the false memory is the one of alien abduction."

"How do the rest of you feel about that?" Winters asked. "Is the abduction phenomenon a memory created because of some earlier trauma? Is it merely coincidence, then, that your experiences are so much the same?"

"It isn't coincidence," Carrie Newcomb, the pretty young hairdresser, argued. "We were abducted. All of us remember it nearly the same, the humiliation, the experiments, the sexual manipulations. If it's motivated by problems from our past, why do all of us remember the same things?"

"All right," Brian conceded, "perhaps for some of you it isn't trauma. Perhaps it's simply a shared hallucination. As Carrie just mentioned, many of the overtones are sexual in nature. Given the climate of repression we face in this country, that might mean the delusions are self-inflicted, invented by a society that has trouble dealing with its unfulfilled physical needs. Freud would most probably think so."

"Well, I think you and Dr. Freud are full of shit," Laura said hotly, eliciting a ripple of laughter from the group. "If you had been there, you wouldn't have a single doubt that what happened to you was real."

Both Brian and Patrick fell silent. Julie noticed that Patrick in particular seemed absorbed by the stories being told. The group talked for a while, each person relating his personal experiences, repeating incidents he had mentioned before, expressing fears or asking questions. It was a painful session, just as it had been before. Carrie Newcomb had tears in her eyes when Willis Small finished his pitiful tale, and Robert Stringer's face looked drawn and pale.

Julie noticed Patrick was frowning, the muscles across his shoulders knotted with tension. She hadn't realized the suffering these people spoke of would affect him in such a way.

Then Laura's voice caught her attention. "There's something I need to say."

Dr. Winters turned in her direction. "Go on, Laura," he urged.

"It's something I remembered, something I have to tell Julie." Laura's eyes swung nervously in her sister's direction.

Brian Heraldson reached for her hand. "Laura, we talked about this. Think about what you're about to do."

Beginning to feel apprehensive, Julie sat forward in her chair. "It's all right, Laura. What is it you have to say?"

"I know you don't want to hear this, Julie. I know deep down you don't believe any of this is real, but you were there with me. I remember seeing you. I don't know why you can't remember, but I know you were there—I saw you."

A chill splintered down Julie's spine. She locked her hands together in her lap. "I couldn't have been there, Laura. Even if your incredible story is true, it couldn't have happened to me—I don't feel any of the things you and the others feel, and…and I don't have that mark on my arm."

"Actually, any physical marks are rare," Dr. Winters put in gently. He gave her a reassuring smile. "I realize the concept is frightening, Julie, but just for a moment why don't we explore the possibility that your sister is correct?"

"I don't…I don't think that's a good idea."

"Julie's right," Patrick agreed. "It isn't a good idea. Laura has enough problems trying to deal with this. Dragging Julie into the picture will only make matters worse."

Laura ignored him. "Please, Julie—do it for me?"

"I think it's time for us to go home." Patrick stood up and reached for Julie's hand.

"It's all right, Patrick. If Laura wants me to try, what could it hurt?" She turned to the doctor. "What should I do, Dr. Winters?"

"I thing the best way to start is just to tell us what you remember. Relax for a moment and just take it easy. Try to think of that afternoon on the beach as if it were passing in slow motion."

Julie nodded. "All right. I can do that." Leaning back in her chair, she closed her eyes, returning her thoughts to that afternoon, imagining the hours they had spent on the beach.

"There was a dog, I remember. A big black dog way down the beach, trailing along near the water. It was really hot and Laura and I were tired. I remember hearing this thick, funny buzzing, then the radio went dead."

"Go on," the doctor urged.

"That's about all I remember. We fell asleep a few minutes later and when we woke up, I had this terrible headache. Over the next few days the headaches got worse, but I don't think they had anything to do with my falling asleep on the beach, and lately they've been fading."

"How long were you asleep?"

"A couple of hours at least."

"On such a hot day, you must have been badly sunburned lying out there in the open."

"No, I...actually, now that you mention it, I wasn't burned at all. I remember being surprised at the time. I wasn't wearing much sunscreen." She frowned, uneasy with the thought. "I don't...I don't know why I wasn't burned."

"Anything else you recall? Odd things you might have noticed later?"

Her frown deepened, digging tiny lines across her forehead. "I remember I had a small pin dot scab at the bend in my elbow. It looked like a puncture of some sort, but of course it couldn't have been. And my wrists were sore. In fact I was a little bit sore all over."

Laura surged to her feet. "You see, Julie? Robert Stringer heard the same thick buzzing sound, just like we did. Neither of us was sunburned because we were *inside* the ship."

Julie said nothing. It was nonsense. It had to be. Yet her heart was thudding painfully.

"The soreness could have come from fighting against

restraints of some kind," Leslie Williams suggested. "That happened to me."

"Wait a minute." Brian stood up beside Laura. "This whole thing is getting out of hand. It's hardly fair to suggest something like this to Julie. Up until now she hasn't had the least thought of any such occurrence."

"Dr. Heraldson is right," Dr. Winters agreed, to Julie's surprise. "A bit of exploration is one thing, the power of suggestion is something completely different. There is no point in placing thoughts in Ms. Ferris's head."

"No, there isn't," Brian finished, casting a reproachful glance at Laura.

"I'm sorry," Julie said to the group. "I realize you can make any number of deductions from what I've just told you, but the fact is I don't remember anything remarkable about that afternoon. I fell asleep on the beach and woke up with a headache. That's as far as it goes." She smiled sadly at her sister. "I can't say I'm unhappy I don't remember, Laura. Even if what you think happened turns out to be true, what you're going through makes me glad I can't recall." She felt Patrick's hand on her shoulder, his touch gentle yet persuasive.

"I think we ought to go home."

Julie nodded.

Laura reached over and squeezed her hand. "Thanks for trying, sis." She managed to smile but it came out wobbly. "In a way, as you said, I'm glad you don't remember."

The two girls hugged, and Julie left Laura in Brian Heraldson's care for the ride back to her apartment. No matter their differences on the subject of abduction, there was a growing attraction between them. Compared to the sort of men her sister usually dated, Julie couldn't help but feel glad.

Walking next to Patrick, she waited while he opened the door to his Porsche and settled her inside, then he rounded the car and slid into the driver's seat.

In silence he started the engine, sat for a moment listening to the powerful roar, then he shifted the car into gear. The evening had been even more bizarre than she had warned him. And some of the things she'd remembered about that afternoon *did* made her think.

Julie wondered what Patrick was thinking.

Layers of pink and orange seeped over the brightening horizon. Since Julie had an early morning meeting with her clients, the Harveys, to gather additional loan information for their condo purchase, Val woke her before sunrise so she would have time to go home, shower and change. Val walked her to her car, kissed her goodbye and watched her drive away, then he climbed into his Porsche and set off for the hills.

He needed some time alone. He needed time to think, to go over the things he had learned at the meeting he had attended with Julie last night. The things he had *felt* when the subjects of the *Ansor*'s testing—victims they called themselves—had spoken of their ordeal.

He had known it affected them, of course. There were medical procedures involved, and any sort of bodily intrusions, no matter how sophisticated, were always uncomfortable. It was the mental anguish he had not until now understood.

In theory, yes. He had known Earth subjects experienced a certain amount of trauma. For a special few like Julie, it could even be life-threatening.

Still, it wasn't until he had joined with Patrick that he could actually understand the intensity of their subjects' emotions, the amount of suffering they endured. It had to be a hundred times worse than he had believed, perhaps a thousand. The sensations he experienced here on Earth, the colors, sights, sounds, tastes and smells had finally given him the ability to relate to their ordeal. The *emotions* he was now capable of feeling gave him an insight into the terror, humiliation and helplessness a Torillian couldn't begin to understand.

Last night, listening to their stories, seeing the pain in their faces, *feeling* the agony they had endured, he finally understood.

The engine purred. He had come to love the somehow soothing sound. Turning the car down an empty stretch of highway, he pulled into a deserted overlook that peered down on the awakening city and turned off the motor. Lights sparkled like tiny stars below him. Somewhere above, the *Ansor*'s lights flashed in the rim of its hull. He couldn't help thinking of his comrades, that at this very moment they might be bringing another subject aboard, setting free all the emotions he had encountered last night and dozens of others he could only begin to imagine.

For the first time it occurred to him to question the *Ansor*'s mission. Was the damage they were inflicting worth the information they were gaining? Where did science stop and humanity—in whatever form—begin?

And what was his responsibility in all of this? Was it his duty to somehow persuade his people to end the testing, at least in its current form?

But the answers did not come and as the sun rose higher, the peace of the morning faded. Val started the car and headed back to Beverly Hills, back to the problems he faced in his office.

At present, his most pressing concern was Sandini and McPherson. He had been holding his so-called "partners" at bay with one excuse after another. Sarah Bonham of the Teachers' Pension Fund was calling him every other day. It seemed their executive committee was just itching—as Patrick would have said—to buy all of Westwind's phony discount paper.

He wasn't sure how much longer he could hold them off. Another week perhaps. After that, he didn't know. He only knew he needed time, time with Julie, time with the other subjects in the abduction group. He wasn't going to get it—that fact was becoming more and more clear.

And there was something else.

The bond was growing stronger between him and Julie. His feelings for her were building, becoming deeper each day. In a short while, he would have to leave her. He hadn't considered that it would be a problem. Now just the thought made his chest go tight and his stomach roll with nausea. He didn't understand it. He only knew that the notion of leaving Julie brought him pain.

He had promised not to hurt her.

Now he wondered if his leaving would cause Julie that same pain.

Julie dashed through the front door of Donovan Real Estate, grabbing her messages from Shirl but continuing past her office. A quick knock at the door and she rushed into Patrick's office, smiling at the sight of his dark head bent over his desk studying what appeared to be Ron Jacobs's most recent real estate contract.

He glanced up, his intense blue eyes climbing steadily to her face, and her stomach did a sweet little curl.

"Hi," she said a bit breathlessly. She wished she could blame it on her harried afternoon, but she knew it was simply the sight of him. He had always been a handsome man. Now, the underlying strength, the purpose that burned in his eyes, made him nearly irresistible.

He smiled, a flash of white against smooth, sun-tanned skin. "You're certainly in a hurry. Something exciting going on?"

"Not exactly. I'm a little pressed for time, is all."

"So what's new about that?" he teased.

She smiled. "I need to take those books I borrowed back to UCLA. While I'm there, I want to look through the latest newspapers and magazines for articles on UFOs. I've done some work on the Internet and I plan to do more, but I feel like I get more out of an actual magazine. I thought I might convince you to go with me."

Patrick frowned. "I thought you were through with all that. After last night—"

"Last night I said I didn't believe I'd been taken aboard a spaceship. For Laura's sake, I'm still trying to keep an open mind." For her own sake as well, she silently added.

Patrick leaned back in his chair. "If you're researching UFOs, there's still the problem we discussed, the one involving the speed of light and the thousands of years it would take to reach other galaxies. I don't suppose you've figured a way around that?"

Julie grinned. "Believe it or not, I might have. During my Internet research, I ran across a woman—an astrophysicist named Meryl Stover. She teaches in the physics department at USC. Dr. Stover believes there are several ways we might be able to reach—perhaps even break—the speed-of-light barrier. I read some of the articles she wrote and then I called her. I told her I was doing some research on space travel, and she was kind enough to give me an appointment to see her tomorrow afternoon."

Patrick smiled but he certainly didn't look happy. "I can't go with you today, but I wouldn't miss tomorrow for the world." His expression changed, his eyes moving downward, traveling over her body in a way that made the heat rise into her cheeks. "And there is tonight, of course."

"T-tonight?"

A corner of his mouth curved up. "I thought we'd eat in. I'll cook, and we can go to bed early. We can go to your place if you like. Then you won't have to get up and drive home."

Julie thought of the invitation addressed to Patrick she had noticed lying on Shirl's desk. "What about the party?"

"What party?"

"Jack Winston's big celebrity party at The Grill? I thought for sure you'd be going." The old Patrick wouldn't have missed it.

"I'm not going…not unless you'd like to go."

Relief trickled through her. Julie shook her head. Jack Winston and his bunch of movie-star groupies were the last people she wanted to see. "No, I…I don't really care much for that sort of thing."

He smiled. "Then it's settled. Your place tonight for dinner and a moonlight walk on the beach. Tomorrow we see Dr. Stover."

The night was even better than Patrick had promised. He had cooked some sort of Oriental noodle soup and served chocolate ice cream for dessert. Patrick's food tastes continued toward the strange, but the meal was good nonetheless. Afterward they walked the deserted beach and wound up making love on a blanket in the sand. Except for Patrick's late night strolls through the house, which awakened her twice, she had slept like the dead and woke up later than usual.

After a hectic morning at the office and a meatball sandwich to go from Prego's, just down the street, Julie joined Patrick for the drive to the University of Southern California. A search of Dr. Stover's office and classroom proved unsuccessful. They finally located the professor in her laboratory, several buildings away.

Meryl "Smoky" Stover was seated at a desk in the corner, hidden behind several stacks of files that almost completely obscured her. Only her crown of sandy brown hair peeked through. She was dressed in white lab clothes, which hung loose over her short, wiry frame.

"Dr. Stover? I hate to bother you. I can see that you're busy, but—"

"That's all right, I'm always busy." She rose from amidst the disarray, a small woman in her fifties, the kind of lined, craggy face smokers often get, probably the reason for her nickname. "You must be Julie Ferris. Come in."

The doctor sized both of them up as they entered the laboratory, smiling with interest at Julie and obvious appreciation at Patrick. She might be middle-aged, but she was definitely female and she wasn't dead yet, her thorough glance said.

"This is Patrick Donovan, Dr. Stover. A friend who is also interested in space travel."

"It's nice to meet you." Taking in their conservative dress, Patrick in his Versace double-breasted, Julie in navy blue slacks and a white silk blouse, it was obvious the woman had her doubts. If so, she didn't voice them. "Well, I hope I can be of some help."

She drew a cigarette out of a pack on the desk, stuck it between her fingers, but made no effort to light it.

"I'm trying to quit," she explained as she walked across the laboratory, the cigarette gripped between her fingers. "Been three months and I'm still going crazy."

"It can't be easy," Julie sympathized, she and Patrick following along in the doctor's wake. The room was large, filled with interesting clutter, the walls lined with colorful graphs and charts. Models and mechanical devices covered the countertops, machinery unlike anything Julie had ever seen.

"You said you read some of my articles," the doctor said to Julie, cigarette still in hand. "If that's the case, you understand a little of how difficult space travel is."

"To be truthful, I'm only beginning to understand. I've been reading a great deal about it. I know how far we would have to travel, that our closest stellar landfall is in the Alpha Centauri system, which is still 4.3 light years away."

The doctor's lips curved. "That's twenty-five trillion miles, in case you haven't figured it out."

Patrick's gaze moved away from the chart he had been studying. "Space travelers face enormous obstacles," he said. "Besides the problem of radiation—a flood of it during magnetic solar storms—there's rocky debris from asteroids and comets which could easily destroy the hull of a ship."

Julie eyed him strangely, but Patrick simply shrugged. "I went to college, too, you know. I'm bound to remember at least a little of what I learned."

"You're both correct. Space travel is fraught with hazards—the body's reaction to extended periods of weightlessness, the problem of communicating through vast empty stretches of space, but the biggest problem is the time it takes just to get there."

"Which, I gather," said Patrick, "is where you come in."

"That's right. My expertise lies in theoretical astrophysics—developing ideas that allow scientists to eventually reach their goals."

Julie studied one of the charts. It diagrammed what was labeled a rotating skyhook, some sort of catch-and-release satellite station that could pluck an orbiting spaceship from a low Earth orbit and hurl it at a much greater speed on its journey into space.

She turned back to the doctor. "The article you wrote said you believe, at least in theory, man can eventually reach the speed of light."

Smoky unconsciously took a pull on her unlit cigarette. "The speed of light—186,283 miles per second. Yes, I believe in time it can be done, just the way speed of sound was reached and eventually surpassed. Still, even at light speed, it would take more than ten years to reach a system with a planet or planets that could support the existence of life."

"Surely such a system is rare," Julie said.

Dr. Stover laughed, a rather unnerving, slightly raspy chuckle. "That's what most people think. Maybe that's what they want to think. The truth is, planetary systems like the one around our sun may be the rule rather than the exception. There are two hundred billion stars in Earth's galaxy alone. Which means there may be hundreds of thousands, even millions of inhabitable planets in the universe."

Julie fell silent, staggered by the thought.

Patrick looked back toward the charts on the wall. "Then it's simply a matter of getting there," he said mildly. "Which brings us right back where we started."

"Distance is definitely the problem. Which is why we'll have to go even faster than light speed to achieve the sort of interstellar travel man dreams of."

"Is that possible?" Julie asked.

"Theoretically, yes." She pointed toward the wall. "Take a look at those graphs up there. Each line shows various methods of spacecraft propulsion."

She ran a thin finger beneath one of the lines. "Metallic Hydrogen and Nuclear Fusion are already in the exploratory stages, but they can't reach faster than thirty percent light speed." She pointed to another line. "Negative Matter could get us up to seventy percent. Combined Matter-Antimatter could go as fast as ninety-nine percent of the speed of light."

"If I remember correctly," Patrick put in, "Einstein believed we could never achieve light speed because we create infinite mass."

Julie's eyes widened. She couldn't believe Patrick was standing there calmly discussing Einsteinian theory as if he studied it every day. All those years, she had underestimated his intelligence. Or maybe he had simply gone out of his way not to show it.

"Albert Einstein never heard of tachyon particles," Dr. Stover said. "We think—if they actually exist—they can't travel *slower* than the speed of light. If that's the case, all we have to do is get beyond the light speed barrier and there's no limit to how fast we can go."

It was mind-boggling, no doubt about it. But the one thing Julie was convinced of was that if highly educated scientists like Meryl Stover and her colleagues believed space travel was possible, and if there really were hundreds of thousands of potentially habitable planets, odds were darned good that some other life form, superior to man, also sought to travel through space and might have already done it.

"We're looking to quantum mechanics for the answer," the doctor was saying. "It's extremely complicated, but we believe, once we've quantumly jumped the light-speed barrier, some sort of tachyon booster could kick in. It could wind up carrying the ship as fast as three hundred times the speed of light."

Julie looked at Patrick, whose face looked decidedly grim.

"Add to that the existence of black holes or wormholes a spacecraft might travel through, and the distance between galaxies could be shortened even more. Or there may be a way to collapse the vast distances in space, or ways to combine several different modes of travel—"

A knock sounded and the door swung open. "Sorry to bother you, Smoky, but that reporter from the *Tribune* is here."

The doctor sighed and rolled her eyes, then nodded to the man at the door. "Apparently duty calls," she said to Julie. "We're always trying to raise money to further our studies. Any publicity we can get is helpful." She called back to her assistant. "Thanks, Tom. Tell him I'll be right there."

"We appreciate your time, Dr. Stover, and I think I'm beginning to get the picture."

"As you can see, there are dozens of possibilities. As I said, so far they're mostly theoretical, but that's the way scientific advances are made."

Julie stared triumphantly at Patrick. "Well, are you satisfied there might really be a way for a spaceship to travel to Earth?"

For a moment his features looked dark, then he actually smiled. "After hearing Dr. Stover, I'd be a liar if I said I didn't believe it could be done."

"There are a couple of good books on the subject," the doctor said. "Stephen Hawking wrote one called *A Brief History of Time. Wrinkles in Time,* by Smoot and Davidson, is another."

"Perhaps I'll read them," Julie said. But as they walked out the door, she was thinking she really didn't need to.

After hearing Dr. Stover, as far as she was concerned space travel wasn't all that far-fetched. The thought occurred, if a spaceship from another world actually did come to Earth, what would the travelers do once they got here?

Perhaps a study of Earth's inhabitants, as Laura continued to insist, wouldn't be so difficult to imagine.

Fifteen

Val sat in the study of his penthouse apartment reading the *Los Angeles Times*. Patrick Donovan had enjoyed reading the paper. Val couldn't read the front page without chills running up and down his spine. Murder, rape, gang violence, child abuse—earth's inhabitants were unaccountably savage. Their primitive drives made them reckless, often governed by emotion or instinct, rather than common sense. In Los Angeles alone, not a single day seemed to pass without total mayhem and dozens of heinous crimes.

Val folded the paper and tossed it onto his desk. There was no crime on Toril. No murder, no mayhem, no hideous disease, no suicide, rarely even an accident. Not even the weather played a part in the life or death cycle as it did here on Earth. There the weather never changed. The clear, acrylic-like dome that housed the cities of the planet were all thermostatically controlled.

Life was controlled as well, planned in an orderly fashion from birth to death. From test-tube conception to the end of a normal five-hundred-year cycle. Any reckless, self-destructive urges had been bred out of Torillian genes ten thousand years ago.

Yet history told of a time when they weren't so civilized, so completely controlled. A time they weren't all that much different from people here on Earth.

And in truth, though the violence chilled him, it also gave rise to certain forms of beauty that no longer existed on Toril. In art and in music, the violence, the passion portrayed made the work come to life. Just as it did the residents of Earth themselves. The challenge to survive brought out the best in people, helped them grow and change and achieve a new awareness.

And he had discovered that as much as he was appalled, he was also drawn to the life-or-death struggle people faced each day on Earth. Watching them battle the forces of a tornado or the destructive power of a hurricane was wildly compelling. A man with the courage to face and overcome cancer, or, like Patrick's father, battle to recover from a debilitating stroke, was an inspiration to Val and to others.

In essence, life on Earth was fraught with risks, but it was balanced by incredible rewards.

Val mulled over the notion as he unlocked his middle desk drawer and removed the journal he wrote in each day. He opened it to the latest entry and picked up a pen, tapped it lightly against the blank page.

Here life is struggle, he began, randomly scratching out his thoughts.

The strong survive over the weak. Individuality is key. People live their lives independent of each other.

They value their differences, even praise them. To us this attitude seems awesome, unsettling, perhaps even dangerous. A human being, free-willed and driven by his passions, might pose a threat that goes far beyond his small place in the world.

He paused a moment, then the pen moved again.

Perhaps it is not man's savagery we fear, but his capacity for independent action.

Val closed the journal, his thoughts moving backward, returning to the charts he had observed on Dr. Stover's wall. Graphs that demonstrated all too clearly several different avenues that would indeed lead to space travel at speeds far greater than the speed of light. Though the actual accomplishment would surely occur at some point in the future, Torillians had reason to be concerned.

But did that also give them the right to interfere?

Val stood up and began to pace the floor, his mind shifting to Julie, to the *Ansor*'s proposed experiments, to how they might affect her—and any number of others. Though they hadn't set out with that purpose, the testing aboard the ship was no less violent, no less savage than the acts he read about in the paper.

More and more, Val was convinced he had to make them stop.

Laura paced the floor of her tiny apartment. The phone had just quit ringing—again—and the answering machine kicked on. "Laura, it's Brian. I know you're in there. Damn it, pick up the phone."

She didn't, of course. Instead she just listened to him demanding, then pleading, determined it would do him no good. She cared for Brian Heraldson, more than cared for. Physically, she was wildly attracted to him. But he was wrong about her, and she wasn't going to let his doctor-patient attitude become the driving force of their relationship.

Not that they really *had* a relationship, she told herself firmly. So Brian had been kind to her. He was a nice man—most of the time. The steady sort women looked for in a man they might want to marry—if she were interested, which she was not. He was also arrogant and domineering, opinionated and determined to sway her to his will.

So what if he was handsome. So what if just noticing the way his bottom lip curved when he smiled stirred funny little flutters in her stomach. Jimmy Osborn was handsome, too. And though he was a little bad-tempered on occasion, he didn't try to run her life.

As luck would have it, Jimmy had called just that morning, right after her fight with Brian. Determined to forget Brian Heraldson and his overbearing ways, she had agreed to a date.

Laura glanced at the clock. Jimmy would be there any minute.

He was only half an hour late—right on time for Jimmy—when she heard his too-loud knock at the door. Hurrying over, she unlocked the double latches, unfastened the chain and pulled it open.

"Hey, babe, what's happenin'?" He was dressed in jeans and a tank top, his thick black hair slicked back, a toothpick stuck between his white teeth. The tattoo of a rose covered a portion of his oversized biceps.

"Hi, Jimmy."

"So...you ready to shit-can this joint and grab a beer?"

She wet her lips, suddenly a little uncertain. She hadn't remembered Jimmy being quite so rough-looking the last time they had gone out. "Yeah...sure...let me get my purse." She grabbed the fringed, quilted shoulder bag she had made herself, stopped a second in front of the mirror to check her appearance—a yellow halter top, jeans, and sandals—and they headed out the door.

They went to Ernie's, a local Venice beer bar that was a favorite of Jimmy's. They played pool and drank pitchers of beer, ate greasy hamburgers and fries. Amazingly, by ten o'clock, Jimmy was ready to go home.

Laura was ready, too. In the course of the evening, she had discovered she was no longer interested in Jimmy Osborn. She didn't enjoy hearing how he'd "beat the shit out of that no-good Buddy Taylor." She didn't like hearing him snicker with his friend, Joe Rizzoli, about the great bod Teresa Wilson had, or how tight her pussy was when Joe had finally screwed her.

All she could think of was that Jimmy was short on brains and that the way the guys talked about Teresa was the way they must talk about her.

She couldn't help thinking of Brian. Whenever they had been together, they had talked about interesting, important things. He had challenged her, made her remember things she had learned in school, made her want to learn more. Even when they were fighting, he made her think instead of just react. And she had to admit there were times he was right.

Jimmy pulled his ten-year-old, dented black Camaro

over to the curb and Laura opened the door and got out, knowing Jimmy would never come around to help her as Brian always did. Besides, she was eager to get home. She had never been so grateful to reach the front door of her apartment.

"Thanks, Jimmy." Standing on the cement step, she unlocked both door locks and walked inside. "I'll talk to you later."

He braced a hand on the door frame above her head. "Hey, wait a minute. You trying to give me the brush-off or something?"

"No, no, of course not. I'm just tired, is all. I haven't been sleeping very well. I thought tonight I'd go to bed early."

"Good idea," he said with a leer.

"That isn't what I meant." She tried to close the door, but he slammed a heavy boot against the jamb.

"Listen, baby, I bought you dinner, remember? I bought you drinks." He shoved hard on the door, pushing her inside, then followed her in. "You ain't gettin' off so easy."

"Get out, Jimmy. I'll give you the damn money for your lousy hamburger, just get out of my house."

"No dice, baby." He grabbed her arm and dragged her hard against him, brutally gripped her jaw and forced her mouth open, then shoved his tongue halfway down her throat. Gagging, Laura raked her nails down his cheek and jerked away, taking several hasty steps backward.

"Get out!" she shouted. "Get out or I'm calling the police!"

Jimmy rubbed his cheek, noticed a trace of blood on

his hand. His eyes narrowed and darkened. "I ain't leavin', baby. I'm gonna stay right here and teach you some manners." His lips curled faintly. "I'm gonna fuck you good, Laura. Maybe next time you'll know better than to mess with Jimmy Osborn."

Laura made a strangled sound in her throat and tried to run, but Jimmy caught her arm and shoved her up against the wall. He grabbed a fistful of her hair and yanked her head back.

"You're gonna get it, baby. You're gonna get it real good."

"Jimmy, don't!" Laura pleaded. "Please let me go."

A slight noise came from the doorway. "You heard what the lady said. Let her go." The door swung wide and Brian stood framed in the opening. "Get away from her and get out of her house."

"Brian…"

His hands were balled into fists, his mouth a grim line. He was taller than Jimmy, but Jimmy was younger, with a more wiry build. And utterly ruthless. If the two men fought, Brian was bound to get hurt.

Jimmy's lip curled. "Get outta here, man. This ain't no business of yours."

"I said to let her go," Brian repeated, legs slightly splayed, every muscle taut.

"Be careful, Brian!"

Jimmy yanked so hard on her hair tears sprang into her eyes. "Shut up, bitch! I'll take care of you when I'm through with him."

He let her go and turned to Brian and the instant she was free, Laura bolted into her bedroom. Her hands were shaking so hard she had trouble with the drawer in her bedside table, but eventually it moved and she jerked it open. The .38 special she had purchased through a friend sat exactly where she had left it.

She gripped the gun with both hands as she had been taught in her one-and-only lesson and tried to hold it steady. Taking a deep, calming breath, she raced back to the living room just in time to see Jimmy Osborn standing in front of Brian, his mouth a tight line, blood-lust shining in his dark eyes.

Laura raised the gun, her hands shaking but steadier than she would have expected. "Hold it, Jimmy! Stop right there." Standing with her legs slightly spread, she kept her arms straight in front of her, just as she had learned. Her knees were trembling, but she held her ground, pointing the pistol straight at Jimmy's heart. "I don't want any trouble, Jimmy. I just want you to leave."

Brian looked incredulous. "Laura, where in God's name—"

"Not now, Brian. Are you leaving, Jimmy?"

He looked at her and a muscle ticked in his jaw. His mouth looked tight against the shadow of beard beginning to roughen his cheeks. "I can't believe it. Little Laura Ferris drawing down on Jimmy Osborn." He chuckled without mirth. "You got more brass than I thought, babe." She tensed when he started to move, but he merely stepped around Brian and walked toward the door. "See ya around."

She didn't stop pointing the gun until Jimmy was gone and the door firmly closed. Then she lowered the weapon to her side and let the tears she had been holding slide down her cheeks.

Brian crossed the room in three long strides. Gently pulling the gun from her fingers, he set it on the table, then eased her into his arms. "It's all right, honey, don't cry. He's gone now. Everything's going to be all right."

Laura sniffed back tears. "Brian, I'm so sorry. I shouldn't have gone out with him. Julie warned me not to. I wouldn't have—" she glanced up "—if I hadn't been so mad at you."

His arms tightened protectively around her. "I'm sorry, honey. That's what I came here to tell you. I know I was wrong to interfere in your life. If I didn't care so damned much..." The words trailed off and Laura smiled softly. She reached up to touch his cheek.

"You shaved your beard."

"Yeah, I thought it might make me look younger. We aren't really so far apart in age, you know. I was hoping you'd like the change."

"I love it."

He smiled and she saw that he had dimples, hidden before by the beard.

"You were really terrific," he said, "even if you shouldn't own a gun."

Laura bristled. "That gun saved your ass, Brian Heraldson."

"I suppose so. But maybe I could have surprised you and saved my own ass. I used to box in college. I was pretty good at it, too."

Laura didn't tell him Jimmy Osborn wouldn't have fought by the Queensbury rules. "Thank you for what you did. You would have fought for me. No one has ever done that."

"No one?"

"Except my sister, of course. Julie's been fighting for me as long as I can remember."

He ran a finger along her cheek. "Tonight you fought for yourself."

Laura smiled. "I did, didn't I?" They walked together over to the sofa and sat down, Laura snuggling against him. "You know something, Brian? As terrible as this abduction thing has been, in some way I feel stronger for it. Do you think that's possible?"

"Maybe. Overcoming adversity often makes people stronger."

"I don't think I've overcome anything, but I'm trying. I'm trying very hard."

"That's all that matters, honey." He kissed the top of her head. "I can't tell you I believe in this alien thing, but I want you to know, I'm with you. I hope you'll consider my advice—as your friend—but however you want to approach this, I'll go along."

Laura slid her arms around his neck. "Thank you, Brian. That's all I could ever ask." She kissed him then, a soft sort of thank-you that mushroomed into something hotter, sweeter, far more insistent.

Laura pulled him down on the sofa and the kiss turned wildly passionate, a fusing of mouths, a stroking of hands on flesh, a straining of bodies to press more closely together.

Brian kissed the side of her neck. "I want you, Laura. God help me, I've tried to fight it, but I want you so damned much."

"I want you, too, Brian. Make love to me...please."

He groaned. Another long, deep kiss. His fingers fumbled with the buttons on her halter top. He slid it off her shoulders, baring her to the waist. Laura frantically worked the buttons on his shirt. His chest was wide and nicely furred, more muscular than she had imagined.

Brian caressed her breasts, then lowered his head to take one into his mouth. "You're beautiful," he whispered, tasting the soft white mound. "I knew you would be."

Feverishly they shed the rest of their clothes then Brian pressed her down on the sofa and came up over her, entering her with a single smooth stroke. Bodies came together, fast, hot, and furious at first, the second time more slowly, much more gently.

Brian fell asleep in Laura's arms, his dark head resting against her breast. She stroked his thick brown hair and felt content in a way she couldn't recall. Perhaps it was knowing he cared. Perhaps it was how much she had come to care for him.

Her eyes slid closed and she thought that she would sleep. She was stronger, now, she told herself, proud of her actions in saving them both from Jimmy. But sleep didn't come, and in the hours before dawn, she found herself listening instead, straining to hear the night sounds more clearly, listening for a dull thick hum.

No sound came that night. No one disturbed her. But sooner or later they would—Laura was certain of it.

Even with Brian beside her, worry rose up, gnawing at her insides, and she couldn't shake the fear.

"Ohmygod! Ohmygod!" Shirl Bingham pulled off her headset and dropped it onto the desktop in front of her. Her hands were still shaking from the call that had just come in. She had to find Patrick or Julie, but both of them were out.

Just then the back door slammed and Shirl sprang to her feet. Miracle of miracles, Julie had just walked in.

"Julie!" Racing through the office toward the rear, Shirl slammed to a halt in front of her. "Julie! It's Mr. Donovan!"

Julie's stomach dropped out. "Oh, God, tell me it isn't his heart."

"Not Patrick! Patrick's father—he's had another stroke!"

The little blood left drained from Julie's face. "Oh, no. Have they taken him to the hospital?"

"Apparently he's still at home. The doctor said moving him would be more dangerous than leaving him where he was. Oh, Julie I feel so awful. Mr. Donovan is such a nice man."

Julie shoved down the fear coursing through her. "We don't know how bad it is yet. We have to think positive, Shirl." She grabbed her purse and her car keys. "Page Patrick, tell him what's happened. Tell him I've gone to see his father." She rushed toward the rear office door, stopped and turned. "Oh, and cancel my afternoon appointments. There's a woman—Mrs. Rosenberg. Her number's in the address book on my desk. I'm supposed to show her houses at three. Tell her there's been an emergency. Try to reschedule for sometime next week."

"I'll take care of it."

"Thanks, Shirl." She was out the door in a flash, into her little silver sports car, shoving her key into the ignition with shaking hands. Oh, dear Lord, poor Alex. He had suffered so much already. And Patrick would be frantic. He loved his father. Their relationship was difficult for him and they hadn't been really close in years, but the love was there between them, fighting to break through.

The tires squealed as Julie revved the engine of the Mercedes and pulled out of the parking lot onto Canon Drive. A few minutes later she was rolling eighty miles an hour down the Glendale freeway, heading for the Flintridge turnoff.

Alexander Donovan's Mediterranean estate sat on Chevy Chase Drive. It stood two stories high, had nine bedrooms, each with its own private bath; a library; a solarium; a billiards parlor; and a separate building for the servants' quarters in the rear. Julie stopped the car in front of the big iron gates, punched in the security code, and the gates swung open. She pulled the car directly to the front door and jumped out, leaving the keys in the ignition. The butler opened the door before she reached it, and she stepped into the red-tiled entry.

It was cool in the house, massive potted palms waving in the slight breeze drifting in through the tall open windows. The soft aqua of the pool out in back contrasted the stark white walls. Only the antiseptic, hospital smell pervading the house hinted that all was not well.

"Come in, Ms. Ferris." The butler, a black-haired, meticulous little Italian named Mario, stood at the door. "We've been expecting you and Mr. Patrick."

"Patrick was out of the office when the call came in. They'll be trying him on his pager and cell phone. I'm sure he'll be here soon." She glanced toward Alex's room upstairs and nervously dampened her lips. "How's he doing?"

Mario shook his head. "Not so good, Ms. Ferris. The ambulance came right away when we called 911, but they decided not to move him. The doctor's up there with him now. And Nathan is with him."

Julie blinked against the quick burn of tears. "I'd better go up, too." She left the butler and climbed the stairs, her limbs heavy, her mouth dry as cotton. She had known there was every chance Alex would have another stroke and that if he did, it might be fatal, but still she wasn't prepared.

At the top of the stairs, she took a deep breath then plunged on down the hall. Nathan Jefferson Jones, Alex's brawny African-American nurse and longtime friend, stood outside the door.

"Hello, Nathan."

"Julie! I'm so damned glad you're here. Mr. D's been asking for you."

"How is he, Nathan?"

His usually round face looked haggard, almost gaunt. "I won't lie to you, Julie. It looks real bad."

"Oh, God, Nathan." She started to cry, felt those massive, muscular arms go around her, holding her ever so gently. She had seen him hold Alex that same way whenever he needed help and a feeling of tenderness for the big man swept through her. "Thank you, Nathan. I'll be all right now."

Straightening her shoulders, she stepped away from him, then nodded and he opened the door.

Julie walked into a room that looked more like an oversized hospital room than any sort of bedroom, had since Alex's first stroke. Boasting a remote-controlled, fully adjustable day bed with metal bars suspended above to help a patient lever himself up, there was also a rolling bedside food tray, an intercom system, and an overhead, adjustable hi-def TV.

Today intravenous tubes hung from wheeled carts,

dripping fluid into Alex's thin arms. Oxygen bottles sat against the wall, and a heart monitor beeped its rhythm near the head of the bed. The room was a jumble of medical apparatus, most of which Julie couldn't name, and amidst it all, a pale, shrunken Alexander Donovan lay still as death beneath the covers, his face as starkly white as the fine cotton sheets.

The doctor approached as Julie walked in. Dr. Cyrus McClean was in his forties with thinning gray hair and glasses. He was the top man in his field, recommended by Martin Cane, the Donovan's longtime family physician. Julie had known McClean since Alex's first stroke and the doctor knew that to Alex, Julie was family.

He took her arm and led her to a quiet corner and urged her into a chair.

"How—how is he?" she asked.

"I'll be honest, Julie. The prognosis isn't good. Alex wasn't fully recovered from his previous stroke when this one occurred. If he makes it through the next twenty-four hours, he might have a chance, but…"

"Go on, Dr. McClean, please. I need to know."

"I'm sorry, but the odds aren't good that will happen."

A thick lump rose in her throat. "You're telling me…you're saying that Alex is dying."

"I'm afraid so…yes."

"Oh, dear God." Tears burned her eyes, began to slide down her cheeks. The doctor pulled a tissue from the pocket of his white coat and handed it over.

"He's been conscious off and on. He's asked for you and Patrick. I'm glad at least one of you is here."

She ignored the censure in his voice. She knew what

the doctor thought of Alex's wayward son. "Patrick hasn't heard. I'm sure he'll be here soon."

Dr. McClean just nodded, and Julie turned toward the man on the bed. Dragging in a long, shaky breath, she squared her shoulders and crossed to his bedside, reached down and clasped his frail hand. It felt just as cold and lifeless as Alex looked, and a wave of pity washed over her. *Oh Alex*. Sitting down beside him, she bent down close to his ear.

"Alex, it's Julie. Can you hear me?"

At first he made no move, just lay there in silence, the only sound the high-pitched *bleep* of the heart monitor.

She swallowed past the hard ache in her throat. "Alex, it's Julie."

A slight movement, then his eyelids fluttered and slid open. He looked at her and made a faint nod of his head.

The ache in her throat grew more fierce. Alex was the father she never had. He had been there since her first struggling days at UCLA. He was her friend and mentor; she couldn't stand to see him like this.

"Patrick is coming," she whispered, fighting desperately not to cry. "You just rest and everything will be all right."

His eyes slid closed. He managed the faintest shake of his head. She felt a whisper of movement as he tried to squeeze her hand, then his fingers fell open, limp and unresponsive. Oh, God, he was telling her goodbye. He believed he was dying and he wanted to say his farewells to the people he loved.

"You're going to be all right," she whispered fiercely, her throat so tight she could barely speak. "You have to be. Patrick needs you. I need you." Her voice broke. "Please, Alex, you can't leave us now."

But his eyes didn't open and his fingers didn't move. Julie bent over him and kissed his sunken cheek, silent tears streaming down her face. "Don't go," she whispered. "I love you so much. Don't go, dear Alex. Please don't leave us."

Gentle hands clasped her shoulders. Patrick urged her up from the chair and turned her into his arms. She hadn't heard him come in, yet she was glad, so glad that he was there.

"It's all right, love. My father wouldn't want you to cry." His touch was gentle but his face looked grim. Harsh lines cut into his brow and the skin was drawn tight across his cheekbones.

"We have to help him, Patrick. Surely there is something we can do."

"You've spoken to Dr. McClean?"

"Yes, but...he sounded so hopeless."

He led her a few feet away. "Whatever happens, it's in God's hands now. All we can do is pray."

She leaned against him, rested her head on his chest. "I don't want him to die, Patrick."

"I know, love, neither do I."

"It hurts, Patrick. God, it hurts so much." They stood there in silence, clinging to each other, Julie crying, Patrick stroking her hair.

Julie lifted her head, used the tissue the doctor had given her to dab at the wetness on her cheek. "I'll be all right, now."

But she didn't look all right. She looked pale and shaken and he wished he could do something to take that haunted look away. Turning toward Nathan, he motioned for the big male nurse to take her out of the room. Val watched her go, feeling the weight of her grief, the painful tightening in his chest that he had felt before. Julie loved Alexander Donovan. Losing him was tearing her apart. Strangely enough, her pain seemed also to be his.

Val waited until she was gone, then sat down in the chair beside the bed, his attention fixed on the frail man lying nearly lifeless beneath the sheets.

"Hello...Father."

Watery blue eyes slid open. Shrewd eyes, perceptive, even in the face of death. His mouth moved, but no words came out. Val wondered what the old man might say if he were able to speak.

"Take it easy. You need your rest. You need to try and get some sleep." So far he had spent little time in the old man's company, just stopped by the house on occasion as Patrick would have done. He didn't want to chance more. If anyone would notice the differences in Patrick Donovan since Val's arrival, it was his father.

He stirred faintly on the bed. One hand was frozen by the stroke, the other started to tremble. He was trying to lift it, Val saw, to reach out and touch his son. Val took the old man's hand and the moment their fingers brushed, a fierce ache constricted inside him. His throat hurt. A lump formed so thick and heavy he feared he would choke.

"Father," he whispered, knowing the emotion he was feeling was grief. It came from Patrick, was the same pain Julie felt, though Val was able to distance himself, keep the unwanted emotions at a manageable length.

It was Julie he was worried about, Julie who would suffer at the death of someone she loved.

In an instant, his decision was made. Knowing he shouldn't, that whatever happened was best left in the hands of fate, Val leaned closer. Alex Donovan's eyes were closed but the thin veined hand still clung to his. Digging into his pocket, Val removed a small silver plate half the size of a dollar bill and a quarter of an inch thick. It was for medical emergencies. The body he occupied was human, after all. Any number of problems might occur.

Val freed himself from the fragile grip, pressed the plate into his palm then once again reached for the old man's hand. He wasn't sure how much good it would do. The stroke had obviously done extensive damage. But perhaps it would help and if Alex Donovan lived, it would also help Julie, make her terrible sadness go away.

He sat there for several minutes more, then removed the silver plate and shoved it back into his pocket. When he stood up, he saw Julie standing at the door.

"What was that?" she asked as he approached.

"What was what?"

"I thought I saw you put something…" She glanced away, a little embarrassed. "Never mind. I can't seem to think straight with Alex the way he is."

The doctor walked up just then. "I think we should let him get some rest." He flicked a glance at Patrick. "Are you planning to spend the night here or…" *Or do you have other more important plans than your father's last night on Earth,* his condemning look said.

Val knew he was thinking of the first stroke Alex had suffered, of the all-night party Patrick had been attending, the girl he'd shacked up with after that. He hadn't gotten home to receive the news till late the next day. In the meantime, his father was very nearly dead.

"We'll be staying, of course," Julie answered defensively, reading the train of the doctor's thoughts. "I'm sure Mario has already made up our rooms."

The doctor continued to stare at Patrick.

"I'm staying," he said.

The older man's mouth softened faintly. "Good. Your father said you had changed since your heart attack. Perhaps he's right."

Val said nothing and neither did Julie. He had definitely changed. He just hoped, if the old man lived, he wouldn't realize exactly how much.

Sixteen

Julie alternated between bouts of weeping and fierce determination. Alex Donovan wasn't the kind to give up, and neither was she. There was always a chance he would live.

But as the hours crept past, the chance seemed more and more remote. At ten o'clock, he slipped into a coma. At midnight, his condition remained the same. At 2:00 a.m., Julie sat in the hall outside his door silently weeping.

Patrick had just gone in.

He came out a few minutes later. "The doctor says he's resting peacefully, which is exactly what you need to do."

"I'm not leaving. I couldn't sleep, anyway, even if I tried."

Patrick stayed up, too, sitting beside her on the sofa Mario had ordered placed in the hall, his shoulder solid and comforting beneath her cheek when she finally did fall asleep. She wondered what he was thinking. She remembered how devastated he had been by his father's first stroke, the guilt he had suffered for not being there when his father needed him. He had been nearly unable to function.

This time he seemed far more in control, resigned in some way to accepting whatever fate Alex might suffer. He was a rock of support for her and Nathan, and his strong, reassuring presence helped them through the hours until dawn. She awakened to find his hand gently stroking through her hair.

Rubbing her eyes, she sat up on the sofa. "I must have fallen asleep. How is he?"

"His condition hasn't changed. The doctor is sleeping down the hall. Nathan's with him. It's my turn in another half hour."

"You've been up all night. I've had a couple of hours rest. I'll sit with him next."

Patrick shook his head. "I'm not sleepy. I'll take a turn and you can go in after that."

Julie blinked and stared at him. Except for his slightly wrinkled clothes—light gray slacks and a short-sleeved burgundy pullover—he looked as fresh as he had when he'd arrived. And thinking of his nightly wanderings, she figured it was probably the truth.

"What time is it?" Outside the window, the first gray light of dawn filtered through the trees around the pool.

Patrick glanced down at the expensive Patek Philippe on his wrist. "Five o'clock."

Hope rushed through her and tears sprang into her eyes. "Then it's almost morning. The doctor said if Alex made it through the first twenty-four hours, he'd have a chance."

Patrick squeezed her hand. "My father's a tough old bird. Maybe he will."

Julie just nodded. She didn't want to get her hopes too high, but she couldn't seem to help it. "I'll get us some coffee," she suggested, no longer sleepy herself.

Patrick gave her a smile. "Just water for me, if you don't mind."

Julie leaned over and kissed his cheek, feeling the rough black stubble of his night-long vigil. "Sorry, I forgot."

In the morning, against all odds, Alex Donovan still lived. He remained in a coma, but his vital signs were slightly improved.

"I'll grant it's a good sign," the doctor said. "But the fact is, recovery in a man Alex's age, in his current physical condition would be almost impossible."

"But you said—"

"I realize what I said. But a single night doesn't mean all that much. The best course is to resign yourselves. At this stage, considering his paralysis and the fact we don't know how much damage there is to the brain, Alex's passing would probably be for the best."

The hope inside her slowly faded. Alex would die or be partially paralyzed, maybe brain-damaged, and bed-ridden for the rest of his life. Whatever happened, Julie intended to be there for him, as he had always been there for her.

For the next three days, except for a quick trip home for her toiletries and fresh clothes, she stayed at the house in Flintridge. Patrick stayed as well, making only a single trip into the office and returning as quickly as he could.

By the fourth night, a bit of color had returned to Alex's face, but the doctor warned them not to read more into it than they should. There was still little chance for any sort of substantial recovery. Alex was simply not in good enough physical condition.

At present, the same could be said for Julie. She hadn't slept for the last three nights, had hardly been able to eat. She knew Patrick was worried about her—and apparently determined to do something about it.

"Get your sweater," he said, coming up behind her late in the evening. "And a scarf. You're getting out of this house for a while—if I have to tie you up and carry you out."

She smiled wearily. "That sounds like a threat, Mr. Donovan."

"It's a promise, Ms. Ferris."

"All right, I give in. I know when the odds are against me. Just give me a moment to change my clothes." Ten minutes later, dressed in jeans and sneakers and a long-sleeved plaid cotton shirt, she stood in the entry, listening to the roar of Patrick's sleek black Porsche pulling up in front of the house. He had taken off the top, she saw as he opened the passenger door and waited for her to slide in.

"We won't be gone long," he promised. "Just a quick spin through the hills. I've discovered sometimes a little fresh air works wonders."

Fresh air. Not something the old Patrick Donovan would have been interested in. But this Patrick took care of his body, and his mind. Apparently, he also meant to take care of hers.

"Where are we going?" She pulled the bright red scarf around her hair and knotted it beneath her chin.

"There's a place I found up in the hills not far from here. It's beautiful at night. You can look out over the whole city and nobody even knows you're there."

Julie said nothing. It did feel good to be out of the house, but guilt gnawed at her. What if something happened while they were gone? "Maybe we shouldn't do this, Patrick. I'd feel terrible if something happened and we weren't there when Alex needed us."

Patrick pushed the car into a sharp, slightly banked turn. "My father could linger as he is for days, even weeks. He loves you, Julie. Do you think he'd want to see you like this? You'll wind up making yourself sick, too."

"I don't know…I'm just so worried." She looked over at him and her eyes filled with tears. "I don't want him to die, Patrick. I just don't want him to die."

She started crying then, choking sobs that came from deep inside her. Patrick cursed as he turned off the road into the private spot he had found overlooking the city. He killed the engine, reached across the console, and pulled her into his arms.

"It's all right, baby. I know what you're feeling. I know how bad it hurts." He pressed a soft kiss on her cheek, another against the side of her neck. "Hush, love, please don't cry. He wouldn't want to see you like this." He rained soft kisses over her forehead, kissed her eyes, then lightly kissed her lips.

Julie looked up at him, saw his beautiful blue eyes darkened with concern, and the hurt inside began to ease. She feel his heartbeat, the warmth of his hands, and the pain began to change, to mesh with the heat of his lean hard body against her breasts. It fused with the fierce need for comfort roaring to life inside her.

"I need you, Patrick," she whispered. "I need you so much." Sliding her arms around his neck, she pulled his mouth down to hers for a kiss. It was soft at first, just a tender brushing of lips. His hands slid into her hair and Patrick deepened the kiss, sensing her urgency, her quiet desperation. His mouth felt hot and moist, tinged with the coppery taste of his desire. Julie's own desire swelled, making her body pliant against his, allowing his tongue to plunge in, accepting its invasion and pressing her own tongue into his mouth in return.

His hands found her breasts and he cupped them through her clothes. He lifted the rounded weight, pinched the ends until they hardened, and began to unbutton her cotton shirt. There was nothing of gentleness in his touch—it wasn't gentle she wanted. She wanted to forget her fears for Alex, to feel the heat of desire, to be scorched by it, and for these few moments be consumed.

The top two buttons on her shirt popped off in her haste to be rid of it and disappeared under the seat. She tugged Patrick's pullover off, then ran her fingers over his shoulders and across his broad chest. It was heavily furred and ridged with muscle, his stomach flat and narrow with a row of muscular indentations down each side.

His teeth nipped into her neck and a shot of pleasure rippled through her, then he lifted a breast into his palm, settled his mouth over the fullness and began to suckle the end.

Liquid heat slid through her, collected in the place between her legs. In the cramped little sports car, it was nearly impossible to move, yet she frantically dug at the buttons on the front of his designer jeans, pulled them open and reached inside. He was rock-hard, hot and pulsing.

Patrick's fingers found the zipper on her jeans and his hand slid inside, slipped beneath the small elastic waistband on her panties. He parted the folds of her sex and began to arouse the tiny bud at her core. In minutes she was writhing in the seat as she reached a powerful climax.

She thought she heard him groan.

Through the euphoric haze of her release, she heard his footfalls outside the car, straightened when he pulled open her door and urged her out into the darkness. Julie kissed him wildly as he lifted her onto the hood of the car, jerked off her sneakers, pulled her jeans down over her hips and tossed them away. He grabbed hold of her panties and dragged them down, ripping them away in his haste to have them gone. A long, deep-tongued kiss, and he urged her backward, parted her legs and moved between them. He kissed her breasts, nipped them with his teeth, laved and tasted her nipple.

Fire seemed to burn where he touched, to move along the path he trailed from her breasts to her navel. He laved the indentation with his tongue, then moved lower, through the dense auburn curls at the juncture of her legs, settling his mouth over the throbbing bud below.

Julie cried out when he began to suckle there, to taste and stroke, then delve deeply inside her. In seconds she was writhing, lacing her fingers in his wavy black hair, softly moaning his name. He didn't stop until she arched upward, coming fully to climax again, her body trembling all over.

She should have been sated, but the ache had been so fierce, her need so strong that when Patrick eased her off the hood, turned her onto her stomach, and bent her over the fender, heat roared through her again. Freeing himself from his snug-fitting jeans, he drove into her swiftly, raising her hips to take more of him, pounding into her with a need that seemed as great as her own.

It was madness, she knew, yet she didn't want it to end. Not until she felt the tightness building inside her, felt each of his thrusts as if he were a part of her, as if they were a single person bent on finding pleasure.

"Patrick!" she cried out, his hands at her waist, gripping her hips to lift her and fill her completely. Pounding, pounding, a rain of sensation poured through her, pushing her over the edge. Her body coiled tighter, tighter, then the coil sprang free.

Wicked, glorious pleasure. Ecstasy so sweet she could taste it on her tongue.

Patrick came, too. Every muscle tightening, his heart thundering, a low growl of pleasure erupting from his throat. He sank inside her again, bent forward and kissed the nape of her neck, held her until their trembling bodies stilled. Then he lifted her off the car and turned her into his arms, kissed her tenderly one last time.

His hand combed lightly through her hair. "You know this wasn't the reason I brought you out here."

"I know."

"I can't say I'm sorry it happened."

She reached up and touched his cheek. "Neither can I. Thank you, Patrick."

"For what? Making love to a beautiful woman?"

"For knowing just what I needed."

"My pleasure," he said with a teasing grin. He picked up her discarded jeans and handed them over. In the sliver of moon shining down, she could have sworn he blushed when he handed her the ruined panties.

"We'd better go," she said and Patrick nodded.

Julie let him help her into the car and close the door, then watched his long-legged strides as he rounded the

Porsche and climbed in. All the way back to the house, her eyes kept straying to his dark, handsome profile, the black flaring brows, the bright blue eyes and solid jaw. She thought of the way they had just made love, the feel of his mouth and hands on her body, his hard length inside her. She had never felt more complete, never felt more of a woman.

Julie leaned back against the headrest, gazing up at the stars. The truth was plain, even if she didn't want to see it. She was in love with Patrick Donovan. Wildly, insanely, passionately in love with him. Just like every other woman he had ever known.

The thought was terrifying.

As horrifying as Laura's fear of alien abduction. Maybe even worse.

Miraculously, five days after his near-fatal stroke, Alexander Donovan began to recover. He came out of his coma asking for his son, whose smile was wide and warm. By the end of the second week, Alex Donovan was sitting up in bed, and to Dr. McClean's amazement, his brain seemed undamaged. He had even begun to regain the use of his paralyzed left hand.

Nathan took over after that, beginning gradual physical therapy. Routines settled back to normal, and everyone went back to work.

Even Laura was working. She had taken a part-time job as a waitress in a local Denny's restaurant. The hours were flexible, which she needed, since she had decided to return to school. She only needed a few more credits at city college to earn her Associate Arts degree. She could take the necessary classes and still be home well before dark, which gave her a certain comfort, though her fears never really ever left her.

And she had another worry. Julie. Her sister's biggest problem wasn't aliens—it was Patrick Donovan. Julie was obviously head over heels for the man and there wasn't a doubt she was going to get hurt.

Patrick just wasn't a one-woman man. As far as Laura was concerned he never would be. It simply wasn't in his nature. Laura was worried about her, just as she was worried about herself.

Since the second abduction incident, there hadn't been another, yet she couldn't shake the feeling of constantly being watched. She had argued with Brian about keeping the gun she had purchased. They had been seeing each other a lot, their feelings for each other growing stronger. She didn't want to jeopardize the relationship they seemed to be building, and Brian had been so adamant about the gun she had finally given in and let him keep it for her.

Now she wished she'd stood firm.

Brian might not think she was emotionally stable enough to handle a weapon, but he hadn't faced an army of big-headed, black-eyed, ugly little gray men.

Not that those were the ones she most feared. It was the others, the gray men's superiors, that frightened her the most. She didn't know who they were or what they looked like, but she knew they were the ones in charge.

Once, during her second time on board the ship, she remembered the thought popping in: *Higher life forms don't mix with the soldier populations.* She didn't know how the thought got into her head, but she knew where it had come from. And she feared, sooner or later, she would have to face her powerful abductors again.

Laura shivered to think of it. At times she envied her sister, existing from day to day as if nothing had ever happened, pleasantly unaware. Laura remembered every brain-numbing, blood-curdling moment of her ordeal.

There wasn't the least chance she would forget.

Val pressed the heavy barbells above his head. He worked out at the gym next door to the office at least three times a week. It was strange in a way, since he knew it was only a matter of time until he'd be leaving Patrick's body to its Earthly end, a cold grave six feet under. It made him sad to think of such a healthy male specimen rotting away, but there was nothing he could do. Patrick's soul was long gone, had left just minutes after his heart had given way. The husk of a man was all that remained.

In the meantime, Val continued to hone the cords and sinews, the tendons and muscles that seemed more and more a part of him. Perhaps it was simply that he liked his human appearance, liked the flex of muscle over bone when he moved. Perhaps even more, he liked the look in Julie's eyes when she touched him, the intimate things she whispered when they were alone.

He thought of the night in his car above the city, the wild way they had mated. Nothing he had read, no specimen he had ever studied, had prepared him for the sweeping power of their joining.

Or the way he had felt when they were through.

Fiercely protective, passionately involved. Bonded to Julie in a way he wasn't prepared to handle. In a few more weeks he would have to leave her. It made his chest ache to think of it, made a sharp pain twist up in his guts.

For the first time it occurred to him that he didn't really want to go. He liked this wild, primitive planet with its fiercely passionate people. He liked not knowing what challenge each new day might bring. He liked accepting that challenge and overcoming it.

But he was a scientist, commander of the science wing aboard the *Ansor*, a powerful man among his people. The High Council would demand his return and he would be forced to obey.

In the meantime, he had a job to do. Which was why, when he finished working out, he drove straight to Julie's beach house, why he was sitting on her bright-colored sofa helping her sort through the stack of magazine and newspaper articles about UFO sightings she had pulled off the Internet.

The articles posed little threat. No matter what in the stack he read, no matter how many people reported the sighting, they were always treated the same, as if the person or person who'd had the encounter was crazy— six bricks shy of a load, Patrick would have said.

Even worse were the reports of alien abduction. It seemed the victims were assaulted twice—once by the "Visitors" who invaded their bodies and minds; a second time by society's ridicule, the refusal to believe what these people had endured.

He thought of Laura Ferris and wished he could ease Julie's worry about her. But the fact was Laura hadn't the strength Julie had and the abduction had affected her severely. All he could do was try to keep Julie's fate from being the same. Or worse.

"Listen to this—" Wearing jeans and a sweatshirt, she sat cross-legged on the floor at his feet. "'According to a study led by Nicholas Spanos, a psychologist at Carleton University in Ottawa, people who claim to have sighted UFOs are neither psychologically disturbed nor especially prone to fantasy.'" She glanced up. "Apparently they did a study of people who had reported sightings or close encounters and used a control group of people who had not. Both groups were found to be psychologically the same."

"That's impressive. People crazy enough to believe in UFOs aren't any crazier than the rest of us."

She punched his leg. "You are such a skeptic."

"Yeah, well, I'm not alone. It says here that two psychiatrists associated with the Harvard Medical School believe flying saucers are misperceptions of sexual organs. Hallucinations stemming from primal modes of thinking from childhood. They say a flying saucer is actually a representation of a mother's breasts. A cigar-shaped object is simply a phallic symbol. Flying objects are, and I quote, 'extremes of gratification and omnipotence,' unquote."

Julie looked at him as if he had lost his mind. "Tell me you are making a joke."

He chuckled softly. "'Fraid not."

She came up on her knees, pretty mouth set, and shook a finger in his face. "If you believe for a single moment—"

Val grinned and held his hands up in surrender. "I don't. Even I'm not that much of a disbeliever."

She laughed softly, settled back down on the floor and began to rummage through the papers spread out on the carpet. She picked one up and began to read.

"Okay, how about this? 'The tiny town of Rachel,

Nevada, has become a tourist destination for UFO enthusiasts. Though only 53 cars a day travel the 98-mile-long State Route 375, so many sightings have been reported it has been renamed the Extraterrestrial Highway. The road runs near Area 51, a part of Nellis Air Force Base where, some UFOlogists believe, the government is testing captured alien spacecraft.'"

He arched a brow. "Captured alien spacecraft? Now you're the one who is joking."

"Maybe, maybe not. I've heard about this Area 51. It's supposedly so secret they bought up all the land around it for miles so you can't get near enough to see it."

"That's what governments do," he said, "try to keep its defenses secret. That doesn't mean they're testing alien spacecraft." Though Val supposed they could be. Over the years, several Torillian crafts had gone down and never been recovered. And there were other space travelers who had visited the planet through the years.

"Look at this. I printed a list of sites off Google. There are dozens of Web sites devoted to people who claim to have seen UFOs. *UFOsightings.com* has accounts by NASA astronauts. And look at this…there was a major sighting at O'Hare airport in Chicago fairly recently. Listen to this. 'In November, a gray, metallic, saucerlike object was spotted hovering above Chicago's O'Hare International Airport. As many as twelve United Airlines employees spotted the object and filed reports.'"

"It was probably a weather balloon," Patrick said, the usual answer to a sighting, and Julie tossed him a look.

"'Airline officials say they have no knowledge of any such occurrence and the Federal Aviation Administration is not investigating.' I find that amazing."

Patrick just shrugged. "I imagine they get a lot of false reports. They hardly have time to investigate them all."

"Here's an old magazine article from *Omni,* back in the days when the magazine was still in print. It's a special issue on alleged extraterrestrial visitations. It says in 1969, after sixteen years of investigation, the government ended its official interest in UFOs. But later a number of people came forward claiming that a secret military underground continued the study."

She glanced down at the pages she had printed. "A retired army major named Robert Dean said NATO issued a classified report in the sixties stating that UFOs were real, extraterrestrial, and had visited the earth. A scientist named Bob Lazar claimed he worked in the late 1980s on an extraterrestrial spacecraft being researched and tested in Nevada, and a retired Air Force colonel named Charles Halt said he witnessed and investigated UFOs over England."

"Does it say how much these men got paid for their stories? I'd say that's a pretty important factor in deciding whether or not to believe what they're saying."

Julie frowned. "I suppose that's true, but—"

"But nothing. You, my love, are far too gullible."

"Here's something interesting…apparently it was a big deal back in the 1970s. Thousands of cattle across the country were mutilated. There were all kinds of investigations but no one ever really found out who was responsible."

"You think they were caused by aliens?"

"The government, of course, says it was all a giant hoax, that the deaths were caused by wild animals. A few might have been caused by members of some sort of cult."

She shuffled through the pages spread around her, found the item she wanted and read the words. "'A book called *An Alien Harvest*, by a woman named Linda Howe, suggests there is strong evidence of extraterrestrial involvement. Howe claims the high heat and rapid pinpoint incisions made into the flesh of the cattle that were killed could only have come from sophisticated laser equipment weighing more than five hundred pounds."

"Or by natural decomposition, which is what probably what most scientists believe." Fools that they were, Val thought. For years, cattle had been used as laboratory test animals for research—until they began to use people.

Julie sighed. She thumbed through copies she had made from magazines at the library: *Close Encounters, National Review; Seeking the Otherworldly, Skeptical Inquirer. Newsweek* had a story on alien abduction, *Omni* had several.

There were items of interest in *Aviation Week* and *Space Technology*. Another issue of *Newsweek* had a major feature on the possibility of long-ago life on Mars, the current work being done, and the government's commitment to actually landing people there.

She rummaged through her pile, held up a small article from the *Los Angeles Times*. "I ran across this on the Internet this morning. I printed it off because of the date. It's a UFO sighting that was printed in the paper the day after Laura claims she was abducted on the beach. I haven't got round to reading it. I just copied it and tossed it into the pile."

Val reached for the article but Julie held it away from him. "I get to read it first." She turned to the scrap of paper, just a small article on one of the back pages. "It says, 'An object described as a silver, saucer-shaped disk was spotted yesterday afternoon over Malibu Beach, California.'"

Her head jerked up. "Malibu? My God, Patrick." Her head went back down. "Several witnesses reported the sighting, including a United Airlines pilot whose name has been withheld. The pilot said the trail of the object was visible for about two minutes after it passed." She fell silent, madly scanning the rest of the article. He could see the pulse beating rapidly in her throat.

"This can't be coincidence, Patrick. Someone reports a UFO over the ocean near Malibu beach the same day Laura claims she was abducted. Maybe—"

He snatched the newsprint out of her hand and read the article to the end. "Maybe it was a failed missile launch from Vandenberg Air Force base, just like it says." He handed her back the copy and Julie read it again.

"I know that's what it says, but…"

"But you'd rather believe your sister was abducted by aliens."

Julie leaned back against the sofa, using his legs to prop herself up. She blew out a long breath of air. "It just bothers me, is all. A lot of people believe in this stuff, but the people who don't seem to have all the power. If they wanted to cover things up, they probably could."

"Why would they want to do that?"

"Any number of reasons. Public panic, I suppose. Or maybe they just don't want to deal with the ramifications of admitting such a threat exists. I mean, we're already facing terrorists all over the world. Maybe its just too much for people to handle. Maybe—"

"And maybe UFOs don't exist. Maybe the sound you

heard that day on the beach had something to do with the Vandenberg missile launch."

Julie sat up straighter, her head cocked in thought. Then she rolled away from him and grabbed up the phone.

"What are you doing?"

"I'm calling the newspaper. It doesn't give the exact time of the sighting in the article. I want to know when it was. Then I'm calling the paper in Lompoc, since that's where the air base is. Somebody ought to be able to confirm the time of the missile launch and the time it was aborted. If they can't, I'm calling Vandenburg."

"Don't you think that's going a little too far?"

"Maybe. I guess we'll have to wait and see."

It took the better part of an hour before she had the information she wanted. Long enough for her eyes to be shining with a mixture of satisfaction and what he would guess was fear, and her hands were shaking.

"I told you, Patrick. I said they could cover things up. The sighting was at 3:07 in the afternoon. The missile was launched at four o'clock and aborted at four-thirteen. The Vandenberg missile wasn't even off the ground when the UFO was reported."

He shook his head. "That doesn't mean what was sighted was actually a spacecraft."

"No, but it damn sure wasn't a missile."

Val said nothing. He didn't like the way this was going, but at present there wasn't much he could do. "So what now?"

"I'm not sure. I only went into this hoping to find some way to help my sister. At first I was sure she was just being paranoid. She's always had emotional problems. I was certain they had escalated into something more. Now…I just don't know. After listening to her sessions with Dr. Heraldson, after sitting in with Dr. Winters's abduction group, I can't say I'm a hundred percent convinced this isn't real. I told Laura I'd try to keep an open mind and I think I've done that. At least now if she tells me little gray men have taken her aboard their spaceship, I can listen with a sympathetic ear."

"You're saying you believe her."

"No, I'm not. I'm saying there's a chance it's the truth. A lot bigger chance than I ever would have guessed." Julie shivered, and Val reached down and urged her up on the sofa, then lifted her onto his lap.

He looped a curl of her glossy dark red hair back over an ear. "Even if it were true, love, if space travelers really existed, it might not be so bad. In most ways people are the same, no matter where they come from."

"If it's true, they're hurting people. Innocent people are suffering and there is no one who can stop them."

He eased her back against his chest, smoothing his hands over her hair. "Maybe they don't mean to hurt anyone. Maybe as intelligent as they are, they just don't understand."

Julie eyed him strangely, but she made no reply, just nestled against his chest. He could feel fine tremors racing through her. When she raised her head, her face looked a little bit pale.

"Take me to bed, Patrick. I don't want to think about this anymore."

Neither did he. But unlike Julie, he didn't have any other choice.

Seventeen

Julie sat at Alex Donovan's bedside, holding the old man's once-paralyzed hand. He was sitting propped up in bed, smiling, his cheeks robust instead of hollow, looking more fit than he had in years.

"It's a miracle," Alex said. "I ought to be lying out there next to Martha, six feet under, but for some damnable reason, God saw fit to keep me alive."

"It *is* a miracle, Alex. And no one is more grateful for it than I am."

"How does Patrick feel? He hasn't come around all that much since the stroke. At times it's hard to know what that son of mine is thinking."

"Patrick barely left your side the whole time you were sick. He loves you, Alex. He always has. Surely you don't believe he feels anything less."

Alex pointed toward a small rubber ball lying on a tray beside his bed and Julie handed it over. "There is the matter of his inheritance." He began to squeeze it with his still weak left hand, determinedly working the muscles and tendons. "Before his heart attack, there were times he seemed to need money very badly."

"He was trying to get Brookhaven built, and having terrible financial problems. But he never considered involving you, Alex, or asking you to help in any way. He knew you couldn't really afford that kind of investment. Besides, I think one of the reasons he wanted to build those condos was to prove himself to you. He wanted to make you proud of him."

Alex grunted something unintelligible. "It was difficult to be proud of a son whose sole purpose in life was to immerse himself in excess…or perhaps find ways to destroy himself."

"He's different now."

"Is he? I'm extremely proud of the man he's become since his heart attack. But I'm terrified the change is only temporary." He reached a thin hand out to touch her cheek. "I'm worried for you, Julie. I'm afraid you're going to be hurt."

Julie felt the sharp burn of unexpected tears. "Patrick's changed," she insisted. "He never touches alcohol or drugs. He keeps himself in shape. He's stronger now than he ever has been, more confident, more self-assured." She swallowed past the lump that rose in her throat. "I love him, Alex. I tried not to, but I do."

Alex sighed. "I know you do. I can see it in your eyes whenever you look at him. And you're right, he is different, more of a man than I ever believed he could be. Donovan Real Estate has actually begun to make money again, thanks to my son. And you, Julie. For years you wouldn't give him the time of day. Now you tell me you're in love with him. Under different circumstances,

I couldn't be more thrilled. But is it really possible for a man to change so much?"

Julie tried to smile but it came out a little wobbly. "I hope so, Alex. I pray every day that the man I love is real and not just an illusion."

"I'm praying for it, too, Julie. For my son…and for you."

Business was in full swing by the time Val arrived at the office the following day. Without looking up from the call she was taking, Shirl thrust a handful of messages into his hand and pointed down the hall. She pressed a palm over the receiver. "There are a couple of guys in your office. I tried to get them to wait for you out here but they insisted. I thought it was better if I just let them in."

Val glanced toward the closed door and knew in an instant which men were waiting. "You did the right thing, Shirl. I'll take care of it."

She nodded and frantically started taking messages again. It was amazing how much busier the place had gotten over the past few weeks. It was a shame Patrick hadn't taken the time to manage his staff as Val had been doing in his place. It wasn't that difficult and Patrick had been good at it. It bothered Val to think what would happen to the business once he was gone.

He reached the door to his office, paused for a moment outside, then stepped in and pulled it closed. The same two men waited, one lean and well-dressed, leaning back in the chair behind his desk, the other stout and sandy-haired sprawled over the arm of the sofa. This time he knew their names.

Val flashed a mocking half smile. "Ah, Mr. Ceccarelli. So good of you to drop in. You, too, of course, Naworski."

The tall, gray-haired Italian eyed him with a look of surprise mixed with respect. The Italian was dressed as impeccably as before, in the standard double-breasted blue pinstripe suit. An old memory surfaced and Val smiled to think the man must have watched too many *Godfather* movies, some of Patrick's favorite boyhood films.

"You've been doing your homework," said the man behind his desk. "Good for you, Donovan. I'm impressed."

It hadn't been all that hard to discover who they were. Ralph Ceccarelli and Jake Naworski were fairly well known around L.A., if you knew where to look for them. Val had simply paid a man who knew the right sort of places to look.

"I don't like faces without names," Val said simply.

Naworski came up from the sofa. "Yeah, and we don't like the runaround you been givin' those folks from the Teachers' Pension Fund." Where Ceccarelli looked slick, Jake look rumpled, his khaki slacks bagging in the knees, his yellow pullover grease-spotted over the belly and slightly wrinkled.

"I'm a busy man, Jake," Val said. "Surely you can't fault a man for trying to earn a living."

Both men moved toward him, stopping just a few feet away, trapping him between them. "The most important business you've got right now is getting that money you owe paid back to Sandini and McPherson. The pension fund is all set to buy that phony trust deed paper. They just need a little push from you and the deal is as good as done."

Ceccarelli smiled wolfishly. "Sarah Bonham will be

calling again the end of the week. She and her people want a tour of the project and you're gonna give it to them. While you're at it, you're gonna tell them what a great company Westwind Corporation is and what a fantastic deal they're making."

"That's right," Naworski put in. "You're gonna tell 'em those condos are selling like nightgowns at a Macy's Mother's Day sale."

Val said nothing for a moment, then he smiled. "I don't have a problem with that. If that's what you want then that's what you'll get. As I said, a man's gotta earn a living. I'm still in for a share of the profits, over and above the debt, and I could sure as hell use the money."

Ceccarelli clapped him on the shoulder. "Now that's more like it. In a matter of weeks, the deal will be over, the money you owe repaid, maybe a little in your pocket, and all of this behind us."

"You may have to take a little heat," Jake added, "once them teachers find out those notes they bought ain't no good, but Mr. Sandini'll make sure you don't do time." His round face broke into a smile. "He's always loyal to his friends."

The two men left a few minutes later, shaking his hand as they walked out the door. Val closed it firmly behind them. He wondered how much longer he could stall Sarah Bonham.

And what Sandini and McPherson would do when they discovered he had advised the pension fund to pass on buying Westwind's worthless paper.

On legs that felt weak and unsteady, Julie reached the refuge of her office, closed the door, and sagged back down in the chair behind her desk. Her hands were shaking, her heart trying to club its way out through her throat. She hadn't meant to eavesdrop on Patrick's conversation. She had only just seen him walk in a few minutes earlier, only intended to say a quick hello and get his opinion on a deal she was trying to make.

Or perhaps she just wanted to see him.

But the door wasn't tightly closed and something in the tone of the men's voices caught her attention. She lingered when she should have walked away, paused just long enough to overhear them talking about the Westwind Corporation's phony trust deed scam.

And Patrick was obviously involved.

Julie shook her head, trying to clear the haze of fear from her mind, to make the pieces fit together. She thought of the Brookhaven condo she had tried to sell the Harveys. Patrick had warned her against it, been adamant she find them something else when he desperately needed every sale.

Now she knew why.

She had known he was desperate for money. The old Patrick's involvement would not have surprised her. He was used to living high and he would do anything to continue that lifestyle, but this man, the Patrick she had fallen in love with—

Julie couldn't stand to think she could have been that wrong.

Her shoulders sagged. If Patrick was a crook, a man willing to cheat innocent people out of their life savings—out of their homes—what else might he do? Would he lie about his feelings, convince her he cared when all he wanted was to amuse himself in bed?

Her afternoon appointment could wait. As soon as Patrick left the office, Julie was going to go through his files. If he was acting illegally, perhaps there was a way she could stop him before he got caught, convince him to do what was right. If he wouldn't, if he hadn't really changed at all—if he had lied to her, used her, duped her into caring for him—dear God, she would…she would… She didn't know what she would do but she would never want to see him again.

Two hours passed. Julie paced the floor of her office, unable to concentrate, worried, then angry, then worried again.

At noon, Patrick stuck his head through the door. "How about lunch? Can you get away?"

She barely glanced up from the files on her desk. "Sorry, I'm busy. You go ahead. I'll see you when you get back."

He frowned, picking up on her crisp tone of voice. "Is everything okay?"

She forced a smile. "Yes, of course. Just busy. I've got an appointment at two and I'm not prepared."

He smiled, a small dent, not quite a dimple, creasing his cheek. God, he was handsome. Her heart hurt just to think what they had shared might be a lie.

"I won't be long," he said. "Want me to bring something back?"

She shook her head. "No thanks, I'm not hungry." That was the truth. Her stomach was churning, gnawing at her insides. The thought of food made her slightly sick. She waved as he headed out the back door, then jumped up from her desk and hurried toward his office.

A quick glance to see if anyone was watching, then she opened his door and slipped in.

It was immaculate as always. The file drawers were closed, each file carefully coded and put away, his desktop Spartan, only a silver-framed photo of his mother and father when they were young, and a black leather desk blotter with matching onyx pen and pencil set, a gift from one of his girlfriends. He had always been organized. Since his brush with death he was even more so.

Julie hurried toward the file cabinets that were locked at the end of the day but during working hours were usually left open. Rifling through the Pendaflex hanging files and a sea of manila folders, she searched for the name Brookhaven, found it, pulled the file and scanned the contents, then found Westwind Corporation and scanned that, too.

On the surface, there was nothing in any of what she read that didn't look legitimate. But studying the way the sales were constructed, she began to have a pretty good idea how the setup might work. She had overheard enough to know there was fraud involved and Patrick was right in the middle of it.

If what she suspected was correct, most of the sales of the Brookhaven condos had never taken place, which meant the high-interest loans Westwind was supposedly carrying back were fake. The buyer of those loans—the Teachers' Pension Fund if she had heard correctly—would be purchasing worthless paper.

For a while, the money could be manipulated and the truth covered up, but sooner or later, the fraud would be discovered. Westwind would undoubtedly be dissolved by then, its "employees" scattered with the wind—just like their name. But Patrick's association with the company was bound to come out.

Dear God, he could go to jail! At the very least his business would be ruined, the Donovan name dragged through the mud.

It horrified her to think what would happen, but mostly it frightened her to think that Patrick hadn't really changed. If anything, he had gotten worse.

She was back at her desk when the intercom buzzed. Julie ignored it, just sat in her chair staring through her office window, trembling and wondering what to do. She tried to think how she might come up with proof, confront Patrick with something he couldn't refute, but her mind seemed unable to function.

The intercom buzzed again. "Ms. Ferris? It's your sister. She's on line one. You usually like me to put her through."

Julie leaned over and pressed the button. "Thank you, Shirl." She lifted the receiver. "Laura? Hi, honey, how are you?"

"Pretty good, sis. I hate to bother you…I know how busy you are…but Brian and I are going out of town for the weekend, heading up to Lake Arrowhead. Brian thinks it'll be good for me to get away for a while and I had the weekend off. I just didn't want you to worry if you tried to call."

"I would have. I'm glad you phoned." Julie hesitated. She had thought more than once of mentioning the UFO sighting she had discovered in the newspaper. Would Laura be heartened that a bit of evidence in her favor had been unearthed—or more paranoid than ever that the "Visitors" might be coming back for her? "I take it you and Brian are getting along okay."

"He's great, Julie. A little too bossy at times, but he's sweet and caring. And he's, well…very sexy, too. I'm lucky to have him."

Compared to Jimmy Osborn, the man was a prince, but Julie didn't say so. Laura felt bad enough about that incident as it was. "Call me on my cell when you get there and leave a number where I can reach you."

"I will."

"Have a good time, Laura."

"Thanks, sis."

Laura rang off and Julie sank back against her chair. Between Laura and Patrick, she was turning into a nervous wreck. The latter stuck his head through the door.

"Are we still on for dinner?" He was smiling, looking for all the world as if he didn't have a care. Julie wanted to strangle him.

"I'm afraid not, Patrick. Owen called. He's decided to buy some of the property adjacent to his house and he wants me to handle the deal. We're getting together tonight to go over the terms of the offer." She hadn't agreed to Owen's dinner invitation when he had called, but she meant to call him and accept it now. Anything to avoid being with Patrick. She needed time to think.

Patrick frowned. "The man's going to wind up owning half of Malibu just so he'll have an excuse to see you."

Her chin hiked into the air. "Owen doesn't need an excuse to see me. We've been friends for years."

"I told you before, he isn't interested in being just a friend."

Julie glared and Patrick's frown deepened.

"Or maybe you like the fact he's so interested. Maybe all that money makes him interesting to you."

She didn't miss the note of jealousy. Patrick looked astounded by it, but at the moment she didn't care. "Money isn't everything, Patrick. But you don't believe that, do you? You've always thought money was an end in itself and you'll do just about anything to get it—won't you?"

"What the hell are you talking about? All I did was ask you to dinner."

Julie grabbed her bag off the sofa, her BlackBerry off her desk, and several files she needed to work on at home. She stuffed them into her briefcase and headed for the door. "Have a good evening, Patrick. I'll see you tomorrow."

"Wait a minute. I thought we were—"

But she only waved and kept on walking. She and Patrick had been together nearly every night for the past few weeks. Not tonight. She wasn't ready to confront him and she wasn't about to pretend that nothing was wrong.

Damn you, Patrick Donovan. Evidence or not, tomorrow she intended to have it out with him.

She wondered if he would tell her the truth.

Owen Mallory stood by as the stately, silver-haired maître d' pulled out Julie's chair. Owen waited for her to be seated, then sat down himself. They were dining at a little French restaurant in Palos Verdes called La Rive Gauche. With its simple French provençal decor and excellent cuisine, it was a favorite of his, and not too far a drive from Oceanside, his Malibu estate. Especially not far in the back of his new white Mercedes limo.

His gaze traveled back to Julie, ran over the short black sheath dress that tastefully accented her curves. She wore small pearl earrings, and a single strand of pearls that drew his gaze to her breasts. She had a very nice bosom, he thought, having dreamed on several occasions of how those lovely white mounds might feel in his hands.

"Would you like a cocktail before dinner?" he asked, thinking she had a pair of great legs, too. Solidly muscled yet shapely, lightly tanned, just enough to make them sexy.

"I'll have a Stoli martini straight up," she said, and Owen arched a brow. Julie was a white wine drinker. Rarely anything stronger. "It's been a long day," she explained. "Obviously, not one of my best."

"Obviously." He turned to the waiter. "I'll have the same."

They drank their drinks, discussing the offer he wished to make on the property next to his, then ordered dinner, a salad of seasonal greens and raspberry vinaigrette, rack of lamb for two, garlic mashed potatoes, and French cut string beans with slivered almonds.

When they finished their martinis, he ordered an expensive bottle of Bordeaux, which the wine steward opened so that it could breathe. Still, it wasn't until halfway through the meal—and the bottle—that Julie began to relax.

He studied her over the top of his wineglass. "Why don't you tell me what's bothering you, my dear? You've been nervous as a kitten all evening. It's obvious that something is wrong."

He took a sip of his wine, watched the legs of the

wine forming against the bowl of the glass. "Trouble, perhaps, between you and your…boss?" He knew she had been seeing Patrick Donovan and no longer simply in a professional vein. It galled him she would become involved with a man like that, no matter how handsome he was. He had always believed Julie had better sense.

"No trouble," she said. "At least not exactly." She hesitated a moment. "There is Laura, of course. I'm terribly worried about her. She seems a little better lately, but I'm not sure how long it will last."

"She still believes all that rubbish about flying saucers?"

"I'm afraid she does. Who knows, maybe it's the truth. It's possible, I suppose. It doesn't really matter. The important thing is for Laura to put it behind her. To find some sort of stability in her life that will make her happy."

"I realize your sister has problems. The fact is you've been worried about your sister since the day we first met. But I don't think that's what's wrong. I have to believe this is something else."

Julie leaned toward him over the table, and the candle in the center flickered with the movement. Even softened by the glow, her pretty face looked tense. "You're right, Owen. And now that you've brought it up, I could use your help."

He leaned back in his chair. "Go on."

"There are some men I need to find out about. A friend…one of my clients…is involved with them. Do you think you might be able to help me?"

"I imagine I could do that." *For a price,* he wanted to add. *Getting rid of Patrick Donovan and looking at me with half the interest you do him.* "What are their names?"

"Sandini and McPherson. I don't know any more than that. They're big money real estate players, though. At least I think they are. And perhaps a little on the shady side."

Owen took a sip of his wine. The bouquet was excellent, with just a hint of blackberry. He set the glass back down on the table. "And who, may I ask, is this *client* you're so worried about?"

"I-I'd rather not say. At least not yet. Not until I know a little bit more about what's going on."

He smiled. He liked the idea of having Julie in his debt. He liked having just about anyone obligated to him. It made getting what one wanted far simpler in the long run.

And for several frustrating years, he had wanted Julie Ferris.

"I'll see to the matter first thing in the morning. I have people who are very good at this sort of thing. I'm sure we'll have the answer in a couple of days."

She reached across the table and squeezed his hand, her fingers small and feminine against the white linen cloth. "Thank you, Owen. I hope you know how much I value our friendship."

Friendship, indeed, he thought. He was determined to have far more than that, but he didn't say so. He didn't want to frighten her away and he knew without a doubt that he would. Timing was everything. He had waited this long. He could wait a little longer.

Perhaps giving her the information she wanted would do the trick.

Coupled with the fact he also intended to discover exactly what men like Sandini and McPherson had to do with Julie Ferris.

* * *

Jealousy. Val knew what the word meant. In theory. He also knew it was an emotion Patrick Donovan had rarely experienced and never over a woman. Which meant there was nothing for Val to go on. In this, he was on his own.

It was almost midnight. He had been pacing the floor in front of the sofa for more than an hour. For the third night in row, Julie had been too busy to see him. She was avoiding him, plain and simple. But why?

The only thought that came to mind was Owen Mallory. The man was handsome, intelligent, and rich as Croesus. Why shouldn't a woman like Julie be attracted to a man like that? He knew very well that Mallory was attracted to her.

Which was where, he supposed, the jealousy came in.

It was an ugly emotion. A gnawing sort of anger with no definable source. It felt like a fist to the stomach, tied him up into knots and wouldn't let go. The thought of Julie with Mallory made him want to shout with rage, to storm over to Julie's and beat down the damnable door.

It wasn't like Patrick to behave that way, and it certainly wasn't like Val. Jealousy was far too volatile an emotion to have survived through the ages on Toril. So where had it come from? How could it even exist? And what the hell should he do about it?

Val glanced at the clock. By now, Julie was probably in bed. He could try to call her again, but she wasn't answering her phone. At least she wasn't picking up for him.

Maybe she's with Mallory. Maybe they're sleeping together. He didn't want to think it, but he couldn't seem to help himself. Patrick wouldn't have had a qualm about involving himself with more than one lover. Maybe Julie felt that way, too.

Damn it, he needed to know.

He was supposed to be studying Julie Ferris, he rationalized. To do that he needed to understand how that mind of hers worked. As a scientist, if their relationship was over, he needed to understand why.

Logic was the final prodding he needed. Val grabbed his camel-hair sport coat off the back of a chair, snatched up his car keys, and headed out the door. One way or another he was going to end this ridiculous behavior.

At least once he knew the truth, he wouldn't be jealous anymore.

She meant to wait for word from Owen, she really did. She had successfully avoided Patrick for three days, but Owen still hadn't called. When Patrick appeared at her front door just minutes before midnight, his jaw set and refusing to leave, she had no choice but to let him in.

"I want to know what the hell is going on," he demanded. "I want to know why you've been avoiding me. Is it Mallory? If it is, at least have the decency to say so."

Julie eyed him a moment, saw the turbulence in those stormy blue eyes and something more. She had hurt him, she saw with a bit of amazement, wishing she had been honest with him from the start. He might be involved in shady business dealings but so far he had played fair in his dealings with her.

"It isn't Owen. Owen and I are just friends. I told you that before."

"Then what is it?"

Her head came up. She looked him square in the

face. "In two ugly words—Sandini and McPherson. I know you're involved with them in some sort of crooked real estate deal."

For a moment he just stood there. Then the tension drained from his shoulders and a faint smile curved his lips. "That's it? That's what you're mad about?"

She felt like slapping his face. "This might be funny to you, but it's deadly serious to me. Innocent people are involved in this. How could you do it, Patrick? How could you sell yourself, sell everything you've worked for down the drain for a few lousy bucks?"

"I take it you were listening when my 'associates' came in the other day."

"I didn't do it on purpose, but yes. I heard most of what they had to say."

"Then you realize the reason they came to see me is that I wasn't cooperating with them."

"I gathered that, yes. I also heard you tell them you'd be happy to cooperate in the future—more than happy, since you're in for a share of the profits."

"I told them that, yes. Put simply—I lied."

"What!"

He made a sound. She could swear it was a chuckle. "I never intended for that deal to go down the way it did. I borrowed money from Sandini and McPherson with every intention of paying it back. When Brookhaven failed and I wasn't able to pay back the loan, they took over the project and formed the Westwind Corporation. Once I understood the fraud they were planning, I've done everything in my power to be certain that they fail."

"But you said—"

"I know what I said. I told you—I lied. I'm not going

to convince the Teachers' Pension Fund to buy those worthless notes. I'm going to convince them not to."

Julie said nothing. She wanted to believe him. She wanted it more than anything in the world. She searched for the truth in those beautiful blue eyes and there was nothing furtive, nothing insincere in the steady look he gave her.

"If you don't do what they say, what will happen?"

"I'll lose a lot of money, but I've already done that. The business is running in the black again. I'll survive."

"And?"

Patrick glanced away, for the first time looking uneasy. "They won't be happy about it, but they'll still own Brookhaven. Sooner or later the market will change and the units will sell. They'll be able to recoup their money."

"Not all of it."

"No, not all of it."

She wondered what he wasn't telling her. She would find out, she vowed. Perhaps what Owen discovered would fill in the blanks. "Is that the truth, Patrick? You're really not involved in this? You're not going to help them?"

"You can go with me when I talk to Sarah Bonham. I'm going to advise her against buying those notes."

Relief rushed through her, so strong tears pricked her eyes. Her heart ached in an odd, throbbing cadence that went far deeper than relief. "Oh, Patrick." She reached for him and he hauled her into his arms. She could feel the bands of muscle across his chest and the solid, reassuring rhythm of his heartbeat.

He nuzzled the side of her neck. "God, I've missed you. Next time you get mad at me, promise you'll tell me the reason. I can't stand this thing you call jealousy. I don't know how anyone can."

Julie laughed. There were times since his illness Patrick had the oddest way of phrasing things. Julie found it strangely endearing.

"I should have come to you," she said. "Next time I promise I will." She leaned toward him and he kissed her, a fierce, possessive kiss that made her blood heat and her body tingle all over. Then he was lifting her up, carrying her off to the bedroom, pressing her down in the middle of the bed and coming up over her. He didn't stop kissing her; he couldn't seem to get enough.

They made love wildly, till both of them were physically and emotionally drained. Julie slept soundly till just before dawn, then woke up in Patrick's arms, one of his long legs thrown possessively over hers, pinning her to the mattress. Her body felt sweetly sated, pleasantly battered.

She smiled as she lay beside him.

As the minutes crept past, only the persistent nagging worry about Patrick's intention to oppose Sandini and McPherson kept her from returning to sleep.

Eighteen

Val leaned back in his chair, surveying the computer screen in front of him. He was working on a listing for Fred Thompkins, trying to establish the value of a Hollywood Hills estate that had once belonged to Errol Flynn, but he couldn't seem to concentrate. His mind kept straying to Julie, to the scene he had made at her house.

He had barged into her home in the middle of the night, been demanding and overbearing—all in all, behaved like a complete and utter madman. What was happening to him? Where was Valenden Zarkazian, scientist, leader—rational, logical, always in control? Even Patrick had never behaved so insanely.

But then, Patrick had never been in love.

Val winced as the word popped into his head. Between Patrick's perceptions, the television shows he had watched, and the books he had read, he knew the symptoms.

It was like a disease, he believed. An Earth disease, and Val was certain he had somehow unwittingly contracted it. It occurred to him he might administer some form of medical relief in the hope of curing himself, but he was fairly certain it wouldn't work.

He wondered if the disease would go away when he returned for good to Toril, but in the back of his mind, he was afraid that it would not.

It was an odd disease, wondrous in some ways, making a man feel like he could leap buildings, or perhaps even fly.

Like Superman, he thought with a smile, dragging a boyhood memory from the back of his mind. The smile slowly faded. Pain went with love. He had sampled a bit of that pain when he had thought he'd lost Julie to Mallory. It hurt, damn it. A physical ache down deep inside.

How many months would he carry that ache when the time finally came for him to leave her? How many years?

Would the ache stay with him forever?

And there was Julie to consider. She cared for him, he knew. He didn't know exactly how much. Would she suffer as he would, after he was gone?

He had promised not to hurt her.

Now it seemed very clear that he would.

A knock at the door interrupted his thoughts. The door swung open and Nathan Jefferson Jones stuck his big bald head through the opening.

"Say man, what's happenin'? You real busy?"

Val smiled. "Not that busy. What's up?"

The door opened wider and Nathan wheeled Alex Donovan into the room. "It's his first trip out of the house since his stroke. Man's lookin' real good, ain't he?"

Val smiled as he rose from behind his desk and started toward the frail man seated in the wheelchair. His thick snowy hair was freshly trimmed, his face clean-shaven, his slacks and yellow short-sleeved shirt perfectly pressed.

"You look terrific, Father." He had almost said Dad. Patrick hadn't called him that in years. Not since before his mother died. "I've been meaning to get out to the house. I'm glad you stopped by." Amazingly he was. Even if it could be dangerous. No one else had questioned Patrick's subtle ongoing personality changes, but Alex always seemed to look deeper than anyone else.

"Julie's been by fairly often," the old man said as Nathan discreetly backed out of the office and closed the door. "I was hoping you would come with her."

"We thought we might come out this weekend. I didn't realize you'd be up and about, able to leave the house."

Alex smiled, gouging grooves in his thin cheeks that had once been dimples. "Amazing, isn't it? The doctor says it's some sort of medical phenomenon. He wants to write it up in one of his journals."

Val just nodded. "You know what they say, the Lord works in mysterious ways." It was all he could think of to say. He certainly couldn't admit his part in the old man's recovery. He was happy to give the credit to God, who rarely got as much as He deserved.

"Shirl says Julie isn't in."

"She's out with a client. She'll be sorry she missed you."

Alex studied him in that shrewd way of his. "Maybe it's for the best. I really came to see you." He leaned back in his wheelchair, an imposing figure even in his weakened condition. "What are your intentions toward her, Patrick?"

Val blinked several times. "I beg your pardon?"

"You heard me. I asked you about your intentions. Do you plan to marry the girl?"

Marriage. The thought had never crossed his mind. Of course he couldn't marry her. He couldn't marry anyone. He was leaving, returning to Toril.

"I realize you're concerned about her, but I think that's a matter best left to Julie and me."

The old man grunted. "That's what I thought. You haven't the least intention of marriage. You wanted her in your bed. You have for years. As soon as you tire of her—"

"You're wrong, Father. We haven't talked about it, but if I could marry Julie, I would."

A thick white eyebrow shot up. "You're saying you're in love with her?"

He didn't want to say it out loud. He had only just faced the fact himself, but he owed Patrick's father the truth. "Yes. Unfortunately, at present, marriage isn't an option."

"Why the devil not?"

Val sighed. "Business reasons. Brookhaven is still up in the air. Money is tight. Besides, I'm not even sure Julie would marry me if I asked her."

Alex didn't respond to that. He seemed to be studying Patrick's face. "Thank you for your honesty," he finally said. "I was worried about her, is all. From now on, I'll leave things up to the two of you."

Val simply nodded.

"You've changed since your heart attack," Alex said. "Mostly for the better."

"Mostly?"

He chuckled. "There are times these days you're a

bit too serious, but other than that…" He reached out and clasped his son's hand. "I'm proud of you, son. I wanted you to know that. It takes a damned big man to turn his life around the way you have."

An odd lump rose in Val's throat. Patrick would have loved to have heard those words. "Thank you, Father. You'll never know how much that means." It would have meant the world to Patrick. Oddly, it seemed important to Val, as well.

"Well, I suppose I had better be going. I still get tired fairly easily."

"As I said, I'm glad you came." Patrick opened the door and Nathan stepped back in.

"Ready to go?" Alex nodded to his nurse, who grasped the handles of the wheelchair, whirled him around as if he were weightless, and shoved him effortlessly out the door.

He grinned at Patrick over one gargantuan shoulder. "Take care, my man."

"Will do," Val said and watched them till they disappeared. Still Alex's frail image lingered, their conversation returning again to mind. *Marriage. Bonding with Julie.* It wasn't possible. Yet the thought tormented him. He would be leaving soon, returning to Toril. It was past time he took a mate, yet how could he bond with a female on Toril when his true life mate was a woman he had known here on Earth?

He wished Alex Donovan had never brought up the subject. Perhaps he could have left without the notion ever occurring. Perhaps it wouldn't have tortured him as he knew it would now.

For the next two hundred and fifty years.

* * *

Standing in the entry of her Malibu beach house, Julie opened the door and was surprised to see Owen on the porch. She motioned for him to come in. It was six o'clock in the evening. She had come home from work early to change and meet Patrick for dinner, "someplace special," he had said. Her expensive tapestry and leather overnight bag sat packed and ready on the sofa for the night she would be spending at Patrick's apartment.

"Good evening, Julie." Owen walked farther into the room. He was dressed casually, in beige slacks and a pale blue rib-knit sweater, his light brown hair still damp near the collar, as if he had hurried over as soon as he got out of the shower.

"I was just going to call you. I found your message on the machine. I was hoping you had uncovered something on Sandini and McPherson."

His gaze darted to the overnight bag. She couldn't miss his frown of disapproval. "Going somewhere?"

Her lips tightened. "I'm sure you can guess where I'm going." She sighed. "I realize you disapprove of my involvement with Patrick, Owen, but that's my business, not yours."

"I just don't want to see you get hurt."

"Everything involves a certain amount of risk. I'm willing to take the chance."

"Perhaps you won't be, once you hear what I've learned."

Julie eyed him warily. She was hoping he wouldn't uncover Patrick's connection to Sandini and McPherson. Obviously he had. She should have known better than to involve him. Owen was nothing if not thorough.

"So what did you come up with?"

He tossed a manila file folder down on the light pine table next to the sofa. "They're heavy-duty players, just like you said. They're headquartered in Chicago."

"Chicago?"

"That's right. They've got underworld connections, Julie. Big-time underworld connections. Patrick is in very deep with these boys and they don't take that lightly. These fellows play for keeps."

"Y-you're not saying Patrick might be in some sort of danger."

"I'm saying he's in trouble. He was from the moment he got involved with those two men. Patrick owes them money—big money—and they mean to see it paid back."

Julie wanted to reach for the file but her hands had started shaking and she didn't want Owen to see. "What...what will happen if he can't?"

"I can only tell you this—you don't get involved with men like that—not if you want to stay healthy. And you don't play games. If you do, you're going to lose."

Julie said nothing. She had known there was more to the story than Patrick had told her. Now she knew what it was. He didn't have the money to repay his debt and he wasn't going to help them defraud the Teachers' Pension Fund. He was pitting himself against them, and in doing so, he was putting himself in danger.

Dear God, he could get himself killed!

She let her unsteady hand fall to her side, nervously smoothed down her skirt. "Thank you for telling me, Owen. At least now I understand what's going on."

He came forward, reached out and gripped her shoulders. "Patrick's no good for you. He never has been. Can't you see that?"

"Patrick's not involved the way you think. He simply owes them money. He's different now, Owen. He's a changed man, a good man. And the truth is, I'm in—"

He shook her, breaking off the sentence before she could finish. "Don't say it, damn you. You want to love someone, love me. I'll take care of you, see you have everything you've ever wanted—clothes, jewels, furs. We'll travel together, visit countries all over the world. Can Patrick give you that? No! All you'll get from Patrick Donovan are headaches and a broken heart." He pulled her toward him, brought his mouth crushing down over hers.

He was a big man, tall and thickly built, a handsome man in an older, more mature fashion, yet she felt not the slightest spark. She tried to turn away but Owen caught her chin and held her immobile, forcing his tongue into her mouth, determined to make her respond.

She finally went still, passive and cold in his arms, and Owen ended the kiss. He was breathing hard, staring at her with hot, dark eyes. They were filled with anger and accusation.

"Why him and not me?" he ground out, his voice thick and hoarse.

"I'm sorry, Owen. I value your friendship, but I'm not interested in anything more."

A muscle ticked in his cheek. "You'll be sorry for this. You need me, Julie. Someday you'll figure that out. When you do, I might not still be waiting." He grabbed the file off the table, turned and stormed out of the house, his shoes clomping over the flagstones in the entry.

Julie watched him leave, a tight knot twisting in her stomach. Patrick had tried to warn her but she wouldn't listen. Now she had lost a friend and she doubted she would ever get him back. Not unless she was willing to change his role from friend to lover and invite him into her bed.

Her thoughts careened to Patrick, the man who filled that place in her life now. Was he really in danger? Was there some way she could help him?

Julie was determined to try.

It started with a tangle in her hair. Not just a few knotted strands but a snarl of long blond hair at the back of her neck that Laura worked on for more than ten minutes trying to smooth out.

Standing in front of the mirror in the bathroom of the condo Brian had rented for their romantic weekend at Lake Arrowhead, she cursed the snarl, wondering where it had come from. Last night she and Brian hadn't even made love. They had been so tired after a day of hiking and boating, after a four-course dinner at a place called Casual Elegance, one of the best restaurants in town, they had curled up in front of the fire in each others' arms and fallen immediately asleep.

Brian had awakened before midnight and carried her into the bedroom. He had helped her undress. She'd crawled into bed, curled up in his arms, and quickly gone back to sleep. A deep sleep, she recalled. Undisturbed. Both of them enjoying the intimacy that had nothing to do with sex. She had slept in one of his old faded T-shirts, wound her heavy blond hair into a single thick curl and pinned it on top of her head.

So where had the tangled knot come from?

It bothered her for some reason, chewed on her mind all morning, distracted her through breakfast. She sat across from Brian in the kitchen, at a small Formica table in the corner of the sunny yellow room. They were eating the scrambled eggs and bacon he had surprised her by cooking, but her mind kept returning to the snarl she had found in her hair.

A memory began to unravel, to free itself much like the knotted strands she had finally managed to untangle, a memory of her and Brian in bed. Of peaceful dreams that faltered, shattered by the faint, scraping, invasive sound of intruders.

Laura swallowed a bite of her eggs, but this time they wouldn't go down. She half rose out of her chair, her eyes no longer seeing Brian's handsome, beardless face, but something else. Something that had happened last night, something she was only beginning to recall.

"Laura?" Brian leaned toward her across the table. "Honey, are you all right?"

She didn't answer, just stood staring, seeing the inside of the spacecraft, hearing the echo of unfamiliar sounds, feeling the Visitors gathered around her.

"You were sleeping," she whispered. "We both were. Such a peaceful sleep. I don't remember ever feeling more content." She moistened her lips. They felt dry and rough. "That's when the Visitors came."

Brian's fork clattered loudly onto his plate. "Laura, my God. Don't tell me you believe—"

"I tried to wake you up, but I couldn't," she continued as if he hadn't spoken. "I couldn't wake you, no matter how hard I tried." She turned her head from side to side, making her long blond hair swirl around her face. "I was so frightened. It was like you were dead but I knew that you weren't."

Brian just sat there, too stunned to speak. Laura sat trembling in her chair. "They were here in the condo. I remember now. They came while we were sleeping."

Brian tried to pull himself together, to force the dumbstruck look from his face. "Laura, that's absurd. I was here. I was lying right beside you."

She numbly shook her head. "I told you, you didn't wake up. They must have done something to you, made it so you kept on sleeping."

"This is insane."

"I know. I know it's insane, but that's what happened. I remember them lifting me up, taking me into the ship. I remember that room, the rounded metallic walls, the eerie blue glow of the lights. I remember the sounds—the whir of machinery, the icy touch of metal against my skin."

Brian just sat there. He looked defeated as she had never seen him. Still, she went on, unable to stop the words from spilling past her lips.

"It was the same as before, and yet it was different. I was afraid at first. I struggled, but it did no good. I remember my hair had come down and tangled itself around my neck. I was perspiring, the dampness seeping into the strands. One of them approached the table I was lying on. A female, I think. She didn't speak out loud, yet I knew what she was trying to say. *Don't be afraid. We don't want to hurt you. We just want to learn.* The fear began to ease. My thundering heart began to slow. I knew where I was. I knew what was happening, what they wanted. I was angry. I felt invaded, violated. But I was no longer afraid."

Brian reached over and took her hand. His fingers felt icy cold, colder even than her own. "I wish I could believe you, Laura—God knows I do. But I can't. As a psychiatrist, I can think of a dozen disorders that might explain these sorts of delusions. As your lover and a man who cares deeply about you, I simply want to help you in any way I can."

Laura's eyes swung to his. "You can help me by opening your mind to the possibility that what I'm telling you might be the truth."

He only shook his head. "I wish I could, honey. I was there, remember? If you had been taken, I would have known."

"Or it might be that you were just not meant to know."

His grip on her fingers tightened. "I suppose I could grant you that." He lifted her hand and pressed his mouth against her knuckles, which were so tight they looked pale. "We'll go home this afternoon. After…last night…I don't imagine you're interested in spending another evening up here."

Laura simply nodded. She didn't want to be there—no. But more than that, she wished she hadn't told him. She was falling in love with Brian Heraldson, and she knew without doubt her continued belief that she had been abducted would destroy any love he might feel in return, cut it out as cleanly as if it had been surgically removed.

"I don't think they'll come for me again," Laura said, her eyes not quite meeting his. She got up from the table, her half eaten plate of eggs cold now, congealed in an ugly yellow lump on her plate. "They've learned what they needed to know. From now on they're going to leave me alone."

It was a lie. She had no idea what the Visitors meant to do, but whatever it was, she wouldn't tell Brian about it.

Not if she didn't want to lose him.

He gently caught her shoulders. "Do you really believe that, Laura?"

"I felt it when I was with them. I felt that my part in this was over."

The darkness in his features eased. Brian's mouth curved up, as if hope for them had just been resurrected. "That's good, honey. That's wonderful." He pulled her into his arms, held her tightly against him.

Laura said nothing, wishing the lie were true. As far as Brian was concerned it *was* true. No matter what happened, no matter what they did, she would never speak to Brian of the Visitors again.

Worry made Julie irritable that Tuesday. For the past three days, she had been thinking of Patrick and his involvement with Sandini and McPherson. She hadn't told him what Owen had discovered. Patrick had been trying to protect her, to keep her from worrying, the way she was right now.

Besides, what good would it do? It wouldn't change what he had decided to do. The right thing, the honest thing. They simply had to find a way to protect him from his two unscrupulous business associates.

To that end, she was now in the study of his penthouse apartment, having gone to dinner with him last night and stayed over, as she did as often as she could. Patrick had left for work early. He had a meeting with Fred Thompkins about the listing Fred had taken on the old Flynn estate. He'd made love to her before he left, kissed her, and left her snuggled in the middle of the bed, taking advantage of a morning free of her usual myriad appointments.

Then the notion had struck: Perhaps there was something of importance in his study, something Patrick had overlooked that in some way might help them. She didn't think he would mind her intrusion. As far as she knew, there were very few secrets between them.

Still dressed in her robe, she rummaged through the low, sleek black teakwood secretary behind the desk in his home office, then through the two tall file cabinets over in the corner. Nothing exciting. She felt a little guilty going through the personal items in his desk drawers, but she rationalized that it was for his own good and if she didn't find anything that would help, he would never know the difference.

The middle drawer was locked.

She tugged on it a couple of times just to be sure, then knelt down and studied the lock, saw that it was a simple device she could probably open with the fingernail file in her purse.

She chewed her bottom lip, guilt trickling through her for real this time. Breaking into Patrick's private locked files was definitely going over the line, but if she were going to help him she needed to know every minor detail of what he was involved in. So far she had seen only the documents he kept at the office, which made no mention at all of the money Patrick owed or the names Sandini or McPherson.

She went for her purse, dug out the nail file and used the sharp, pointed end to turn the lock on his desk drawer. The drawer rolled open. Inside she found the file she'd been looking for, a manila folder marked simply *BROOK-HAVEN*. Julie smiled triumphantly and flipped it open.

Scanning the contents, she carefully read the details of Patrick's loan—eleven million three hundred thousand dollars. Not exactly small change. Then again, the old Patrick had never thought about money in anything but very large terms.

Julie read on, saw that the debt was payable at an astounding twenty percent interest, as well as a percentage of ownership of the project, which increased in proportion to the length of time the loan remained unrepaid. There was a copy of the deed given in lieu of foreclosure Patrick had signed over to the Westwind Corporation just before his heart attack, copies of notes, agreements, everything that wasn't in the file at the office.

Julie read through the contents again, searching carefully for something that might help, blew out a frustrated breath, and closed the file. She knew it all now, every gruesome detail, knew that Patrick had sold his soul to the devil to build Brookhaven and try to make the project work.

And nothing she read gave her the slightest clue as to how she might be able to help him—since she didn't, at present, have eleven million dollars conveniently on hand.

Julie sighed as she leaned forward, intent on shoving the file back into the drawer, but something blocked the way. Reaching down, she pulled out a leather-bound volume, a five-by-seven inch notebook, smooth red leather, bordered with a thin line of gold.

It was a journal, she saw as she cracked it open, the lines on each page penned neatly in what appeared to be Patrick's own hand.

She meant to put it back, she really did. She didn't intend to snoop through Patrick's personal ramblings, but her name, appearing as it did on the page that had fallen open, drew her eye unerringly, gripping her and refusing to let go.

The words didn't make sense. None of it made any sense. Not at first. Not until she turned to the first page and began to read from the beginning. Even then she couldn't seem to grasp the meaning of what was written with such precision on the lined white pages.

She sank down in the chair behind Patrick's desk, studying the entries, one for each day, beginning the day Patrick had returned home from the hospital. She had to start over several times, unable to absorb what was written, unable to fit the words together to make any kind of sense. Refusing to accept it when she did.

It was insane. Impossible. Some sort of sick delusion, the same kind of alien fantasy her sister was experiencing.

But that thought only added to her confusion, for in the journal Patrick spoke at length of Laura's abduction, and the date at the top of the page was prior to the first time Laura had mentioned it. How could he possibly have known?

Julie's hand trembled so badly she dropped the notebook. She picked it up and set it down on the desk, closed it for several long, mind-dead seconds. Then she opened it again and forced herself to continue to read.

Humans experience their world in a different way than we do. They are governed by feelings, not logic. They are not objective in the same manner we are. It went on to talk about violence among humans and individual rights, a strange and frightening treatise, made even more terrifying by the story unfolding on the pages.

Entries that claimed Patrick wasn't Patrick at all. That he was part of some terrible conspiracy that revolved around the horrifying experiences Laura claimed to have suffered. And in the journal, those experiences included Julie—just as her sister had said.

Oh, my God.

She turned off her cell phone and spent the next two hours reading and rereading the journal. She tried to tell herself it wasn't real, that Patrick and Laura had both contracted some sort of mental disorder. Then she thought of the way Patrick had changed, become a different man since his heart attack.

The journal explained it all, even his odd behavior: his nocturnal sleeplessness, his bizarre tastes in food, his sexual inexperience. She thought of the strange terminology he sometimes used. Even his features looked different, sterner somehow, more manly than he had looked before.

It couldn't be real, yet what if it was?

Suddenly she had to know the truth.

She was almost ready to go. She had showered and applied her makeup before going into Patrick's study. Now she tossed off her robe and hurriedly put on her clothes, barely able to fasten the hooks on her bra with her hands shaking so badly. She tried to step into the skirt of the crisp white linen suit she had brought to wear to the office, but her knees were trembling so badly she had to sit down to put it on.

She finished dressing then paused in front of the mirror, her face looking even paler against the white of her linen suit. Adding an extra dash of blush never occurred to her. She just wanted to see Patrick—or Valenden—or whatever his name really was. She had to know if what the journal said could possibly be true.

Stuffing the notebook beneath her arm, she headed out the door, her hands so unsteady she dropped the car keys twice on the way to his parking garage. She nearly flooded the engine before she got the damned car started. She threw the Mercedes into reverse, shot backward out of the space, then slammed the brakes on too hard and jerked herself forward against the seat belt, knocking the air out of her lungs.

"Calm down, Julie," she said out loud. "You've got to get there in one piece if you want to get this whole thing straightened out." As if that could actually happen.

She dragged in two deep breaths and slowly, purposely released them. Her hands calmed a little. She put the car in drive, drove through the garage at a moderate speed and out onto the street.

It didn't take long to reach the office. She parked in her usual spot at the rear of the building and turned off the engine, but couldn't find the courage to open the door and get out. Patrick's Porsche was parked in the lot not far away. He was in there. A Patrick she didn't really know.

Or a man from another world.

It couldn't be true. Her logical, functioning mind knew that, yet the pieces fit so neatly together, everything Laura had said—confirmed. And explained in detail in Patrick's journal.

Her head tipped forward till it rested on the steering wheel. "God, please help me get through this." What-

ever she discovered, it wasn't going to be good. Not unless Patrick knew nothing at all about the journal, and
recognizing his writing as she had, even that would be
hard to believe.

She got out of the car and crossed the parking lot, entering the back door as quietly as she could and making
her way directly to his office, grateful no one had seen her
come in. She could only imagine the look on her face—
terror, sheer, stark terror. And a pain that ran soul-deep.

What if all of it were true?

It was impossible. Surely. There had to be some other
explanation.

Patrick glanced up as she walked in without knocking and quietly closed the door.

He smiled. "Julie…" Then he saw her face. "My
God, what's wrong?" He was out of his chair in a heartbeat, worried about her, ready to help, strong, purposeful, determined.

Everything he never was before.

Julie's gaze met his and her whole body went rigid.
"Stay where you are. Don't…don't come near me,
Patrick."

He frowned darkly, digging deep lines across his
forehead. Then he saw the journal she still clutched
under her arm.

"Julie…"

She held it up with a trembling hand. "Explain it,
Patrick. Tell me this is some sick joke of yours. Tell me
none of this is real. That you made it all up."

Patrick said nothing.

"Are you crazy, Patrick? Are you insane?"

He stiffened, tension making his broad shoulders

look even wider. He took a deep breath and slowly released it, his eyes still fixed on her face. Resignation settled over his features. "No."

Julie's throat went tight, a hard lump rising, part of it anger, some of it fear. "If you aren't crazy, then I must be. This can't be real. Laura was never abducted. There is no such place as Toril."

He said nothing. The silence was so deep, the air between them filled with such clarity she knew in that moment the journal was real.

"Oh, my God."

"I'm sorry," he said gently. "In life, there are always things that are bigger than we want to believe. Frightening things. Things we don't understand. I hoped you would never know the truth. I hoped you would never find out."

"It—it can't be the truth. It isn't possible."

"I'm afraid, love, that it is."

She moved her head from side to side, trying to deny it when his eyes said clearly that the things in the notebook were true. There was pain there, too, she saw, and regret and something else she could not name.

"Who are you?"

"My name is Valenden Zarkazian. I'm commander of the science wing on board my ship, the *Ansor*. But I imagine you know that already. I imagine you read it in my journal."

Her mouth felt dry. Feathery dry, parched until her lips would barely move. "I read it. I read it over and over and over. I couldn't make myself believe it. I didn't want to believe it."

"I know it's hard. I realize—"

She held up a trembling hand, shaking her head at the same time, unwilling to hear the words. "Did…did you kill him? Did you murder Patrick Donovan?"

His grim expression darkened even more. He firmly shook his head. "No."

"I don't…don't believe you."

"It's complicated, Julie. If you'll give me a chance, I'll try to explain what this is all about." He took a step toward her.

Julie backed away. "You want me to listen to you? Why should I? I don't even know who you are—*what* you are. When I think of the way I let you touch me…of the things we did in bed…it makes my skin crawl."

He reached out to her, trying to stop the hateful words. "Don't, Julie, please. I'm begging you—give me a chance to explain."

Adrenaline rushed into the pit of her stomach. "You can explain it to the authorities. I'm sure there is someone in the government who'll be interested to learn what you and your friends have been doing."

"Don't be a fool. You know as well as I do that no one will believe you."

She lifted the notebook above her head, turned, and jerked open the door. "You forget, Patrick—or whatever your name is—this time there's proof." She waved the notebook. "I've got your journal."

She started to walk out of the office, but the doorknob twisted out of her fingers and the door slammed closed in front of her. The notebook felt hot in her hands, then suddenly jerked upward and flew across the room. Patrick neatly captured it between his waiting hands.

She was shaking all over. She turned to stare at the

closed door that once more barred her way. "Am I…am I your prisoner?"

"Good, God, no!" The doorknob turned and the door swung gently open. "That was little more than a parlor trick. You can leave whenever you wish. I was only trying to protect you." He looked at her and this time she didn't turn away. "There is only one thing I ask before you go."

"What's that?" she whispered, the adrenaline beginning to fade, the ache of loss returning to take its place. The Patrick she had loved was gone. Lost to her forever. In truth he had never existed.

"Before you walk out that door, I want you to consider all the things we've shared. If you ever felt anything for me, if you ever cared for me in the least, give me a chance to explain."

Julie raised her head and looked him straight in the face. "Goodbye, Patrick." She couldn't seem to stop calling him that. Dear God, she had loved him so much. It didn't really matter. Nothing did. The world was nothing as she had perceived it. It never would be again.

She walked through the door and he made no move to stop her.

Her legs felt wooden but she forced herself to walk away, out into the hallway, outside into the sunshine. It should have warmed her, but it didn't. Her heart felt encased in ice. Her stomach felt leaden. She didn't know where to go, where to turn.

He was right. No one would believe her. Everyone would think she was crazy. She had read volumes of books and dozens upon dozens of articles. No one would believe her story held a grain of truth.

No one but Laura.

For the first time in all of her twenty-nine years, Julie needed her sister. Laura was the only person on earth who could possibly understand.

Nineteen

Val hunched over his desk, his elbows propped on top, his head hanging down. He raked his hands through his hair, but it tumbled forward again, forming a stubborn curl over his forehead.

He had been sitting this way for nearly an hour, his heart throbbing dully, feeling sick to his stomach. Every time he closed his eyes he could see Julie standing in the doorway, his journal clutched under her arm. He could see her pale face, stricken with grief and fear. He could remember the way she had looked at him—as if he were some kind of monster. Or perhaps some kind of bug.

Poetic justice, they called it—since that was the way he had first looked at her.

Someone knocked at the door, and Val lifted his head. "What is it?"

The door swung wide and Shirl Bingham stuck her head through the opening. "Are you all right, Patrick? You've been ignoring the intercom for almost an hour. I thought maybe—"

"I'm fine. I just had some things to go over." He stood up, shoving back his chair, the wheels banging sharply against the side of his desk. "I'll be out for a while. You can reach me at home later."

Shirl eyed him with concern. "Are you sure you're all right? You don't look so good."

A corner of his mouth curved faintly but he couldn't make himself smile. "Thanks."

"You know what I mean. I was thinking maybe your heart…"

"My heart is fine." But of course his heart wasn't fine at all. It was broken. He had read the term and now he understood it, and it was even more painful than the words implied. His heart had been sliced neatly in two by a fiery little redhead with the courage to confront him with the truth.

Val left the office, sick with despair and regret. He didn't go home, drove instead up into the Hollywood hills, the top down on the Porsche and the wind whipping his hair, the sun beating down on his face. Thick white clouds floated above his head, cumulous clouds whose beauty until today never failed to make him smile.

Today, not even the perfect California weather could soothe his turbulent emotions. He had lost someone dear to him, and the sort of grief Julie had felt when Alex fell ill had seeped into his bones. He was worried about her but he knew she wouldn't let him help her. He felt frustrated and angry, and more alone than he had ever felt before.

For the first time since his arrival on Earth, Val wished for the quiet serenity of Toril.

* * *

Julie sat across the tiny kitchen table in Laura's Venice Beach apartment, her icy fingers wrapped around a flowered coffee mug, its contents long ago grown cold.

"I still can't believe it," Julie said.

Laura reached over and gently squeezed her arm. "I know what you mean. I still can't believe any of this is real, but in my heart I know it is."

"I'm sorry I didn't believe you."

"It's all right. It isn't something that's easy to believe."

Julie sighed, her breath whispering out to mingle with the air in the steamy kitchen. "No it isn't. But I kept reading things, articles in magazines and newspapers that made me think UFOs might be real. So many people claim to have seen them. Half the population believes they exist—did you know that? Half the people in the United States believe UFOs are real, but I just couldn't convince myself. I didn't want to. The truth is I was afraid."

Laura said nothing.

"I feel sick, Laura. Sick and angry and scared. I feel like I should tell someone, the military, maybe, or the police, the FBI—someone. I feel like I ought to do something, but I don't know what."

"Haven't you figured it out yet? There's nothing you *can* do. Not unless you want to put yourself through the kind of agony I've been through. And even if you do, it won't do any good. No one is going to believe you."

"I wonder if they know…the government, I mean. I wonder if they're keeping this all a terrible secret."

"Why don't you ask *him*?"

"Who?"

"Patrick."

Julie shook her head. "There is no Patrick. The Patrick I fell in love with doesn't exist. He never did."

Laura sighed as she got up from her chair and left the room, returning a few minutes later with a box of Kleenex she dropped in the middle of the table. Julie didn't realize she was crying till Laura jerked out a tissue and handed it over.

Julie took it with a look of gratitude and dabbed it against her eyes. "I loved him, Laura. I loved him so much."

"I think he loved you, too."

Julie's head came up behind the tissue. "You're crazy. The man is some kind of creature from another world."

"Maybe he is. Or at least that's what they seem like to us. Especially to me. But the last time I saw them, something changed."

"What do you mean, *the last time*? You're not saying they've taken you again?"

Laura nodded and glanced away. "At Arrowhead. That's the reason we came home early."

"Oh, dear God."

"It was different this time, though. This time, they tried to comfort me, tried to make me understand what it was they wanted."

"You saw the leaders, the superiors? What…what did they look like?" Unconsciously, she shivered. God, she didn't really want to know.

"I didn't see the leaders. I've never seen them. I just felt their presence. They're trying to learn about us, Julie. From what you've said, that's the reason Valenden is here."

"I don't care why he's here. I hate him for what he has done."

"You love him."

"Are you insane? He's a monster."

"Is he? He's in love with you. You could see it in his face whenever he looked at you. I don't think Patrick Donovan was capable of that kind of love. And I think this person, Valenden…I think maybe he is."

Her throat hurt, ached and ached and fresh tears rolled down her cheeks. "How can you say that? He isn't even human."

"Patrick was human, and in his own way I think he cared for you. But he never looked at you the way this man does. He never cared enough to be true to you. I couldn't figure it out. It didn't fit with the Patrick I knew. But if Patrick is partly this other person, this Commander Zarkazian, it all makes an odd kind of sense."

Julie's shoulders sagged. "God, I wish it did."

Laura reached out and gripped her hand. "You have to talk to him. You said he didn't kill Patrick. You said he wanted to explain. Aren't you the least bit curious what he might have to say?"

The mug clattered noisily against the table. Julie looked her square in the face. "I can't believe I'm hearing this. I'm his experiment, for God's sake. What can he possibly have to say?"

"If he's in love with you, maybe he isn't really so different. Not deep down inside."

For the longest time Julie didn't answer. Her voice was locked in her throat and even if she could have spoken, she wouldn't have known what to say.

"I'm frightened, Laura." She felt Laura's warm fingers close reassuringly around her hand.

"I know you are. So am I. Talk to him, Julie. If not for your own sake, do it for mine. Can you imagine how desperate I am to learn more about them? How I wish I could make them understand the terrible things they're doing to me and to the others?"

"I—I never thought of it that way."

"You have to do it, Julie. It's important. More important than anything you've ever done before."

"What if he's dangerous or something?"

"You don't believe that. At least you didn't or you wouldn't have fallen in love with him. Give him the chance he's asked for. Listen to what he has to say."

Julie fell silent. Of all the advice she might have expected her sister to give, this was surely not it. What Laura said made sense, more sense than up until now she had given her sister credit for having. But she wasn't ready to face him yet. She needed time to think. To pull herself together.

Whatever he had to say, it couldn't change the fact that her affair with Patrick Donovan was over. Julie needed time to resign herself to the heartbreaking loss she felt every time she closed her eyes and saw Patrick's beloved face.

Tony Sandini leaned his heavy, big-boned frame back against the curved red vinyl seat in the corner booth at Banducci's Ristorante, his favorite local hole in the wall. Ralph Ceccarelli and Jake Naworski sat across from him, Ralph immaculately dressed as usual, Jake rumpled and looking like he had just crawled out of a four-dollar flophouse somewhere.

Tony snapped his blunt fingers and called the waiter over, a little man with a bald head and little pig eyes. When the waiter reached the table, covered by the mandatory red-checked cloth, Tony shoved his empty salad plate toward him and ordered another bottle of Chianti.

He was out on the West Coast mixing a little business with pleasure. After lunch he would return to his fancy suite at the Beverly Wilshire Hotel and the svelte little blonde who would be waiting. He had met her on his last trip out, an airline stew with a taste for the better things in life.

She had just enough moxie and just enough brains to attract his interest—and an ass and tits to hold it past the first two times he had screwed her.

But that was for later. Business came first. It always did.

"Tell me about the Brookhaven deal," he said to the men. "You spoke to Donovan, got everything worked out?"

"Yeah, boss," said Naworski. "We took care of it just like you said."

"He'll do as he's told," Ceccarelli added. "He doesn't want his pretty face mashed in and he's smart enough to know that's exactly what he'll get if he doesn't do his part."

Or worse, Tony silently added. He wasn't about to let pretty-boy Patrick Donovan off the hook till he'd repaid every dime he owed, no matter what it took. "Things seem like they're movin' kinda slow. You talked to that Bonham woman lately?"

"Donovan's supposed to meet with her this week,"

Jake said. "That guy could charm a nun out of her drawers. Them teachers'll be eatin' outta his hand."

"Jake's right," Ceccarelli agreed. "With Donovan backing the sale of those notes, the deal's as good as done."

"Good. I want this whole thing wrapped up as soon as you can get it done. Once the money's in, Westwind can take the fall. Just make sure there's no way they'll be able to connect the company to me."

"No problem, boss."

"And keep an eye on Donovan. There's something about that guy that bothers me."

"It's his conscience," Ceccarelli grumbled. "Donovan's got one and he's the kinda guy who can let it get in his way."

"See that he doesn't," Tony warned, digging into the plate of linguini and eggplant parmigiana the waiter had just set in front of him. The aroma drifted up and his mouth started to water. God, he loved this place. Food was almost as good as his mama's.

As they ate, Tony's thoughts returned to the blonde he would be screwing after lunch. The image gave him a slight erection and he only ate half what he usually put away.

He chuckled to himself. He'd fuck Patrick Donovan real good, too, if the bastard even thought about screwing him over.

Tony laughed as he finished his tiramisu.

Val pulled the Porsche into the parking garage and just sat there staring through the windshield. He had been driving for hours, trying to clear his head, trying to find some way out. Nothing had come to him. All he felt now was numb.

It took several moments in the deep leather seat before he felt the vibration of the small communications device in his pocket. Pulling it out, he slid open the lid and began to read the transmission. It came from Calas Panidyne, a live feed of the High Council meeting that he had entirely forgotten about.

Damn! He had been so fatigued after transportation to the last council meeting, it had been decided this was a safer procedure. With his thought in turmoil over Julie, the meeting had completely slipped his mind.

Val replied that he was receiving the transmission clearly and would be happy to respond to any questions the council might have.

As highest ranking of the ten members in the group, Calas Panidyne began the session. Val was only mildly surprised when he started by stating that Val had made entirely too little progress during his time on Earth.

One of the ministers disagreed. The transmission read: *Commander Zarkazian is one of the most highly regarded scientists on Toril. The assignment he has undertaken is not only perilous but difficult in the extreme. In a world heretofore unknown to him, it is only natural his progress would be hard to measure. I for one have found the information he has been sending infinitely enlightening. I have begun to understand the people of Earth as I never have before.*

And the rest of you? Panidyne asked. *Do all of you feel that way?*

A female council member responded. *I certainly do, but I am concerned for the commander's safety. No one*

*has undergone Unification for such an extended period
of time. I think the sooner he is returned aboard the* Ansor,
the less chance there is that something may go wrong.

Panidyne agreed. *As a matter of fact, I noticed several behavioral changes in Commander Zarkazian
when he was last aboard. At the time I ignored them, but
now, as you say, his safety may warrant a quicker end
to his mission.*

The council member's reply held a note of sarcasm,
*Which of course has nothing to do with the fact you
would like to bring the Ferris female back aboard the
ship for more testing.*

Val's stomach knotted. Panidyne was fierce in his
quest for knowledge, even more fierce than Val.

*It would seem the most expedient way to accomplish
our mission.*

*But as the commander has several times pointed out,
it is also extremely hazardous for the woman.*

Panidyne made no reply. Instead, his transmission
read, *Your comments, Commander?*

Val took a deep breath, knowing how important this
was. They already had his most current report, which
had been sent from his apartment yesterday afternoon.
Reporting to the council during their session was strictly
a formality, yet it couldn't be dispensed with. And
somehow transmitting live gave him the opportunity to
explain matters that were difficult to express in a for-
mal report.

Cracking open the journal that lay on the seat beside
him, Val reviewed events to the present date, omitting
only the confrontation he'd had with Julie.

One of the council members transmitted the moment

he had finished. *All of us have been properly impressed, Commander, with the information you have gathered. But some of us, including First Council Panidyne, feel your have not sufficiently succeeded in your original assignment—finding out why the subject under study, as well as a number of others before her, were able to resist our highly sophisticated scanning equipment. First Council Panidyne suggests your return and a resumption of testing on the Ferris subject, and many of us concur. No.*

We are concerned for your safety, Panidyne replied. *Unification for this length of time is bound to have certain side effects. None of us know exactly what they are. We suggest you end your mission and let us bring the woman back aboard.*

I said no! The symbols flashed across the small screen with the impact of a blow. *You will not bring Julie Ferris back aboard this ship. You will not destroy her or any other human being like her.*

No reply appeared on the screen. He knew they sat there stunned. No one on Toril showed any sort of emotion, any sign of anger, and even though they couldn't see him, it was clear how strongly he felt.

There will be no need for such an action, Val added, hoping it would lessen his harsh words. *I have come to know the subject more intimately than any other being I have ever encountered. I can tell you what is different about her—about the other Earth subjects who have been able to resist the probe. What these people have in common, what makes them so different, is a thing they call determination. It isn't a word Torillians know. It means to be adamant, to assert one's will in the face of any and all adversity. It means having a strength of purpose so strong it can overcome any obstacle in its path. Combine that determination with courage, perhaps a bit of faith, and you have a force to be reckoned with, a power beyond anything a Torillian has ever been faced with.*

The council made no comment and Val's very human heart beat painfully his chest.

I have come to understand this word determination *as the rest of you cannot. I can feel it even now, thrumming through my body, giving me the strength to send this. That determination is driving me to speak when before I would have remained silent. It gives me the will to oppose you when every fiber of my being, every cell in my body has been schooled against it. It tells me I have to convince you the testing of humans must be stopped, that the destruction of people's lives isn't worth the high cost of the knowledge we are obtaining.*

Val sat there behind the wheel, willing them to understand, wishing he had made the journey and stood before them in person. *If I have learned anything at all during my time on Earth, it is that humanity—in all its diverse forms—is too precious to be tampered with. It is not our right to do so any more than it is another life-form's right to tamper with ours.*

He knew what they were thinking, that he was no longer the being they knew, that he was behaving like someone from another world.

Which in fact, he was.

He was no longer simply Val Zarkazian. He doubted he ever would be again.

The screen lit up. *Your concerns have been noted. Thank you for your comments, Commander.*

The screen went dark. Val hoped the council would remember that their purpose in coming had never been to do harm to the people of Earth.

He thought of the council members, both male and female, he had worked with for dozens of years. They seemed unfamiliar to him now, as foreign as Patrick's penthouse apartment had once seemed. By now the members knew that something about him had changed. Silently he cursed. The fact that he was angry and frustrated showed him how different he actually had become.

Val wondered if that change would enable his colleagues to see what he had been so desperately trying to make them understand.

Julie phoned Laura as soon as she had showered and dressed the next morning. It was earlier than usual. She hadn't been to bed at all last night, had if fact barely slept for the past three days.

At that early hour, Laura's voice sounded groggy and strained. "Hello?"

"Wake up, sleepyhead. Get out of bed and get dressed. Yesterday I closed a big fat escrow and today we're going to spend the money."

"What are you talking about?"

"I'm talking about shopping. You know, shop till you drop? Never say die till the stores are closed?"

"Shopping? Julie, have you gone insane?"

"The whole world's insane. No one knows that better than you and me. All I want is a day—just one single day—to forget how crazy the whole world is."

Laura went silent. If Julie had hoped to hide the misery her jovial words were meant to disguise she must have failed mightily.

"If that's what you want," her sister said softly, "then that's what we'll do."

And so they had the valet at the Beverly Wilshire park Julie's Mercedes and Laura's aging Volkswagen bug, and set off down the sidewalk. The sun was out, but a stiff wind shoved papers along the street. It looked as if a storm was moving in. Shouldering their way through the crowd of Saturday shoppers, they made their way toward the front doors of Saks Fifth Avenue on Wilshire.

As they passed through the cosmetics department, the fragrance of Bulgari drifted across the counter. Julie had always liked the exotic scent, but today it made her sick to her stomach.

"Are you sure you're all right?" Laura asked as they reached the second floor, her pretty features drawn with worry. "You don't look so good."

Julie tried to smile but it came out forced. "You always did know how to cheer a person up."

Laura rolled her eyes as Julie pasted on a smile and headed for the escalator. An hour later, they had bought three new outfits apiece, including a leaf-green silk skirt and blouse for Laura and a cranberry-red Chanel suit for Julie. They bought half a dozen pairs of Ferragamo shoes, lacy bras and panties, bags, hose and cosmetics.

Laura hefted the heavy shopping bag sitting on the marble floor at her feet. "All right, where to next?"

"Let's put this stuff in the car and just start walking. We'll head down Rodeo Drive, see what looks interesting." Both women's arms overflowed with packages.

Julie could barely see above the stack she held in front of her as they walked back to the car.

"Rodeo Drive? That's pretty pricey, isn't it?"

"What difference does it make? We just bought half the stuff in Saks."

"Saks is one thing. Rodeo Drive is something else."

"I told you money wasn't an object. I said we were going to buy anything we wanted. That's exactly what I intend to do."

"Julie, this is crazy."

"That's what you said when I called."

They went into Gucci, but didn't buy anything, Laura rolling her eyes and confiding to the salesgirl she wasn't really the Gucci type. Then they hit Valentino and Tiffany's, and wound up in a dressing room at La Mode trying on outrageously expensive evening gowns.

Standing in front of a tall oval mirror, Julie smoothed the bodice of a floor-length navy blue silk gown trimmed in matching dark blue sequins. It had narrow straps, a slimming waistline, and a long, slender skirt split up the side to mid-thigh. Except for the hem, which would have to be shortened, the dress fit as though it were made for her.

"Wow, sis, that dress looks absolutely terrific." She frowned. "Tell me you're not going to buy it."

Julie flashed an overbright smile. "Why not? You just told me it looks terrific."

"Come on, Jules. You've never bought a nine-thousand-dollar dress in your life."

Julie ran her fingers over the delicate silk. A slight tremor shook her hand. "Lately my life has changed."

She turned sideways, surveying herself in the mirror. The gown was truly remarkable, setting off her dark red hair and green eyes, not to mention what it did for her figure.

But as she stared at herself in the mirror, all she could think was where would she wear it? Owen Mallory could take her to the kind of places where people wore gowns like these. Patrick would have taken her if she had wanted to go.

But Patrick was no longer there.

Something burned behind her eyes. She was looking at her reflection but her image began to blur and she could no longer make out the beautiful lines and curves. Hot tears welled, began to trickle down her cheeks.

She felt Laura's arm around her shoulders. "Let's go home, okay?"

"I have to talk to him."

"I know you do."

"Today. I have to talk to him today. I have to understand, Laura. I have to know why this is happening to me." *To both of them,* she silently corrected.

Laura just nodded. Julie knew her sister wanted to understand, too. Maybe Patrick could help them both.

Standing like a mannequin, Julie let Laura help her change out of the beautiful silk gown into her brown slacks and cream silk blouse. Once she had slipped back into her loafers and fastened the buckle on her belt, Laura handed her a small gold compact.

"Here. You smudged your mascara."

"Thanks." Julie wiped the black streaks away and ran the powder puff over her red nose and flushed cheeks. She put on fresh lipstick and ran a comb through her hair.

"Thanks for coming today." She glanced up at her sister. "I really needed you."

A good six inches taller, Laura bent and hugged her. "It felt good to be needed, Julie. I'm glad I could help you for a change."

Julie smiled, thinking how much stronger Laura seemed lately. "Let's go get our cars. Then I'm going to see Patrick. I'm going to the office and confront him."

"This isn't going to be easy. I'll go with you if you want."

Julie shook her head. "Thanks, sweetie, but this is something I have to do myself."

Twenty

As luck would have it, Patrick wasn't at the office when Julie arrived. She had been primed to face him, her blood running high, every nerve ending alert. He was out with Fred Thompkins, Shirl said. She wasn't quite sure when he was scheduled to return.

The adrenaline slowly faded, and now as she slumped in the chair behind her desk she just felt nervous and tense. Her mind kept going over the things she had read in the journal, the questions she wanted to ask, the answers he might give. Mostly, she just wanted to see Patrick's face, even if the face wasn't really his.

The light stiletto click of a woman's heels sounded but Julie barely heard it. Then the door slammed open and Babs walked in.

"All right, what the hell have you done to him?"

"Who?" Julie sat up straighter in her chair, trying to gather her wits, but it took a gargantuan effort.

"Patrick. He must have lost ten pounds in the past three days. He isn't sleeping. He barely speaks to anyone. He sure as hell isn't eating. I'm worried about him, Julie. I can't believe I actually feel sorry for the man, but the truth is I do. What in God's name have you done?"

In her flashy magenta pantsuit, her striking features tense, Babs marched across the office. She frowned as she drew near, her sleek black brows pulling together over eyes nearly as dark as her hair.

"On second thought, you don't look a whole lot better than he does. Honey, what the hell is going on?"

Julie shook her head, fighting back tears. "Patrick and I aren't seeing each other any more."

"Yeah, well, I already gathered that. What happened? Was the SOB cheating again?"

"No, Babs, it's nothing like that. I wish it was something that simple."

"So tell me."

She wished she could. God, did she ever wish she could. If she even tried to explain, Babs would think she'd gone over the edge. "We've just…we've just decided to go our separate ways. It's the best thing for both of us."

"Somehow I don't think Patrick would agree with that."

"Please, Babs. You're my very best friend. I'd tell you if I could, but this is something Patrick and I have to work out by ourselves." That was beyond the truth. Telling someone Patrick Donovan was really a man from outer space was a good way to wind up in the loony bin.

Babs cocked her head toward the door, catching the sound of approaching footsteps. "Well, here's your chance. I think he just came in, but I doubt he intends to stay for long. You better hurry if you're going to catch him."

Julie just nodded. Her adrenaline had started pumping again the moment she had heard the rough-smooth cadence of his voice.

Shoving back her chair, she took a deep breath for courage, and walked past Babs into the main part of the office. "Patrick?" It came out high and a little bit squeaky. She cleared her throat. "Patrick, could I have a moment, please?"

His eyes found hers. They were a more intense blue than she had ever seen them. "Of course."

She followed him down to his office, but neither of them took a seat. Finally he motioned her toward one of the black leather chairs in front of his desk. Julie sat down and Patrick took his usual seat in the high-backed leather executive chair across from her, deciding, she supposed, to allow some distance between them.

"I'm glad you came." Leaning forward, he rested his elbows on the desk. "I've been worried about you."

"Have you really?" A brow arched up. "Just because I happened to discover the man I loved is actually an alien from outer space—why would you possibly be worried?"

His mouth curved faintly. She noticed, as Babs had said, there were faint gray smudges beneath his eyes and his cheeks looked hollow and pale.

"Were you?"

"Was I what?"

"In love with me?"

A shot of anger rippled through her. "I was in love with Patrick Donovan. Where is he, by the way? You said you didn't kill him."

He sat back in his chair. "Patrick killed himself. I merely borrowed his body."

The breath whispered out of her lungs. She sagged back against her chair. "Patrick is dead?"

"Not exactly. In a number of ways, Patrick is still here, sitting right in front of you. I'm all the things Patrick was—his memories, his dreams, his likes and dislikes. But I'm also Valenden Zarkazian. I don't live the same life Patrick did. I don't believe in that sort of behavior."

Julie digested that, or at least she tried to. She had read the explanation in his journal, but hearing him say it aloud made her somehow more able to accept it. "I don't know what to call you…Valenden or Patrick?"

"At home I'm mostly called Val, but you've always called me Patrick. I used to love the way you said it…the way you looked at me when you did."

She felt like crying. Dear God, she refused to cry in front of him. "I came here as you asked. To hear what you have to say. I have no idea what will happen after that."

He smiled but there was a sad, regretful twist in the line of his mouth. "I'll tell you whatever I can."

And so he began, telling her first about Toril, about how far away it was from Earth, and how Torillian travelers had long ago discovered Earth's existence. He told her about his life as a scientist, about his research, and that they had been studying the planet for quite some time.

"We had no choice but to come here," he said. "Your technology has gotten way out of hand. Your nuclear discoveries, combined with your interest in space travel, makes Earth a threat to other populations. We need to learn about the people of your planet in order to protect ourselves."

"Space travel—if it ever really happens—is still well into the future. You said yourself that even if we could figure it out, it could be years before we break the light speed barrier. How could we possibly pose a threat?"

"Innovation comes when one least expects it. Think about radio waves and how rapidly their discovery altered communications. Think about computers and cell phones and how they've changed the face of the world. A breakthrough could come at any time. Even now your scientists are working in that direction."

He was talking about Dr. Stover and the charts they had seen on the university walls. NASA wanted to send a manned mission to Mars. Expeditions to other planets might follow. Nothing seemed impossible anymore.

"What about Laura and the others?" she asked, feeling a shot of the old anger. "How could you let your people do those awful things? How could you let them hurt her that way?"

He shook his head. "At first I didn't understand. I was one of them. I believed as they did, that what we were doing was necessary to advance the cause of science. Once I understood, I've tried to make them see how wrong it is. I hope I succeeded, but I'm not really sure."

She could see the regret, the pain, and something softened inside her. "How long…." She fought down the high-pitched note in her voice. "How long will you be here…as Patrick, I mean?"

He looked at her with those blue, blue eyes. "A little over a week. My greatest regret is that I'll have to leave you."

Her heart wrenched hard inside her. "Don't say that…please."

"Why not? It's the truth. I love you, Julie. Until I

came here, I didn't know such a thing existed. Now I can't imagine living life without you."

A thick lump rose in her throat. Her heart beat painfully inside her chest, making an ache swell there. She looked at him and saw Patrick. Patrick's beautiful face. Patrick's lean, hard-muscled body. She saw a man of intelligence, a strong man, a caring man. She saw a man of principle who had gained the respect of the people around him.

"I don't…I don't even know what you look like."

"If you're asking if I have two legs, two arms, two eyes, two ears—the answer is yes I do. Torillians are a mental race, Julie. We're not as physical as you, but in other ways we aren't so far apart."

She swallowed past the tightness in her throat. She hadn't thought seeing him would make her feel this way, but she had been wrong. "It said in your journal that you've grown to like it here, yet you still plan to leave."

He straightened a little in his chair. "Earth is a place of great beauty, of even greater passion. It's unlike anyplace I've ever known, unlike anything I could ever have imagined. I'm fascinated by the strength of its people, by the challenges they face each day and overcome. But my time here is almost ended. I have to go back to Toril. I don't have any other choice."

Her heart ached. His handsome face began to blur. Oh, God, she was going to cry. She blinked to hold back the tears, determined that he would not see. "What…what will happen to Patrick when you're gone?"

Concern darkened his features, regret and something more. "He'll die, Julie. Just as he would have before."

Her eyes slid closed. Tears slipped down her cheeks.

Patrick would die. She would lose him all over again. The thought sent a shaft of agony straight into her heart.

"What about you?" she whispered. "What will happen to you?"

He glanced away, the skin taut over his high cheekbones, pain making his features look harsh. "I'm not sure anymore. Since I came here, everything about me has changed. I can't imagine living a life without bright colors and explosive sounds, without exotic foods and violent storms. In the time I've been here, I've known great joy and great passion, experienced great sorrow. I've learned to feel things I never knew how to feel before."

He shifted in his chair, leaned toward her across the desk. "And there is Patrick. Patrick and I have bonded in a way I never expected. The memories he carries will never leave me. Not through all the days of my life." His eyes came to rest on her face, caressing her almost as if he touched her. "But mostly I'll remember you, Julie. And I will love you always, from the deepest part of my soul."

A sob escaped, a cry of anguish erupting inside her. Without a glance at Patrick, she leapt up from her chair, turned and raced for the door.

"Julie, wait!"

But she didn't stop running. She could hear him calling her, hear his heavy footfalls behind her, but she didn't slow. She raced out of the office, across the parking lot to her car, and jerked open the door. Through a haze of tears, she glanced one final time in his direction, saw him standing alone beside the door.

Her heart tugged painfully, felt like it was tearing itself apart. It took sheer force of will to climb into the car and turn the key, to pull the car into gear and drive away. She felt battered, beaten. Felt as if a great hot stone was burning a hole in her chest. There was no hope for them, yet her mind kept whispering his name, urging her to go to him. Reminding her that in a few brief days he would be gone.

It didn't matter, she told herself. Patrick was already dead. She didn't even know this man. He wasn't even human.

But she couldn't make herself believe it. Instead every time she closed her eyes she saw Patrick telling her his greatest regret was that he would have to leave her. That he would love her always, from the deepest part of his soul.

The storm had finally arrived. It was a day late, much to the weatherman's chagrin, but the ground was so dry and parched the Earth itself seemed grateful for the life-giving moisture.

Julie stared out the big glass windows toward the gray, turbulent sea and the brooding clouds beyond. Wind whipped the waves into white-capped peaks and rattled against the windowpanes. Rain pelted the sand on the beach below, turning it a muddy, discolored brown. Soon the dull edge of light beyond the clouds would fade and without moon or stars the house would be shrouded in blackness.

Thinking of Laura, and of the things she had read in the journal, Julie wondered if she should be afraid.

She felt no fear, only numbness. And the constant ache for Patrick that wouldn't go away. She had thought of him every moment since their confrontation three days ago, had told herself a dozen times that the man she loved was gone from her life for good. Patrick wasn't Patrick. The Patrick Donovan she loved did not exist.

But as she had watched the storm, entranced as always by its dark, majestic power, she couldn't help thinking how Patrick would have chafed at the storm's intrusion, and how the man named Valenden would have loved it.

It occurred to her in a way it hadn't before that it wasn't really Patrick that she had fallen in love with. The best parts of him, perhaps: his physical beauty, his charm and warmth—but the qualities she loved most about him belonged to Val Zarkazian. She wouldn't be drawn to one without the other, but together they were a man unsurpassed by any she had known.

The question nagged—did who he was really matter? The man she had loved was the tenderest, most caring individual she had ever known. He was strong and courageous and deeply committed to helping the people around him.

And she was still in love with him.

God help her, no matter who he was, *what* he was, she loved him still.

Julie leaned her forehead against the cold glass pane, absorbing the chill against her skin. Somewhere inside her, the voice she had heard before rose up, urging her to go to him. It challenged her to shove aside every notion she had ever had of the way her life should be, to bury the prejudice she felt and see instead the gift that she had been given.

It taunted her with memories, goaded her with her pain and loss.

Be as brave as he is, the voice whispered. *Claim the love he has offered for as long as you can.*

She moved her head from side to side against the window, trying to deny the voice, to tell herself she couldn't possibly do such a thing. But as darkness settled over the water, the voice persisted, a hollow, nagging echo inside her head.

Go to him, Julie. You love him. If you don't go you'll regret it for the rest of your life.

Lightning cracked outside the window, a wild, jagged yellow shaft of beauty, glorious to her…as it would be to the man she had loved.

Julie turned away from the window, her heart awakening as if from a deep, mournful sleep, her pulse increasing. Purpose burned through her, her steps more certain than they had been in days. Grabbing the car keys out of the woven straw basket on the table in the hall, she jerked open the closet door and hauled out her rarely used raincoat.

Ten minutes later, she was driving the Pacific Coast Highway, listening to the slap of the windshield wipers against the glass, nervously worrying her bottom lip.

Trying to decide what she could possibly say to a man who came from outer space.

Val stood at the window of his apartment, staring out at the storm. Lightning flashed. A few seconds later, thunder rumbled over the empty streets. As long as he lived, he would never forget the wild pagan beauty of a storm.

Just as he would never forget the woman he had met here on Earth. He thought of her now as he had a dozen times, with a heart that felt heavy inside his chest. He wondered where she was and what she was doing. He wondered if she felt half the awful grief that he did.

And more than anything else, he wished he hadn't hurt her.

At least she was safe for a time. The council had acquiesced to his wishes. They would suspend their testing of humans for the balance of time the *Ansor* remained above Earth.

And soon they would be leaving. As soon as he returned to the ship, they would make whatever final preparations were needed to conclude their research and end their mission. Then the ship would begin its journey home.

Home. Oddly, now that he had lived here, he had a hard time thinking of Toril as home. There was no one there he was eager to return to. He had friends, of course, his biological parents, but there, even close relationships were little more than a comfortable bond.

The door buzzer sounded. A visitor stood downstairs, outside the door to the lobby. Val walked to the intercom panel on the wall and depressed the answer button. "Yes?"

"Patrick?"

His stomach clenched. He knew who it was. "Julie…"

"Could I…could I come up?"

His voice came out husky. "Of course." He depressed the door release, admitting her into the main part of the lobby, then waited impatiently as she rode the elevator to the floor at the top. His heart was throbbing, thumping painfully against his ribs. His mouth felt dry. He hoped he could keep the gruffness out of his voice when he tried to speak.

He was waiting beside the doors when the elevator opened directly inside his top-floor apartment. He stepped back as she walked out, giving her room, worried that he might do something to frighten her.

"It's good to see you," he said, careful to keep a respectful distance between them, wishing he could haul her into his arms. God, he had missed her. "I hope you're feeling better."

"I—I'm fine…Patrick. You did say it was all right to call you that. I have a hard time calling you Valenden."

"To tell you the truth, here I feel more comfortable as Patrick. And as I said, I like the way you say it."

She nodded, her face a little flushed, a dark auburn curl looped over one ear. She seemed a little nervous, but in a different way than the last time. Her features looked softer, less tense. Her eyes kept straying toward him, instead of glancing away.

His gaze ran over her clothes, a soft white jersey wool dress that just brushed her curves and fell gently to the floor. Her hair was freshly washed, a deep rich russet, buoyant with color and light. She looked pretty and feminine and he ached just to touch her.

"I'm afraid I don't quite know where to begin," she said. "I've been thinking things over, trying to understand everything that's happened. It hasn't been easy."

"No," he said softly. "I know how hard this has been. I want you to know I'm sorry for the pain I've caused you. I never meant for you to be hurt."

"You mean you didn't expect me to fall in love?"

Something sharp stabbed into his chest, followed by a trickle of warmth. Guilt perhaps entwined with the pleasure he felt in hearing the words. "When I came here, I was a different man. I was only interested in my studies. I didn't even know there was such a thing as love."

"And now?"

"You've given me incredible joy, Julie. All I've done is give you pain."

"I think you're hurting, too, Patrick. I can see it in your face whenever I look at you."

His eyes slid closed. He hurt all right. He had never known such agony. He looked into her face, studied each soft curve and line. "I love you, Julie. Like so much that has happened to me, I never understood what loving someone could do to a man. Now I know."

Julie blinked several times and glanced away, but a tear rolled down her cheek. "I've tried to bury my feelings. I told myself the man I loved was dead, that he died that day on the sidewalk in front of The Grill. But it wasn't the truth. In the past three days, I've had time to think. The storm tonight, somehow it made things clearer…like the rain, washing away the dirt on a muddy street. I was never in love with Patrick Donovan. I was attracted to him, yes, but I never loved him. It's you I love. Whoever you are. Wherever you've come from. I love the man Patrick has become."

He watched as fresh tears rolled down her cheeks. He wanted to go to her, but he was afraid. It took an effort of will to remain where he was.

"These past few days have been a nightmare," she said. "Part of me died the day I lost you, the day I found your journal. Now that I realize the man I love is you, my heart is breaking for the day I will lose you again."

"Julie…" He closed the distance between them, swept her against his chest and held her close, praying she wouldn't push him away. Instead she slid her arms around his neck and clung to him, the wetness of her tears soaking the front of his shirt.

"I love you," she whispered. "I want to be with you for as long as I can. I don't want to waste a moment more."

"Ah…Julie." He buried his face in her hair, held her as she wept against his shoulder. "If I could stay I would. It isn't something I can do."

A slight motion of her head. "I know."

He smoothed her silky red hair. "Stay with me, here in the apartment. We'll take time off from work. Be together every minute we can."

Julie looked up at him, tears clinging to her long black lashes. "I can show you things, Patrick. I can show you beauty unlike anything you've ever known."

He kissed her eyes, her nose, her mouth. "You're more beautiful than anything I've ever known."

"Hold me, Patrick. Make love to me. We've wasted too much time already."

The words surprised him. He drew a little away. "Are you certain? I know things are different between us now. I don't expect you to feel exactly the same."

She smiled with such warmth his heart squeezed. "I want you, Commander. Why wouldn't I? You're two men—Patrick and Val—formed into one. You're every woman's secret fantasy and you belong to me."

He chuckled, a rumble deep in his chest, the first bit of happiness he had known in days. "So…you little hedonist, you want both of us at once. All right, my love. I shall see what I can do."

Julie laughed as he scooped her up, her long white dress trailing over his arm. Smiling, he carried her into the bedroom, set her down on his bed and slowly began to undress her, removing first her rain-soaked shoes, then drawing the dress over her head. He discovered to his pleasure that she wasn't wearing a bra.

Outside the window, lightning flashed, illuminating the bedroom and casting their silhouettes against the wall. Thunder followed, rumbling across the sky, obliterating for a moment the reckless beating of his heart.

He paused as she stood before him dressed only in a pair of lacy white thong panties. He went hard just looking at her, wanting her as he always did. Bending his head, he kissed her, savoring the taste of her, enjoying the feel of her breasts lightly brushing his chest. Her small hands clutched his shoulders, but Val drew away.

"On second thought, I don't believe Patrick would make love to you in here—far too tame for this occasion."

"What occasion?"

"Our very first orgy."

Julie laughed as he lifted her up and carried her into his huge black marble bathroom. "And Val would want to be someplace where he could watch the storm." There was a massive skylight in the room, revealing flashes of the lightning overhead. A big corner window looked out over the city, yet the apartment was on a high enough floor that no one could see in.

Julie smiled at him as he set her on her feet beside the big sunken tub and turned the gold handles on the faucet, adjusting the temperature to suit him. A little tepid for Julie, he realized, so he turned the hot water up a little bit more. A row of clear glass jars sat on a ledge above the tub. He took one down, dumped in a handful of pine-scented bubble bath, then began to strip off his clothes.

Julie's gaze ran over his body, watching the flex of his muscles, the movement of sinew over bone. Appreciation sparkled in the depths of her green eyes. Pride was there, too. And desire. She had not lied to him. It made him want her even more.

As he had discovered, he was a different man now. Where excess had once been unheard of, his passions now ran deep and extreme, a inexorable part of him.

His erection thrust forward, thick and hard, throbbing with each of his heartbeats. His gaze traveled over her beautiful upturned breasts, the soft rosy mounds at the crests. He assessed her tiny waist and the swell of her hips, her well-shaped legs and slender ankles. The lacy thong panties hugged the line between the globes of her bottom.

Standing naked beside her, he ran a hand over the curve of a firm round buttock, cupped it and gently pulled her toward him. She came willingly, her head tilting back as he captured her lips, urged them apart, and took her with his tongue. He groaned at the taste of her, sweetly erotic, warm and softly feminine. He filled his hands with her breasts, molding them gently, pebbling the ends between his fingers. Lowering his head, he took a nipple into his mouth and her hands came up to grip his shoulders.

She was pressed full-length against him, flesh to flesh, his erection hard against her belly.

"I want you," he whispered, lifting her into his arms and carrying her down the steps of the big marble tub. Turning off the water, he sank down in the airy white bubbles, taking a seat on one of the warm stone steps and positioning Julie astride his knees, her legs splayed on either side of his. She sucked in a breath as he opened his legs, forcing her thighs apart and giving him access to the damp secret place between them.

The water lapped against their bodies, a liquid blanket of warmth. Beneath the surface he began to stroke her, delving deeply, his tongue dipping into her mouth with the same hot rhythm.

Desire surged through him, strengthening his arousal, making him as hard as the marble tub beneath him. Julie moaned and arched her back, unconsciously offering her breasts to him, enjoying the pleasure he gave, craving more of it, seeking fulfillment.

He would see that she got it, but not for a while. He wanted her to know passion more intense than any she had ever known. He felt the bud of her desire plump around his fingers, felt the slick, welcoming dampness of her passage. His mouth claimed a breast. He suckled and bit the end, laved and teased her nipple. Several more determined strokes and he brought her to climax, her head falling back as her body arched upward and her muscles contracted.

The storm raged outside, thunder rumbling, deep and heavy, lightning white-hot against the sky. His body burned with that same sizzling fire and desire surged through him. The thunder of his heartbeat throbbed through his veins.

He didn't wait for her to spiral down, but lifted her instead, parting her legs even wider, wrapping her legs around his waist and thrusting himself deeply inside. He paused for a moment, holding her immobile, calming himself so he could go on.

He wanted her so damned badly.

"Patrick…" She whispered the word against his throat as he began to move, gripping her waist, lifting her and surging deeply inside her. The water in the tub began to move in the same pulsing rhythm, lapping over the sides, spilling in warm waves onto the black marble floor.

"Patrick…please…oh, I don't think I can stand it."

But he knew that she could. At least for a few more moments. Long enough for him to fill her again and again, to feel her hands gripping his shoulders, her small teeth biting the side of his neck. Long enough to feel a sweep of pleasure so intense he had to clamp his jaw against it.

He paused for a moment, gathering himself, working to regain his badly slipping control. But Julie wouldn't wait. Instead she took up the hot, stroking rhythm, taking him even more deeply, riding him and wringing a groan from his throat.

Heat burned into his loins, swept over him like a wave. Her muscles tightened as she reached a powerful climax and his own release burned through his blood. He came for long, sweetly satisfying moments, and Julie climaxed again, her nails digging into his back.

She had a passion to match his own, he thought, still drifting in pleasure, waiting for the thunder of his heartbeat to slow. He tenderly kissed her forehead, bent his head and softly covered her lips. She loved him. She had come back to him, overcome every obstacle that should have kept her away, and because of the trust she had placed in him, he loved her even more.

Yet soon he would have to leave her.

Not tonight. Not for the next few days. And until that time, he meant to make the most of every hour, every minute. As soon as his body was ready, he would make love to her again.

Twenty-One

━━━━━━━━━━━◠◡◠━━━━━━━━━━━

Laura hung up the phone and walked through the beaded curtains into the living room of her tiny apartment. Brian lay in a comfortable sprawl on the couch. The Dodgers were playing the Mets, the Mets ahead two to one in the bottom of the seventh inning. She had no classes at city college today and the day off from her part-time waitressing job.

"Who was that on the phone?" Brian asked during a commercial. It felt good to have him there, so natural somehow, to have him around the house. She didn't know why, it just did.

"That was my sister."

"That's the second time she's called in the past two days. What's up?"

Nothing particularly exciting. My sister's just in love with a man from outer space. Other than that there's not much new. "Just girl talk. We went shopping a couple of days ago. She wanted to know how I liked the clothes she bought me."

Brian propped himself up on an elbow. "Your sister's always so thoughtful. She loves you very much."

"Julie's a terrific sister and a very good friend." *The best*, Laura thought, her mind going over the phone conversations they'd had in the past two days. They had talked about the things that Patrick had told her, things about the place he lived, a planet called Toril. Patrick said he had convinced his superiors to hold off the testing they were doing on human subjects. For a while at least, Laura and the others would be safe.

Brian sat up on the couch, noticing for the first time the lightweight plaid wool jacket she carried draped over her arm. "You're not going out in this rain?"

"Actually, I am. I knew you'd be watching the game. I've got an errand to run that will take me a couple of hours. I thought maybe when I got back, we could go out and get some pizza or maybe order Chinese."

There was something about the way he looked at her, his thick brown eyebrows pulled together, the lines of his face going dark. Brian was a lot of things, but he was not a fool.

"Where are you going, Laura?"

She didn't want to lie to him again. She had been lying way too much lately. "There's a meeting at Robert Stringer's. I won't be gone long."

"The abduction group? You promised me you were through with all that."

"I am through with it. As a matter of fact, that's the reason I'm going. I want to say goodbye to the people in the group. I want to end this thing, and to do that, I need to see it through to the finish."

He got up from the sofa and walked toward her, gathered her into his arms. "It's just that I worry about you. I want to protect you, keep you safe from the bad things in the world. But we both know I can't do that. I know this is something you feel you have to do. You're looking for a sense of closure and I think that's good. Do you want me to come with you?"

She shook her head. "No. This time I have to go alone." There were things she needed to say and she wouldn't be able to do it with Brian there. She could just imagine the look on his face, his expression changing from gentle condescension to out-and-out disbelief.

"This is the last time, Brian. I promise."

"All right." He kissed her gently on the lips. "Just remember, if you need me, I'm as close as the phone. Drive carefully and I'll see you when you get home."

I'll see you when you get home. The words had a warm, intimate ring. They were practically living together. Brian spent every spare minute at her apartment or she went over to his. It was only a matter of time before he asked her to move in. She wasn't sure she would. Maybe she would suggest they move into a different apartment, neutral territory they could furnish together. She thought Brian might like the idea.

Whatever the case, there appeared to be a very good chance there was a future for them.

Now that she had dealt with her fears.

Incredibly, she had been able to do that far better than she would have imagined. In the beginning, she couldn't believe the things that had happened to her were real. She felt constantly terrified or angry, felt as if her mind were crumbling and she was staring insanity in the face. Later, all she wanted to do was hide, find some sort of shelter, yet there was no place she felt safe.

Lately, she had discovered an odd sort of peace. The last time she had been abducted, she had seen the Visitors in a whole different light. She had felt oddly as if she were a part of them, as if they were somehow a part of her.

Or perhaps it was merely acceptance. That she had found her way at last in a world that had suddenly changed.

The drive to Long Beach didn't take too long. The group was milling about in the white-carpeted living room when she got there. They turned in her direction, waiting for her as she walked into the foyer. She waved and continued in their direction.

What she hadn't told Brian was that she was the one who had asked Dr. Winters to call this special session of the group. Apparently everyone else was aware.

"Laura, it's good to see you." Dressed in his usual jeans and a long-sleeved white shirt, Dr. Winters walked toward her. Standing several inches shorter than she, he clasped both her hands in his, leaned forward and kissed her cheek. "You missed the last meeting. We thought perhaps you had decided to stop coming."

"Actually, I have. But I wanted to see you all one last time." She turned toward the others who were clustered around her and smiled. "I wouldn't have asked you all to come if it hadn't been important. I didn't want to wait for your next meeting because I know what a struggle it can be just to get through the week."

"What is it, Laura?" Leslie Williams, the black Xerox saleswoman from San Diego, looked at her with a worried frown. "I thought something terrible must have happened, but you don't look upset."

"I'm fine. This isn't about me, it's about you. What I wanted to tell you is going to be hard to believe, but in time I'm convinced you'll see that it's the truth."

"Why don't we all sit down?" Dr. Winters suggested. "Give Laura a chance to say what she's come here to tell us." They all took their usual favorite chairs, Laura ending up on the white wool sofa.

"I don't know where to begin exactly." She met each interested gaze directly, even the nervous darting glance of the schizophrenic, Matthew Goldman. "I can tell you I've been abducted again since the last time I saw you. I can tell you it was different this time. Though the examinations were pretty much the same, I experienced some sensations that I hadn't before, things a few of you have mentioned, the feeling of oneness, the gentle side of the Visitors that I had never seen. But that isn't really important. What I came here to do is deliver a message. As I said, I can't expect all of you to believe it. I only hope it gives you some comfort and in time you'll discover it's true." She took a deep breath and plunged ahead, thinking of Julie and Patrick and the things Patrick had said.

"The message I'm to deliver is that the testing of human subjects has been suspended. The Visitors will soon be leaving. At least for a while, all of us will be safe."

"How do you know this?" Robert Stringer rested his coffee mug on the arm of his chair. "How can you be sure?"

"Where the Visitors are concerned, it's difficult to be sure about anything. I only know the message came from one of the superiors. I believe he is someone we can trust. I believe the Visitors are discovering, perhaps for the very first time, the terrible consequences their testing has had on the people of Earth."

The room fell silent, then erupted with all of them talking at once. Dr. Winters called for order and they started their rounds of questions, quiet Willis Small, the nonfiction author, asking more than any of the rest.

There weren't many answers to be had. She wasn't about to mention Patrick Donovan or Commander Zarkazian. She refused to mention Julie.

"I know it sounds far-fetched. But the truth is, everything that's happened to us is totally out of the realm of credibility. Give yourself a chance to believe it could be true. Put your fears to rest and give yourself the chance to feel safe."

She wasn't certain they would. Fear was a daunting opponent. It gnawed at you even when logic told you it was senseless to be afraid. Yet as she looked at each hopeful expression, she prayed she had done some good.

As for herself, she had meant what she had told Brian. She intended to get on with her life, to count this as just one more of life's never-ending experiences. What had happened had dramatically changed her. But unlike the others, Laura believed it had made her stronger, not weaker. Oddly enough, in her case, the change was for the best.

Laura smiled as she left the meeting and headed for her car. She slid into the driver's seat of her aging white Volkswagen Beetle, sparing only a quick glance at the *Save the Whales—Ban Sonar Testing* bumper sticker riding on the dash, waiting to be put on.

She slapped the little stuffed dolphin that hung from the mirror, a treasure she had purchased from a craft seller down at the beach, watched it dangle back and forth on its string.

She started the engine, the tension draining from her muscles now that her task was completed, thinking of Brian, eager to be home. She couldn't wait to see him, couldn't help feeling an urgent need to be with him. In his own way, Brian had been as true a friend in this as Julie, who had stood steadfastly beside her from the start.

Julie. Thinking of her sister made the smile on her face turn sad. In the end, it was Julie who would suffer the most from this. It was Julie who would lose the person she so desperately loved. For years, Laura had believed her sister wouldn't let herself fall in love. Not after their mother's ill-fated marriage. Certainly not after her own failed attempts.

Then Patrick had come along—a new Patrick, a man of strength and self-assurance—and Julie had tumbled head over heels. Now the odds were good that once Patrick was gone, her sister would never fall in love again.

Laura's thoughts returned to Brian, waiting for her at home, and she felt an almost desperate need to see him.

She hoped the damnable baseball game was over so that they could make love.

A week was so very little time. Not nearly enough days to build memories that would have to last a lifetime. Julie didn't care. Patrick had been returned to her and for as long as he was there, she was going to make every minute count.

As he had suggested, they took time off from work, deciding to explore California, starting with a trip along the coast. Julie had always loved to drive, to see what might lie around the next bend in the road. Flying meant a cabin full of strangers and they wanted to spend their time alone.

As she had expected, Patrick took in the magnificent scenery like a starving man at a buffet. It was one thing to remember the places Patrick Donovan had seen, he told her. It was another thing altogether to experience those places firsthand.

Like the afternoon they drove Highway 1 to Big Sur. They were traveling in Patrick's black Porsche, two small soft-sided suitcases barely fitting in the trunk. They had spent the night at Morro Bay, then stopped at the Hearst Castle in San Simeon and gone on the tour of the estate.

"It's incredible," Patrick said, staring at the front of the huge Mediterranean, revival-style mansion. Upstairs in one of the bedrooms, he craned his neck to look up at the beautiful frescoed ceilings. "I could never have imagined anything so as magnificent as this."

"There are places like this all over Europe," Julie told him as he marveled at the gold candelabra, fine Chinese porcelains, Italian marble hearths, and priceless paintings. "Today people frown on spending this kind of money. I guess they figure the dollars would be better spent feeding the hungry masses."

Patrick shook his head. "There is no poverty on Toril. Some of us have a bit more than others, but the disparity between us is not very great. No one individual could ever amass enough of a fortune to commission beautiful works of art like the things in this house. What the people of Earth don't realize is if it hadn't been for the great division of wealth in your world throughout the ages, none of your magnificent antiquities would exist. No castles, no palaces, no pyramids. You'd find your- selves living in the pale dim world of sameness that I am forced to exist in."

"I never thought of it that way." She paused as the group stopped beside the huge Neptune pool, its bottom shimmering with gold. "I suppose it's different today than it was back then."

Patrick shook his head. "Nothing has changed," he argued as they walked along. "It takes money to accom- plish things. Great fortune often equates with great beauty. That beauty is passed on to us all—or will be, once the art and architecture commissioned by the men of wealth today is passed on to future generations."

Julie said nothing to that. She wasn't sure she agreed with him, but it was an interesting concept. She let her mind digest the possibility while Patrick absorbed their surroundings, beauty Julie saw with fresh, new eyes.

They left the mansion and continued northward. Trav- eling the narrow curving road to Big Sur, they paused to take pictures of the jagged coastline, white plumes of foamy surf shooting up against the rocky shore. In the distance, sea lions basked in the sun, the sound of their husky barks drifting across the turbulent sea.

At a turnout farther along the route, Patrick asked a fellow tourist if he would mind taking their picture, and both of them smiled into the lens of the yellow Kodak disposable camera he had bought. Julie couldn't help wondering if the lens would capture the wistful, happy- sad expression she wore on her face.

They visited Carmel, Monterey, and San Francisco, then headed inland, arriving five days into their trip at

Yosemite National Park. Labor Day had passed, thank God, so the usual number of tourists had thinned to a manageable trickle. They stayed at the famous Ahwahnee Hotel, built of stone and massive timbers on the floor of the sculpted Yosemite Valley, in a quaint, private cottage off by itself.

They slept late that morning, their bodies nestled spoon fashion in a log-hewn bed beneath a colorful Indian blanket, Patrick getting up long enough to build a fire in the small rock fireplace, then climbing back under the covers. His skin was icy cold, so she snuggled up to help him get warm. Snuggling turned to kissing. They made slow, sensuous love and afterward she lay curled in his arms, watching the flames in the hearth.

Their mood was lightly teasing. She playfully tugged at the hair on his chest. "By the way, Mr. Toughguy, I finally figured out why you were never afraid of Sandini and McPherson."

He arched a thick dark brow. "How do you know I wasn't afraid?"

"Were you?"

Patrick chuckled softly. "Not really."

"That's because you knew when the time came to face them you would be gone."

"I knew I would be leaving. I could have left even sooner if the threat they posed had become too real."

Julie's fingers absently traced a slab of muscle on his chest. "The old Patrick...he would have done what they asked, wouldn't he?"

He sighed and leaned his head back against the pillow. "I don't think he would have wanted to...but yes, I think he would have."

"Not you, though. Not even if you were staying. You would have opposed them anyway."

"What they're doing isn't right. People are going to be hurt. I can't condone that."

She bent her head, pressed her mouth against the flat spot above his navel. "I know you can't. That's one of the reasons I love you so much."

He groaned as she trailed soft kisses upward, bit the tiny nub of his flat copper nipple.

"You're playing with fire," he warned, arousal roughening his voice.

But Julie simply retraced her path, moving downward this time, ringing his navel with her tongue, moving lower. He was hard, she saw, her fingers stroking over the thick ridge of muscle that had risen beneath the covers. She eased the blanket back, bent and took him into her mouth.

Patrick gripped the covers, a breath hissing out from between his teeth. Julie felt a shot of satisfaction. He would leave her, she knew. Their time was almost over. In the end she would lose him, but as she continued to stroke him, Julie was determined that he would never forget her.

Twenty-Two

━━━━∽◦❦◦∽━━━━

The days careened past, slipping through their fingers like sand through an upended hourglass. They made every moment count, soaking up each experience with quiet desperation.

As Julie had hoped, Patrick loved Yosemite. They hiked steep trails into the woods, walked paths along babbling streams, and climbed to points that overlooked bottomless precipices.

Arming themselves with plastic garbage bags pulled on over their clothes, they carried a picnic lunch up to the top of Vernal Falls.

"There are no waterfalls on Toril," Patrick said, stopping along the steep trail to admire the rainbows created by the thick spray of water. "There are a few small hills, but no deep valleys, and even those few places lie beneath great domes that keep the temperature constantly controlled."

To Julie it seemed a terrible injustice for a vital man like Patrick to be forced to live indoors.

When they finally reached the top of the steep trail up the falls, Patrick seated himself on a rock near the edge so he could watch the pounding fury of the water rushing over the cliff. With his T-shirt damp and plastered against his muscular chest, his eyes full of wonder and his black hair wet and clinging to his forehead, he had never been more attractive.

She had never felt so close to despair in knowing their time together was nearly at an end.

They returned to their cabin late in the afternoon, made love for a while and then napped. Instead of eating supper in the dining room, Patrick ordered room service, trout almondine for her, chicken noodle soup for him, and they stayed in their charming mountain cabin. Sitting cross-legged on the braided rug, they ate in front of the small stone fireplace, Patrick in a pair of sweatpants, Julie wearing one of his shirts.

"It's been a wonderful week," he said when they had finished, his back propped against the sofa, Julie sitting comfortably between his legs, his arms wrapped around her waist. "I'll never forget it. I'll never forget you, Julie."

A hard lump rose in her throat. "Please, Patrick…if you talk that way you'll make me cry, and I want these last memories to be happy."

His breath came out slowly. He nodded and glanced away. "I just wanted you to know."

The lump in her throat ached harder. She knew. How could she not? It was the most wonderful week of her life. She felt the warmth of his lips against her temple, firm, warm lips, beautifully carved in a face so handsome it made her breath catch every time she looked at him.

"If you could have stayed," she said softly, "do you

think you could have been happy? You're a scientist. Your people are obviously far advanced in intelligence. Do you think you would have been able to spend a lifetime here on Earth?"

His chest rumbled softly. "As you said, I'm a scientist. My specialty is the study of life-forms that inhabit other worlds." His hand smoothed over her hair, long dark fingers slipping through the strands, a firm yet gentle touch. "I've only begun to understand the people of Earth. Can you imagine how much there is for a man like me to learn? I could live here a thousand lifetimes and it wouldn't be long enough."

"I wish you could stay."

"Julie…"

"I know. I promised myself I wouldn't say it." She glanced toward the flames in the hearth, watched the red-orange fire licking upward. "I just wanted you to know."

He didn't speak, but a fine tremor passed through his body.

"I wish we had more time," she said. "I wish we could stay here forever."

"So do I. Unfortunately, we can't," he said gently, kissing the top of her head. "We have to leave here in the morning. It's time to go back to L.A."

A sliver of ice slid through her, seemed to wrap itself around her heart. She tried to stop the tears from pooling in her eyes, tried to brush them away when they slipped down her cheeks. "Couldn't we stay just one more day?"

He only shook his head. "It's time, Julie. It's time for me to go home."

She turned into his arms and he held her as she cried, stroked her hair and whispered soft words of love. When the fire burned low and a chill invaded the room, he lifted her into his arms and carried her over to the bed. They made love with aching tenderness, and a fierce, almost frantic passion.

They packed the car just after dawn, a cold day in the mountains, cloudy overhead, sharp with the sting of the coming fall.

"I wish you could have seen the trees in autumn. The leaves turn such lovely colors, russet and yellow, bronze and crimson."

His hand came up to her cheek. "And a dark red with hidden streaks of gold, the color of your hair."

She tilted her face into his palm. "It's beautiful. I know you would love it."

"You're beautiful—and I know I love you."

She went into his arms, trying not to cry, then giving way to her tears and sobbing softly against his shoulder. "I feel like I'm dying. I feel like I'm breaking in two."

He didn't answer, but he tightened his hold around her. "I don't know how I'm going to live without you."

They stood that way for long, silent moments, holding each other, the car engine running, shrouding them in white billows of cold morning air. In silence, each of them pulled away.

Julie forced an overbright smile and opened the passenger door. "We had better get going. L.A.'s a long way away."

Patrick simply nodded. He held the door while she slid into her seat, then rounded the car and climbed behind the wheel. Mostly in silence, they drove the curving road down out of the mountains into the San Joaquin

Valley. The scenery was as breathtaking as it was on their way in, but this time Patrick didn't seem to notice.

They reached his apartment late that evening and Julie stayed over. Neither of them mentioned his leaving, but it hung like a pall over their heads, a deep jagged wound that neither of them could mend. In the morning he went to the office, determined, it seemed, to finalize Patrick's affairs as best he could before he left.

He spoke to each of the people he worked with, praising each of them in some special way, letting them know how important each of them was to him.

Saying goodbye in his own quiet way.

Julie wondered how much longer she could continue without breaking. The only thing that kept her going was the knowledge that this was as hard for Patrick as it was for her. She knew the pain he was suffering. She didn't want to make it any worse.

They spent the night together then returned to the office the following morning, Patrick working hard on last-minute details.

"I want to leave this place in the kind of shape my father would have wanted. I want to make this as easy on him as I can."

Patrick didn't notice the slip, but Julie did. *My father.* The words sent an arrow of pain into her heart. Dear God, nothing had ever been so hard.

She worked beside him, sifting through escrow files, clearing up loose ends, helping him any way she could. She promised she would do her best to help the staff relocate, or assist Alex in finding someone else to manage the office after he was gone. But every time she looked at him, all she could think was *who is going to help me?*

She knew she looked awful. The color was gone from her cheeks and she hadn't been able to eat. Patrick didn't look much better. He wasn't sleeping at all and just barely eating. She guessed he no longer cared about his health. Why should he? Any day now, he would be gone.

Babs looked at them both with dark worried eyes, but so far she had said nothing. Julie was grateful. She was living on the edge and she wasn't sure how much more she could take before her slim thread of control finally snapped.

It was almost noon when he stuck his head through the door. "It'll be lunch soon. You need to have something to eat. Why don't we go get a sandwich or something?"

He didn't even like sandwiches. But he was obviously worried about her so she said yes just to please him. "Where shall we go?"

"There's that little café on Wilshire…Joey's. That's usually pretty good."

She almost smiled. Patrick was the last man on earth who would know anything about "pretty good" food. The thought made her smile. She must be so tired she was getting rummy.

Outside the office window, a breeze snapped the flag beside the sign above the door. She took the sweater off her arm and slung it around her shoulders, grabbed her purse, and walked past him out the door. They walked along the sidewalk and turned left at the corner, making their way along Wilshire Boulevard. Traffic buzzed past, horns honking, people swearing at each other the way they always did, but Julie barely heard them.

They had almost reached the restaurant when Patrick suddenly stopped. Julie turned to look at him, saw him take another unsteady step and stumble backward, landing hard against the rough brick wall.

"Patrick! My God, what is it?"

Leaning heavily against the wall, he dragged in several panting breaths, his face as gray as the cement beneath his feet. He grimaced as another sharp pain speared through him.

"Patrick! For God's sake—what's wrong?"

He jerked violently as another spasm shook him, his body slamming backward against the bricks. "They've started…the removal process. I didn't think it would begin…until sometime tomorrow."

Julie's heart constricted. They couldn't be taking him. Not now. Not yet. *Dear God, don't let them take him now.* He grunted and clamped his jaw, and Julie gripped his arm to help him steady himself.

"They're hurting you. Why are they hurting you?"

"They're…taking me…all the way out," he panted. "The other times, part of me remained in Patrick's body. No one's ever…been in this long. Apparently…Division is harder than Unification."

Julie clutched his shoulder, which was corded with tension and felt hard as steel. "Tell them you have to stay," she pleaded, frantic now, seizing on the chance she had suddenly glimpsed. "Tell them it hurts too much—you'll have to stay here. Tell them—"

He pressed a trembling finger against her lips to stop the words. "I have to go. You know that. They won't let me stay." A violent spasm shook him, doubling him over, his stomach knotting in agony. His legs buckled beneath him and he slowly collapsed to the cement.

"Patrick!" Julie knelt beside him, desperate now, knowing it was useless yet unwilling to let him go. "You can't go now. Now yet. Please…please don't leave."

A well-dressed couple stopped a few feet away, studying the stricken man with concern. "Somebody better call an ambulance," the husband said. "Looks like this guy is having a heart attack."

Several people stopped and turned, began to press forward. A heavyset woman peered through the circle of onlookers, jerked her cell phone out of her purse and quickly dialed 911. Through the window of the café, Julie saw someone pointing frantically toward the street and a waiter rushed off to make the same call.

Julie sat down on the sidewalk beside where Patrick lay, his body shaking all over. With trembling hands, she lifted his head into her lap and began to smooth back his hair. "I'll never forget you, Patrick. Never."

He found her hand, struggled to lift it, pressed it against his lips. "Goodbye, my love. Wherever I am, you'll always be with me."

"Patrick…" She bent her head over his, her tears falling freely now, a flood of wetness that ran down her cheeks. "I love you," she whispered. "Patrick, I love you so much."

But Patrick couldn't hear her. He couldn't hear the wail of the ambulance siren as it raced down Wilshire Boulevard in a futile attempt to reach him. He couldn't hear her heartbreaking sobs as she whispered his name.

Beneath her cold hands, his heart beat only faintly. A meager breath feathered past his lips.

"No…" Julie whispered, burying her face against his chest. "It's too soon. The day isn't over. Please don't take him yet."

But they didn't hear.

The ambulance attendants tore her away from him as they frantically worked over his chest, but as soon as he was loaded onto the stretcher, she reached out and took hold of his hand. In the back of the ambulance, they forced oxygen past his lips, used defibrillator paddles to try to get his heart beating again, but nothing they did would work.

They must have known there was no hope of reviving him for they let her hold on to his hand all the way to the hospital. All the way there, she watched the flat white line of the heart monitor, listened to the dull beep of defeat. The siren screamed as she bent over his body and pressed a final soft kiss on his lips. Then she sank down in the chair beside his lifeless body and sobbed against his chest, a river of tears soaking through the front of his shirt.

Val stood in the transporter room aboard the *Ansor,* dizzy and disoriented, his body still shaking all over. Grief weighed him down like a shroud and his usually crystal-clear mind refused to work. Along with his overwhelming sadness, he couldn't seem to see. He closed his eyes and tried to fight the numbness, the ache that throbbed like a wound in his chest. He tried to block the pain that he had brought with him, the knifing sorrow of losing Julie.

His throat ached. He felt a gauzy robe draped around him, blinked and at last he could see. All ten members of the High Council stood in the chamber, forming a semicircle around him. They had come to observe the final stages of the first successful Unification that had lasted such a long length of time.

"Commander?" Calas Panidyne moved closer. "Commander Zarkazian, are you all right?"

He tried to speak, but the words lodged in his throat. He wasn't all right. He felt torn apart and it wasn't from the physical battering he had taken.

"Commander?" One of the ministers walked toward him, her robes floating softly out behind her. He couldn't remember her name. "What has happened to you, Commander?" She studied his features, reached out and ran her fingers over his face. They came away covered with wetness.

"That cannot be what it looks like." He heard the note of awe in a second minister's voice. "It simply cannot be."

"He's...*crying*." A member of the group came closer. "There are pictures in the archives that show what it looked like." But Val knew it couldn't be true. Torillians hadn't cried for ten thousand years.

"That's not possible," Panidyne argued. "Tear ducts are nothing but useless glands. They evolved out of use eons ago."

Val reached up and touched his face, felt the astonishing wetness. He thought of Julie and wanted to cry all over again.

The female minister gently touched his shoulder. "Something terrible has happened to him, can't you see? What is it, Commander? Can you tell us what happened?"

"Yes, Commander, please." Another minister pressed forward, third council, one of the more aggressive members of the group. "When you were here before, we saw that you were different, that your time on Earth had changed you. Can you explain what has occurred?"

He wiped away the last few drops of wetness, thinking of Julie, of the grief still pulsing through him. Even as Patrick, he had never cried.

He looked at them with a face full of sorrow. "As you said, my time on Earth changed me. Part of me is human now. I believe it always will be."

Silence fell over the group.

The female minister was the first to speak. "And what you are feeling…is that what made you cry?"

He nodded.

"What do you call such a feeling?"

"The emotion is known as grief. It comes from excessive sadness."

"And this sadness arises because you had to leave?"

"Yes."

"You aren't saying you wished to remain?" Panidyne seemed incredulous. "You're a respected, well-known scientist on Toril. Surely you wish to return to the life you led before."

He only shook his head. It was useless and yet he could not stop himself from speaking the truth. "Toril is no longer my home. Another place calls out to me as no place ever has. Earth is where I wish to live. I believe I will die on Toril."

Soft murmurs rolled through the small group of observers. There was not the slightest chance they would let him remain, yet at the look on the ministers' faces, a kernel of hope took root in his chest. He was afraid to let it grow, knew that it would only mean more pain.

Hope and fear. Emotions that only made him realize how human he had become.

They talked for a moment more, then Panidyne turned in his direction. "If we were to grant your wish and allow you to remain, you would lose your Torillian strengths. Your lifetime would be no longer than a human's. Your body would be susceptible to the same diseases, the same failings. Your children would merely be human."

As Patrick he might have smiled. "I am aware of that."

"And yet you wish to remain?"

"Above all things."

Panidyne turned back to the members of the council. For long moments they discussed the pros and cons of such a move. "Perhaps, in some way," Panidyne suggested, "we might later benefit from having one of our own on Earth."

One or two disagreed but only briefly. The sight of the unexpected tears on his face seemed to be forever burned into their minds.

They spoke quietly among themselves, then Panidyne ended the discussion. "So then we are agreed?" He returned the look each minister gave him. When his attention returned to Val, there was an unreadable expression on his face.

"Our decision is to let you remain on Earth, Commander. Perhaps it is an unwise choice, but under the circumstances, all of us have agreed. However, if we are to rejoin you with the human, we must do so quickly. There is little time left to spare."

Hope and joy crashed through him in thundering waves. He was almost afraid to believe it. The female minister urged him forward, toward the transporter he had arrived in, and the others fell in behind. The joy in him grew. He was going back to Earth. Returning to Julie. Going back where he belonged.

Patrick was going home.

Twenty-Three

The wail of the siren echoed off the buildings along the Boulevard as the ambulance wound its way toward Cedar Sinai Hospital. The traffic had been heavy, slowing the vehicle nearly to a halt, making the long journey seem to take forever. Julie heard the siren only vaguely. Sitting next to the gurney on which Patrick lay, her cheek pressed to his chest, her fingers clutching his hand, the world was a vague, distant blur. Her mind was gratefully numb, dull with grief and loss.

In a corner of the ambulance, one of the attendants stared out the window, giving her privacy for her sorrow. The ambulance attendants had exhausted every avenue in an effort to restore Patrick's heartbeat. Now he lay quietly on the gurney, each of them resigned to failure.

Julie almost felt sorry for them. It was hardly their fault Patrick couldn't be saved. In truth, he had died long ago.

Against her cheek, his skin felt cool, no longer warm and enticing. Still, she didn't move away. Soon he would be gone from her forever.

They had almost reached the emergency entrance to the hospital when a sharp beep sounded and Julie lifted her head. Another beep cut into the silence, then another. Several more echoed loudly through the speakers of the heart monitor.

"What the hell?" The attendant jerked to his feet, started toward the machine, whose wires were still attached to Patrick's chest.

"What…what is it?" Julie tried to make sense of what was happening, why the young attendant was madly shouldering her out of the way, but her mind was still too numb to comprehend.

"Get the paddles! His heart is trying to start up again."

"No way," said the second attendant. "Not after all this time."

The first attendant grabbed the paddles of the defibrillator. "Stranger things have happened." He was ready to go into action but his gaze stayed fixed on the heart monitor, which had set up a sharp rapid series of pulses, then begun an even throbbing that made a constant, high-low pattern across the screen.

"What's happening?" Julie asked, staring down at Patrick.

"His heart has started beating on its own." The attendant grabbed the oxygen mask dangling near the side of the gurney. Julie gasped as Patrick's lungs sucked in a great breath of air even before the mask had time to reach him.

"Holy shit!" The attendant's eyes seemed to bulge from their sockets. "He's started breathing!"

"H-he's breathing? H-he's alive?" It was impossible. He couldn't be alive. Val Zarkazian was gone.

Which meant Patrick Donovan should be dead.

The attendant checked Patrick's pulse, found it growing stronger every second. "I've never seen anything like it. We tried everything we knew and we couldn't bring him back."

Julie said nothing. She didn't understand what was happening and suddenly she was afraid. Patrick was breathing again. It looked as though he was going to live. But Val had sworn he wouldn't be returning. What if the man on the gurney wasn't Patrick. What if it was somebody else? Nothing seemed impossible anymore.

She waited tensely as the ambulance attendant worked over his patient, inserting a fresh IV, making sure the patient's condition was stable. All the while Julie sat in the shadows, afraid to believe yet unable to stop the aching hope that was building inside her chest.

Dear God, if all of us really are your children, won't you please help this one?

Perhaps He heard her, because a few minutes later, Patrick's eyes cracked open, an intense cerulean blue. For a moment he seemed uncertain where he was, and Julie held her breath, praying a miracle had happened—that it wasn't some horrible intergalactic joke.

Let it be him. Oh, dear God, please let it be him.

His gaze sought hers, caught and held. The harshness eased from his features and a corner of his mouth curved up. She grabbed onto his hand. He lifted it a bit shakily and pressed her fingers against his lips.

"I'm just Patrick now," he said, his voice deep and rough. "And I'm eleven million dollars in debt. Will you marry me?"

Tears burned her eyes. Julie's heart crumbled inside her chest. It was Patrick. *Her* Patrick. No man had ever looked at her the way he did. She tried for a smile but her lips trembled instead. She finally forced the answer past the thick lump in her throat.

"Of course, I'll marry you. How could a woman say no to a man who has crossed a galaxy to be with her?"

His fingers tightened around her hand. "I love you," he whispered as the ambulance rolled into the emergency entrance of the hospital. Then the doors flew open and a dozen white-uniformed medical personnel swooped into the rear of the ambulance.

He was grinning when they wheeled him away.

Twenty-Four

Tony Sandini stood next to Vince McPherson in the locker room of the Chicago Health and Fitness Club. Vince had been playing a little racquetball while Tony indulged himself in a long relaxing massage. They had just finished a nice hot shower and were getting ready to go into the snack shop for something to eat.

"So what's the word on the Brookhaven deal?" Vince dried the back of his neck, then began to work on his curly dark brown hair. He was in good shape for a man in his late forties. He couldn't imagine letting himself run to fat like his friend Tony did. "That Bonham chick with the pension fund give the okay yet on the Westwind trust deed sale?"

Sandini grunted. "As a matter of fact that was one of the things I wanted to talk to you about. The pension fund turned down the purchase. We got to find somebody else or give up and try somethin' different."

"Something different like what? Wringing the money out of that stupid bastard, Donovan? If you recall, that's what I wanted to do in the first place."

Tony dragged the towel back and forth across his beefy shoulders, shaking the thick slab of fat on his belly. "If this Westwind scam woulda' worked, we'd of all made a pot load of dough. The way things are going, it looks like we shoulda' done it your way."

"You think Donovan went against us with the pension fund?"

"I don't know, but I gotta hunch he might have."

Vincent pulled on his shirt, a nice white cotton knit, and began to fasten the buttons at the throat. "I hear the prick's back in the hospital. Another heart attack or something."

"From what I heard, he's off the drugs and booze. Pretty-boy Donovan's probably screwin' himself to death."

McPherson chuckled. "I hear Woody Nicholson's out on the Coast. Why don't we send him over to see Donovan, deliver a little *get well card*, if you know what I mean? Tell him to let Donovan know, in no uncertain terms, he's got ten days to come up with the money he owes us, or he isn't gonna like what happens."

"Good idea. I'll take care of it myself." Tony zipped his pants, then sucked in his belly to fasten the button at the waist. McPherson thought he could probably knock the eye out of a cat at fifty yards if that button ever came unsewed.

"You think Donovan'll be able to pay us?" McPherson asked, slamming his locker door.

"He'd better," Tony said, his eyes suddenly cold. "If he doesn't, he'll be havin' another heart attack—and you can bet this one'll be fatal."

Julie poured water into the paper cup on the table beside Patrick's hospital bed and handed it over.

"Thanks," he growled, accepting the cup and knocking back the pills the stout nurse, Mrs. Fielding, commanded him to swallow. As soon as the "tyrant in white," as Patrick called her, left the room, he sat up in bed and spit out the pills he had hidden beneath his tongue.

Julie laughed as he dumped them into the waste bin, swore an extremely earthy phrase, and fell back against the pillow.

"I realize you're grouchy and eager to get out of bed," Julie said, "but you'll just have to struggle along for a couple more days. There is no way Dr. Cane is going to release you until he's sure you're going to be okay."

"I'm in perfect health," Patrick grumbled. "Every damn test I've taken has told them that, but they keep dreaming up something new."

"They're just doing their job. Be grateful you've got health insurance." A company plan Patrick had actually kept paid and Val had upgraded after he took over the company. His deductible was sky-high, but right now the policy was looking pretty good.

"Another couple of days and I'll be stir-crazy."

"A couple more days and you'll be out of here."

He grinned at that. Reaching out, he captured her hand, bent his head and kissed her palm. "When are we going to get married?"

Julie smiled. He had asked her every day since his return. So far they hadn't set an exact date. "How about the end of the month? Is that soon enough to suit you?"

"Tomorrow isn't soon enough to suit me and you know it."

She leaned over and kissed his forehead. "I thought

we could have a small wedding in your father's back-
yard. Just friends and family, maybe a small reception."

"If that's what you want, it sounds perfect. Do you
want to live in your house or mine?"

"Mine, if it's okay with you. I thought maybe, in a
couple of years, we could sell the beach house and get
something with a…a little more room." She stumbled
over this last and glanced away. They had never spoken
of children. She had been on the pill since the first time
they had slept together, but now things had changed.

Unfortunately, she wasn't sure how Patrick would
feel about kids.

She wasn't even sure he would be able to have children.

"Are you saying what I think you are?" He laced his
fingers through hers, gave them a gentle squeeze. "Are
you talking about having offspring?"

Offspring. Only Patrick. "It's all right if you don't
want them. It doesn't change anything between us. I just
thought…hoped…maybe…if you could…you might
want a family."

He said nothing for the longest time. Then he smiled
and a faint dimple formed in his cheek "If I could? Why,
Ms. Ferris. I thought I had proved that point a sufficient
number of times, but if you wish to see further evidence—" He pulled back the covers, inviting her to join
him, and Julie laughed.

"That isn't what I meant, you scoundrel, and you
know it."

He smiled at her. "I would love to give you children,
Julie. They would be human in every way and I would
do my best to be a good father, though it isn't something
I know very much about."

Julie leaned over and kissed him. "You'd be a wonderful father. You're kind and generous, you're loyal and caring. But would our children…? I would want some part of them to be yours, Val."

She rarely called him that. She did it now to make a point. She loved him, not the man who was once Patrick Donovan.

"The children would be ours—yours and mine. We would make them so. Our teachings, our morality, our patience and love, that is what makes a child grow into a fine man or woman. Together we can give them those things."

A lump rose into her throat. She loved him so much. She started to tell him so when a soft knock sounded at the door and Nurse Fielding pushed it open.

"He's right in here," the woman said to the tall, bone-thin man who walked into the room as if he belonged there. He moved with purpose, his face hard-edged, his mouth little more than a gash in his narrow, slightly sallow face. It was visiting hours. The floor was open to anyone who might want to come, yet she didn't recognize this man who must have been a friend of the old Patrick's. And there was something about him, something of menace that sent an icy chill down her spine.

"You Donovan?" Ignoring Julie, the man walked—no, swaggered—farther into the room. He was dressed in black slacks and a plaid shirt. A navy blue windbreaker hung loosely from his narrow, bony frame.

"I'm Patrick Donovan." He sat up straighter in the bed, his expression suddenly wary, and a knot began to form in Julie's stomach.

"Woody Nicholson's the name. I got something for you from your associates—Mr. Sandini and Mr.

McPherson. A get-well card of sorts." Standing next to the bed, he whirled on Julie, slapped her hard across the face, jerked her against him and locked an arm around her throat.

Stunned, she gasped in a breath. "Let me go!" Struggling to be free of his choking hold, she felt the cold prick of a knife blade pressed against her throat.

"Leave her alone!" Patrick commanded. "It's me you want—this has nothing to do with her." He was breathing hard, crouched on the edge of the bed, his hospital gown off one shoulder, his muscles corded with tension, but the knife at her throat held him still.

"Sandini said to tell you the pension fund deal fell through…but then you know that already, don't you?" A ruthless smile twisted his lips. "You've got ten days to dig up the money you owe. After that…" He squeezed Julie's throat and she clawed at the arm locked around her neck. "Well…you get the picture. Only next time it won't be her, it'll be you, and *you* won't be walking away."

Nicholson let her go and Julie staggered backward, gasping for breath, her throat bruised and swollen.

"See you around," the man said calmly, sliding the knife into its sheath beneath his jacket as he turned and walked out the door.

Julie didn't move and neither did Patrick, not until the heavy door swung closed, then he was out of the bed and pulling her into his arms. "I'm sorry. God, I'm so damned sorry."

Julie shook her head. "You have nothing to be sorry for. None of this is your fault. You only did what you had to. We both knew there might be consequences."

His face looked thunderous, his eyes a cold, savage blue. "I wanted to kill him. Before I came here, I never even knew what anger was. Tonight I wanted to kill a man."

Julie reached up and cupped his cheek. "You felt helpless. You wanted to protect me. Under the circumstances, there is nothing wrong with the way you felt."

His mouth curved into the faintest of smiles. "You're telling me I was only being human?"

Julie managed to smile, too. "I guess you could put it that way." Patrick's smile widened, but Julie's slid away. "What are we going to do, Patrick?"

He sighed and together they sat down on the edge of the bed. "The only thing we can do, I guess. Find a way to come up with eleven million dollars."

"Plus interest," Julie added darkly.

"Plus interest." Patrick tilted her chin with his hand. "Don't look so glum. Business has been better lately—"

"Since you've been running the company."

He smiled. "Yes, I'm happy to say. Donovan Real Estate has assets—"

"*You* have assets.

"All right, *I* have assets. Somehow I'll find a way to raise the money."

But deep in their hearts, both of them were afraid he wouldn't be able to come up with enough. And he only had ten days.

Patrick shut another cardboard box and taped it closed with a roll of packing tape. He carefully marked the contents *kitchen utensils* with a black felt pen, glanced to where Julie bent over the sofa, folding a stack of linens, and drew a happy face below the words.

"Ready for another?" she asked, walking toward him with another empty box. He was packing his things, carting them little by little over to Julie's beach house. They had decided not to wait until after the wedding to move in together. Both of them knew only too well how precious time could be.

"One more and we can start on the living room." He reached for the empty box, but Julie dangled it just out of his reach. She laughed as he made a futile lunge for it, then let it drop a few feet away.

As she looked at him, her warm smile slowly faded, replaced by a far too serious expression.

"What is it, love?" He reached for her hand, pulled her down on the floor beside him. "Tell me what's the matter?"

"You know what's the matter. We've gone over every possible avenue we can think of and we still haven't come up with nearly enough money to satisfy Sandini and McPherson."

"We've still got time. I've got an appointment with Beverly First National in the morning. Dan Witherspoon has become a friend. He'll help if there's any way he can."

"Let me go to Owen. If he would loan you the money—"

"Damn it, we've talked about this. Owen Mallory is the last person in the world I'll ask for help."

"I know you and he don't get along, but—"

"That is putting it mildly. The man is in love with you. I'm the last person he'd want to help."

"You don't know that…not for sure. If I asked him, maybe—"

"No. That's the end of the subject. Owing money to Mallory would be worse than owing it to Sandini and McPherson. He wouldn't do it anyway—not even for you."

She looked like she might argue. Instead she gave up a sigh. "Maybe we should talk to your father. I know we agreed not to bring him into this, but maybe there is some way he could help. I don't know much about his finances—"

"Neither do I. He was always somewhat guarded about his money, but I'm sure he can't afford anything as substantial as this. And even if he could, I wouldn't ask him. His health is extremely fragile. The strain might cause him to have another stroke."

Julie shivered. He knew she wouldn't argue with that. She loved Alex Donovan. She wouldn't want to see him hurt. He settled an arm around her shoulders and drew her against him. Tipping her chin up, he outlined the bruise on her cheek. "Don't you understand? I don't want anyone else getting hurt."

Julie swayed toward him. "I'm frightened, Patrick. Those men are determined. They might do something—"

The lobby buzzer sounded, interrupting whatever else she might have said. Patrick stood up and hauled Julie to her feet. "I'll go find out who it is." Padding silently across the thick white wool carpet, he pushed the button on the intercom next to the door.

"Yes?"

"Patrick...son, it's your father. Nathan and I would like to come up for a moment, if you don't mind."

"Of course, I don't mind." He pressed the admittance button, then waited for the elevator to arrive. The door slid open and Nathan wheeled Alex into the living room.

"I know it's a little late for unexpected house calls, but something's been bothering me and I needed to see you about it. I hope we haven't interrupted anything important." He glanced around at the half-filled cartons and boxes.

"Getting Patrick moved, is all." Julie smiled as she leaned down to kiss his cheek. "It's always good to see you." He had come to the hospital, of course, but kept his visits brief. His health remained good, his complexion robust, but tonight he seemed edgy, somehow disturbed.

"If the two of you don't mind," he said to Julie and Nathan, "I'd like a moment with Patrick alone."

Julie gave Patrick a sideways glance, then smiled. "I'll go fix us a pot of tea—assuming I can still find the teapot. Nathan, you can help me."

"You got it."

They walked into the kitchen, Nathan towering over Julie, so wide he filled the doorway. As soon as the door swung closed, the wheelchair spun in Patrick's direction and Alex Donovan turned the full force of his still intimidating gaze on his son.

"I'm glad you're feeling better," Alex said, his shrewd old eyes fixed firmly on his face.

"Much better, thank you."

Alex glanced around at the heavy items Patrick had obviously been lifting with ease, and those perceptive old eyes assessed him even more closely. "The doctors are amazed you aren't dead. They say it's a medical miracle the way your heart started beating on its own. And there was the matter of the length of time you were dead. There should have been brain damage…something. Instead, they say you're the picture of health. In fact, considering the trauma your body's experienced, they say it's astonishing how healthy you are."

Patrick shifted uneasily. "No one is happier about it than I am."

"Except perhaps Julie."

Patrick said nothing. He didn't like the way Alex Donovan was staring at him, as if he could see beneath the surface to the man he was inside.

Alex's eyes remained on his face. "Amazing, isn't it? Two miracles in one family in just a few months."

"Yes, it is."

"And let us not forget the miracle of my recovery."

Patrick said nothing.

Alex sighed. "I'm an old man, Patrick. When you live to be as old as I am, you stop seeing everything in black and white. You stop knowing what can and cannot happen, what's possible and what is not. You start to realize there are things that happen we'll never understand. Things that sometimes can't be explained. That doesn't make them any less real."

Patrick worked to make his voice come out even. "What is it you're trying to say?"

Alex picked up a silver framed photo of Patrick and his mother when Patrick was a boy. "I know about the Brookhaven deal," he said, still concentrating on the photo. "At least I know part of it. I know my son was involved in some sort of fraudulent real estate scam. I know his involvement might have ended up sending him to jail. At best it would have destroyed the company and ruined the Donovan name."

"I'm sorry. I never meant for any of that to happen."

"I know you didn't. I also know you have done the right thing and advised the Teachers' Pension Fund not to buy those worthless notes. I also know the Westwind Corporation has packed its proverbial bags and headed out of town."

Interesting. Even he hadn't heard that bit of news. "I did what I had to. It was the right thing to do."

"Yes, it was. In the months since your first heart attack, you seem to have made a habit of doing the right thing. You've saved Donovan Real Estate from going bankrupt. You've won the respect and admiration of the people in your office, the love and respect of a woman I love like a daughter."

Alex looked him straight in the face. "If you were my son, I'd be proud of you. I'd go to my grave a happy man. Unfortunately, I know it isn't true."

The words sank in like a blow to the stomach. And yet he didn't deny it. He respected Alex Donovan too much to do that.

"My son was greedy and selfish," Alex went on, "but he was still my son and I loved him. What happened to him? Is he dead?"

His stomach felt tied in knots. He had prayed this day would never come. He wasn't quite sure how to answer at first, then decided simply to tell the man the truth.

"He would have died the day of his heart attack. Because of who I am, part of him still lives—his hopes and dreams, his memories of you and his mother when he was a boy, the happy times the three of you shared. If

Julie and I have children, Patrick's blood will run through their veins. They'll be your grandchildren, children who will carry on your heritage."

"I thought perhaps it was merely a physical coincidence…that the two of you simply looked the same. It didn't take long to realize that wasn't the truth…that in most ways you *are* him." He fumbled with the photo. "I don't suppose you'd be willing to explain how all of this has happened."

"I'm afraid I can't do that."

Alex just nodded. He looked older, more frail than he had when he came in, yet as always there remained an underlying strength. "Does Julie know?"

"Yes."

His face showed a moment of relief. "I've watched you these past few months. I saw Patrick in you and for a while I was fooled. I appreciate your honesty. And now that I know the truth—or at least a portion of it—I believe you are the best of Patrick. And I also believe that in some strange way, I am a very fortunate man."

His throat went tight. He had never had a father yet he felt tied to this weathered, aging man as if he were truly his son. "Thank you."

The old man nodded. He lifted a hand and waved it toward the kitchen. "I imagine our tea is ready."

Patrick smiled slightly. "I could use a good strong cup…though I only drink decaf."

Alex chuckled softly. "My son drinking tea. I never thought to see the day."

His smile grew warmer. "I imagine both of us have a number of surprises yet in store."

The old man chuckled again. "Thanks to you and your 'miracles,' perhaps I'll be around long enough to see them."

The study was sumptuous, masculine, and expensively done in gold and dark forest green. Heavy Oriental carpets warmed the polished wooden floors, and behind his massive rosewood desk, a row of mullioned windows overlooked the pounding sea. Owen Mallory leaned back against his expensive leather chair and adjusted the telephone receiver to a more comfortable position against his ear, the panoramic vistas behind him the farthest thing from his mind.

"You listen to me, Witherspoon. I don't give a damn what you promised Patrick Donovan—you loan that bastard enough for a cup of coffee and I'll withdraw every dollar I've got on deposit with Beverly First, and use my influence to see that my associates do the same."

A long silence followed. When the banker didn't answer fast enough, Owen started speaking again. "If you can't handle my request, Dan, I'll have to speak to Adrian. I'm sure your boss won't have any trouble at all seeing that my request is complied with."

Witherspoon sighed into the phone. "All right, you win. I'll take care of it myself. You've left me no choice but to do what you want."

Owen inwardly smiled, pleased with the results of the conversation though he had never really doubted the outcome. The bank simply had too much to lose. "Thanks, Dan. I knew I could count on you. We'll have lunch at the club the next time I'm in Beverly Hills."

Witherspoon made no reply, his disdain more than

clear. Owen didn't care. He hung up with a shot of satisfaction. Less than an hour ago, Julie Ferris had left his office, asking him on Donovan's behalf for a loan against Donovan Real Estate and other of Patrick's assets; the rest, she had told him, was coming from a loan with Beverly First National Bank.

Owen smiled. He had agreed, of course. *For a price.*

"We're friends, Julie—you know you can count on me. I'll be happy to loan Patrick the money—on one condition."

She turned a little wary. "What's that?"

"That you stop seeing him. That you never go near him again."

"What!" Julie jumped up from her chair. "That's insane, Owen. You know Patrick and I are going to be married."

"Marrying Donovan would be the biggest mistake of your life. Tell me you'll stop behaving like a lovesick fool and I'll see he gets the money. Otherwise he can forget it."

Julie clenched her fists. "I can't believe I'm hearing this. You're supposed to be my friend."

"I am your friend, Julie. I'm trying to help you."

She looked at him hard. "No—you don't want to help me. You just want something else you can't have." She braced her palms flat on his desk and leaned forward. "You know something, Owen, I never believed what people said about you, stories about how ruthless you are, what a complete and total prick you can be. I thought you were kind and generous. I felt lucky to count you among my friends. The truth is, if I ever behaved like a fool it was believing in you—in being so stupidly naive."

She whirled away from him, grabbed her purse, and started walking toward the door.

"Donovan will only end up hurting you," Owen called after her. "When you've had enough, come back and see me."

"Don't hold your breath," she tossed back over her shoulder, jerked open the door, and slammed it closed behind her.

Owen thought about their unfortunate confrontation as he leaned back in his chair. She had always been a challenge. Perhaps she was right and he only desired her because he couldn't have her. It really didn't matter. Whatever the reason, he wanted her.

And if he couldn't have her he intended to make damn sure Patrick Donovan wouldn't have her either.

Twenty-Five

Julie paced the floor of her living room in front of the big plate glass windows overlooking the sea. She was waiting for Patrick, nervously anticipating his return from the bank, hopefully with the money he so desperately needed.

She glanced at the clock, which ticked ominiously yet seemed to move almost painfully slow. She had watched it since the moment she'd gotten home, thinking Patrick would surely be arriving right behind her. But so far he had not appeared and the bank had been closed for nearly two hours.

The sound of a racing engine as his Porsche pulled into the driveway announced his impending arrival, and Julie hurried toward the door. Yanking it open, she rushed out to greet him before he'd had time to reach the porch.

"Patrick, I've been worried sick." She slid her arms around his neck and he hugged her tightly against him. "What happened? Did the bank give you the money?"

The muscles in his shoulders went tense. His face

told her the answer, his expression taut and grim. "Something came up with the bank at the last minute…some sort of glitch with the credit. At least that's what Dan Witherspoon said."

Her chest squeezed. "The money's due tomorrow. What are we going to do?"

He only shook his head. "I was worried about the bank, so I've also been working with Federal Savings. I've got half of what we need. In time I'll be able to raise the rest."

"Time is something we haven't got."

"I know. I'm hoping the nice fat cashier's check I'm going to give them tomorrow will be enough to buy us a little more time." But his face said he wasn't sure it would, and neither was she.

"You look exhausted." Julie forced herself to smile. "Why don't you go sit down and I'll fix us something to eat?" She had started supper earlier, parmesan noodles and skinless breast of chicken, something for both of their palates, but when Patrick didn't come home, her concentration had evaporated and she still wasn't finished.

He nuzzled the side of her neck. "Why don't I help? There must be something I can do."

Julie smiled in earnest this time. "My darling, Patrick, I'm sure I can think of something—though it might not have to do with food."

The meal turned out to be good but neither of them ate very much. They cleared the table together but as soon as they were finished, he dragged her into his arms.

"I thought there was something you wanted me to do," he teased, capturing her mouth in a kiss. They made passionate love on the sofa in the living room, then went into the bedroom and made love again. There was a fierceness to their mating, a shadow of the same impending doom that they had experienced before.

Lying beside him in her light-pine, four-poster bed, Julie snuggled deeper in his arms. "Patrick, I'm frightened. We've come so far. I can't bear the thought of losing you now, not after all that we've been through."

"You're not going to lose me."

But she might and he knew it. Anger trickled through her. She slammed her fist down on the covers. "It isn't fair. You didn't even make that stupid deal."

Patrick arched a sleek black brow. "Didn't I?"

"Well, only part of you did."

"True. A fairly small part at that, but still it's my responsibility. And tomorrow I'll convince my *associates* I intend to make good on my obligation."

Julie said nothing. Perhaps half the money would be enough. But thinking of Woody Nicholson and the scene at the hospital, she didn't think Sandini and McPherson were going to be that easy to convince.

As they usually did, in the morning they took separate cars to the office. They each had a job to do. Patrick had appointments and Julie had property to show that afternoon. A brief kiss through the open car window, and Patrick pulled out of the driveway. Waving, he headed toward the office.

Julie watched him only a moment, then hurried into the garage and opened the door to her big Lincoln Town Car, the car she drove whenever she was working with clients. Today she was taking Dr. Frank Sullivan and his wife to see the old Flynn mansion—Fred Thompkins's prize listing in the Hollywood Hills.

Thinking of the wealthy older couple, she pulled onto Pacific Coast Highway not far behind Patrick, her thoughts quickly returning to him, her mind overshadowed by fear of what might happen to him today.

She could just make out his shiny black Porsche as he weaved perilously in and out of traffic. His newly acquired passion for speed combined with the racing skills of his youth helped keep him from disaster, thank God.

Watching him roar off from a stoplight, Julie smiled, then she frowned at the sight of a long white limousine appearing out of nowhere, speeding equally fast alongside him. The cars were running close together when the limousine began inching into Patrick's lane. He swerved onto the shoulder to avoid the bigger car, but the limousine followed, nearly slamming into the side of his car before both vehicles returned at a slower pace back onto the road.

The stoplight changed in front of her and she was too far away to try to make it through the intersection on yellow. She watched Patrick's car fade into the distance, the limousine right along with it, and said a quick prayer the light would hurry and change.

It didn't. It seemed like the longest red light in Malibu history. She finally rolled through the intersection, pressing hard on the accelerator, but her timing was off now and she hit another stoplight down the road.

That was when she saw it, Patrick's car, parked at an odd angle on the shoulder of the road. The driver's seat was empty.

"Oh, no." Julie changed lanes, then swerved the Lincoln hard to the right, pulling to a halt just in front of Patrick's Porsche. Shoving the Lincoln into park, she jumped out onto the busy road, running toward the low-slung black Porsche. Cars whizzed past, blowing sand and grit into her face, the wind ripping open the navy bolero jacket that matched her skirt. Julie rounded the Porsche to the side away from the oncoming traffic and opened the passenger door.

Nothing was there that said where Patrick might have been taken—nor was the briefcase with the cashier's check he was carrying.

Jerking her gaze toward the sea of cars disappearing down the busy highway, she thought she caught a glimpse of the long white limo but she couldn't be sure.

The Lincoln was still running. Julie raced back to the car and climbed in, then sat there shaking, trying to decide what to do. Her instinct was to tear onto the highway, try to catch up with the limo, flag them down and do whatever it took to help Patrick convince the men he would find a way to repay them.

But reason said there were a dozen cars that color and a dozen roads the limo could have turned onto and simply disappeared. She might drive for hours and never find them. If Sandini and McPherson weren't satisfied with being paid only half of the money—and she was convinced they wouldn't be—then time was of the essence. There had to be something else she could do.

Julie pulled the Lincoln onto the highway, her mind running through every desperate possibility she could think of, none of which seemed to have the least amount of merit. There was Owen Mallory, of course, but now that she knew the kind of man he really was, and after their last ill-fated meeting, she no longer believed he would help her. It even occurred to her that Owen might be behind the Beverly First's refusal to make the loan, since she had told him the name of the bank.

She didn't want to believe it, but it might just be the truth.

Which left her with only one possible alternative. Alexander Donovan.

It was risky. God knew Alex was living on the edge, a frail old man growing older by the day. Yet Alex had always maintained a certain quiet strength. He was a successful businessman, a man who knew more about finance than anyone Julie had ever known.

And he had come to love this new Patrick, Julie believed, as if he were truly his son.

Her fingers shook as she dug her cell phone out of her purse and frantically punched the auto dial for Alex's home number. He was their last hope and she couldn't help wishing that she had called him sooner.

If anyone could help Patrick now it was his father.

The butler, Mario, answered the phone on the second ring and quickly put her through to Alex, alerted perhaps by the urgency in her voice.

"Alex? It's Julie."

"Good morning, my dear. I've been hoping you would call."

She tried to control her voice. "How…how are you feeling?"

"Fairly chipper lately. My arthritis is acting up, but it isn't too bad, and at any rate there's not much I can do about that."

"I—I've been meaning to drop by, but with Patrick moving in and getting ready for the wedding, I've just been so busy." Her throat began to close up. She prayed that he wouldn't hear the distress she was trying to hide, but Alex was a difficult man to fool.

"Julie, my dear girl. I can tell there is something wrong. Please don't be afraid to tell me what it is."

"Alex…it's Patrick." Her voice broke. "He's in trouble over the Brookhaven deal. He owes some money to a couple of men—"

"Sandini and McPherson?"

She straightened, pressed on the brakes at yet another stoplight. "Yes, how did you know?"

"I've known for some time. I heard rumors before his heart attack and hired a private investigator. I spoke to Patrick about it that night at his apartment, but he never mentioned the money. I suppose I should have guessed."

"He didn't want to worry you."

"Those men, Julie…they aren't the sort to be trifled with. Patrick should have come to me."

"I tried to convince him. You know how stubborn he can be."

"Where is he? I'll speak to him and together we'll work this thing out."

Her throat went tighter. "That's the problem. They've taken him, Alex. He only has half the money, but they expect him to pay it all. I'm terrified of what they might do."

Silence descended over the phone. "Listen to me carefully, Julie. Are you at the office?"

"I was headed there. I'm in my car on the way."

"All right. Once you get there, stay close to the phone. I'll be there as quickly as I can."

"But w-what about Patrick?"

His voice roughened. "I lost my son once. I don't intend to lose him again." With that Alex hung up the phone.

* * *

Tony Sandini leaned his corpulent frame against the red leather seat in the white Lexus stretch limo. The window was closed between the driver's compartment up in front and the rear of the limo, where he and Woody Nicholson sat on either side of Patrick Donovan. Jake Naworski and Ralph Ceccarelli sat across from them on a seat facing the opposite way.

Tony bent forward, waving the cashier's check Patrick had handed him into the guy's too-handsome face.

"So what have you got to say, pretty boy? I know you can add, and we both know this don't add up to what you owe."

Patrick sat up a little straighter. "It's almost half," he said, surprisingly calm for a man in his situation. Then again, maybe the bastard didn't understand the situation as clearly as Tony did. "Give me a little more time and I'll see you get the rest."

Tony chuckled, jiggling the fat at his girth. "You've had time, Donovan. More than you shoulda' had in the first place." The car turned sharply just then, pulling onto a narrow dirt road, rutted and overgrown with weeds. They were somewhere deep in the Malibu hills, on a chunk of private land away from the traffic where no one could see them, hear the bastard scream, or the thud of their silenced weapons. The kind of spot Tony preferred for this kind of work.

The car slid to a halt and he waited a moment for the dust to clear.

"Get out of the car." Grinding down on the door handle, he hefted his big bulk out of the limo. Woody Nicholson prodded Patrick in the ribs and they got out and stood in front of him, bone-thin Nicholson shoving his Glock nine-mil into Donovan's side, a smile of anticipation splitting Woody's sallow face.

"I don't like you, Donovan," Tony said, shifting his attention back to the man in front of him. "I never did. You promised to make us some money or we never woulda' made you that loan. Instead all you've done is cause us trouble."

"I told you I would pay you and I will. I just need—"

Nicholson buried his fist in Patrick's stomach, turning the last word into a grunt and doubling him over. Donovan dragged in several deep breaths and started to lift his head, but Nicholson hit him again, splitting his lip and flinging blood all over his expensive white shirt.

"You beginnin' to get the picture, pretty boy?" Tony's own hand unconsciously fisted. "You don't mess with Tony Sandini—nobody does. We gave you time to get the money you owed and you haven't done it. You ain't paid." He grinned. "But you will."

He turned to Woody and motioned toward the trees off to the left, a thick copse of sycamores near the edge of a steep ravine. Nicholson grabbed his arm, but Patrick twisted away.

"I thought you were smarter than this, Sandini," he said. "Shooting me is going to cost you six million dollars—to say nothing of the trouble it's going to cause. Give me another two weeks and you'll be money and trouble ahead."

"And you'll be lounging on a beach in Mexico with one of your big-titted blondes. You friggin' lowlife—what kind of fool do you think I am?"

Patrick might have answered, but Jake Naworski

wrenched an arm up behind his back so hard he clamped down on his jaw in pain.

Tony tipped his head toward the trees and the men dragged Patrick off in that direction. He was tougher than he looked. Jerking free, he managed a couple of good solid punches before they started pummeling him again. A wild blow landed on Ceccarelli's chin, knocking him into the dirt.

Tony smiled to think of Ralph with mud on his pristine, extravagantly expensive navy blue suit.

Tony watched a moment more, then headed back to the limo just as his cell phone started to ring. He recognized the number. Tony frowned, wondering what the hell McPherson could possibly want since they had spoken less than an hour ago. Sliding his substantial bulk back inside the car, he pressed the phone against his ear and listened to his partner on the end of the line. The whole time, he kept wishing he was back at the hotel getting a blow job from his little blond stew instead of sitting out here in the dirt.

Unconsciously nodding, he called out to the driver. "Hey, Mickey—if it ain't too late, tell them guys to hold off on Donovan. Tell 'em to bring him back over here."

The driver took off at a run and Tony returned to the phone. "You sure this guy's gonna pay us?" he said to his partner.

"According to my sources, Alexander Donovan's got more money than he can count. Apparently he's always been secretive about it. He figured if his son knew how much he really had, the guy would sink even deeper into booze and drugs. At any rate, he's offered to pay the bill and throw in a million for good measure. He says the money'll be waiting at Donovan's office by the time you get there. Just drive the guy back, drop him in the parking lot, and the money is ours."

Tony shrugged against the seat of the limo. "What the hell? Money's money—why should I give a damn where it comes from?"

He ended the call with McPherson and hung up the phone, turned at the sound of footsteps in the dirt outside the car. Woody Nicholson's bony frame appeared at the open car door, his jacket off, his knuckles scraped raw and oozing bright red blood.

"You sure you want him back?" Woody asked.

Tony grunted. "Sorry to put a crimp in your fun, but pretty boy here, just went from a lowlife to a precious commodity. Get his ass back in the car and let's get the hell outta here."

Seconds later, Patrick slid in through the opposite door wearing the evidence of Nicholson's handiwork—a black eye, bruises, a fat lip, and a bloody nose. Tony chuckled. At least he wouldn't be quite so pretty anymore.

No one spoke as they drove to the real estate office. Jake and Ralph clearly looked as if they'd been brawling, but Jake usually looked that way. Ralph's shirt was bloody and the pocket of his suit was torn. Tony had to give Donovan credit, he wasn't such a pussy after all.

It didn't matter. Not if that money wasn't there when they reached the office.

Tony tossed a hard look in Patrick's direction and leaned back against the red leather seat of the car.

Patrick sat rigidly as the limousine turned down Canon toward the parking lot of Donovan Real Estate.

Julie's car parked in the distance caught his eye and he was glad to know she had arrived there safely. Then again, maybe her being there wasn't good. He didn't think the men would hurt her, but he couldn't be sure.

So far he wasn't sure about anything.

Like why they had brought him back here. One minute he was standing on the edge of a sharp ravine, his arms pinned at his sides, being beaten bloody by that slimeball Woody Nicholson and his two cronies. They were going to shoot him, he was sure, shove his body into the bottom of the ravine. God only knew how long it would have been until someone had found him.

Then, just when he thought his time had run out, the limo driver had appeared and he was dragged back to the car—albeit reluctantly—by Nicholson and his friends. Mopping the blood from his face with the handkerchief Sandini lent him, Patrick almost smiled. It certainly wasn't a situation he would have faced on Toril.

Gazing out the window through the black tinted glass, he waited as the limo drove toward the rear office door. Julie stood tensely beside it, next to Nathan Jefferson Jones, positioned like the linebacker he was, behind Patrick's father. The huge man wheeled Alex forward just as Tony Sandini swung open the heavy car door and stepped out onto the blacktop.

"You got it?" Tony said to the frail man in the chair.

"Every dime I promised," Alex said. "Assuming you have safely returned my son."

Sandini motioned toward the limo. "Get him outta there." Nicholson shoved him across the seat and Patrick climbed out onto the pavement, Nicholson and Ceccarelli sliding out behind him.

As soon as Patrick's feet hit the ground, Tony reached over and grabbed the suitcase out of his father's lap and handed it to Ceccarelli, who held it while he popped the shiny brass latches. It didn't take long to count the money, bundled as it was. When he finished, Tony jerked his head toward Patrick.

"He's all yours, old man," he said to Alex.

Nicholson shoved Patrick forward. "Have a nice day," he said with a smirk.

Patrick didn't answer. It wasn't exactly a nice day, since he felt as if he'd been run over by an eighteen-wheel truck. On the other had, he was still alive—which made it a wonderful day.

As the limo drove away, disappearing down Dayton into the crowded streets of Beverly Hills, his gaze swung to Julie and his father.

"Patrick!" Julie was instantly in his arms, hugging him fiercely, and he tightened his arms around her. "Thank God you're safe."

"A little the worse for wear," he said when she reached up to touch his bruised face and swollen lip, "but fine nonetheless."

"You don't look fine. God, Patrick." She went back into his arms and clung to him and he didn't make her stop.

"I'm all right," he said. "Really."

Reluctantly, she let him go and his gaze went in search of his father. The old man's eyes were fixed on his face.

"You should have come to me," his father said in the same tone of voice he had once used on his young disobedient son. "Fathers are supposed to help their children. Remember that and don't ever be afraid to come to me again."

Something tightened in Patrick's chest. Memories

washed in, times in his childhood before his mother died when he had known his father cared, known that his father really loved him.

"How did you know? How did you raise the money? How did you get it so fast?"

Alex chuckled softly. "Julie had sense enough to call, thank the good Lord. As for the money…it seems I'm worth a good bit more than I might have previously let on." He chuckled again, a rumble in his thin chest. "Quite a bit more, actually."

Patrick said nothing, absorbing the old man's words, understanding why Alex had done what he had. Then he sobered. "I'll pay you back, Dad. I promise. I'll pay you every penny. I won't let you down again."

His father looked stunned. Patrick hadn't called him Dad since he was a little boy. Alex stared at him and his eyes grew moist with tears. "I know you will. I never doubted it for a minute. I'm proud of you, son."

Patrick felt the gentle touch of his father's hand, and an odd warmth settled in his chest. For a moment he found it hard to speak. "Thank you, Father." He glanced into Julie's upturned face, saw the happiness shining there. "I owe my life to both of you."

They smiled at him and Patrick smiled, too, his heart full of joy and love, emotions he had only begun to discover. He was thinking he had heard the phrase no place like home, but until today he had never really understood it. Now for the very first time, he realized what the saying meant.

For even with all of its problems, even after all that had happened, there was surely no place like the home he had found here on Earth.

From The Author

I hope you enjoyed *SEASON OF STRANGERS*, the third in my paranormal series that started with *SCENT OF ROSES*, followed by *THE SUMMIT*. The books are about ordinary women who have extraordinary experiences. If you liked *SEASON OF STRANGERS*, I hope you'll look for the others in the series.

Next I'll be writing about the rugged Raines brothers of Wyoming—handsome, powerful men who dragged themselves out of poverty by their bootstraps to become the successful men they are today. Each brother's story is a romantic suspense beginning with Jackson, who gets caught in a dangerous intrigue with a lady named Sarah Allen, who once scorned him and now desperately needs his help.

Gabriel and Devlin's stories are also filled with adventure, suspense and romance.

I hope you'll watch for the books, beginning with *AGAINST THE WIND*, out next year. You can find information on my Web site at www.katbooks.com.

Until then, all best wishes and happy reading,

Kat

#1 *NEW YORK TIMES*
BESTSELLING AUTHOR
DEBBIE MACOMBER

What do you want most in the world?

Anne Marie Roche wants to find happiness again. At 38,
she's childless, a recent widow and alone. On Valentine's
Day, Anne Marie and several other widows get together to
celebrate…what? Hope, possibility, the future. They each
begin a list of twenty wishes.

Anne Marie's list includes learning to knit, doing good for
someone else and falling in love again. She begins to act on
her wishes, and when she volunteers at a school, little Ellen
enters her life. It's a relationship that becomes far more
important than she ever imagined, one in which they both
learn that wishes can come true.

Twenty Wishes

"These involving stories…continue the Blossom Street
themes of friendship and personal growth that readers
find so moving."—*Booklist* on *Back on Blossom Street*

Available the first week of May 2008 wherever books are sold!

From The Last Stand trilogy

BRENDA NOVAK

Four years ago Skye was attacked in her own bed.
She managed to fend off Dr. Oliver Burke, but
the trauma changed everything.

And now her would-be rapist is out of prison.

Detective David Willis believes Burke
is a clear and present danger—and
guilty of at least two unsolved murders.

But now Burke is free to terrorize Skye
again. Unless David can stop him.
Unless Skye can fight back. Because
Oliver Burke has every intention
of finishing what he started.
And that's a promise. Trust me.

"Brenda Novak's
seamless plotting,
emotional intensity
and true-to-life
characters...make her
books completely
satisfying. Novak
is simply a great
storyteller."
—*New York Times*
bestselling author
Allison Brennan

*Available the first week of June 2008
wherever books are sold!*

MIRA®

www.MIRABooks.com

MBN2412

USA TODAY Bestselling Author

TAYLOR SMITH

MIRA®

Gun-for-hire Hannah Nicks takes on an assignment that promises easy money and a vacation on the Mexican Riviera. Hired by a gallery owner, Hannah sets out to transport a minor artist's painting. But when Hannah arrives at the delivery point, she finds a massacre. She hides the painting, fearing it is a death warrant, and flees back to the States.

But it only gets worse for her in L.A.: the gallery owner has been killed and Hannah is a suspect. In order to prove her innocence, she must hunt down the person who framed her and uncover a deadly secret....

the night café

"A graceful, compellingly written thriller...
[The] gloriously intricate plot is top-notch, and her writing...is that of a gifted storyteller."
—*Publishers Weekly* on *The Innocents Club*

Available the first week of June 2008 wherever books are sold!